I0608705

Becoming Magdalene

The Transforming Journey of a Disciple

Jennifer Ristine

En Route Books and Media, LLC
Saint Louis, MO

⊕*ENROUTE*
Make the time

En Route Books and Media, LLC
5705 Rhodes Avenue
St. Louis, MO 63109

© Copyright 2024 Jennifer Ristine

ISBN: 979-8-88870-422-6
Library of Congress Control Number: 2025946532

ACKNOWLEDGMENTS

I gratefully acknowledge many unnamed family and friends who have been patient sounding boards, encouragers, revisers, constructive critics and editors over the last years as this work has developed into its present form. Thank you to my sisters in Christ, the consecrated women of Regnum Christi who endured countless moments of sharing, be they retelling of chapter scenes, cover page options or advances on this final product, if we can even say that this is the last.

I send a warm thanks to all who invested time in editing and giving very specific feedback. Thank you, Lisa Small, Consecrated Woman of Regnum Christi and sister in Christ for your editor's eyes. Thank you, Mary Driscoll, movie script analyst/writer and co-conspirator in two movie scripts that we hope will someday see the light of day. Jennifer Malneritch, thank you for your keen sense of character development and critiques. Magda Pettey and Jodi Longo, France pilgrim partners, you were an important part of God's providential plan, connecting me with Dr. Sebastian Mahfood, OP, a patient publisher. Wayne and Mary Ristine, my parents, thank you for encouraging me to persevere, something I learned from your testimony of life. Fr. Anton Vogelsang, LC, I appreciate your constancy, a chapter a day, to assure theological soundness amidst creative license. My profound gratitude to Fr. Robert Presutti, LC, for spiritual guidance. You facilitated a deeper pathway of listening to the Lord in my life, which bears fruit in the "soul" of this book.

Finally, thank you, to my good friend Saint Mary Magdalene. I look forward to a long "coffee chat" in heaven where you tell me all the things I got wrong, what I intuited correctly, what was inspired, and above all, finally set the record straight about your personal journey. Last, but never least, thank you God, Father, Son and Holy Spirit. Jesus, you walk with me through the dark valleys and make the flowers grow. Your Spirit keeps the lamp lit in the depth of my heart. And Father, you make all things new. Please, may this work serve to glorify you and build your Kingdom in the heart of each reader.

TABLE OF CONTENTS

AUTHOR'S NOTE

Despite Mary Magdalene's being one of the most referenced women in the New Testament, she remains a paradoxical mystery. Contradictory theories abound. While living and working in her hometown, Ancient Magdala, from 2014-2018, I addressed a plethora of traditions and stories about her in my first book, *Mary Magdalene: Insights from Ancient Magdala.*

Now I venture to explore her interior world. From discoveries and insights, I enter a deeply personal and spiritual realm, using my "gospel imagination" to glimpse into the unknown. Using creative license, with some foundation in reality, I explore Mary Magdalene's transforming journey, pondering a pathway of maturing freedom and love.

This is historical fiction with a twist. As you read, listen. Listen to the echo of God's voice in your heart. Ask the Holy Spirit to speak in his small still whisper.[1] Do the scripture passages used in each chapter resonate in your own heart? Do you identify with Mary Magdalene's experience? How? Why?

The story loosely follows a timeline of events, primarily offered by the evangelist Matthew. However, liberties are taken to include passages scattered throughout the gospels. As John the evangelist testified, Jesus did many things that were not recorded in the gospels. The same applies to the multitude of personal encounters he had with each of his disciples, Mary Magdalene included. While we find the real Jesus in the pages of sacred scriptures, we also come face to face with him anew in prayerful "graced" imagination.

My hope for you, dear reader, is to instigate a personal journey of ongoing conversion and deepening discipleship. Mary Magdalene is not the hero of the story. It is God the Father, Jesus her Lord and Savior, and the Holy Spirit. They are the hero of our story as well. While Mary Magdalene was an historical figure, she remains a friend in heaven with whom we can relate. She is a guide of sorts in the battle between life and death, a hidden battle often obscured from vision, even if we profess to walk in faith.

Mary is not merely an enigmatic Gospel figure, but a woman who, like us, struggled with her own humanity and the temptations of the world, yet hung onto the sense of being called to something more, something noble, something good and meaningful. She discovered her purpose of life in and through Jesus. She was beloved in his eyes all along, but she became, through a graced transformation, the Magdalene whom Jesus chose to be the bearer of the greatest news in all of human history.

Her simple announcement of Christ's resurrection has had ripple effects in more than two thousand years of believers. She is the Apostle to the Apostles, a role that perhaps Jesus conceived of even upon seeing her in her broken state. She offers us hope. We, too, are becoming the disciples, the men, the women, the persons we are called to become. We are called to a transformative journey of ongoing conversion and deepening discipleship. May the Spirit accompany you on your path, deeper into the heart of Christ, our Rabboni and Savior.

Guide to reading with the *Companion*

Read *Becoming Magdalene* for enjoyment and for personal enrichment. If you wish, go beyond pleasure reading, listen for echoes of the Spirit in your own heart. As you read, you will witness the interior movements of the various stages of the Ignatian spiritual exercises in the life of Mary Magdalene. The *Companion to Becoming Magdalene* can assist you. In it, I provide an explanation of each week's spiritual exercises' dynamic to be read before parts of Mary's story. Take note of whatever strikes you. Then, use the questions at the end of each section for personal journaling or shared group discussion. I also recommend particular meditations for each stages. The *Companion* will assist you in further reflection and application of Mary's transforming journey.

Chapters	Part	Spiritual Exercises
Prologue-6	Part 1	Principle & Foundation
7-9	Part 2	First week 1
10-14	Part 3	First week 2
15-22	Part 4	Second week 1
23-30	Part 5	Second week 2
31-38	Part 6	Second week 3
39-44	Part 7	Second week 4
45-50	Part 8	Third week
51-60	Part 9	Fourth week
Epilogue	Part 10	Contemplation to Attain Love

PROLOGUE. THE LETTER

Southern France, Provence area

Anno Domini 77, Sainte LeBaume, Gaul

Dear John, my beloved brother in the Lord,

It is finished. As her Rabboni once proclaimed these words from the cross, now Magdalene proclaims it with her death. Our little light has gone out of this world, but darkness did not overcome her. I believe John, that her story, as Jesus predicted, will be told for centuries. The lamp she kept lit for her beloved, the fire that he himself kindled within her, will continue to burn wherever we share it. Of this I am certain.

But she would be mortified if she were made an idol, as I myself did to her so many years ago, before we both followed the Lord. And so, I send these pages, as promised. I pray you are still in Ephesus and they will arrive safely. Maximin has helped me. Having been her spiritual father for over thirty years, he knew the more intimate details of the transforming journey of her soul. I merely applied my skill at storytelling, weaving together the various memories and confessions of which I was a privileged recipient in the last month of her life.

I will fade away now to tell the story of how she became the Magdalene. Many say she is named after the town, but you and I know the truth John. She was like a mighty tower, in her beauty and personality. But her magnificence was her profession of the greatest news ever told! "I have seen the Lord! He is alive!" It is fitting then, that these were also her last words. The last testimony from this beloved disciple, an apostle even to the apostles.

How was she so predilect? She knew slavery, despair, and the agony of restless searching. But I am sure she would say to me now, "No little Joanna! I knew freedom, hope, and joy, for I was lost and now am found; I was despised, but now I know I am loved; I was in darkness and now I live in the light." And so it is fitting that I begin her story in darkness, on the verge of being vanquished, awaiting the eternal light that enlightened her path. It is the light of Christ, who enlightens our own.

Your sister in the Lord, (Little) Joanna

CHAPTER 1. THE GARDEN

Early on the first day of the week,
while it was still dark,
Mary Magdalene went to the tomb.
John 20:1

Darkness enveloped all things. But Mary would not be deterred; neither by the moonless black of the hour, nor by the disciple slumbering in front of the door of their present lodgings, a protector against possible intruders. She could wait no longer. She grabbed a small lantern that fit into the palm of her hand, leaving a larger one for Mary Jacobe, Johanna Chuza, and Salome who planned to set out at early dawn. Baskets sat on the table like sentinels, ready for action. They held linens, spices, fresh flowers and flasks of fresh oils and nard water. She grabbed the basket she had prepared the night before and slipped quietly into the dark of early morning.[2]

Not even the cocks crowed this early. Determination mingled with waves of anguish and hope. This strange combination brought tears as well as fierce determination. She would not succumb to the interior darkness that sought to swallow her whole. Having successfully maneuvered her way out of Mary Mark´s house, she passed by several dormant living quarters and shops and made her way toward the scene of horror just two days prior. Scents of early morning bakers and the quiet of sleeping dwellers scoffed at her loss and suffering. It was one of life's cruelties, continuing on in defiance of broken hearts and pained existences as if nothing extraordinary had happened. As if her Rabboni had not been unjustly condemned and crucified, taken from her without a fair trial.

As she left the inhabited area, she lit her small lamp from a few simmering coals left behind by late night loiterers. Basket in one hand

and lamp in the other, she entered the edge of a garden. She chose a path that would lead her to the burial tomb where she had reluctantly left him at her friends' insistence. A faint light of the sinking moon converted rocks and bushes into hovering obstacles, making everything feel surreal. Surreal described the past few days. She wished they were merely a nightmare from which she would soon awaken. Since their last supper together she felt as though she had lived a thousand days' sufferings compacted into three.

She stumbled down a hill, her goal fixed on the unseen tomb gifted by Joseph of Arimathea. The scant beginnings of twilight outlined the heights of two adjacent hills. The sight of one stung her with memories of torture. The other resurrected memories of finality, a resting place for her Lord. At the base of the hills her feet splashed through puddles, remnants of the quick and unexpected outpouring from the heavens unleashing its fury. It had rained at the start of Sabbath, that horrid Friday, and again last night. Angels´ tears, she had thought. The heavens are crying and mingling with her own.

She began the ascent to the hill on her left, turning her back on the skull-like shadow of Golgotha. Low lying bushes hedged her in. Their claw-like thorns clung and tore at her clothes, trying to hold her back. She couldn't stop the course of events that had led to Jesus´ crucifixion, but she would not be thwarted in her efforts now. Exertion and the balmy weather, a sign of winter finally being vanquished by spring, left her sweating. A chill ran down her spine as a cool breeze wafted out of an open unused cavern. Upward she climbed. Exhaustion, darkness, thorns. Not even her lamp sufficiently enlightened her way as she navigated the rough terrain. But nothing would deter her.

She stubbed her foot against a protruding rock, the contents of her basket threatening escape before she regained her balance. It jogged her memory of another rock that might be a stumbling block. *The tombstone. How will I possibly remove it? There had to be a way!*

Suddenly, the earth growled and trembled beneath her feet, a loud cracking and crashing deafened her hearing. Swaying back and forth, she relinquished the hold on her basket, grabbing the nearest branch of an olive tree until the earth finally stilled. Movement and voices ahead put her on alert. She squatted, hoping to remain unseen and cautiously gathered the scattered remnants of her basket as best she could. She was so close now. A few olive trees and larger brush shielded her from seeing the tomb and whoever was shuffling about speaking in hasty whispers. The sound of metal and leather clued her in to the noisemakers. Soldiers. She froze. She remembered. Friday, before the Sabbath had descended upon them, soldiers had sealed the tomb and positioned themselves as guards.

Mary recalled her surprise that Friday afternoon. Something had changed in the soldiers' treatment of them during the three long hours of agony to the closing of the tomb. Three soldiers in particular had driven off the more aggressive antagonists. She had known Gaius, but the other two had been unfamiliar faces. Despite her grief, she had heard their names: Abedanar and Cassius, she now remembered. Cassius had allowed them a semblance of peace as they prepared Jesus' body for burial. The soldiers' silence had been surprisingly reverent and respectful, leaving them undisturbed to go about cleaning, anointing and wrapping Jesus' body.

Are they still here? Will they help me move the tombstone? She heard words of three or four men fly back and forth in haste as they moved about. Earthquake. Not natural. A curse. The stone. Broken. Check the tomb. Gone! Report to Pilate. You stay. No. I'm getting out of here! She heard their footsteps making haste. And then, she was alone. Alone again in the dark.

A barely flickering lantern became her weapon against the darkness practically consuming her. She held it up as if to fend off any threats. Cautiously, she broke through her cover stepping into a clearing before the tomb. She dropped her basket in surprise. Indeed, it was open. There on the ground lay the tombstone, in two pieces! She looked about in confusion and concern. *Did the earthquake do this?* She stooped to peer in, the moonlight barely offering shadows, her lantern even less. Silence. Coolness of the cave. She stepped in, first to a larger chamber, then felt her way into the second smaller chamber, where they had lain the body of Jesus. Holding out her lamp to light the small crevice, her heart stopped. A heavy blow was struck. Her breath left her. A linen cloth lay on the ground next to the stone slab, the resting place for Jesus' anointed and embalmed body. A smaller cloth used for covering his face was rolled up and placed off to the side. *But where is Jesus?*

Panic seized her. A double wave of loss and grief hit her as the oil lamp slipped from her hands, crashing to the ground, leaving her once again in darkness, questioning, searching, wondering, where was her beloved Rabboni?

She fumbled forward, reaching out to the cave walls and shuffling her feet until she felt the cloth upon her sandaled feet. She sank to the ground and grabbed the linen cloth, bringing it to her wet cheeks and stifling a cry. She leaned against the cave wall as she faced the out-cropped ledge where they had lain Jesus. A wailing mourn escaped her lips. Jesus was no more! *Where is he? Who took him? Did the soldiers? How dare they?!* Perhaps she could find Gaius and he would help her? He had been strangely quiet and cooperative the last two times she had crossed his path, far from the arrogant man of former days, whom she had thought she loved. A time that seemed so long ago. A time before she truly knew love.

CHAPTER 2. ROOTS & REJECTIONS

Do not hide your face from me,
do not turn your servant away in anger;
you have been my helper.
Do not reject me or forsake me,
God my Savior.
Psalm 27:9

Approximately two years prior...

A crisp late winter day dawned as Mary stepped out of her Galilean home on the northern outskirts of town to embark upon some necessary errands.[3] She loved her villa. It afforded easy access to the town's marketplace to the south, was a short distance away from a bathing spring to the northwest, and a quick walk to the harbor or quiet area at the sea's shoreline to the east. It sat on the edge of town. Fig and walnut trees, as well as date palms lined the perimeter of the property, offering privacy to the large plot of land. And her land further to the north boasted a fertile vineyard.

Her villa was the one thing she maintained pride in. She couldn't say the same of her reputation. She shook off that thought as she arranged the empty bags over her shoulder which would soon hold the fruit of her morning's errands. Breathing deeply, she took in the fresh outdoor aroma of early morning Magdala as though preparing for an ensuing battle. She quickly braided her thick, long dark hair. She was usually attentive to her toiletry, but today she wanted an early start in and out of town. She was hoping to beat the morning crowds and return to her villa, her safe haven.

Before she was born, her father had built a comfortable villa on this land for periodic trips to the countryside. It was a good eight-day journey from Jerusalem, which, in her younger years, they made at least once, sometimes twice a year. Her parents died just shortly after her fourteenth birthday. But her father, surprisingly, had foreseen that she would inherit this villa when she came of marriageable age. Martha, her older sister by thirteen years, was given the house in Bethany; and Lazarus, her older brother by fifteen years, was designated as overseer of both, along with his own properties he had acquired further outside of Bethany.

She often wondered when her father had made the decision to give her this property. He knew how much she loved the sea and probably saw Magdala as the safest place for her to run around and play her little games. Perhaps her father thought it would save her from trouble, being far away from Jerusalem and in the countryside. How wrong he had been. He hadn't counted on the proximity of Tiberias and its influence, newly built when Mary was just eleven years old.[4]

Eleven years old. She had still been a child of playful innocence. That year of her life marked a before and after, the beginning of a downward spiral when her father began showing signs of fatigue and illness and they traveled to Magdala no more, at least not as a family. At her behest, her father still sent Mary a couple times a year under the watchful eye of Babs and Tams, their trustworthy steward and his wife. Little by little it dawned on her that her father no longer had the strength to endure the travel. At the age of thirteen, her agony began. She watched him waste away from some mysterious illness, and her mother from sorrow. They both passed away around her fourteenth birthday, one upon the heels of the other. Oh, how she missed her father more than anyone. No, she thought, whenever he had decided to bequeath her Magdala, he would not have envisioned the influential company of Roman officers and Herod Antipas' court.

The inheritance went against the grain of custom, especially considering that it would normally go to the eldest son. But Lazarus never complained. He treated the whole situation as though he was guardian of both of his sisters and their inherited properties. Mary would have none of that. A rift began between her and her siblings when they attempted to presume a maternal and paternal authority over her.

When she turned fifteen, Lazarus began to hint at marriage prospects. Mary only exerted a greater independent spirit, making it clear to everyone that she was the arbiter of her own destiny. She determined then and there to leave for Magdala, for good. Lazarus, at his wits end, finally took her and installed her in the villa. But when he came to check on her and manage the estate, she insisted on being her own overseer.

Truth be told, she loved and respected her brother and sister, but the more she lashed out in anger the more she pushed them away. Martha's efforts to tame her only made her spitefully look for ways to be the opposite. And her deep pain and anger over her parents' death converted her brother into an easy target every time he attempted to fill her Father's shoes. Finally, his trips became less frequent, relying on the trustworthy proxy of Babs and Tams. They had no children of their own and would have gladly treated her as their own, had Mary allowed them. But she would be a child to no one.

A knot formed in her throat at the thought of how she longed for the presence of family, and yet she repeatedly rejected their attempts to reconcile. She was exasperated with her sister Martha for her righteous attitude and constant insistence that she return to Bethany and leave her past behind. Mary chastised herself. It was her own fault that she felt so alone. Their attempt to "save her reputation" only made her retreat from them even more. She didn't understand her own reactions.

Her father must be rolling over in his grave at the sight of her present situation. She cringed at the thought of how he might look upon her now if he were alive, his beloved Mary, stained. She wasn't so sure if she was considered beloved by anyone right now. Unmarried, alone and on the verge of being twenty-three, she had renounced the desire to be under anyone's direction. Her independent streak was certainly an attribute cultivated by her father.

Her father had been a just man and a seeker of the truth, although not Jewish. He met her mother when he moved from Arabia, having been awarded several tracts of land from the Roman emperor for his service of war to the Syrian king. He was well known for his generous and open-minded streak. He even donated a portion of his newly acquired land to the Temple when he had fallen for her mother. She was a Jewess from the sect of the Pharisees, and Mary´s father converted for her sake. The other lands in Galilee and near Jerusalem, he had retained and they were presently occupying.[5]

He had always fostered education for his children in the traditions of her people. But he also appreciated a good debate. He wasn't afraid to express ideas outside of the vision of more narrow-minded scholars. Mary had fond memories of listening to vivacious conversations and silently rooting for her father. He would give her a wink and afterwards explain to her some of the finer points of the argument. He was, at times, considered too open-minded. After a few too many heated debates with prominent religious leaders in town, he was respected, perhaps more for his wealth, but also suspected of leaning too close to the unconventional side.

She probably got some of her "spit-fire", as he called it, from him. But her beauty was from her mother. Or so her father used to tell her. Her mother would shush him whenever he commented on Mary's luxurious dark hair and smooth olive complexion.

"You are feeding the vanity of an already precocious and vain child," mother would warn, as she scolded father.

Mary knew from a young age that she held a certain sway and alluring power over others, even over her father. And so, he easily indulged her, or so her mother often said. At a young age, her admirers were beguiled by her beauty, then shocked with the quick wit and intelligence of her tongue. She often experienced the compulsion of trying the art of persuasion, be it to convince a young boy to climb the date palms to fetch her a fresh juicy morsel or talk a merchant down to a good price with her radiant smile and gleaming eyes when she accompanied her father to market as early as nine years old. It was all an innocent art until five years ago. That's when rumors began that she had played with fire and imprudently fallen into disgrace. *But rumors were not truth*, she told herself. *Or were they? Should I have known better? Had I been deceived?* She often wondered now.

Townspeople blamed Lazarus, her brother, for her present situation. They often murmured that if only he had forced her into marriage, she wouldn't have been so prey to temptations. But Lazarus hadn't had the heart to press further after a few attempted failures. While he had entrusted Tams and Babs to take charge of her, he soon realized who was really in charge. Mary liked being the master of her own life. As for the management of the villa, she actually thrived in that role. And despite her young age, she had natural gifts for organizing, directing and managing a household and a modest wine-making negotiation. It gave her a sense of purpose and helped to fill an emptiness or, at least, distract her from the painful hole in her heart from her parents' deaths.

Tams and Babs loved her like their own. But they were more like grandparents who consented to her whims and desires, than parents who disciplined her. They simply did her bidding, putting on the appearance to the townspeople, for the sake of propriety, of being guardian to the young girl.

Mary managed to learn the way of finance and business. She inherited her father's sagacity in these matters and was quickly managing the estate herself. Unconventional from the start, the townspeople's reactions varied in their acceptance of her when she began doing her own dealings by the age of sixteen. Many women that age had already married. She continued insisting that she had no plans to do so. At least not to someone who would curb her independence.

Barely having reached the age of eighteen, she met Gaius, a Roman officer. He held a post in Tiberius as a liaison between Pilate and Herod's soldiers. She had slowly allowed herself to be lured in by his unique charism. He was different. He was ambitious, but not manipulative. He was a soldier with his rough crude side, but an officer, capable of a commanding yet noble side.

She knew she could easily win him over with her beauty and charm. But she initially held her ground at his obvious advances towards her and was surprised how he had respected that. She began to sense that he held her in esteem. He affirmed her savvy ways of managing the villa. His persevering presence answered a desperate aching need. He conversed with her as an equal and sometimes reminded her of her father. But father, he was not. While older than her, he was handsome and captivating.

On his initial pretense of checking out fine wine for the officers, he visited frequently. Little by little, from their brief encounters to his intentional visits, she found a kindred companion, an unexpected friend. He won her over with his persistence, intelligence and kindness. They could speak of anything, and while he did not adopt her religion he would listen and consider her beliefs from a rational point of view, making comparisons to his own knowledge of religion.

He introduced her to the pagan gods. They were curious stories, she thought. Believable when a person had a desperate need for what each god promised to offer. She thought there was an uncanny similarity between pagan festivals and her own peoples' celebrations of various moments of harvest and the offering of first fruits. Gaius only half-heartedly believed in the gods himself, but he paid his dues to each according to the season of the year, putting in an appearance so as to comply with his duty as a representative of Rome.

Tams, like a concerned grandmother, began to comment on his frequent visits, questioning his intentions. Mary dismissed her as overly judgmental. Tams and Babs both eventually confronted her when Gaius invited her to frequent Herod's court. But she dismissed it once again. He introduced her to various leaders in his circle of friends.

At least one good thing came out of that event that she did not regret. Mary had met Johanna Chuza. She was quickly attracted by Johanna's maternal presence and impressed by her husband's devotion to the gods, even if Mary herself did not believe. She also sensed some hesitation in Johanna, yet, in her barrenness, she had turned to the gods of fertility for their intervention and blessing.

She also met little Joanna, Johanna's vivacious niece. (Sorry John, I had to put myself in at least once, so the reader sees that I knew her before she met Jesus). Only two years younger than her, little Joanna took to Mary as pagans to idols, emulating her and visiting her whenever she was staying with her aunt. Mary quickly discovered that girls her age either adored or envied her, one of two extremes. The first fed her vanity. The second she tried to ignore, realizing their jealousy.

She increasingly participated in the social life in the court. A final straw for Tams and Babs was Mary's attendance at Vinalia Urbana, the spring wine festival honoring the Roman gods, Venus and Jupiter[6]. Gaius had acquired a contract for her to supply the wine for the festival. She made a pretty fortune from it. He also invited her to the festivities. Mary did not return until the early morning and was still overly inebriated as she stumbled into the house. Tams silently put her to bed and even tendered her aching headache all day and through the next night. But as soon as Mary's health was restored, she spoke up. It was the first time Tams had ever spoken harshly to her, striking her with fear.

"You know not what you do Miriam! Gaius has charmed you into that, that pagan territory. You play with life and death! Their gods are no gods at all, but evil spirits, eager to possess a willing victim that pays it homage. Do not betray your God. Do not betray the memory of your father and mother. They taught you about the one true God of Israel."

Mary tried to dismiss it, mumbling that it was just a party. She did not worship any gods. But Tams did not let up.

"You are deceived if you think these are innocent celebrations. There is nothing innocent about them. They are mere seduction. You walk into the enemies' lair. Every time you go there with Gaius, you are in danger. Don't you see? You open the door to further danger. I fear for your life Miriam!"

Mary had been struck dumb by the length and force of her speech, but also her genuine fear and concern. She told Gaius, who laughed and called Tams a well-meaning, but superstitious old woman. Mary dismissed Tams' warnings and merely did her best to hide any further involvement in Gaius' courtings or in visits to Herod's palace in Tiberius.

Of course, Mary mixed with Gaius' people, but he never mixed with hers. If she could even call the townsfolk "her people". Mary had maintained her attendance in the synagogue until rumors began to circulate, calling her unclean, accusing her of consorting with the enemy and of being a pagan worshiper. They even went so far as to call her a prostitute and possessed. She was distraught to learn that the insinuations and accusations came primarily from the leaders. Gullibly, she believed that people would not persist in their harsh judgments and that it would soon peter out. But with the passing of time, friends became foes. Some business acquaintances closed their shop doors.

The rejection was strongly felt. Increasingly accusing stares in the synagogue left her no motivation to frequent it. And to the horror of her brother and sister, she left it altogether. While she never quite felt she belonged among the pagans, she at least found them to be a more welcoming crowd. She had never consorted in their pagan worship, she thought to herself, trying to justify her attendance. She was but a mere bystander, initially. She only joined in a couple of times, like a child playing at some form of magic ritual. She often wondered if that constituted participation, but she dismissed that fear with the excuse that something in her could not believe in their gods. She held fast to her one God, despite feeling it a distant dream-like and childish belief, a memory from a past life of carefreeness and innocence.

Her wandering memory returned to her present reality. Here she was now, having rejected her own family, steeped in a soiled reputation, having been rejected by her people, and worst of all, abandoned. She knew not where she stood in this life. She scolded herself for allowing her memories to drag her into dark moods. Recalling life's daily errands, she drew in another breath of crisp fresh air, hoping it would push out the anguished spirit that threatened to overcome her resolve to live another day.

CHAPTER 3. ABANDONED

Can a mother forget her infant, be without tenderness for the child of her womb? Even should she forget, I will never forget you. See, upon the palms of my hands I have engraved you...
Isaiah 49:15-16 (NABRE)

Mary continued onwards into town for her morning errands. She passed carefully over a burgeoning stream that a rock-hewn channel attempted to corral to the sea. She wondered at the people that had ingeniously designed the system to prevent flooding in this northern part of the town. "Town" was an understatement. Magdala was on the verge of being a small city, just under the population of Capernaum. The town was likely started by a handful of simple Jewish families nestling themselves between Mount Arbel and the Sea of Galilee only about three hundred years ago. It was a prime spot for simple farmers, fishermen, and cave dwellers. Lush vegetation and fertile soil welcomed farmers to these lands. Fresh water from underground streams flowed almost all year round, with exception of the harsher years of drought. This year was proving to be far from dry. The farmers' good fortune brought a lighter feeling, momentarily lifting a heaviness of heart.

Mary recalled her father's animated and spontaneous history lectures. He was a master story teller, weaving facts into his tales. But her present mood made his history lessons look bleak. They were all the same to her - God's election, foreign domination, struggle to overthrow it or escape bondage, a renewal of the covenant, and the cycle started again. Would her people ever be free of "the enemy"? Now the enemy was Rome. And she had fallen for a Roman, a terrible transgression in the eyes of many. But sometimes she wondered if her people were their own worst enemy, considering the squabbling fights from within.

She recalled one of her father's repetitive lessons of the struggle right here in Magdala. A little over one hundred years ago, the Hasmonean dynasty annexed Judea and Galilee, leading to an influx of Jewish settlements to this northern area of Israel.[7] By her interpretation of history, power among the Jewish leaders led to the downfall of the Hasmonean dynasty. They were weak from inside and allowed the enemy to take advantage. Was not her life analogous to her own people's plight, allowing the enemy to overthrow what was once a more peaceful life. Could she still call them "her people"? Was she still one of them, having felt rejected by many? Where did she belong? She felt so lost. Yet, ironically, she still called Magdala her home.

She recalled more of her father's history lessons. Magdala was like a little paradise at the base of Mount Arbel when many families chose to resettle here. But, eventually the Romans encroached upon their paradise, not so long ago. They captured Magdala under General Cassius' leadership. Despite the Roman governors' conquest, Magdala recovered, harboring Jewish families who maintained their religious traditions while assimilating various cultural trends of the Greco-Roman influence. She wondered when the next conquest would be. The Romans seemed to have the upper hand at present. They were confusing the people, at times pretending to permit independence, only to turn around and squeeze more life out of them. She and Gaius had often spoken of this conflict. At times she felt him to be an ally to his people. But then she would detect a presumptuous arrogance at being the elite race. There was no convincing him to see her point of view when his stubborn streak set in. They had that in common.

Mary, she scolded herself now, *leave Gaius in the past where he belongs.*

She thought it curious that despite animosity against Roman domination, the differing cultures within Magdala seemed to be tolerably integrating or at least living amongst one another while each held onto their own traditions. Perhaps that was why she had received such harsh treatment from some corners and maintained semi-cordial relationships with others. While mixed relationships were not common, the factions tolerated one another, for the most part.

Like her father, Mary had practiced many traditions of her faith, but she didn't condemn or flee from engaging in conversations with the so-called "pagans from the other side." The town itself had benefited from the interchange. She had frequented the Hellenistic style baths and walked through the streets patterned off the borrowed Hippodamian grid. She also appreciated that the more prominent dwellers were installing mosaic floors in their villas. At present the new synagogue was continuing with plans to imitate the modern Greco-Roman trends.

Despite Magdala's growth, it still had the small town feel. Everyone knew everyone's business! She was reminded of that as she passed by the synagogue that she had watched being erected when she was a child. The leading priestly family had appealed to her father, a wealthy landowner, to contribute funds for the building of the new synagogue. Her father was never one to shirk his civic and religious duties whenever they were in town and he offered a substantial contribution back then. Now there was a campaign to raise the money for further embellishment: a meander-style and rosette mosaic floor pattern. They hoped to install a rosette similar to a priestly house near the Temple. More modern and forward thinkers were proposing expensive and bright colored frescoed walls with various shades of red, yellow, ocher, purple, green, pink, orange, black and white pigment. It would be an expensive feat indeed; one to which her father would have surely contributed, if he were still alive. But now, despite the fact that she could have contributed generously, they didn't dare ask her for monetary assistance. It would be considered scandalous to take her money for such a project. She was fine with that, considering the fact that she hadn't stepped foot into the synagogue for almost four years. Memories dragged her back into the past once again.

"Miriam," Gaius tenderly consoled her as she was distraught over the accusations flung at her in her last synagogue attendance. "Abandon them. You do not need any of them." He huffed a mischievous laugh, grabbing her possessively. "They slight your great fortune in finding love."

His smile made light of the situation. It relieved her angst enough to make her laugh and send him an equally playful and haughty look, letting him know that he was the more fortunate one.

"Believe in a God or gods as you will," he continued in a more serious tone, "but you don't need those vipers telling you how to live your life."

And that did it. She never set foot in synagogue again.

Now she wondered where her fortune really lay. Her memories of Gaius would creep in unbidden.

Why can I not let him go?! Be gone you old memories! You serve me no more!

Their friendship, if that is what you could call it, had lasted almost three years with no indication of a commitment of marriage, although she believed he was considering the prospect and was faithful to her. She had thought that it was true love, something that would last. She had considered the unconventionality of the relationship but had not heeded other's warnings that it could not be.

And then, from one day to the next, he disappeared. Sent on assignment to Rome, she was told. An immediate and urgent order. His friends said not to worry, they would take care of her. She had never trusted them, especially not Vespasian, his supposedly best friend. They were all crude and ignorant. She had often judged them as such and told Gaius. Nonetheless, they were his people, his closest allies. And so she had welcomed them into her house, against the disapproving looks of Tams and Babs and the further town gossip that it produced.

Eventually word arrived through various channels that he did not know when he would return. Then she was told he was not to return any time soon. Time passed and news circulated that he had taken a Roman wife, and Mary was seen as free game to his acquaintances. At least before he left there had been an unspoken understanding. They didn't dare disrespect her while Gaius was around. But then, he was gone. Hope extinguished. And those she had once called Gaius' friends took advantage, without her consent.

18

Gaius' actions struck her as betrayal. Used and discarded. Deceived. She fell into her usual cycle of spinning and tormenting thoughts.

Had his signs of affection been true? Had I been a mere plaything, an amusement for his temporary period in Tiberias? I am a Jew after all, and a Jewish wife would not be favorable for his ambitious career.

She suddenly felt just like those women she had pitied on the street years ago in the marketplace. Her mother had warned against associating with them.

Am I like them? No, I had been faithful to him. And I thought he had been the same to me.

Devastated, angry, confused. The deception seemed to rewrite her entire story under a new lens. Abandoned. She had been abandoned. Buried emotions from the death of her father and mother surfaced like a monster suddenly disturbed from a long slumber. They exacerbated the grief she felt over Gaius. Somewhere over the years she had told herself that she was abandoned by her parents and by the God whom they had taught her was a God of power, of life, of love.

Where was God's power when her father had been ill? When both of her parents died?

Part of her knew that it was unreasonable to think and feel that way. The other part of her did not listen to reason. Reason didn't change the deep sense of abandonment that festered like an open wound.

Betrayed. Deceived. Abandoned. She turned her confusion to wrath, directing it at God in a subconscious way.

What God would permit this? To a girl of fourteen who needed her father and mother. To a young woman willing to give her life to her beloved.

Mary no longer recognized the precocious yet innocent little girl, the favorite of her father. Now she felt that her mother's predictions had come true. The constant warnings and scoldings seemed like distant prophecies.

What has become of me? I have become what they all said I would be!

She had slowly spiraled downward, fitting into the mold of people's accusations and murmurings. She recalled her fascination with the women of the court when she was young. Her romantic idealism and daydreams of being a woman of great influence led to a superficial admiration of their stylish dress and expensive adornments. She had imagined that they were above society's norms, not subject to man but his equal. How naive she had been. Now she had a taste of the lies behind the masked appearances. They were no better off than the women of ill repute on the streets. She had pitied them both and perhaps could be accused of holding her own self-righteous judgments against them, even as she herself socialized in Herod's court. Back then, she wondered how they had succumbed to being beggars of men's affection. Little did she know back then that she would fall into a similar trap. An internal debate surfaced again and again in her conscience.

I was a victim. No, I was a sinner. But I had been duped. No, I had chosen my own path.

Deep down, she knew she made excuses for herself in an attempt to reconcile her own consent, as thwarted and vulnerable as she had been in Gaius´ tempting lair.

After all, she frequently rationalized, *I had remained faithful to one. And he had spoiled it all.*

Since he abandoned her, feeling loved had been replaced by a sense of shame and regret. She tried to bury everything and little by little she felt her heart numbing. She wondered if it was turning to stone. But no, stone does not feel the black torments that beset her.

Paradoxically, her beloved Magdala, in which she had once found favor in the eyes of others, had become a place that drove her back into the "spider's lair", time and time again. She loathed to return to Herod's court. But it was there that she still felt strangely accepted, untouched by the eyes of judgment, for they too had much to be judged by their lifestyle. It was nonsensical, even to herself.

At present, her predominant mood bordered on disconsolate. She knew she was beautiful, but instead she felt ugly and forlorn. Despite her naturally social disposition, loneliness was nipping at her heart. Her spirit was constantly agitated and restless. She tried to shake off the prevailing mood as she glanced skyward. She tried to replace the feeling with another deep breath of crisp air and let the sun warm her face.

The day was starting out gloriously sunny. It was a good respite from the winter rains.

A respite, she thought, *how I wish I could find rest from the torments within.* For the moment, she would attempt to console herself with activity. She forced herself to pass by the synagogue and entered the market-place, unsure if she desired distraction or refuge from unwelcome company.

CHAPTER 4. TRANSGRESSIONS

My people have become lost sheep;
Their shepherds have led them astray.
They have made them turn aside on the mountains;
They have gone along from mountain to hill
And have forgotten their resting place.
Jeremiah 50:6 (NASB)

Nostalgic sentiments surfaced in her morning walk through the marketplace, ushering in memories of sunrise visits to the harbor with her father. He preferred to purchase the fresh fish down at the harbor as the early morning catches arrived. She continued his tradition.

All was relatively quiet as shopkeepers prepared for their day's clients. She had beaten the rush. Later, the streets would be bustling with locals, as well as Romans and Greeks who sought out Magdala's renowned fish products. The Greeks had made a name for Magdala calling it Tarichaea, "the place of salted fish." Magdala relied on purchases from travelers far and wide. The town's economic vitality depended on it.

Mary knew that Magdala held ties to the pagans, both culturally and economically. Some Jews would prefer to pretend they didn't need the foreigners. Despite the Roman invasion having begun generations ago, resentment still rankled many residents. They felt and feared further violations of their freedom. She laughed to herself at the irony. Some Jews hated the Romans and Greeks and yet greed made them barter and cater to their enemy's request. Resentment was an underlying tension that seemed impossible to heal. Her own life paralleled the nonsensical dynamic that existed in her country, and among many people in her town.

Mary shook her head as though to free herself from heavy ponderings. Her attention turned to one of her favorite stores: the vial shop. Although closed, the wavering scents elicited memories of her mother. It was always a treat to visit and inspect the variety of diverse containers holding precious ointments and perfumes. But other goods tantalized her senses as she passed by piles of fresh produce tempting her hungry stomach. The fertile land of Gennesaret, just north of Magdala, brought delicious produce to the marketplace: walnuts, dates, olives, figs, grapes, peaches, and much more was in abundance. She quickly pulled out a few coins, leaving them on the counter as she scooped up a handful of fresh dates to appease her growling stomach. She was glad the shopkeeper was busy in the backroom. His permanent scowl was too much for her this morning. The day's weather had promised respite from the anxiety she had felt of late, and she didn't want to spoil it more than it already was from her previous darker memories.

As she moved on, a less pleasant smell overpowered the sweetness of her breakfast. Pigeons and mourning doves flitted about, to the extent that their small wooden cages permitted. Her heart swelled with empathy as they cuckooed and flapped their wings in their little manmade prisons. They were destined to be sacrificial offerings. The caves in the local Mount Arbel were ideal conditions for harvesting pigeon-doves. As a child she had watched the annual loading of wagons that carted the unsuspecting creatures off to Jerusalem for the festivities at the Temple. The memories ushered in a nostalgic sense of foreboding mystery. But it quickly eluded her as one particular pigeon caught her attention with its incessant squawking, unaware of its fate. Leaving the caged birds behind, she came to a boardwalk leading her to the harbor.

Ah, her beloved town of Magdala, a place rich in people and culture. Paradoxically, it was, at present, a place from which she longed to escape. Yet she stayed. *Perhaps it is myself that I wish to escape?* Magdala was the closest thing she felt to home and familiarity. It linked her to memories of better and happier days. But then she would be overcome with loneliness as it reminded her of all she had lost.

Mary arrived at the bustling and noisy harbor as the sun, almost blinding her, climbed steadily over the hills on the opposite shore.

Trading had commenced. Greek mixed with Aramaic as buyers and sellers negotiated. Magdala was a convenient distance to the other harbors, ideal and accessible for trading, but a safe enough distance from the idol worshippers that inhabited the Decapolis across the sea.

A boat building industry had gained ground among the other fourteen harbors and anchorages along the Galilean seashores. Although when it came to fixing the worn battered boats, she noticed that each fisherman found their own way. They were resourceful men. She watched them haul in nets, taking stock of the fruits of their late night and early morning labors. Workers sorted fish into pools and basins, preparing the day's catch for market or processing, for sale and for shipping.

Men from all corners of Mary Magdalene's known world were in and out of this harbor. The Gentiles hailed from the Decapolis. And all were under the scrutinizing eye of Roman inspectors. She enjoyed the diverse group, despite their roughness. They were technically below her social class, but one thing she appreciated about this group of "dregs," is that Jew or Gentile, their common trade as fishermen obscured their differences as they taunted each other in a spirit of camaraderie and competition. A sense of freedom tweaked at her conscience at that thought. She wished to belong to a group in which social paradigms were known and acknowledged but made no difference in the way you were treated. Her heart ached to experience a new world in which all the prejudices and barriers between people faded away.

"Miriam." A man's familiar voice called out her Jewish name.

Aharon, an old friend of her brother, was standing at the water's edge. One hand grasped the edge of his boat as he balanced himself after jumping out. And one hand waved her over.

"I've got a good one for you Miriam! Come!"

His tall and scrawny appearance was comical with his jovial presence. Since he got married, the harbor was about the only time she heard him speak. Otherwise, his wife filled in any silent space in their house. Theirs was a match that resembled the one she had thought she might have one day. Although he was Jew and his wife had been the pagan. Somehow, that was accepted by her people more than the other way around. She called out a greeting.

"Thank you, Aharon! You always come through for me. Let me see that catch."

His partners gave her a quick nod of acknowledgment. They didn't pay much attention to her. She was used to the spectrum of gazes wherever she went: indifference, politeness, lewdness. Like most women, she disdained the lewd looks, knowing that her social standing was well above mere fishermen. The looks of indifference she matched with her own. But politeness often caught her off guard. It softened her heart, making her feel dignified, as her status should have afforded her. Somehow, it made her believe in the beauty she naturally possessed.

With Aharon, she felt beautiful, but not in a way that she was tempted to flaunt it or use it to her advantage. He was like an innocent child, like a brother, treating her as a sister. It was her only link to Lazarus, whom she had stubbornly avoided and refused to acknowledge for the last several years.

Aharon held out a nice sized fat catch. She opened her bag and watched the healthy looking fish slip into the pouch she brought for this occasion. Behind Aharon, an abundant catch covered most of the boat's hull. A few random fish thrashed about attempting to escape their fate, but for the most part, they lay still, ready for sorting.

"It seems that the fish were happy to board your boat last night, Aharon!" Mary teased.

"The Lord has blessed us abundantly. Demetria will be happy! But Miriam," exuberance rose to the point of almost bursting, "we are all going to be doubly blessed with the arrival of the Messiah."

Aharon checked and controlled his emotion, then continued, "I think I met him. Yesterday. Not too far from here." He slapped a hand over his mouth as though attempting to contain whatever words wanted to escape.

"Aharon, don't be fooled. Too many false hopes have come and gone. Don't be so gullible."

Aharon ignored the fact that she was dismissing his news.

"Well, I better not say more. Demetria will have my head. I am sure she will want to share this news. But Miriam, it is promised us, as the Baptist has been preaching. The Kingdom of God is at hand. He called for repentance. And now this Jesus of Nazareth is calling for repentance as well. I want to take Demetria to hear him preach. Perhaps you could go with us and meet him. Perhaps he could help you?"

She loved Aharon, as kind as he was to her, but every time he attempted to speak to her of repentance, she felt a wall go up in her heart. Her own resistance bewildered and confused her. For a moment, with Aharon and Demetria, she could forget the past that hovered over her, binding her in scandal. Being with them was like a slight taste of home. She would feel the distance shortening between her present state and her family's traditions that she had begun to neglect years ago. But when Aharon turned to the theme of repentance, she recoiled. She knew he meant well, but it did nothing for her.

I am what I am, and there is no way out, the frequent dark thought echoed in her ear.

Aharon, while zealous in his faith, was also sensitive. He saw her countenance change and scolded himself for his impetuous comment. But he cared for her, having been friends with her brother for many years, back in their early childhood, even before Mary was born.

"Well Miriam," he said gently. "Please stop and see Demetria. But brace yourself. I am sure she will be a torrent of excitement after what I told her yesterday when I returned from Capernaum."

"Thank you, Aharon. And thank you for the good catch you set aside for me. I will leave payment with Demetria." Mary offered a polite nod and turned from the shore.

Aharon watched with a heavy heart, believing in Mary's goodness, but perceiving the web in which she was stuck. Four years ago, he had sent a message to Lazarus, warning him about the rumors flitting about Magdala. Aharon had heard she was frequenting Tiberias, consorting with people within Herod's court. He had been worried and kept a distant but vigilant eye on her, sending news every once in a while to her brother. Mary was always a free-spirited and independent girl, now a woman. A stubborn woman at that, who went after what she wanted.

She had managed to keep the villa in excellent shape, refusing her brother's assistance. He admired her tenacity, despite her flaws in pride and vanity.

He wasn't sure what she had gotten herself into, but she had changed. He also knew her Roman friend had finally disappeared. But this past year she began to look despondent, depressed. Sometimes she even looked frenzied. She had stopped attending synagogue about four years ago and she no longer took the treasured journey to Jerusalem for the Great Festival. She had lost her youthful happiness. She had even lost some of her playful mischievousness. Her unconventional ways had often won her a scolding, harmless as they were. But eventually, he wasn't sure Mary's activities were so harmless. Something had taken over the innocence she once possessed.

Aharon had appealed to his wife, hoping she could talk Mary out of any temptations she was walking into. But, while they had become friends, Mary wouldn't reveal to her what was truly happening. And Demetria didn't know how to convince Mary to return to synagogue. Lazarus was no help. He seemed at his wit's end with her and finally, whether from health or exasperation, stopped visiting altogether. Or when he did come, he would not stay with Mary. He kept his distance, as though he was spying on her without her knowing, and respecting her wishes to keep away.

Aharon stood perplexed and disappointed as Mary left. A wet net slammed into his body, startling him back to the task at hand.

"Why bother with her Aharon?" His gruff partner had no patience for his attempts to convert others. "She is a lost cause like the rest of those pagans you keep preaching to whenever you get the chance. Why don't you spend your energy where it does some good! That net needs mending and I did it yesterday."

Aharon scowled at his partner and picked up the edge of the net to haul it ashore, but as he looked up to watch Mary walk away, he lifted up a prayer for her.

The fisherman's words had carried upon the wind and stung Mary. *Lost cause? Is that what I am? So much for a pleasant day.*

Shame and misery crept in once again, masked by seething anger and an attempt at cold indifference. She went on, bracing herself for her visit with Demetria. As she walked out of the harbor, snatches of conversation caught her ear. An internal tug of war was going on as she fought against a growing curiosity about the charismatic, itinerant, and newly arrived rabbi. He had recently settled in Capernaum and despite his call to "repent", similar to the Baptist's, he was attracting more and more followers.[8]

Well, I will not be one of them. Be assured of that! Her streak of stubbornness cried out. *I forge my own way,* she convinced herself. She raised her chin, defiant to an invisible crowd, and once again attempted to purge her mood with the rich scent in the air.

CHAPTER 5. CURIOUS NEWS

"For I know the plans I have for you," declares the Lord,
"plans to prosper you and not to harm you,
plans to give you hope and a future."
Jeremiah 29:11

Demetria's house, which served as the town's bakery, was a mere five minute walk from the shore.[9] Wafts of freshly baked bread tickled her nose, replacing the smell of fish and dirty fishermen as she strolled along the path to the large complex. The full effects of Demetria's early morning labors engulfed Mary as she stepped into the room that served for transactions with the customers. The robust and vivacious baker was as close a friend as Mary had in this town. From their first encounter, there was an unspoken acceptance of one another. Besides the connection with Aharon, their friendship was likely due to the fact that neither of them felt completely accepted by some of the prominent leaders. Though Mary never shared intimate details of her life, Demetria treated her as though she were a best friend. She was Greek, from one of the cities of the Decapolis, but soon became one of Aharon's "catches". She accepted the one God when she married him.

Demetria looked up and smiled with eager eyes, as though relieved to have a friend with whom to share her news.

"Miriam, come, I must speak with you," she whispered excitedly, in the midst of her transaction with a customer. She gestured with her head to wait for her in the side room, then hurried back as soon as she sent the customer on her way. Mary, clued into the reason for her enthusiasm, decided to not give away Aharon. She would receive the news as though hearing it for the first time from Demetria's lips.

"Guess what I heard from Aharon?"

Before Mary could respond, Demetria launched into her story.

"Aharon was over at the Cursi harbor and heard a story about a herd of swine racing down the embankment and into the sea nearby. It turns out that Jesus of Nazareth, that man who John the Baptist announced, healed a man possessed by a legion of demons."

Demetria's animation increased as she spoke with as much of her arms as her mouth and facial expressions.

"He was a crazy man, yelling and screaming, foaming at the mouth, and haunting the graveyard. Now he is perfectly sane! Jesus cured him by sending the evil spirits into the swine. Can you believe it?! Aharon thinks that we should go see him. See Jesus, I mean, no the demoniac, and hear him teach. He has been spending more and more time in this area."

Mary didn't have to act surprised after all. She was stunned at the news. She had heard rumors of Jesus, but like hearing the news of John the Baptist, had dismissed them both as another zealot making noise. She had been expecting her to share news at her amazement over this rabbi-fellow, but demons? Healing a person of demons? Before she could ask more, Demetria raced on.

"And then just yesterday Aharon returned from Capernaum. He saw hundreds of people upon the landing near the hill by the seven springs and that same Jesus standing up along the hillside preaching. Aharon went on to Capernaum for business, but when he was on his way back the people were still there, gathered into groups. He asked some other fishermen what was happening. Turns out, the people were famished, and Jesus gathered what few provisions they had among them, then worked a miracle, turning a handful of fish and bread loaves into a king's feast. They had twelve baskets full after feeding everyone! Imagine! A handful of fish and loaves turned into twelve baskets full!"

Demetria paused long enough to take a breath. Excitement gave way to vexation as she blurted out with sudden realization, "He's going to put me out of business if he keeps that up!"

Mary's amazement over the miracles trumped any compassion for the loss of business her baker-friend ranted on about. She remained in stunned silence. Demetria's mood changed again as quickly as a winter shower passes over Magdala.

"Well, expelling demons and multiplying bread. That is something to see isn't it Miriam!"

Mary's heart was wavering between disbelief and curiosity. It sounded like a child's tale. She was still imagining the possessed man when Demetria's storytelling demanded her attention again.

"That's not all Miriam! Jesus has rallied together several fishermen. I had heard, several months ago, that he told them to just leave their nets and follow him. But it is confirmed. Told four of them and they left their business and families and everything. He tempted them with a big miraculous catch of fish, so many fish their nets were close to bursting!"

She paused briefly, suddenly distraught. "So help me if Aharon gets any ideas of following that rabbi and leaving me high and dry!"

Just as quickly, Demetria's countenance changed again, displaying a myriad of emotions.

"Oh Miriam, I'm so curious! I want to see him! But I'm scared. What if Aharon gets the same urge as those other fishermen, always preaching as he is, eager for converts. Is he going to just pick up and leave me behind?"

Mary was trying to process all she had heard and at the same time muster up compassion for Demetria's distress. She was familiar with her friend's quickly changing and exaggerated emotional states, but she wanted to assure her.

"Don't worry Demetria! Aharon would never leave you. He loves you and is an honorable man. Besides, if he even thinks about it, I will smack some sense into him."

A customer hollered from the other room and Demetria returned to the business at hand.

"Oh Miriam, your bread. You must have places to be yourself. Keep your eyes out for that Jesus of Nazareth. He must be a sight to see. How I would love to hear him! Here you go Miriam, one fresh loaf for you. Have a good day. Looked like a promising one today with clear skies at dawn, but now I see a dark horizon to the west. Storm must be headed our way. Tired of these rainy cold days. Spring is late in coming, isn't it! Hope the storm blows over fast. Bye Miriam."

Mary barely got a goodbye out of her mouth when a loaf of bread was shoved into her arms and Demetria walked away to attend to her customer. Mary dropped some coins into a money jar as payment for the fish and bread and left the bakery, pondering what she had heard.

I wonder if I will see this Jesus of Nazareth when I go to Capernaum for business? Do I even want to run into him? A cautious curiosity brewed inside. Her own emotions confused her. Mary's heart was agitated.

What kind of man expelled demons and provided for thousands of hungry people? She wondered at this Jesus of Nazareth whose compassion provided for such an abundance of people. Then images of a self-righteous man preaching repentance quickly turned her curiosity to irritation.

He probably just rants and raves about repentance like the crazy Baptist I've heard about. It seems to have become a fad. An interior resistance stifled a barely lit kindling in her soul. Restless, so restless. She longed for solitude, a strange desire when she already felt so alone in the world.

She glanced to the northwest. Clouds were indeed forming, but the sun still shone brightly above Magdala. A steady breeze had picked up. She calculated that she still had time to take refuge on the beach, to withdraw to one of her favorite places. Heading north, parallel to the harbor, she walked a few minutes to the edge of its reach. At the end of town, she turned right, onto a path that wound through tall sea grass and onto a patch of sandy beach. The tall grass was enough to shelter her from sight. The wind, lapping of the water, and squacco herons flitting about drowned out the noise from the harbor. There, she sought refuge from the restlessness of her own heart.

CHAPTER 6. RESTLESSNESS & LONGINGS

But now, thus says the Lord,
who created you, Jacob, and formed you, Israel:
Do not fear, for I have redeemed you;
I have called you by name: you are mine.
Isaiah 43:1

The narrow beach strip, surrounded by tall sea grass, was Mary's place of peace, a sort of safe haven amidst the restlessness that stirred within. The sun baking on her skin tempered the cold breeze. The fresh fragrance of the grass and sea and the view of the towering hills on the opposite seashore filled her senses. Memories of childhood began flooding her mind, a temporary respite from a gnawing loneliness. She recalled one of the many visits to Magdala with her family. One of her favorite memories was to this shoreline.

Her father had just purchased a small pocket net that was attached to the end of a long fishing pole. Everyone in the family laughed at his attempts to catch a fish, teasing him that he better not quit his old occupation for this newly desired trade or they would end up poor and on the streets. He just laughed and continued to wade the waters, back and forth, waiting for that one fish, as though it had a date with his net. It became a game with the family finally joining him, trying to hunt with the hope of corralling them towards him and his net. She remembers everyone's surprise when suddenly, down dipped his net into the waters and with an upward thrust, out came the net with a good sized catch! The whooping and rejoicing was a sight to see!

Mary recalled her strangely comforting thought. As she had watched the prized fish thrash around, she had thought how lucky the fish was to have been taken up in her father's net. It would be truly valued and appreciated. It would nourish the family with a feast tonight. If a fish had feelings, this fish would be proud to be caught! It belonged to a good family now. It had a purpose.

Belonging and purpose, that is what she missed. She recalled Demetria's tales of Jesus "catching" the fishermen.

Is that why they left everything and followed him? Belonging and purpose? Do all things have their place and purpose in this life? My life feels more like nonsensical chaos right now. Everything feels out of place.

Remnants of psalms rose slowly to her consciousness, like submerged treasures striving to surface from underwater depths. She remembered standing on the beach after the family fish-catching adventure. The sun was dropping behind Mount Arbel at their backs, turning the horizon all hues of pink. She leaned into her mother, snuggling deeper into her arms, and listened to her sing a prayer of praise with joyful awe. It was a rare moment of affection.

All of Mary's life, her mother had suffered from variable moods and bouts of extreme fatigue, as her sister had called it, which took her into isolation in her parents' room. But during the short weeks of her mother's life, after her father's death, she became even more distant, a mere stranger who eventually slipped out of this world. She preferred the scarce memories of her mother from before her father became ill, when her cheeks were ruby red from the sun and wind, and her father made her laugh with his teasing.

Her mother could recite and sing a multitude of verses for every occasion. *What were those words she had spoken?* Mary longed to conjure up the feeling of comfort it had brought years ago.

> Bless the Lord, my soul!
> Lord, my God, you are great indeed!
> You are clothed in majesty and splendor, robed in light as with a cloak.
> You spread out the heavens like a tent; setting the beams of your chamber upon the waters.
> You make the clouds your chariot; traveling on the wings of the wind.[10]

Her father had loved to speak of God's majesty. But he was particularly fond of remembering God's providential love for his people, ironically speaking as if he had been Jewish all his life. But he had learned everything from her mother's father, or perhaps even her own mother, and had assumed it as his own. He would often make her recite his favorite words from the prophet Isaiah. Her father believed it spoke not only of God's faithful action in the past, but of a time to come. When they had recited those words, her hope always ripened into joy.

> But now, thus says the Lord,
> who created you, Jacob, and formed you, Israel:
> Do not fear, for I have redeemed you;
> I have called you by name: you are mine.[11]

You are mine. She used to feel as though she belonged. Now she felt ungrounded, rootless, so to speak. Blessings of all that she had received flashed by her eyes. The firm hand of her mother she had not necessarily appreciated, nor the seriousness of her father. But she loved his humor and playfulness. And how they had provided for her and her siblings! They were never for want of anything. She recognized that she often took their generous nature and the comforts of life for granted. While her sister seemed to freely give away their possessions to the town's poor that occasioned their doorstep, Mary had a particular interest in befriending those women from the marketplace that her mother didn't dare approach.

Mary's impulsiveness and naivety practically sent her mother to her deathbed when, at seven years old, she had wandered off and then was found vivaciously chatting with "the scandalous women". She was attracted by beauty and saw something in those women. She didn't understand it at the time, but later she understood that she saw potential but lost beauty. Their wit and sassiness didn't hide their sad eyes which made Mary even more curious. She sensed kindred passionate souls like herself in many of those stolen encounters.

Mary would suddenly find herself yanked away by her mother who had lost sight of her as she went about business at the marketplace. The women began to recognize her, seemed delighted to see her, and slipped her little treats. Her mother didn't know what to do with her. Her father simply laughed, thinking that they were harmless experiences and gave her a wink, revealing that he was secretly proud of her for not turning her back on women whose circumstances were less fortunate than her own. Her mother perceived the attraction to this lost group as a bad omen and a sign of an unruly heart and misguided zeal.

The thought of how far she had fallen from the ideal her mother had constantly placed before her agitated her spirit, matching the changing lake scene. The winds had picked up speed and were pushing the waves higher as an approaching storm announced its coming. But Mary remained immovable as she sat before the sea. Despite her mother's strictness at times, she recalled her deep faith and trust in God. Words of a psalm flooded in again as she remembered more lines.

> You fixed the earth on its foundations, for ever and
> ever it shall not be shaken; you covered it with the deep
> like a garment, the waters overtopping the mountains.
> At your reproof the waters fled, at the voice of your
> thunder they sped away, flowing over the mountains,
> down valleys, to the place you had fixed for them; you
> made a limit they were not to cross, they were not to
> return and cover the earth.[12]

God's power over the earth and waters confused her. *Why could he not have used His power to stop her parents from dying? His people from slavery and domination of a foreign power? My own heart from being deceived and broken? Men from violating my intimacy and trampling my dignity?*

She felt her own circumstances as a cruel fate. If she had God's power, how would she use it? She thought of the rabbi, Jesus, and the stories about his demon expulsion and multiplication of bread and fish. *Did he have God's power? How were those things possible if he was not from God?*

A jumping fish broke her musings, and she turned to another line in the psalm. Despite not having murmured those prayers for a very long time, they flowed out as though carved upon her memory.

> How many are your works, Lord! In wisdom you made them all; the earth is full of your creatures. There is the sea, vast and spacious, teeming with creatures beyond number-living things both large and small.[13]
>
> All creatures look to you to give them their food at the proper time. When you give it to them, they gather it up; when you open your hand, they are satisfied with good things. When you hide your face, they are terrified; when you take away their breath, they die and return to dust. When you send your Spirit, they are created, and you renew the face of the earth. May the glory of the Lord endure forever; may the Lord rejoice in his works - he who looks at the earth, and it trembles, who touches the mountains, and they smoke.[14]

She trembled at the thought of her life depending so much on the breath of God sustaining her. Fear of His wrath overcame her. *Why does he not just wipe me off the face of the earth? That is what I deserve. But then, so did the first couple that walked the face of the earth.*

An image of the story of creation, so often told by her mother, brought the first couple to her imagination. Her first instinct was to dwell on their terrible transgression, their sin of disobedience from distrust, as her mother had called it. But then she recalled her father's take on it. The first couple had walked in friendship with God in the garden of paradise. The thought of that privilege overwhelmed her with a sense of intimacy, a stark contrast to her loneliness.

For a brief moment nostalgia swept over her. Her deep loneliness disappeared and took on another form. A welcomed solitude. Like the first couple, alone with God in the garden. *What would that be like? To walk with God? To look into his face?* Not even Moses was permitted that lest he die. She imagined it would be terrifying, yet glorious. *To come face to face with God, alone before your Maker.*

The sense of solitude was now pervaded with presence. She didn't know if it was her overactive imagination or a sensation of something real, a flitter of something old and new, familiar yet elusive, inviting her to leave a heaviness and hardness of heart behind and experience…*experience what? Innocence? Freedom?*

To have God's eyes upon her suddenly turned from terrifying to awesome. No pretense would be needed! No hiding. No struggle against expectations. No shame or fear. She longed to be seen and known without judgment, to be loved by a Providing Creator, to trust that God was all-powerful and good and loving.

Just as fast as the wave of nostalgia had crashed upon her, it petered out. Awareness of her present reality overwhelmed her. *No, I am alone. Mother and father are gone. I am like Adam and Eve, as my mother had predicted, fallen.* She felt abandoned and shunned, alone and independent, by circumstance and by choice, with no place in this world.

She rose to go, but the last verse of the psalm brought her to her knees as it slipped from her lips, "May sinners vanish from the earth, and the wicked exist no more! Bless the Lord, my soul."[15] With it, the echo of Jesus' words crying out, "Repent!" lashed against her conscience. Tension and fear of being condemned rose up to suffocate her. She longed to know the heart of God, the one who walked in intimate friendship in the garden of paradise, where innocence reigned. She didn't want to resist. But she felt so little, frail, alone. *Could I possibly be welcomed into that garden, belong and be loved in an intimate way?*

"You are mine," echoed again in her mind. *To belong, to be God's. Is that within my reach? How could God work such a thing?* With a sigh, she muttered her own spontaneous prayer, desiring to trust in the God she remembered from her childhood - the One who stopped the floodwaters and started all anew, who brought her people from slavery to a promised land where she lived today, who preserved the Israelites from destruction time and time again despite many exiles and conquests.

How she ached to know this God again. How long it had been since she had prayed!

Another Psalm came to her, consoling her as she released the tension she felt within. "Find your delight in the Lord who will give you your heart's desire. Commit your way to the Lord; trust in him and he will act."[16]

Despite an agonizing mix of feelings, hope shone like a barely visible beacon on a distant shore. The agonizing plea of her heart was enough to let God in. *Maybe that Jesus of Nazareth could show me the way to delight in the Lord and commit my way to him.*

And then a strong, cold wind descended upon her, loosening her braid until her hair swirled in a tumultuous mess. Drops of rain spattered on her face, mingling with the tears that had escaped unperceived. A drop in the temperature and darkened horizon told her it was time to run for cover. Mary had business in Capernaum that she had hoped to attend to, or at least, that was her excuse for deciding to walk to that town, secretly hoping for a chance run-in with the rabbi and miracle worker. Activity, she told herself, that is what she needed. But that must wait for another day. Time to head home and shelter from this day's shower.

CHAPTER 7. FLIRTING WITH DEATH

And do not fear those who kill the body
but cannot kill the soul.
Rather fear him who can destroy
both soul and body in hell.
Matthew 10:28

Mary woke with memories of yesterday. Her sleep had been as restless as the raging storm throughout the night. Her solitude on the beach had helped her momentarily regain peace, but this morning she was more disturbed than ever. Life was too complicated right now. Once, long ago, she was simply Miriam, the beloved yet precocious daughter of faith-filled and generous parents. Her family had been well-respected and well-to-do. Born into affluence, she lacked nothing, materially speaking anyways. Temperamentally sharp, her feminine curiosity, her expansive spirit, and her grandiose desires shaped the once-young and noble heart. Yet circumstances and ongoing concessions had opened the door into a lair of temptations. *Have I fallen and become trapped in an unholy life?*

She had become the woman "possessed by seven demons." That was how many referred to her. No matter if they accused her of being possessed by seven or seven hundred. When she slipped into despondency or ill humor, it was as if she could not recognize her own self. She saw no way to climb out of the darkness. She just had to wait out the terrifying storm that wreaked havoc on her interior world and certainly frightened others by its manifestations of ire and irascibility.

Mary tried to put those unpleasant thoughts aside but couldn't shake the feelings that they had engendered. She made her preparations for the day, expertly weaving her thick hair off her face into a lengthy braid. Heavy clouds hung over Magdala, but the heavens held back the season's deluge for the moment. She decided to go to market once again today, which always promised adventure depending on who she encountered. The murmurings of others assaulted her whenever she walked about in her hometown. She would escape it now and again by wandering anonymously into nearby towns, meandering amidst passersby coming to and from the market. She had even tried to seek refuge from the piercing judgments leveled against her by returning to Herod's court. Hers was a familiar face there.

She tried not to care about others' opinions; a seemingly sturdy wall forged a barrier between two interior worlds in her heart. One held unspoken desires for goodness, wholeness, love and courage. This one showed itself occasionally, bringing a glimmer to her eyes and a short-lived resolve in her spirit as she glanced heavenward. In those moments, hope warmed her heart as the sun warmed her face. The prospect of something more, something beyond her present existence seemed possible for a fleeting moment, like yesterday's visit to her safe haven on the beach. But before long, the storm would overtake her, sweeping over her like a tidal wave. Reality, her reality, would rear its ugly head, snuffing out the little light that fought for its life, leaving her in darkness, doubt, anger, and confusion and engulfing her in despair and shame. This was the prevailing mood of the present.

This morning, she desperately hungered for rescue from death's grip upon her soul. Was she exaggerating to call it death? It certainly did not feel like a life she wanted to endure. *What have I become? Who am I?* She didn't want to face the answers but couldn't help asking. Hope eluded her as a sigh of defeat disclosed her interior turmoil.

At times she would fight against the piercing shame that welled up in the face of judgmental glances from others. There was something of truth to these accusations, yet their attitudes towards her were not justifiable. In the face of judgment, she defended something deep within, although she knew not what or why. She tried to convince herself that she neither wanted nor needed their acceptance. They would never see who she really was. Without being able to formulate or understand it, she sensed that something inside herself remained good, intact and needed to be protected. She longed for a time when someone would look upon her and see her for who she really was in this deep interior recess. But unable to grasp this obscure reality, she remained on the defensive, often putting up walls of rebellion, indifference, distrust or anger.

A vicious cycle had ensued over the course of the last few years: an immersion into escapes and fleeting, vain compensations, then guilt and shame consuming her, followed by a desperate hunger for rescue from the death she felt inside. Life continued like that, spiraling into a chasm of confusion and darkness. And so she remained as she was, as though trapped in a cage where interior freedom seemed beyond her grasp.

Activity, I need to do something! She gathered her money bag and colorful linen cloak. It was a bold color and a gift from Gaius. She fluctuated between tearing it apart and holding onto it like a life-line of hope that those days were not full of lies. Mary felt like a living paradox. She wished to hide from all and remain unseen. Then, she felt a daunting boldness, an almost reckless frenzy to prove herself as part of society. Today was one of those latter days. Her cloak reminded her of how often she did just that.

She used to gallivant proudly through the marketplace, draped in the scarlet red cloak, accompanied by an entourage of followers, other young women, girls really, whom she had befriended in Herod's court. Little Joanna among them. But time had proved who her true friends were. Only little Joanna had stuck around after Gaius disappeared. And eventually life circumstances sent even her off to Jerusalem as soon as she was married, like most of those who were once her little band of admirers. *Probably for the best. I am not worthy to be admired anymore.*

She set off towards the marketplace, entering the streets lined with booths that held enticing treasures: the last of fall's fruits, spices alluring the senses, flax for weaving linen and sails,[17] glass vials of various sizes, pigeons galore raised in the local caves, and fish, always fish! She weaved her way through the streets on her way to her favorite store of exotic perfumes. She expected no kindness or mercy from these quarters. Not even pity could be detected in the sideways stares directed at her. *I don't care what they think of me,* she tried to convince herself as she went about her business. *I have a right. It's my town too. Besides, most of those hypocrites craved riches and would not refuse a coin, no matter the hand from which it came.*

Sometimes she felt like a ghost passing through this world. Was this really her flesh? Her heart? Her house? Her money? Her town? Her people? Why did she feel so estranged? She seemed to float invisibly among the people, laughing, taunting, delighting. Herself, yet not her. Existing, but not really present. Searching questions pushed their way to the surface time and time again: *Who am I really? What is the purpose of my existence?* She held the answers at bay, fearful of disappointment if she let that dark voice within answer.

Is there no help for me? the religious authorities, Gaius, the men who treated her as they did. But inwardly, as she sought to put the blame on someone else, as she tried to appear like she had it all together, she spiraled into self-accusations. She knew that the blame game would not solve her problems. But what would? Change was beyond her strength. And deep within, she knew the truth. *Change is beyond me. Who then can help me? Who can take me out of my misery if even God refuses to look upon me?*

She shook her head from her inward introspection and picked up her pace as she continued through the town. Her walk towards the main road inevitably took her past the synagogue, reminding her of the leading Pharisee, Simon. He derived pleasure in pointing out infractions of those who were not law abiding citizens. There was no end to what you couldn't do or had to do to remain righteous according to his standards. A sickening weight sat in her stomach as she recalled her spells of rebellion against the strict laws and traditions of her religion. It had not been so until she felt herself rejected. Then, she knew that her curiosity and prideful daring may have taken her too far into the realm of the pagan.

Mary spotted the Pharisee as she approached the basalt purification bowl that decorated the roadside between the marketplace and synagogue entrance. His sneer was enough to communicate his feelings about her without making eye contact. She kept her head down and covered as she passed, not daring to walk close enough to touch him, for she knew she was judged as impure. But her defensive and rebellious spirit was boiling under the surface. She felt the urge to bump into him just to defy him. He would have to start his purification process all over again.

She resisted, passed him by and turned left into a store of overpowering scents from distant lands. All the selections cost a hefty coin, but she spared no expense on these amenities. A new item caught her attention, a beautiful alabaster flask. She made her request to the shop owner: a pint of spikenard, an import from India, to be stored in the alabaster jar. Its musky, earthy smell was strong but a great remedy for her nerves. She also handed over her glass vial to be refilled with the rich aroma of myrrh. She enjoyed mixing it with wine for tempering indigestion and it could even be applied to her face to maintain a healthy, youthful looking skin. It reminded her of her father's anointing at his burial, the first time she had participated in the ritual. What a strange combination of uses was myrrh, from bettering life to anointing at death.

Deed done. *Where to now?* She wanted to get out of Magdala. Yesterday she had thought of going to Capernaum tempted by curiosity from the news of this supposed Messiah figure. But she ignored that inclination and walked in the opposite direction. Tucking her newly acquired treasures into a pouch hanging from her belt, she maneuvered her way through the market on the main north-south road. Continuing her hurried walk across the city, she approached a wealthier side of town where two villas stood tall. She longed to remind the dwellers that she belonged to this social class. She had means, resources, wealth. But the villas only served to accuse and taunt her, reminding her of the luxurious and private purification baths that were housed within. While the common people used the sea for their ritual baths, these two elite families had their own indoor ones. She was familiar with the practice, having done this in her past life. But now, immersion would make no difference. The mark on her name and person were indelible and permanent. How she wanted to escape!

Thoughts of escape had come often over the last year. When travelers and traders passed through Magdala she would imagine what their life was like. Were they free to travel and do as they wished? Were they bound by a culture that held them to the same suffocating standards that she sometimes felt? She was weary, weary of wealth and beauty that made her an object of desire and possession by some, weary of judgments and expectations of others, feeling stuck in an oppressive web. How she longed for an altogether different kind of life. What that 'different' was, she could not conceive or name.

Mount Arbel towered above her on the right.[18] She tried to draw comfort in its protection as its massive fortress-like structure stood as a lookout upon the city of Magdala. Mary's feet kept carrying her south, past the villas, past the water well and public square, out into the countryside, past the cemetery, and toward Tiberias. She didn't understand herself. The place of painful memories became a place to which she was continually drawn. Perhaps she still hoped to see Gaius. Perhaps she found some solace in familiarity. Some unseen power moved her steps, taking her back time and time again. Her heart numbed more and more each time she went. Today was another one of those days-the numbing walk, as if she was not going by her own free will.

Less than an hour's walk and she had arrived. Herod's palace stood as ostentatiously as Herod himself. When he was present, it was a circus of feasts, pleasures, entrancements, intrigue, and seductions. She had witnessed his eclectic and fanciful "commitment" to religion. On Passover he would appease the Jewish leaders, only to turn back to pagan idol worship when the God of the Jews did not answer his every demand.

Mary had witnessed those pagan events and wondered if her presence at the ceremonies constituted participation. She had experienced a dark frenzied thrill. Yet fear, remorse and despair soon followed. She didn't know why she kept going back. Today she found herself once again entering the palace. Sensual music flowed toward her, luring her with claw-like hands and pulling her into the inner chamber where the smells of a feast made her mouth water.

She entered the large hall through a luxuriously veiled curtain. An acquaintance quietly appeared at her side. It was Johanna, whose husband, Chuza, administered Herod's estate. Johanna was a woman who stood above the others in integrity. Mary admired her. She was one among the court, yet seemed to hold her own, as if she lived above all the chaos that reigned in the palace. If there was anyone with whom she had once felt most kin to, it was this woman. Johanna looked her way and greeted her with a kind smile and nod of the head, then turned her gaze back to the dance floor with a guarded and questioning look, as though awaiting a turn of events and not quite sure how to judge it.

A young girl danced seductively as Herod smiled and laughed, his beady black eyes bouncing back and forth between the girl and his newly found passion, Herodias. The song ended and the girl approached Herod. The young dancer and the newest attraction of the court was Salome, Herodias' daughter.

Mary couldn't hear the exchange taking place on the dais where Herod and his new lover, Herodias, were lounging, but she saw the girl's surprised demeanor as she went between the two. After receiving some sort of indication from Herodias, the girl turned back to Herod and spoke, chin up and spine straight. She held a commanding, haughty stance. Herod's face turned ashen. He recovered quickly with a weak but arrogant laugh. A quick order brought silence to the crowd.

"Bring me the head of John the Baptist on a platter."

She felt a hand grip her arm. Mary turned and saw Johanna's pale expression as she released her grip. Brows furrowed, mouth pinched and shoulders obviously tensed, Johanna determinedly walked out of the room. Mary didn't know John the Baptist personally, but she guessed he was not guilty enough to warrant beheading. She had heard that Herod was fascinated with him, despite being annoyed at his moral finger-pointing. Herod had imprisoned John. Would that really be the end of him? Just like that, from the request of a young seductive dancer and jealous, power-seeking woman?

Murmured whispers, a tense atmosphere filled the seconds that flew by. Would they really behead the man? Mary looked around, wondering if it had been a joke. But no. In walked a large soldier, bloody sword in one hand, and platter with the head of a man in the other. Mary's stomach wrenched inside of her. She was suffocating. *Out! I have to get out of here!* She ran from the room, through the palace to the exit and fled Tiberias. She ran and ran. She did not care where. Finally stopping to catch her breath, she collapsed, retching and sobbing.

What is wrong with me? That preacher they called John the Baptist is no one to me; he was a mere spectacle, a mad man who irritated me with his crying out to all for repentance. Yet, she knew he was a righteous man, not like some of the hypocrites that spoke about living the law while their hearts were far from righteousness. Or the fanciful madmen like Herod.

She took deep breaths and tried to reorient herself. Looking around, she realized that she had run right into the edge of Magdala's cemetery,[19] an ironic spot to contemplate the end of life she had just witnessed. *What had become of him? Would there be any reward or justice for such a just man? Did his life vanish without purpose? For what? And Herod's party would just keep on. What a cruel fate.* The senselessness of it all overwhelmed her as she sobbed herself to exhaustion and then slumbered right next to a recently carved cavern standing empty and waiting for death's next chosen victim.[20]

CHAPTER 8. A CALL TO LIGHT & LIFE

He will wipe every tear from their eyes. There will be no more death or mourning or crying or pain, for the old order of things has passed away.
Revelations 21:4

Emotional exhaustion led to deep sleep. Nonetheless, it was a sleep disturbed by a partial dream merging with memory. Mary was standing outside the Temple as a young girl. Her father had entered into a discussion with a man named Nicodemus, a middle-aged man like her father. He exuded confidence, without arrogance. Her father had a curious and eager look about him, as though delighted by what Nicodemus was sharing with him.

A small group of men, called Sadducees, as her father later explained to her, stood nearby vigilantly listening and interrupting. They didn't like the direction of the conversation. Mary overheard tidbits, trying to grasp the words flying out between the two parties as emotions rose. Her father had taken up the debate on Nicodemus' side. She was curious about the meaning of it all: "A life after death," "incorruptibility of soul," "a resurrection of the dead," "those who sleep in dust will awake to some everlasting way," "awakening to an everlasting renewal of life or an everlasting contempt and shame."[21]

The thought of life after this earthly one intrigued her. She used to pester her father insistently, asking how could this be? His answer was like a riddle as he quoted the prophet Isaiah. "But your dead will live, Lord; their bodies will rise—let those who dwell in the dust wake up and shout for joy—your dew is like the dew of the morning; the earth will give birth to her dead."[22] She finally gave up asking, believing that he knew no more than she did on the matter.

The memory faded and another scene emerged. No longer a memory, it felt surreal. Her father emerged from a rock-hewn grave in the ground. He was not looking at her, but upwards. As she turned in the direction of his gaze, a bright light blinded her momentarily until a majestic face came into focus. His hand stretched out toward her father, revealing a gaping wound with bright light emanating from it. She looked toward her father again, willing him to look at her, wanting to call out to him, but finding no voice. Sorrow and longing for his embrace overwhelmed her.

She heard a voice, not with her earthly ears, but somehow it was clear. The words of the prophet Isaiah were spoken. "There will be no more gloom for those who were in distress. In the past he humbled the land of Zebulun and the land of Naphtali, but in the future he will honor the Galilee of the nations, by the Way of the Sea, beyond the Jordan. The people walking in darkness have seen a great light; on those living in the land of deep darkness a light has dawned."[23]

Her father and the majestic man disappeared from her dream, but residues of hope and joy fill her heart. This man of light, did he bring life? Would she see her father once again thanks to him? She looked downward into the earthly grave where her father had stood. The open ground brought a foreboding sense of loneliness and death. Memories of Herod's palace invaded her mind. A gentle, kind but firm whisper resounded within, *Not for you Mary!* Stunned, her gaze lifted upwards. Another path opened before her: unseen, but known, an outstretched hand lay open before her. It felt daring and pregnant with the promise of life. She longed to reach for that hand.

The fog and darkness of the approaching dawn kept Mary teetering between reality and her dream world until the cold finally penetrated and she woke to the sound of nearby rustling through the brush. She tuned into the voices drifting into the graveyard as the passers-by came into view. Her presence was still hidden by the grayness of the early morning's twilight.

"They might not even give us his body, or worse, if they associate us with him, we might be the next to lose our heads."

Mary saw the moving figures. She remained crouching, half hidden behind a broken off cover of the empty carved out tomb in the ground.

The voice came from a big, tall, rough-looking character. Behind him, a skinnier man piped up, "I can think of worse ways to die James."

A younger voice piped in as he led the pack, "We are not going to die Andrew! Not now anyway. I know a lady in the court."

"A lady? John, I didn't know...," The man named James began to tease his young companion but was quickly interrupted.

"Stop, not that kind of lady!" John retorted. "She is a respectable married woman whose husband happens to be an official of the court. She is the one who sent word to us. I am certain she will get us in and out with no trouble."

James suddenly stopped in his tracks, "Hey look out for the wild pigs moving around over there."

Andrew, behind him, wasn't as agile and slammed into the massive wall of his body, falling backward to the ground.

Getting his bearings, Andrew declared, "That's no pig, that's a person. Wait. It's a woman." He jumped up, embarrassed to have stumbled in her presence.

Having nowhere to hide, Mary had at least managed to brush the dirt off of her clothes, residue from her restless night on the ground. She attempted some altering of her disheveled hair before they all fixed their eyes on her. She stood tall, trying to appear confident and unafraid as she stepped forward from her partial hiding place. She did not want to appear as an easy prey for the men.

James questioned with incredulity, "What are you doing there woman? Are you alone? Have you lost your way? Come out."

The younger one spoke more gently, "Mam, do you need assistance?"

His gentleness disarmed her. Having overheard their conversation about the Baptist, her distress was returning. She spoke impetuously, "Are you going to collect the body of John the Baptist?"

Forgetting the circumstances of their meeting, their attention was drawn back to their task at hand. They all piped in randomly, "Yes." "Why?" "Have you heard of what happened?" "We are on our way now." "Did you know him?" "Are you one of his followers?"

"Yes, I mean No," said Mary, overwhelmed by the bombardment of questions. "Yes, I saw it happen. I was there in the palace last night. But no, I am not one of his disciples. It was horrible and unfortunate. It was not just."

John proceeded to explain their relationship with John the Baptist and mentioned that they were hoping to return the body to Jesus of Nazareth and provide a proper burial.

"Do you know Jesus of Nazareth?" he asked her.

That name again. Jesus of Nazareth. Everyone was ranting and raving about him. She had yet to actually see him. John spoke enthusiastically before she could answer.

"Come and see him. Come and hear him preach. He heals the blind and casts out demons. He even forgives sins. We believe our Rabboni is the awaited Messiah. He will restore all things to the way they should be. You must come. We have been traveling with him, but we never know where he will head off to next. He is traveling from town to town. You must come see him. He is not far from here now."

Mary was taken aback by his loquacious speech, to her, a stranger. The morning sun was still below the eastern hills and on the verge of appearing. Dawn was making the men's hazy appearances more pronounced, and hers as well. She felt exposed. She wanted to escape their company. "We will see. I must be off," she muttered indifferently.

She turned without any formal farewell. Despite her hasty departure she overheard James' rough bark of a laugh and harassing tone as he thumped John on the back, "Way to go Thunderman! You scared her away!"

CHAPTER 9. HINTS OF PROMISE & PEACE

Today, if only you would hear his voice,
Do not harden your hearts.
Psalm 95:8

Mary made her way back to Magdala. She didn´t want to return to the villa just yet. Tams and Babs would surely be up and she did not want to face their silent and fearful glances. She loved them and while they attempted to take care of her, the truth was, she was taking care of them as they had aged and were now less capable of carrying out their previous tasks. And Mary sometimes wondered if she had driven them to ill health with their worry over her.

She looked for comfort in her usual spot upon the seashore. Despite the cold, the clouds were dissipating, and the early morning sun was bursting forth from behind the majestic hills, practically blinding her and making it difficult to see to the shoreline across the sea. She closed her eyes and let her senses be inundated with all that was familiar: the rhythmic lapping of the waves, the wind rustling the tall seagrass sending a chill up her spine, the familiar smell of the sea in the early morn, and the sounds of multitudes of birds flitting about. She laid back and took in the blue domed sky with wisps of pink, orange, yellow and purple-tinted clouds streaked across the horizon. She tried to let the beauty push out the frightful memories of the previous day. A semblance of calm finally broke through her anxiety and fear.

Recalling her dream, she remembered that hand reaching out to her and the intuition of an invitation. She questioned once again: *Who am I? What have I become? And who am I to become?* And once again, she had no answers. But slowly, fear gave way to hope of a better future, of a promise that the blessedness that once was would dawn again in a new and splendid way. She held onto that feeling, as though she were fixing her gaze on a sure but distant beacon of light. It offered a moment of relief for her weary soul.

She welcomed this brief lucidness as a promise amidst too much darkness. Like a pebble tossed into the placid sea's waters it rippled through the memories of her life, readjusting her vision and bringing different scenes of her past into focus. They all connected, the good, the bad, the beautiful and painful events. A glimmer of hope enkindled belief that all would be well again, health and righteousness would be restored, her brokenness would be fully healed. *How? By that Jesus of Nazareth, whom I have heard enthusiastically proclaimed, more than once in the last couple of days?* She did not know, but for the first time in a long time she was determined to be alert, patiently yet eagerly anticipating the fulfillment of what felt like a promise.

Remnants of Psalm 95, as though fresh from her childhood, rushed to her lips.

> Come, let us sing for joy to the Lord; let us shout aloud to the Rock of our salvation…For the Lord is the great God, the great King above all gods.
>
> In his hand are the depths of the earth, and the mountain peaks belong to him. The sea is his, for he made it, and his hands formed the dry land.
>
> Come, let us bow down in worship, let us kneel before the Lord our Maker; for he is our God, and we are the people of his pasture, the flock under his care. Today, if only you would hear his voice, Do not harden your hearts…

The verses turned to prayer as she cried out, "O Lord, melt this hardened heart if you hear my plea!"

As she prayed, a solitary doubt crept in like a sinister voice, "Why would the Lord even glance upon you?" The small light of hope and vague promise of new life instantly squelched, replaced by doubt and fear of an angry God's rejection. "Not for you," the accusatory voice grated upon her nerves. Shame converted to rebellion as she felt the doors of her heart close once again. She stood up, straightened her cloak, and walked away from her silly dream of peace and freedom, light and love. Her semblance of hope blew away with the wind.

CHAPTER 10. GOOD NEWS KINDLINGS

Hear, you deaf! And look, you blind, that you may see.
Isaiah 42:18

Having rested from her exhaustion, Mary woke the following day with the desire to keep busy. Rainy days kept her close to the villa and she filled them with chores that Tams and Babs used to do. Tams attempted to shoo her away from the menial tasks of laundry and cooking. But Mary knew that Tams wore out easily, so she pretended to accompany her, relieving her of the majority of the burden by sending her on little errands to distract her while Mary did the heavy work. Her moments with Tams and Babs brought a touch of normalcy to her life, if she didn't let dark thoughts pull her into their lair.

She checked on the few workers she had hired, mostly to relieve Babs of the weight of the wine making venture. She never heard him complain, but she had observed a gradual slowing in his gait and clumsiness as a result of constant pain in his aging joints. She found ways to make him feel like the protagonist who played an essential role by letting him inspect the new hires' work, correct them or give them advice.

As the days passed, her restlessness increased. She had refrained from leaving the villa, afraid of her own reaction and where her feet might take her. She did not want to return to Herod's palace. But she needed to get out. A day trip to Capernaum, that's what she needed.

A break in the rain finally tempted her to venture out. Capernaum sold some of the finest linens, made from flax harvested in Bethsaida. It was time to make a new cloak and throw away the memory of Gaius. If she were honest with herself, she was hoping to run into Jesus of Nazareth. Curiosity had definitely gotten the better of her. But she avoided admitting it to herself and turned her mind to the fine purchase she hoped to make.

Many thought her bold to walk the distance unchaperoned. By the light of day, she was bold. She preferred her independence. But when she ran into the Roman soldiers, she entered into a dangerous game. She became like an outside observer of her own behavior. She executed a rebellious luring, testing her capacity to win them over. It brought a momentary, but fleeting thrill, a sensation against the numbed existence her life had become. But as soon as she entered into the temptation, shame overwhelmed her. Anger made her want to lash out instead of luring them. She would come to her senses and then make known she was not to be messed with.

Speaking of messes, today the road was muddy from previous rains, causing her to tread carefully lest she slip. Time passed quickly as she pondered all she had seen, heard and felt in the last few days. And the walk proved invigorating with the crisp sunny morning.

As she approached Capernaum's marketplace, she recognized Johanna. Their eyes met and they made their way to one another.

"Miriam, are you well?" Johanna asked with a concerned look on her face.

Mary was touched by her maternal gesture. It struck a chord that almost opened a floodgate of tears threatening to break through. An overwhelming urge to confess the mayhem of emotions and thoughts practically choked her. But she swallowed it whole like a bitter herb, holding it all back. She wouldn't know where to start. Instead, she detracted from the question.

"Fine Johanna. Did you just arrive?"

"Yes, but I have come from Bethsaida. Myself and a servant accompanied some young men who came to fetch John the Baptist's body. I wanted to stop back here on my way home and visit with Eva and Salome, the mother of some of those young men."

Mary recalled the men she had met on the graveyard path. So, Johanna had been "the woman" that the young disciple knew.

"I am on my way to see them now." Johanna hesitated then spoke gently, observing Mary's reaction. "Eva was recently cured of a deadly fever. Miriam, have you heard of Jesus? Jesus healed her. Come, she lives near the synagogue. Would you accompany me?"

Jesus. Healed. Come. Mary's legs felt momentarily paralyzed. But she nodded her assent and willed herself to take a step. They walked side by side.

Mary was attracted by Johanna's goodness and admired her inner strength and beauty. She was confident, yet not full of false pride. Her husband held an important post and yet she was not pretentious. She wore no mask of falsehood, but at the same time she was prudently guarded whenever Mary saw her in Herod's palace. Today she seemed different, as though freer and unreserved.

Johanna broke Mary's ruminations.

"That was a disturbing event at the palace Miriam."

Johanna's voice gave away her compassion and her searching glance awaited Mary's reaction. "You should be careful who you associate with in the court. There are some treacherous men there. I am glad little Joanna is finally away from there, as much as I miss her. I have often thought that it is not safe for you, especially since…" Johanna faltered. Mary knew what she meant to say, *Since Gaius left.* Johanna saw the pain etched on Mary's face. "It is not safe for you. What takes you there Miriam? Why do you keep coming back?"

A tumult of answers brewed within. *How I wish I knew! How could I even describe it?* It was like something beckoned her there, sometimes against her will and she just let it take over. She was too weak to fight it. At the same time, she felt attracted to the place. She still received the attention of several men. They admired her beauty and acknowledged her worth. What she was worth, she couldn't answer. Overwhelmed by her own lack of understanding, she shrugged her shoulders and answered, "I have friends there."

They had already reached the house. Johanna was silent for a while, then turned to Mary, asking quasi-rhetorically, "Do you truly Miriam? They are good friends?"

Mary's brows furrowed with a quizzical look as Johanna turned to the house to knock. With barely a rap, the door flew open and a boisterous jolly woman greeted them as though anticipating their arrival.

"Johanna! There you are, come in, come in! And you have brought a lovely friend. Welcome!" Kisses all around and a quick introduction to another woman working quietly in the kitchen's corner didn't interrupt this woman´s banter. "The boys are not in now. You can tell from the lack of crowds. I don't get a moment's rest when they are here. I think that must be why Jesus cured me! He knew those boys needed a mother every time they passed through Capernaum."

Johanna stifled a chuckle and raised her eyebrows, "Are they here frequently? I would love to see Jesus."

"Lately they have been staying here overnight. Long enough to give me plenty to do, to feed them and wash their tunics. Thank God Salome came to help out."

Salome nodded and smiled. She raised a red-stained hand as if to say, "Here I am! Count on me." Pomegranate husks were scattered all around her, evidence of Salome's intense work at deseeding the luscious fruits. Mary wondered if she was normally silent or was merely reconciled to being a listener to her loquacious friend.

Eva continued almost without a breath, "Speaking of food, let me get you something!"

She bustled around preparing tea and putting together a small feast as she continued her monologue. "Oh, but I am not complaining! It is a joy to have them here. They know how to laugh and have fun and when to listen and be serious. At first, we were left to ourselves to enjoy Jesus, but now the people flock to see him. You wouldn't believe what happened since I last saw you. Oh Johanna! He is surely the one spoken of by the prophet Isaiah, 'He himself bore our sickness away and carried our diseases.'[24] We have been concerned about trouble with the centurions, but one day to the next they left us alone. People say that Jesus cured the centurion's son without even stepping into his house. Faith, they say. Faith is enough for Jesus to work a miracle!"

Salome looked up toward nothing in particular and nodded her head contemplatively. "Faith," she repeated, "Faith. My sons certainly have that."

Eva jumped in again, "Her sons John and James, big James they call him, have been with Jesus since he began coming here. Poor Salome lost her youngest son to the Baptist and now both of them to Jesus."

Salome piped in while she could, "But I am not complaining. My husband and I had prayed that these times would come."

These times, Mary wondered to herself. Salome looked quite youthful for a middle aged woman with at least two adult children. But she could have married very young. She had a strong, healthy looking stature and a kind face, one that seemed content, confident and welcoming.

Eva picked up the thread of conversation as though it was never interrupted. "Johanna, you should have seen the paralytic man! The crowd was so thick they climbed to the roof and pulled apart a hole to lower him into this house to get Jesus' attention. With just a word from Jesus the man stood, picked up his mat and walked home! Simon and Andrew spent half a day trying to repair that roof for me. Good boys those two. Like my own sons."

"Simon is her son-in-law, but his wife passed away last year," Johanna quietly commented to Mary.

"Jesus rattled a few people though," Eva continued. "He alluded to himself as the Son of man who has power to forgive sins. To forgive sins! Only God! At first, I wasn't too sure about Simon and Andrew going off to follow that fellow, but Johanna, I think he is the one. No, I don't think it, I believe it! He is truly the one we have been waiting for. He will restore all things to their righteous state. I am sure of it! Salome agrees with me. Thank the Lord, because she couldn't stop those sons of hers even if she said no."

Salome continued slowly nodding and assenting to all she heard.

A rising restlessness had been building in Mary. She couldn't contain it any longer and burst into Eva's monologue, "But how can this be? How will he restore all things? What does that mean?" Her expression gave away her incredulity.

The women looked at her somewhat surprised, followed by tenderness. Her host spoke up.

"My dear, I do not know how, but everywhere we witness his power. The blind see, the deaf hear, the lame walk again, he casts out demons, and even forgives sins. Our people have never seen that. He is wise and humble, gentle, yet stern. John the Baptist's death was tragic, but he came as another Elijah, crying out in the wilderness, 'Prepare the way of the Lord.' The prophet Micah had foretold that a ruler of Israel would come from Bethlehem. Jesus and his people are from there, despite everyone saying that he is a Nazarene. He was born during Herod the Great's census and his parents traveled to that city where he was born. At least this is what Simon has told me."

Johanna piped in, "Yes, I do believe he is the shepherd that Micah speaks of who comes in the majesty of the name of the Lord, bringing security and peace to the ends of the earth. We will witness great things! I am hopeful."

Mary's heart was racing as she was listening. She wrestled interiorly with their claims. *Did they believe blindly? He could forgive sins? How long before he ended up like John the Baptist with his head on a platter?* She knew enough of her religion to know that he was bordering on blasphemy. She thought of the Pharisees. *Oh, how I would like to see him outtalk and outsmart some people in her town! But he, the Messiah?* Despite her incredulity, she did not want to show disrespect to her host and Johanna's conviction. She would take her leave. Besides, she had other things to do. She said her goodbyes with the excuse that she must finish her errands and head back home.

After goodbye kisses all around, Johanna gently took hold of her elbow. With concerned eyes she quietly pleaded, "Miriam, about our earlier conversation, please, do take care."

Mary nodded, smiled politely and departed.

CHAPTER 11. THE POWER TO FORGIVE SINS

You, Lord, are forgiving and good,
abounding in love to all who call to you.
Psalm 86:5

Her two purchases lay wrapped in her bag: two long pieces of fine linen. She had determined to make a more modest cream colored cloak with the hope of setting aside her ostentatious red garment. On a whim, she had also purchased an elegant white piece, fit for a bride. Not that she saw herself as such, but it had sparked a longing, and she had envisioned a bridal cloak as soon as she saw it. Perhaps she would make it and give it away. It certainly would not be in her future.

Having also taken care of various business dealings, assuring contracts and deliveries of their villa's products, she turned home. The walk afforded her time to ponder. She wondered about Jesus' capacity to forgive sins. Her people were familiar with the frequent necessity for atonement. She recalled the stories of Abraham and Moses who mediated on behalf of the people for God. She could use a "Moses" in her life right now.

Moses had climbed the mountain to beg God forgiveness for the idolatry her people so easily fell into. But Abraham and Moses never professed to have the power to forgive sins. Forgiveness always required a sacrifice, not merely words. Her father had taught her all about the sacrifices offered for the atonement of sin. As a child, one of her favorite times of the year was Rosh Hashanah to Yom Kippur. The outdoors would be filled with deep sounds of the shofar. The ram's horn trumpet signaled God's voice sending a message to be vigilant. Memories of the shofar conjured up the story of the ram that God provided for the sacrifice in place of Abraham's son. Nostalgic feelings of awe opened the door to childhood memories.

She recalled the nine full days of hope-filled anticipation before Yom Kippur, the great day of atonement.[25] Far from a fearful time of condemnation for one's sins, her family would rejoice over the liberation that the special day's sacrifice brought. She didn't care much for blood, but there was something sacred about the innocent animals that were sacrificed for the sins of all. Besides, she didn't have to see it. She loved the mystery of the high priest entering the Holy of Holies to sprinkle the blood of bulls and goats to atone for people's sins. And then the sweet smelling incense filled the air, like a prayer lifted to God on high.

There were many things she didn't understand about her traditions, but she understood too well the words of Ezekiel, "The soul who sins is the one who will die."[26] As an innocent child she knew that sinners were deserving of death, but that "God was compassionate and gracious, slow to anger, abounding in love and faithfulness, maintaining love to thousands, and forgiving wickedness, rebellion and sin."[27] But those sinners always seemed like someone else, not her.

She remembered her father's reaction to her mother when they crossed paths with a recently divorced woman. Her mother had quietly commented that the woman should go quick and offer sacrifice. Her father, obviously restraining a scalding remark for her mother, launched into a slew of scripture verses as though they were overdue for their Sabbath lesson. She quickly realized that the lesson must be for her mother more than for her. She was only eight. She hadn't even realized the woman was divorced.

"Listen carefully daughter, for Hosea spoke, 'I desire mercy not sacrifice, and acknowledgement of God rather than burnt offerings.'[28] And Samuel called out Saul for his disobedience despite Saul's sacrifice. He told Saul, 'Does the Lord delight in burnt offerings and sacrifices as much as in obeying the Lord? To obey is better than sacrifice, and to heed is better than the fat of rams. For rebellion is like the sin of divination, and arrogance like the evil of idolatry. Because you have rejected the word of the Lord, he has rejected you as king'.[29] So daughter, reflect well on your own righteousness for God sees the depth of the heart. Think twice before you pass judgment on another."

That had silenced and humbled her mother. At the time, she had wondered if there was something she hadn't seen in that divorced woman? Had her father been inferring that the woman was obedient to God while she, Mary, was not? Well, she was a bit naughty sometimes, especially when it came to avoiding her chores. Her mother was forever telling her father to correct her. He rarely followed through with that plea. But that day, her father's words changed the way she looked upon others. It amplified her scope of understanding God's merciful act of forgiveness. As her thoughts drifted back to the present, she wondered what had happened to that understanding of God? *Oh, to be a child again!* It had seemed so easy to believe in God's forgiveness when she was a child.

With the exception of her interior world, the walk from Capernaum was uneventful. She returned home. She pulled her purchases out of the bag and set the cream colored fabric on the table as a reminder to sew a new cloak as soon as possible. Touching the elegant white linen, she chided herself, embarrassed that she had even thought to buy such a fabric representing innocence and beauty. She tucked it away in a storage chest and went to rest, anticipating what events the next days would hold. Perhaps she would stay away from Tiberias for a while. Secretly, she dared to hope that she might meet this Jesus of Nazareth she kept hearing so much about.

CHAPTER 12. UNEXPECTED VISITOR

The eyes of the LORD are everywhere,
keeping watch on the wicked and the good.
Proverbs 15:3

Midmorning, one unusually fine day, Mary heard a knock on her door. She didn't often have visitors at this time of day. She had been accustomed to night time visitors, but even those had thankfully been petering out. She wasn't expecting anyone. She opened the door to Johanna who lifted up a basket of pomegranates and apples upon greetings and kisses.

"Johanna! I wasn't expecting you. Welcome. Come in please. I can make some tea."

Johanna was hardly able to restrain her excitement. She stepped over the threshold, but immediately put the basket to the side, turned to Mary, and gently grabbed both her arms. Her barely contained exuberance spilt out like flood waters breaking through a dam.

"No tea Miriam. I saw Jesus on my way here. I heard him speak. He is not too far from here. Come. Let's go see him."

Johanna waited for her reply with hopeful and expectant eyes. Then Johanna's excitement turned to concern. A questioning look tried to penetrate Mary's reaction. Mary, suddenly feeling lightheaded, realized that she had been holding her breath since she heard the name Jesus. Her feet were like lead anchors. Fear gripped her.

Johanna smiled compassionately, picked up the fruit basket and held it out to Mary. She spoke calmly and slowly, as though giving her time to register the news.

"A little gift for you from Salome and Eva. They enjoyed meeting you. You left so quickly the other day that they didn't have a chance to offer you anything."

64

Mary took hold of the basket, but her mind was incapable of response. She breathed deeply and mustered up a nod and slight smile.

Johanna continued, "I've come straight from Capernaum. I must have been about thirty minutes outside the town when I saw a gathering of people at the alcove, just beyond the olive trees. You know the spot? Where the stream cascades down the rocks and creates an inlet? Jesus was sitting in a boat in the alcove, teaching a large crowd that had gathered. It was just far enough out for his voice to carry to the shore."

Johanna tried to maintain a quiet demeanor as though not to frighten Mary, but her voice sped up as her face lighted with excitement at the memory.

"He spoke a parable, Miriam, a wonderful parable about a farmer who went out to sow seed. Some seed, he said, fell on the path and birds came and ate it up. Some fell on rocky ground, but the shallow roots caused it to wither and die. Then some seed fell among thorns and was choked to death. But then, he said, some fell on good soil where it produced an abundant crop. Whoever has ears, let them hear."[30] Johanna paused, allowing a patient and non-expectant silence to fill the space between them.

Mary heard, or she thought she did. Her heart felt like all those places where the seed tried to plant itself, but something prevented it from taking root and growing. She wanted to be good soil. *How I long to be that good soil!*

Rumbled sounds of an approaching crowd had gradually been growing louder as they stood in silence. It finally drew both their attention. They stepped out of the house and made their way to the street to see the commotion. People appeared from everywhere. They were streaming past them, some running, others stepping out of houses with curious eyes. "Jesus." "The Nazarene." Scattered voices announced his coming.

Johanna looked at Mary with expectation then turned in the direction of the crowd. Mary found her feet following Johanna as the stream of people thickened and she eventually lost sight of her in the gathering multitude. She turned from the noisy stream of people and backtracked until she found a quieter side street that wound around the back of the synagogue. She followed it around to the side where she could hear the people congregating. As she rounded the corner and entered the mass of people a slight opening gave way for her to slip in and catch a glimpse of a man holding a toddler. Many were looking upon him with delight and eagerness.

Jesus? Is that him? He is so…unassuming. Tall but not standing above most men. Strong but not bulky like some of the soldiers.

Despite the gathering crowds seeking his attention, he appeared jovial, calm, and gentle as he laughed and tousled the hair of a little five-year old that tugged at his garment. He handed the toddler back to its ecstatic mother then lifted up the insistent child. Mary observed cautiously, pressing her way through the crowd, trying to make her way closer to hear him.

From the opposite side of the street, black and white garments forced their way through the crowd. The Pharisees. His joyful interchange was interrupted by silence all around as the religious leaders approached him. The atmosphere ignited with potential conflict. But Jesus received their remarks and questions with an undisturbed countenance. They were accusing him of driving out demons by Beelzebul. He finally set the child down, assuring that he returned to his mother, and began to address them. His speech penetrated the air.

"If I, then, drive out demons by Beelzebul, by whom do your own people drive them out? Therefore, they will be your judges. But if it is by the finger of God that I drive out demons, then the kingdom of God has come upon you."[31]

They continued to taunt him. She heard bits and pieces of Jesus' response about an unclean spirit roaming and searching for rest, then returning to its home and finding it swept clean. Then she caught his words fully. They pierced her heart.

"Then it goes and brings back seven other spirits more wicked than itself who move in and dwell there, and the last condition of that person is worse than the first."[32]

The Pharisees agitatedly cited laws in an accusatory tone. He spoke again with an authority to make one tremble.

"Woe to you Pharisees! You love the seat of honor in synagogues and greetings in marketplaces."[33]

His voice was not raised and yet it seemed to resonate through the crowd, striking awe. *Jesus must see right through them*, she thought. Her self-righteous sentiment cheered him on. It went unchecked until she heard his next line.

"Woe to you, teachers of the law and Pharisees, you hypocrites! You give a tenth of your spices—mint, dill and cumin. But you have neglected the more important matters of the law—justice, mercy and faithfulness."[34] His words called them out and yet, they seemed to speak to her too. *I am no Pharisee, but can he see into my heart too?* The Pharisees, agitated, threw warnings his way and left discomposed.

Jesus stepped towards the synagogue entrance. She still felt the weight of his message when suddenly, he glanced in her direction. She froze, caught off guard. *Does he know my thoughts?* A psalm echoed in her mind. *Lord, you have probed me, you know me...you understand my thoughts from afar.*[35]

Unassuming, non-judgmental, inviting. *Invitation to what?* She could not hold his gaze. Her head drooped in confusion, and she realized she was still holding onto the fruit basket Johanna had given her. As she raised her eyes to catch another look, Jesus had disappeared into the synagogue. She found herself being jostled to and fro as a current of people vied to enter the synagogue. Even if she had wanted to follow, there was no way to get through that crowd. A bedraggled woman and young son were shoved into her from the massive movement. Mary's initial reaction of irritation gave way to pity at the sight of them. Without a thought, she handed the fruit basket over to the woman. Then she spied a Pharisee eyeing her with curiosity. She turned and ran home, overwhelmed at the prospect of any more encounters.

CHAPTER 13. CURIOSITIES & POSSIBILITIES

Woman, you are set free of your infirmity.
Luke 13:12

The next day, the day of Sabbath, she was agitated with an impetuous but conflicting desire. Tams and Babs, faithful to their weekly Sabbath plea, had invited her again to synagogue. This time they attempted to entice her with curiosity over the new rabbi. They had heard that he was going to teach in the synagogue and encouraged her to join them. She dismissed their invitation, and they left early enough to secure seats. But she wrestled with the possibility until a growing desire won out over fear. She had to see him again.

The synagogue was filled to overflowing when she arrived. A few familiar faces revealed their surprise and curiosity upon seeing her. Others scrutinized her presence. *How long it had been since I entered the synagogue!* They judged her as having rejected the faith of their Fathers. Little did they know that faith still had its grip on her by way of the memories of her parents. That was the extent of it these past years, but she did not think that she had completely abandoned her faith. It felt more like God had abandoned her. And she just couldn't tolerate the judgments any longer. She didn't feel she belonged there anymore.

Voices hushed as Jesus entered with several men. She recognized the three whom she had briefly met in the cemetery. A young girl approached him, pointing to a corner of the synagogue. She grabbed his hand and began tugging him toward a little disfigured woman. A man and woman aided the old woman, taking her by the arms and leading her to Jesus. They met in the middle of the synagogue where all were witnesses to the strange encounter. Mary recognized the woman, disfigured with a hunched back for as long as she could remember. Mary's eyes fixed on Jesus' face as he towered over her small frail frame.

She was moved by his presence and demeanor toward her. *What compassion! What kindness! Did he know this old woman? I don't think so.*

Then Jesus laid his hands on the old woman's shoulders. No pretension, no pompousness. He looked upon her tenderly, then solemnly spoke.

"Woman, you are set free of your infirmity."[36]

Immediately the crippled woman stood up straight, raising her little stick she had used for balance and sang out, "Praise be to the Lord God, the God of Israel, who alone does marvelous deeds."[37]

The leader of the synagogue stepped forward, fuming red. Everyone else remained in awed silence or praised God, but he and a small crowd of his followers were indignant that Jesus had cured on the Sabbath. The leader approached Jesus and expelled a heated admonition, but it was drowned out in the increasing volume of praise and wonder. Jesus responded to the official. She leaned in to hear the exchange. Something about watering ox and ass on the Sabbath. The crowd had finally calmed as he continued to speak.

Then he turned towards the entrance of the synagogue where she had slid in, partially hidden behind the mass of people. He spoke to all.

"This daughter of Abraham, whom Satan has bound for eighteen years now, ought she not to have been set free on the Sabbath day from this bondage?"[38]

The noise level once again increased and those who had opposed him shrunk away at the site of the onlookers rejoicing at his splendid deeds and words.[39] As she watched the commotion and the old woman standing straight and praising the Lord, she felt strangely removed from the entire scene, as though she were an outside observer detached from participating in the happy event. Men and women were crying with astonishment. Pharisees were aghast and trying, without effect, to still the excitement.

Suddenly, she caught Jesus' gaze and all faded away. *Is he looking at me? Why is he looking at me like that? A summoning appeal? A beckoning?* She felt as if she were standing on a precipice being encouraged to take a leap without looking. She wavered between fear and daring. She tensed, wanting to hold onto what was familiar. Yet longing to be brave and face the unknown. She wanted to be healed by his gentle touch and simple words, like the crippled women. She wanted to let go and be reckless in a new and different way. Amidst the interior war waging within, a suffocating terror crept in. The noisy commotion once again flooded her senses and she fled from the synagogue, avoiding his eyes at all costs.

CHAPTER 14. ENCOUNTER MERCY

I will sprinkle clean water over you to make you clean; from all your impurities and from all your idols I will cleanse you. I will give you a new heart, and a new spirit I will put within you. I will remove the heart of stone from your flesh and give you a heart of flesh.
Ezekiel 36:25-27

She ran towards the sea, her feet taking her to a familiar spot, her safe space, through the tall sea grass to her hidden refuge on the beach. She walked up and down the shoreline. Time passed quickly as she relived the scene over and over in her head, a myriad of confusing emotions running through her veins. Morning had come and gone. Midafternoon crept in and the sun shone high in the sky, making its way toward Mount Arbel. Soon it would sink behind the towering hill. It was unusually hot for this time of year, but perhaps her panic in the synagogue and her racing heart as she paced the shoreline had made her break out in a sweat. She stopped, breathed deep and sank to the sand. The coolness under her knees and beneath her hands was a relief from the heat of the sun.

Courage, she needed courage. She had heard and seen enough of Jesus of Nazareth to begin to hope that he was the way to a new beginning. Her past life could be left behind. She could leave the nonsensical indulgences, the endless search for meaning, and the yoke of her reputation that only drove her deeper into despair. If only he would help her. If only she had the courage to ask. Fragments of a psalm surfaced from her memory as a silent plea to the heavens.

> Turn away your face from my sins; blot out all my iniquities. A clean heart create for me, God; renew within me a steadfast spirit. Rescue me, my saving God. Restore to me the gladness of your salvation.[40]

Hope lingered as she sincerely lifted that prayer to the heavens. She thought of the people's lives being changed from Jesus' touch, his words, a mere glance. She longed for a change, for a new heart, a new spirit. *How?* She leaned forward, as though bowing to the God she longed to cry out to. Hands wide open on her lap, she inclined to cover her face, feeling so small, like a babe in a fetal position. A song from the words of the prophet Ezekiel flitted to her mind.

> I will sprinkle clean water over you to make you clean;
> from all your impurities and from all your idols I will
> cleanse you. I will give you a new heart, and a new spirit
> I will put within you. I will remove the heart of stone
> from your flesh and give you a heart of flesh.[41]

Yes Lord, please! I need a new heart and a new spirit!

The rustling of the sea grass startled her. She knew, even before she looked up. It was him. She sat up, turning her face toward the sound. The sun shone in her eyes, blinding her to his features. She only made out the outline of his figure. He approached her until his body cast its shadow upon her, giving her, at last, a direct view of his face. Her heart seemed to stop. He was alone. How had he managed to escape the crowd? Had he intentionally come in pursuit of her?

"Miriam."

Simple, one word, no scolding, no condemnation. His tender, yet firm voice washed over her as a gentle swab over a fresh wound. Bewilderment turned to conviction. He knew her. He saw her. He knew her pain and her sinfulness.[42] She could hide nothing. He saw her impurity. Yet, he was willing to be near her. Yes, he could set her free. She wanted this.

"Rabboni," she whispered.

She was struck dumb, uncertain of what to speak, how to act. But no more resistance. She extended her arms like a toddler toward its parent. She raised herself to her knees as though to stand. He stopped her, extending his hand. He touched her forehead. And she let go. She let go of anger, hatred, envy, fear. She felt naked before him as her sins flashed through her mind. She saw the pretenses, lies, pride and vanity, false masks and binding mental schemes that had their tight grip on her. She felt herself letting go, letting go of enslaving and false securities. The idols she had erected in her heart, the pleasures and pastimes that captured her desires now vanished like dust. She was breathless and then, in an instant that breath returned, filling and renewing everything within. She saw the truth of her brokenness, the unjust violations against her, her innocence and deceptions, her longing for something noble, good, right. A desire for freedom, real freedom, claimed its hold on her as she surrendered. A locked interior door slowly opened. Penetrating joy suffused from the center of her being. Light overcame darkness. Peace permeated her whole being.

Sounds of approaching people roused her to her surroundings. She wanted to stay with him, just as they were. One last glance saw Jesus smiling down upon her. He extended an open hand this time. She slipped her hand into his and he pulled her to her feet. Gratitude overwhelmed her. She flung her arms around him as tears freely flowed and she clung to him like her life depended on it.

"Thank you. Thank you," was all she could mutter, until she realized she had embraced him impulsively and she stepped back, setting him free.

"Fear not Mary," said Jesus with a consoling smile and lighthearted chuckle. He turned and disappeared into the reeds separating the beach from the town's edge, leaving Mary with remnants of overflowing peace. She sunk to the ground and poured forth tears of joy and relief, marveling at a new sense of freedom she now possessed.

CHAPTER 15. CONSOLATION & INVITATION

Behold, I stand at the door and knock; if anyone hears My voice and opens the door, I will come in to him and will dine with him, and he with Me.
Revelations 3:20

Dawn nudged Mary out of a content slumber. A new day. Remnants of yesterday's peace converted her typical morning from dread of the future and regret of her past to the wonder of a fresh day. She set her mind scheming as she slipped on sandals and began preparations for the day. How could she express her indebtedness to Jesus? Having accomplished her routine ablutions and fully dressed, she pulled her mass of hair over one shoulder and began to braid. Her dexterous and graceful fingers moved to the pace of her ruminations. Fingers over fingers, then undoing it and starting again. Disapproval was taking its toll on her hair. What payment measured up to the liberating gift she had received from Jesus? Her resolve was withering as she discarded one unsatisfactory idea after another for how to repay him. A knock at the door suspended her movement and imagination.

Who could that be? Could it be him? He wouldn't come to my house would he? Does he even know where I live? He knew my name, so he must know something about me.

She hesitated, then lifted the latch ready to face him, bracing herself as she opened the door. Realization turned to a sigh of relief yet disappointment as her half frown greeted Johanna who stood patiently outside. Johanna's face quickly changed from a joyful greeting to a quizzical eyebrow lifting.

"Well, good morning to you too, Miriam!" Johanna teased.

"Oh, sorry Johanna. I just wasn't expecting it would be you."

Johanna understood. "Ah yes." She continued with her gentle and maternal spirit. "I am sorry that I lost you in the crowd on Friday and didn't return to see you. I had promised Chuza I would be home before Shabbat.[43] I finally convinced him to return to celebrating the Shabbat with me. Of course, this doesn't mean he is going to synagogue. It has been years since he stopped going, Miriam. More years than even you have been away. So, I know it is not an easy step. Of course, he is not completely convinced about Jesus being the Messiah, but he has been listening to my stories and has finally agreed to return to celebrating the Shabbat dinner with me."

Johanna was unsure if Mary understood the significance of this change in her husband, but she let it go. Mary was obviously distracted. She continued along another vein, suspecting the reason for her inattention. "I returned to you as soon as I could. Did you see Jesus and hear him preach?"

The name of Jesus brought her back and lifted her spirits with anticipation once again.

"Oh Johanna, do come in. I have so much to tell you." Mary dragged Johanna into the house and forgoing the customary hospitality, she began pouring forth the tumult of her recent emotions and experiences. Johanna's countenance sincerely welcomed Mary's vulnerability and intimate sharing, melting any reserve. She recounted the last two days, between getting lost in the crowd, Jesus' first glance, the synagogue healing, and finally her own liberation on the beach. Tears freely flowed between the two women. Tears of joy, of wonder, of gratitude. As she wound up her story, silence fell between them. It was pregnant with awe as they contemplated the beauty of Jesus' healing presence. Healing, Mary thought. Healing and so much more. How could she put into words what he had accomplished in the depth of her heart?

Johanna broke the stillness. "Mary, you must come with me, today. Chuza and I are to dine with Jesus at Simon the Pharisee's house. Pharisees and scribes have arrived from Jerusalem. I think they have come to investigate Jesus. Herod caught wind of the dinner and secured a place for Chuza. He is insane. Herod, not my husband. Well, my husband sometimes," she joked. "Anyways, I think Herod believes Jesus is John the Baptist come back to haunt him."

Concern for Jesus, then surprise over her sudden desire to defend and protect him, washed over Mary. Johanna also recognized fear.

"Don´t worry. Chuza is prudent and cautious, not speaking about any of my associations with Jesus. Well, not that I have had so many meetings with Jesus personally. It is mostly a sideways connection, knowing John, his disciple, and his mother Salome. And I met Eva through them. Chuza just tolerates my connections with them. But Herod wants a spy. I am glad he chose my husband. I don't think Chuza is anywhere near ready to call Jesus the Messiah, but he is respectfully curious. Do come Miriam. With the crowd that is gathering, what is one more. You can come as our guest."

Simon the Pharisee. Dare I cross the threshold of his house. In his eyes I would taint it with my presence. But to see Jesus again. Oh, what would I say to him? What would I do? I could offer him a gift. Surely, he needed resources, financial support. I would offer him my livelihood if he would accept it.

She looked toward her shelf of treasures, glass vials, the beautiful new alabaster flask and expensive ointment of spikenard. *Would he accept that? He could sell it and sustain himself for weeks on the cost of the ointment alone.* The face of Simon the Pharisee entered her imagination and a pit formed in her stomach. A vile taste rose to her mouth. She turned back to Johanna, "I don't know Johanna. I will think about it. But thank you."

"Very well Mary. You know where he lives. We dine in four hours. Be assured that you are welcome as my guest, despite what Simon and others may think."

They said their goodbyes leaving Mary alone to muster up the courage and overcome the conflictual feelings of desire and disgust of seeing Jesus in Simon the Pharisee's house.

CHAPTER 16. REVERENCE REDEEMS

Therefore, I tell you, her sins, which were many, have been forgiven;
hence she has shown great love.
Luke 7:47

The time arrived. Her resolve settled. She would go. Mary grabbed her alabaster flask of spikenard and set out, remembering the pretty penny she had paid for it and wondering at the appropriateness of the gift. She stopped a distance from the house and discreetly concealed herself, glad for the new and more modest fabric she had converted into a new cloak. She had barely finished it in those brief four hours between Johanna's visit and the present moment. The realization of her vain intention made her wonder if Jesus had really changed her yesterday. Here she was, determined to not let vanity or fear of one man's opinion deprive her of this opportunity. And yet, vanity had driven her to use every last second to sew a new cloak. The thought of showing up to Simon the Pharisee's house with her scarlet red cloak was abhorring. It would likely serve only to reinforce his judgment of her as a flaunting prostitute.

She observed the guests arrive. Johanna and Chuza, unfamiliar Pharisees, people from the upper echelon and social class in town whom she no longer associated with. Then, Jesus, followed by a group of his disciples. They stood out like a band of rough rebels. Their difference from the rest gave her courage to draw nearer to the doorway. Random townspeople shuffled towards the house, curious to catch glimpses of Jesus and snatches of conversation that wafted from the windows. Her resolve to enter as an invited guest was fading fast. Yet she did not flee. She would remain outside, she determined. She situated herself between the door and a window, like the others, to savor any message that came from the Rabboni's lips.

Introductions and familiar greetings passed as soon as Jesus entered and they quickly reclined at the table. Mary noticed. No gesture of deference, no sign of the traditional hospitality was offered him. He had been slighted. An unexpected rage began brewing within her. She had always possessed a high sense of justice for the treatment of others and little tolerance for arrogance snubbing an undeserving victim.

It didn't take long for an antagonizing Pharisee to pipe up.

"Why do your disciples break the tradition of the elders? They do not wash their hands when they eat a meal."[44]

Jesus replied to their pointed interrogation. She managed to hear snippets of it, something about breaking God's command for the sake of tradition and nullifying God's word. His voice raised slightly with passion and she caught the rest.

"Hypocrites, well did Isaiah prophesy about you when he said, 'This people honors me with their lips, but their hearts are far from me; in vain do they worship me, teaching as doctrines human precepts.'"[45]

Tumultuous passions welled up inside Mary as she hung onto every word. Memories of her past sins, how she had been defiled, how she had defiled herself, seen now in the light of Jesus' merciful embrace yesterday, overwhelmed her. An overpowering sense of gratitude made her yearn to honor him in a way not offered by the host. The crowd pressed in on the house as the air thickened with tension. Then Jesus spoke as though addressing both those within and the eavesdroppers outside.

"Hear and understand. It is not what enters one's mouth that defiles that person, but what comes out of the mouth is what defiles one. [...] From the heart comes evil thoughts, murder, adultery, unchastity, theft, false witness, blasphemy. These are what defile a person, but to eat with unwashed hands does not defile."[46]

Mary's hand ached. She had been clutching the alabaster flask with all her might. Tears streamed down her face and resolve set in. She pushed through the crowd and had no need to walk far.[47] Jesus was reclined at the side of the table, not even at the head as an honorary guest. Impulsively she dropped to her knees, her head bowed in a gesture of reverence. Tears flowed inconsolably. Her hair, partially loosened from her unsuccessful attempts to braid back its fullness, cascaded to the floor and she improvised the show of hospitality that was not afforded him earlier. With one hand she wiped his now bathed feet with her hair, still grasping the alabaster flask with the other. She felt the gentle touch of his hand on her head and bowed further in a gesture of reverence that she knew would win her scorn from onlookers. She didn't care. No gesture could equal the outpouring of love and reverence she felt for him now. She kissed his feet, uncorked the flask and anointed them with the rich fragrance.

A familiar and agitated voice threatened to belittle the purity of her gesture. Simon the Pharisee. She only caught a few words as her tears continued to flow. "Prophet", "Sinner", words were exchanged and a story was told by Jesus. Then she looked up. Their eyes locked, but his words were for the Pharisee.

"Simon," he said, "do you see this woman? When I entered your house, you did not give me water for my feet, but she has bathed them with her tears and wiped them with her hair. You did not give me a kiss, but she has not ceased kissing my feet. [...] You did not anoint my head with oil, but she anointed my feet with ointment."[48]

He broke their gaze and turned to Simon, "So I tell you, her many sins have been forgiven; for this reason, she has shown great love. But the one to whom little is forgiven, loves little."

Turning back to her, he spoke tenderly, "Your sins are forgiven. Your faith has saved you. Go in peace."[49]

Peace flooded her senses as she felt hands gently lifting her to her feet. It was Johanna. Mary looked around the room, all eyes on her, some horrified, others admiring her boldness. She turned to Jesus once again. A slight smile and nod encouraged her to go, not pushing her away, but accepting the gesture of love she had displayed. She allowed Johanna to lead her away from the scene as she held on to a renewed interior peace and freedom.

CHAPTER 17. ZEALOUS BEGINNINGS

And everyone who has left houses or brothers or sisters or father or mother or wife or children or fields for my sake will receive a hundred times as much and will inherit eternal life.
Matthew 19:29

Johanna had accompanied Mary to her villa. She barely remembered the walk, having been emotionally spent. But Johanna, with motherly tenderness, prepared her for bed and stayed with her until Chuza collected her. When she heard the knock at the door, Mary hoped it was Jesus. But he did not come.

Now, the next day, she was alone. She spent her day in quiet thought. Tams and Babs seemed to sense a new mood. For the most part, they left her to her solitude. Tams entered once with bread and cheese, looking at her expectantly, with bright and hope-filled eyes. She stood silently, staring at Mary as though waiting for her to speak. Mary simply thanked her. Tams nodded then turned to walk out of the room. But as she left, she turned and watched Mary as she slowly closed the door, an uncontainable smile breaking out over her face, acknowledging that she knew the secret, she knew the good news.

All through the remainder of the day and night, waves of peace nurtured Mary's spirit. But it was interrupted by occasional restlessness. A longing gnawed at her. What would she do now? Her reputation hadn't changed even if her heart had. She could not stay still. It was a different kind of restlessness now. Not heavy and weighing her down. Not desolate as before. She felt on edge and itchy to do something bold, good, noble, adventurous, new. Twenty-four hours had not passed before Mary had made a firm decision. She would join Jesus, wherever he went.

Mary informed Tams and Babs that she would be gone for a while, wondering if she was being rash and presumptuous in her decision. *Will Jesus even let me go wherever he goes?*

Tams' expression turned to panic. Bab's mumbled, "But where? Why? What are we to do?"

Tams' confused concern increased as she pleaded, "Miriam, don't go. I thought maybe you had met Jesus and he helped you? Why are you leaving? Please, don't go to that palace. Please Miriam!"

Mary grabbed both of their hands to reassure them. "No, do not worry about me. I hope I never go back there again. I can't explain it all now. But I feel different. Jesus has forgiven me. I want to follow him."

"But you are a woman," Babs piped in.

Tams shot him a scolding look.

He shot his wife a look back. "Well, it is true. His disciples are all men. She can't just go off with him. That will cause even more scandal."

Mary wanted to put them both at ease, but she would not change her mind simply to avoid more gossip. "I will go if he will allow it."

They were speechless. Mary began shoving some basic supplies in her leather bag as she gave orders to Babs and Tams, handing them coins to be offered to one of the workers' wives to come and assist in the household.

Tams refused, "I can get along just fine."

"This is not up for discussion," Mary insisted with a firm but kind stare until Tams nodded slowly.

"Do not worry about me. You know I can take care of myself," said Tams as she pocketed the coins.

Babs murmured a sarcastic response, "Well, *that* is something that could be discussed." Tams elbowed him and left for the kitchen.

Babs awkwardly patted Mary on shoulder, wished her well and left her to her final arrangements.

As she quickly finished her preparations, Mary nurtured a new sensation of hope, joy, and freedom with the memory of her encounters with Jesus: his gaze, his soft smiling eyes, his voice and personal words to her that resonated in the depth of her heart in a way nothing had affected her before.

She went to her hidden stash of money, a reserve that could comfortably last anyone a year, and transferred a hefty amount to a hidden pouch inside her leather bag. She didn't know how long she would be gone or what Jesus would need, but she would gladly give him her possessions for his journeys. She had a secure inheritance and wealthy property. He could do with it as he wished. She was not going back to the life she had before. It was as simple as that. She had nowhere else to go, but with him. She didn't think beyond the task of finding him. Decision made, she turned to leave as Tams and Babs entered again. Tams loaded her arms with at least three days of bread and dried fruits. Babs assured her all would be well at the villa. She kissed them goodbye and off she went to follow Jesus.

Doubt seeped in as soon as she stepped across the threshold of her villa and into the town. *Am I crazy? What if his other followers reject me? No, I don't care. I must find him.* Determination replaced the momentary fear.

She went toward the synagogue with the hope that he was teaching today. Absence of movement outside the building indicated he was not there. She caught sight of Demetria in the marketplace.

"Demetria, have you seen Jesus?"

Demetria responded with exuberance. "Yes, he has left on the north road. Not too long ago. I insisted that Aharon pack him and his disciples a supply of dried fish and bread. We were able to walk with him to the outskirts of town and have just returned. What wonders we have seen Mary! Do you believe he is the Anointed one? My Aharon believes."

Mary interrupted with a quick kiss to her cheeks and a thank you and set out at a rapid pace, leaving Demetria startled, and for once, speechless, by her abrupt departure. She set out northbound.

Am I too late? I must hurry or I could lose him when the roads fork. If I don't catch him before that I could be walking for hours in vain.

Half running, half walking, a stream of people made for another obstacle as they were returning to town. She inquired if they had seen Jesus of Nazareth. Strange looks accompanied the clue that they had indeed come from seeing him off as he headed north. Conversations revolved around Jesus as the oncoming crowd thickened. "Surely he is the Messiah." "He better watch what he says around the leaders."

But as the crowd thinned out, she began to wonder if he had taken a different path. She continued walking as a familiar woman with a little chattering boy came closer. She recognized them. It was the mother and child to whom she had given her fruit basket outside the synagogue, the first time she saw Jesus. The woman caught sight of her and nodded a greeting.

Her boy was chattering animatedly. "Ima, when do you think Jesus will come back?"

Mary stopped them. "Have you just come from him? Is he much further?"

"Yes, we just left him at the crossroad. He is on his way to the northern coastland. Tyre, I believe."

Murmuring a thank you, she hurried on, catching up with a tail end of the people who were still walking with Jesus.

There he is!

Relief and nervous anticipation slowed her steps as she blended in with the crowd. She caught peeks of him up ahead, but she remained slightly behind. They turned westward and entered a cavernous valley. The cool morning was giving way to the heat of a high sun, despite the lingering cold season. Little by little people split off, saying their farewells, and returning home. The thinning crowd no longer disguised her presence. One of the disciples walking closest to Jesus was the first to recognize her.

Simon whispered as he motioned with his head for Jesus to look behind him. "Jesus, the crazy lady is following us."

Jesus raised his eyebrows at Simon. "Crazy? She's no crazier than you Simon!"

A younger disciple laughed as he too looked back and recognized the woman. Simon looked at her with distrust. The younger disciple, the one the others teased and called Thunderman, upon seeing her, raised his hand in a gesture of greeting. Like a little kid eager for Hanukkah, he strode over to her.

"I remember you! You were the woman in the graveyard, no?"

Mary hesitated answering. He hadn't mentioned the incident from yesterday, at Simon the Pharisee's house. Was he too embarrassed to mention it or hadn't he recognized that she was also that same woman? He searched for something in his satchel. His muscular arms and legs contrasted with an almost adolescent face. He pulled his large hand out of the bag and opened it to expose the alabaster flask that once held the gift she had poured out on Jesus' feet.

"Oh, and I think you left this behind yesterday." His eyes held no judgment, only an innocent child-likeness.

She relaxed and smiled. "Thank you."

"I'm John. What's your name? Are you going to join us?"

"I'm...Miriam, my name is Miriam."

The dwindling group, now about fifteen people, had stopped and were curiously watching the scene. Her eyes went to Jesus.

"Mary, Mary of Magdala," he said, fixing his gaze on her alone. No other words were spoken, but it felt like he was offering her an invitation and a question at the same time. Her heart wanted to speak, but her tongue was tied.

You know me. I don't know how, but you know me. I wish to follow you. Will you accept me?

He gave a slight nod and gestured with his hand to join the band of growing disciples.

"Come Mary. If you can stand this crowd of vagabonds, you are welcome to join us."

A smile broke out on his face as muttering complaints and chuckles rippled through the motley crew. Her heart rejoiced at his words.

She blurted out, "I can help you Rabboni! I have wealth and property. I am willing to sell it if you need assistance."

"Yes, so we shall see Mary. As I have told the others, I tell you. Anyone who has left houses and land, or family for that matter, for the sake of my name, will receive a hundred times more, and will inherit eternal life."[50]

Jesus turned and continued walking, conversing with the disciples at his side along the way. Mary was perplexed. *Does he want my money or not? Does he think I wanted something in exchange? I just want to follow him, to know and help him.*

John was still at her side. He broke her train of thought by offering to carry her satchel, which looked bulky, but wasn't so heavy. Two women approached. She recognized one of them. Salome, the woman busy at work in Eva's house. The mother of two of these disciples, she remembered. John's mother? She could see some resemblance in her tall and strong constitution. Salome greeted her as a long lost friend and introduced her quiet counterpart, Rachel. Despite having determined to not care about gossip or more scandal associated with her name, relief at the company of other women made her realize that perhaps she did care somewhat. But doubts or regrets? None whatsoever. She had no idea what the next day would bring, but a certainty was growing. She was walking where she needed to walk. She was following the one person with whom she needed to be.

The trek through a cavernous winding trail, up and down hills, seemed to go on and on. But there was a lightness in her step. She kept up, eager to not miss a word, mostly observing and sometimes participating in the random conversations. Periods of silence followed banter. A humorous moment would suddenly turn into a lesson that left all pondering. She marveled. She looked at the modest sized caravan of people following Jesus. A sense of belonging filled her heart. A thought crept in, catching her off guard, but delighting her. *My new family?*

Her adventurous spirit finally found a home she hadn't even known she was missing, until now. She was eager for all that this new life would offer. A bubbly joy energized her as she schemed all the ways she could contribute. Purchase lodging and food wherever they went. Get some good bargains for them. *What will tomorrow bring?* Enthusiastic anticipation ran through her veins as she turned her attention once again to Jesus who caught her musing. His eyes answered with a delighted smile and a raising of his eyebrows. An invitation and a challenge to "come and see."

CHAPTER 18. ROOTED RESOLVE

Therefore, do not worry about tomorrow,
for tomorrow will worry about its own things.
Sufficient for the day is its own trouble.
Mt 6:34

Blisters had already formed, exploded and bled. More than once. Pale and exhausted on the third day of travel, Mary trailed behind as they entered the city of Tyre. She had hoped they would lounge in a decent place of rest and she longed for good food after the rough conditions of travel and simple meals. The disciples seemed used to this daily routine. They amused themselves along the way, distracting her many times from the weariness of the long trek.

Jesus stopped, allowing her and the other women to catch up. The disciples didn't even notice Jesus' intentional pause. They were trying to outmatch one another in recalling the history of Tyre. The underdog of the disciples, as she liked to call him, was outsmarting them all. He had been a tax-collector, but had an aptitude not only for economics, but also history and scripture. Matthew taught them like a young scholar.

"Tyre and Sidon have had their share of scandalous history over the centuries. Remember the Sidonian princess, Jezebel? She was given over in marriage to Israel's King, Ahab. But she insisted on maintaining worship to the baals."

"You know where it went from there," John interjected. "Isaiah didn't speak of Tyre as a prostitute for nothing."

"Yes," continued Matthew. "Eventually, Tyre's trade with Egypt made Israel rich. Now it's filling Rome's coffers."

A couple of the disciples harassed Matthew. "Yeah Matthew, and you didn't benefit at all from that?!"

She wasn't sure if they were speaking in jest or trying to be derogatory, but Matthew appeared to brush it off. Before he had a chance to respond, a Canaanite woman approached Jesus. Mary watched in dismay as she pleaded for her daughter, possessed by demons. The disciples tried to convince Jesus to send her away, but the woman only insisted more, bowing before him and offering him homage. Compassion overwhelmed Mary. She waited, confident that Jesus would help her. But Jesus' reply to the woman's supplication startled her.

"It is not right to take the food of the children and throw it to the dogs."

Mary knew that his reference to the children referred to the people of Israel and the dogs referred to the gentiles. His statement was harsh enough to discourage anyone. But the woman pleaded even more for just a scrap from the table. In desperation, Mary would have asked for the same, just a scrap. She would have done anything to alleviate the woman's distress and was about to plead with Jesus when he replied with obvious admiration for the supplicating woman.

"O Woman, great is your faith! Let it be done for you as you wish."[51]

That was it? He could just say the word and it was done?

Confused, she watched the woman bow in gratitude. She turned to Mary and the other woman, grabbing their arms and kissing their cheeks, thanking them as well. Then she left as quickly as she had come, leaving Mary to wonder if anything miraculous had even taken place. *Was her daughter really healed?*

Mary marveled at the woman as much as at Jesus. Blind trust and faith, as well as persistence, had won an answer from him. The woman had begged not so much for herself, but for another. And apparently it was granted. Was that the power of faith in Jesus? Intrigued by this new revelation, she congratulated herself for having decided to follow Jesus. Pride swelled in her heart.

What is this? She wondered to herself at this new sensation - a feeling of investment, of being a part of what he did and said. She wasn't an observer anymore. She would be seen as "one of them", one of Jesus' followers. *Is that what I want?* He was loved and adored in one instant, but rejected in the next. To follow Jesus would be to ride the tides of the present, with a heart ready for the unexpected in every instance.

They didn't stay long in Tyre and Mary began to suspect that Jesus had retired from the Galilee area to calm Herod's and the Pharisees' growing animosity. Her feet had barely healed from the journey to the coast when it was announced that they were returning. She questioned his purpose for coming all this way. Was it a worthless trip? With the exception of that one beggar woman and a handful of others who came to speak with him, she did not see the same success as in Magdala.

The long walk back was more excruciating than her journey to Tyre. Frosty mornings woke them. Afternoon storms wet them. And still, Jesus walked on. She was miserable, tired, and more often than not, hungry. She had offered several times to obtain lodging and food for them, only to be thanked, but not accepted. Adding to the physical discomfort, a rising interior irritability was taking hold of her. Any power of persuasion and appeal was in vain. The disciples were impervious to it. And jealousy nibbled at her conscience when Salome or any of the other disciples monopolized Jesus' time. She did what she could to maintain composure and avoid revealing the constant grumblings, complaints, and judgments that assaulted her mind.

On the third day, the rain finally subsided as they crested another hill. A breathtaking panorama broke through her festering agitation. Deep blue water sat cupped in shades of green landscape as the sun's rays peaked through the parting clouds. The eastern mountains were a familiar site. And to the west, Mount Arbel beckoned her to hope for respite. It marked Magdala, nestled comfortably at its base. Home. Bed. Comfort. Still a day's walk away.

Villagers' farms were scattered below. Places of refuge she did not want to merely pass by. She drew near to Jesus. She would ask to go ahead with a couple of others to purchase lodging and food. But her efforts to make a simple request turned into a spew of frustration and anger as she unleashed a barrage of sentiments.

"Jesus, I am a rich woman. You have not availed of this offer, not once! Every time I ask, you simply dismiss it. Why can you not take it! Let me go and secure comfortable lodgings. I have brought sufficient coins and goods to provide for decent shelter and plenty of good meals. And I have a house in Magdala. I can purchase fresh clothing while ours are laundered. I can host you all or sell my property to provide for your needs."

Jesus looked kindly upon her. She thought she had finally persuaded him, but his response deflated her.

"Thank you, Mary. The time will come, but it is not yet ripe. Do you not see the birds of the air?"[52]

Jesus pointed to the sky toward the Sea. Raptors glided just above them, while flocks of starling, cranes, finches and larks were scattered here and there. Their numbers were daily increasing as they entered the full migratory season to the nearby wet valley for nesting.

"They neither sow nor reap nor gather into barns; yet your heavenly Father feeds them. Are you not of more value than they?"[53]

He spoke up for all to hear, "Which of you by worrying can add one cubit to his stature?"

Nathaniel elbowed Little James in jest, "You could use a cubit or so."

Chuckles abounded as Jesus continued, "So why do you worry about clothing?"

Again, he pointed to the landscape around him burgeoning with patches of wildflowers. Carpets of trumpet-faced white, purple, blue, and red poppy-like anemone were all waiting for the sun's rays before showing their faces. Light purple cyclamen was also on the verge of revealing its splendor. And tufts of chamomile were sprouting up amidst the rocky terrain.[54] Jesus spoke, "Some of you have heard me before, as I told you,"

> Consider the lilies of the field, how they grow: they neither toil nor spin; and yet I say to you that even Solomon in all his glory was not arrayed like one of these. Now if God so clothes the grass of the field, which today is, and tomorrow is thrown into the oven, will He not much more clothe you, O you of little faith? Therefore, do not worry, saying, 'What shall we eat?'

or 'What shall we drink?' or 'What shall we wear?' For after all these things the Gentiles seek. For your heavenly Father knows that you need all these things. But seek first the kingdom of God and His righteousness, and all these things shall be added to you. Therefore, do not worry about tomorrow, for tomorrow will worry about its own things. Sufficient for the day is its own trouble.[55]

"Is it not?" Jesus asked.

The disciples all mumbled and nodded their assent.

"Come, we are heading toward Bethsaida."

The disciples began the trek downward toward the Sea as Mary remained atop the hill whose peak offered the grand vista. She looked toward Magdala. How easy it was to contemplate returning to the comfort of her villa. But was it really so much comfort to her? Then she looked further and could see Tiberias sitting on the edge of the Sea, not far beyond Magdala. It stood taunting her, a reminder of her past life, of feeling so lost. *And of truly being lost,* she thought. No, her feet did not want to take her there as she had blindly let them so many times before. Despite her bewilderment at Jesus' ways, her heart began burning as she recalled his words. She longed to know and trust in a heavenly Father. Just moments before, Magdala had appealed to her longing for familiarity, security, and comfort, despite the imprisoning life she had left behind there. Did her past life truly have its grip on her still?

Jesus had let the other disciples pass him by as they continued down the trail. He returned to her side, looking out toward the Sea. As though he could read her thoughts, he spoke, gently but firmly.

"We will take a different route."

He paused and she did not respond. A cool dry breeze blew past them. Mary shivered as her saturated clothes stuck to her skin. The sun had mercy, offering some warmth to her chilled bones. At last, he spoke again, softly provoking a response.

"Mary. Do you wish to return to your home?"

"No!"

Conviction of her chosen path remained firm and the luring attraction of Magdala dissipated like smoke in the wind. She squared her chin, not at Jesus, but at some invisible enemy as she turned to look him in the eyes. She was met by compassion and encouragement.

She declared, "I will follow you, Jesus."

His eyes intimated joyful gratitude as he nodded and motioned her forward, "Onward Mary. We travel on. Together."

CHAPTER 19. GLIMPSING THE INCONCEIVABLE

In my vision at night I looked, and there before me was one like a son of man, coming with the clouds of heaven. He approached the Ancient of Days and was led into his presence. He was given authority, glory and sovereign power; all nations and peoples of every language worshiped him. His dominion is an everlasting dominion that will not pass away, and his kingdom is one that will never be destroyed.
Daniel 7:13-14

The trek toward Bethsaida was muddy but manageable. She felt lighter and a new wave of fortitude maintained her heart facing forward, rather than groping for the past. She remained at the back as Jesus slowly wove his way to the front again. She noticed how John had fallen back, keeping an eye on her like a kind guardian. He was a gentle giant. A strong fisherman, but gentle as a lamb. Child-like at times in his impetuosity, but mature and profound in his spontaneous reflections. He also noticed when something was amiss. This was so rare among men, let alone the company she used to keep, she mused. He broke her silent concentration on the muddy trail.

"Mary, I heard your offer. That was kind of you. But it seems our master is not in the least bit worried about the things that daily concern us. Although I have to admit, he knows how to treat us to good things when we are least expecting it. Like the abundance of choice wine at his friends' house in Cana. They had completely run out early in the party and Jesus worked his first miracle at his mother's request. He turned several large jugs of water into fine wine, the best I've ever tasted. You have to ask Nathaniel about that. His family had provided the wine. We teased him that Jesus will put him out of business if he doesn't keep the festivities well stocked in the future."

They chuckled and Mary took note that Nathaniel and her had something in common, a wine business. She had been trying, little by little, to get to know each one. In their short time together, a fondness was growing for her travel companions. However, two in particular had proven more difficult to penetrate. Judas, the one they call Iscariot, was a peculiar man. She sensed he did not like conversing with her. Perhaps it was because she was a woman. He would not share anything personal with her except to boast about his accomplishments or order her about. Simon was another difficult one for her. He acknowledged her but acted as if she were not trustworthy. For the most part, he just left her alone.

Matthew had also lagged behind, and from his position in front of them, was eavesdropping, as was his custom, she noticed. She was getting used to that, almost expecting it. Actually, he was endearing in an odd sort of way. With his being a tax collector, she detected that he felt different from the others. He appeared to brush off the teasing remarks, but she wondered if it didn't take its toll. She detected that he tried hard to fit in and then withdrew and became a humble observer. She felt empathy for him.

He piped in. "Don't you remember John, when the scribe offered to follow Jesus, but he replied, 'Foxes have dens and birds of the sky have nests, but the Son of Man has nowhere to lay his head.'"[56]

"Yes, I do recall that scribe," replied John. "I guess he didn't like our vagabond plan, or not knowing where our next lodgings would be. You don't see him with us today, do you?!"

Matthew continued his train of thought. "And then another disciple said he would follow but wanted first to go bury his dead father."[57]

John gave Mary a silent shared glance of perplexity, wondering where Matthew was going with this story. Mary listened, grateful for a distraction from the distance still lying between them and the next town, and for the walking stick that John had picked up and fixed for her so she could keep her balance on the moist trail.

"Then I remember how he told us we were to go out and proclaim the kingdom was at hand, and cure the sick, raise the dead...well, he told us to do it, not that I have done it yet. And then he said, 'Do not take gold or silver or copper for your belts; no sack for the journey, or a second tunic, or sandals, or walking stick.'"[58]

Mary wondered at having to give up all those things. Actually, that would constitute everything she was carrying at the present moment.

John berated Matthew gently, looking at Mary as he did.

"Matthew, I don't think he meant it like that, literally."

Matthew cut him off, getting more excited as he spoke.

"He also said we would be persecuted and hated in some towns because of his name, and we wouldn't finish the towns of Israel before the Son of man comes.[59] Do you hear what he told us John? The Son of Man. The Son of Man spoken of by Daniel! I remember reading it when I was younger and imagining the Ancient of Days on his throne of flaming wheels[60] and then 'One like the son of man' came before him and 'received dominion, splendor, and kingship; all nations, peoples and tongues serve him. His dominion', said Daniel, 'is an everlasting dominion that shall not pass away, his kingship, one that shall not be destroyed.'"[61]

Matthew was becoming more animated as he continued.

"Do you get it? Do you hear what he is trying to tell us? Jesus is the Son of Man, come to establish an everlasting kingdom. He keeps telling us, 'My heavenly Father will provide.'[62] Why would he even need to worry about anything if that dominion will be given by the Ancient of day, his Father."

Mary remembered being fascinated with Daniel's prophecy as well. Her father had spoken of it along with a story of Enoch who prefigured a messianic son of God. And he had often quoted the scribe of Ezra who wrote about God's son, the seed of David, who comes to save and to judge the world. She had since learned that interpretations abounded over the passages. But as fascinated as she was about it, her Father would always hush her when she asked how God could have a son, and wondered, with her child-like imagination, if God could also have a daughter.

Mary noticed John's silence. He was pensive, pondering Matthew's revelation. His eyes were fixed to the path, watching every step, but his mind was obviously racing. John quietly mumbled something Jesus had said.

"The one whom God sent speaks the words of God. The Father loves the Son and has given everything over to him. Whoever believes in the Son has eternal life."[63]

He looked as though he were trying to sort out a puzzle. Finally, he looked up as though it dawned on him.

"Matthew, do you recall in the feast of Dedication, at the Portico of Solomon, the Jews insisted he reveal to them if he was the Christ or not, the Anointed one?"[64]

Matthew shook his head, excitedly waiting for John to process a conclusion.

John continued, "Jesus said, 'My sheep hear my voice; I know them, and they follow me. I give them eternal life, and they shall never perish.'[65] I remember thinking that I wanted to be one of those sheep that hear his voice. But then he startled me by saying, 'The Father and I are one.'"[66]

Clarity of vision dawned upon him as he bobbed his head up and down. "Yes, yes. And I remember when he spoke of the work of the Son. He was referring to himself. He said, 'For just as the Father raises the dead and gives life, so also does the Son give life to whomever he wishes.'[67] In Naim, he raised the widow's son from the dead. And he also said that the Father gave him power to exercise judgment, because he is the Son of Man."[68]

Incredulously, John shook his head and as if speaking to himself, "We know that this power is reserved only for God."

John stopped in his tracks, brows deeply furrowed, and looked up toward Jesus, a distance away at the head of the pack. Like a passing rain shower, fright and awe, marvel and bewilderment played upon his countenance. He spoke slowly, timidly, "One like the son of Man come down from heaven. The Father's son who can give life. An everlasting dominion."

Just then they saw Jesus stop and turn around, looking back to the stragglers.

"John, Matthew, Mary, what are you about? Care to fill us in on your intriguing conversation?"

They all swallowed, none brave enough to speak, none capable of comprehending, let alone speaking of the mystery they just daringly surmised. Each one piped up some sort of answer, "No." "Nothing." "Coming."

Jesus was certainly intriguing, beyond all other persons Mary had ever met, but to practically call him a divine figure, a god, well, she might as well go back to Herod's court to worship one of his gods. She shook off that thought. Perhaps Matthew and John had meant something else. It seemed that no one dared to pick up the conversation again. It had come to a halt as they integrated back into the pack and entered a village. To her relief, they had arrived at a resting place at last.

CHAPTER 20. FRATERNAL CORRECTIONS

We urge you, brethren, admonish the unruly, encourage the fainthearted, help the weak,
be patient with everyone.
1 Thessalonians 5:14

Days turned into weeks and weeks turned into months as they made their way through different villages surrounding the northern side of the Sea, frequently returning to Capernaum. She was grateful to be close enough to Magdala to send messages back and forth to Tams and Babs. She inquired about their well-being and the needs of the villa. Messages came back. "Do not worry, all is well." They were happy for her and her choice to follow Jesus. And eagerly hoped that she would eventually make her way with Jesus and the other disciples to Magdala once again.

Mary experienced her first Passover in Capernaum with her new-found community. Memories of the celebration with her family flooded in, renewing old sentiments of a child-like faith. Everything was new and exciting. At first, she was a mere observer, feeling a bit awkward about her role among the diverse group. With time, her natural ways of being came to the forefront. But her ways, initiatives and suggestions were not always welcome, nor were they tempered by her new and converted heart. Her skills at taking charge ruffled feathers. Differences of opinions led to arguments.

Jesus never seemed to intervene. He just let the personality dynamics play out and continued to give of himself wherever they went. Mary's only dismay was his disappearance for a few days. He travelled to Nazareth with Nathaniel and Philip. It rankled her that she had not been told or invited. It was then that she realized he was her reference point and anchor for everything. Interiorly, she felt lost without him, despite being among new found friends.

Johanna occasionally joined the group when they were in Capernaum. On one occasion she brought little Joanna with her. (Sorry John, I just have to mention myself here, once again. Not for my own sake, but to tell you how much Mary had changed and how much she helped me as my faith in Jesus was just beginning to bud.)

Little Joanna had matured. She still possessed her child-like admiration for Mary and even more so now, seeing her among Jesus and his disciples. Her aunt Johanna had been very influential in awakening a fascination for Jesus when they were together in Jerusalem or Tiberius. Now a wife, yet saddened without children, her husband had permitted her to visit Johanna for several weeks to recover from fatigue. Mary guessed (correctly, I must add) that it was melancholy more than any physical illness. And likely a result of lack of attention from her husband, who was many years her elder.

She watched little Joanna improve over the course of the days that they spent in Capernaum together with Jesus. They were both grateful for the blossoming friendship, one based on the genuine and mutual empathy of two adult women rather than its previous connection rooted in vain adoration. Mary listened attentively to little Joanna, encouraged her and let her accompany her in the work that she was doing with the disciples. It was strange but wonderful to see her past and present life weaving together like new patches on old clothes. She wasn't sure how they fit together, but she was starting to realize that following Jesus was not an escape from her past. She was finding herself, her old self, or better said, her true self, in a new reality.

Mary rose each day eager for what she would witness and hear. She went to sleep tired and content. The rhythm was beginning to suit her. People streamed in from villages near and far, wherever they went. She attended to their needs as they waited to speak face to face with Jesus. Sometimes she would intercede for them in some way, helping them skip further ahead in line so as not to have to return without having heard or met Jesus. Her childhood desire reignited in her particular fondness for troubled women, as she called them. It was a miracle that they had even come. They were often accompanied by a husband, father, or brother. But she found a way to single them out, hear their stories and often escorted them personally to meet Jesus. Jesus' eyes twinkled with delight, no matter how tired he was, whenever he would bring one of her "treasures", as he called them.

As the crowds grew in number, and the waiting lengthened from hours into days, the people tended to gather in circles. Women formed separate groups from the men. She took the opportunities to sit with them. She listened to their stories to see if they too had need of a similar healing that Jesus had offered her. And she encouraged their belief in Jesus. She marveled at all she saw and was amazed that she could be part of this tremendous work.

***

Eventually they made their way to the eastern shore, the "other" side, as they called it. It was the pagan side. Even here, the multitudes flocked to see him. She was dumbfounded that they praised the God of Israel. Initially, a new sense of purpose enlivened her spirit daily as she cared for the needs of the people. But the persistent crowd eventually began taking its toll on her patience. She longed for a moment alone with Jesus, or at least with a smaller more intimate group.

One day she overheard Simon speaking to Andrew. He wanted to send the people home. She looked around. Some were not dressed sufficiently for the long wait they had to endure in the cooler weather. The days were bearable, but evening chills set in. She understood the plight of the people and Simon's reasons, but Andrew talked him out of sending them home. When more days had passed and the crowds only increased, Simon became more impatient. He began to take matters into his own hands and began encouraging the people to return home. Mary's anger rose until she could hold it in no longer.

She separated him from the people and spoke firmly.

"Simon! Stop trying to shoo the people away. Why don't you do something about their needs instead. Go get blankets to protect against the cold!"

Simon was taken aback at the first attack, but responded in a likewise manner, short of temper. He didn't appreciate her increasing boldness at giving orders. Words flew back and forth as pride matched pride. Finally, Andrew and Salome, having watched tempers escalate, mediated the heated discussion and Simon and Mary finally backed off from lashing out at each other. But Mary was satisfied. She watched as John, Andrew, Matthew, and an irked Simon finally helped to pass out blankets, thick tunics, and wool coverings. Where they managed to find them, she didn't know.

Salome and Mary continued walking the crowd together. Her ire was still cooling off. Mary was grateful for Salome's companionship. Over the weeks, Salome had proven to be a good listener and every once in a while, gems of wisdom flowed from her heart that left Mary with much to ponder. A comfortable trust had grown between them as, little by little, they had shared bits of their past lives with one another.

Salome had married very young and was only able to give birth to her two sons, Big James and John. She was older than Mary, but probably not much older than Martha, Mary thought. She reminded her a little of Martha, but without the judgmental attitude. It seemed that everyone was related to Jesus somehow. Salome was distantly related to Jesus' mother. She had the bearing of a gentlewoman, although she was from simple stock. She was observant, thrifty, and always ready to serve where needed. She was also extremely proud of her sons. Her husband must be something of a rarity, Mary thought, since he allowed her to be so long away from home.

Rachel was her companion and only seventeen years old. Not quite a servant, but not quite a daughter, Rachel had been welcomed into Salome's home a year ago, when she found herself homeless upon the death of her parents. Despite the possibility of an arranged marriage, Rachel had chosen to follow both Salome and Jesus.

Salome allowed Mary to temper her still hot fuse, waiting for a prudent moment to speak.

"Mary, you and Simon are like two mules pulling in opposite directions when really, you have the same goal in mind."

The comment left Mary speechless.

Salome continued, rushing forward while Mary was silent, mouth agape.

"I know that you have been hurt and deceived by men in the past, but you take it out on certain disciples. Or shall I say, one in particular, Simon. He has the same intentions and interests as you. What a force you would both be if instead of two stubborn mules you were two yoked oxen pulling in the same direction."

"I have no desire to be yoked to anyone," Mary huffed. Then added, "Except Jesus."

"That is not what I insinuated, Mary."

Mary knew she didn't mean to imply some sort of arrangement between them. She tried to hold back her tongue and let Salome speak.

"You don't know your own strength of character Mary. You go all day attending to the people and I don't think that you realize how much they notice and admire you. You stand out among the rest. Not just for your height! But for your gifts and at times like this, for your passion. But, I fear what they think of us when we argue like that. You have a special heart that listens and sees what others do not. But please Mary. Do not be so harsh with those who do not see what you see, or feel what you feel."

Salome paused, gaging Mary's reaction and hesitated to continue. Mary, often quick to answer back, remained silent, considering Salome's insightful observation. Salome took that as an open door to continue.

"I am afraid for you Mary. Your passion is your gift, but perhaps it is also your curse. Remember the proverb, 'When pride comes, then comes disgrace, but with humility comes wisdom.'[69] Mary," she said with a gentler and cautious tone, "sometimes you make demands on others that border on Roman tyranny. But," she held up her hand, fending off Mary's comeback, "I know you mean well."

Lightening her expression after this serious, but gentle reprimand, Salome offered a smile of solidarity as she exclaimed under her breath, "And that Simon, he has a streak of stubbornness similar to your own." She huffed a laugh, shaking her head and sighing. "But Mary, you were a little harsh on him. Not that he can't take it. I think it's actually why

Jesus keeps entrusting him with all he does. He knows Simon's determination, a bit too much determination if you ask me. But please, be more gracious in your speech toward him. How goes that proverb? 'He who is gracious of speech and pure of heart, will have the king as a friend.'"[70]

Mary shot back, "You have a verse for every occasion, don't you Salome! And I don't care what others think!" Mary checked her reaction as she heard the sassiness of her own tone. She looked heavenward and closed her eyes as she took in a deep breath. Letting out a slow sigh, she felt herself letting go and surrendering. The sting of correction slowly morphed into gratitude as she pondered the goodness of Salome's heart-felt and sincere reprimand. She let out a little chuckle, shaking her head at Salome's crafty use of proverbs and with a warmer tone she addressed her sincerely, "Thank you for your wisdom, Salome. I will take it to heart."

They embraced and Salome went back to work. Mary stayed in their semi-solitary space where Salome had pulled her apart from everyone. She recollected herself, wading through the multitude of emotions she had just felt in the brief moment of their conversation. Mary knew Simon meant well, they just didn't always see eye to eye. She hadn't thought of the fact that they had a similar character. Always ready to act, ready to put in motion a plan when they saw a need. Their plans just differed at times. Or better said, their way of carrying it out differed.

Mary had been learning to examine her heart, see when her independence, pride, and desire for her own way held its grip on her. When that happened, she had noticed, she could only see one way forward, her way. In the little time she had been among this group of followers, she had come to feel part of whatever they were doing and found herself attentive to Jesus' needs and the needs of those who came from far away to see him. She had begun to take charge in small ways, being used to giving commands and having them heeded in her own household. Some might have called her bossy, but at least her vain habit of manipulating to get her way was slowly giving way to intentionally seeking to serve others, to serve Jesus. Her mother would have been proud of her. Pure of heart, she had called it, similar to Salome's words of wisdom. She realized that, lately, she had been feeling different inside. She felt free of nonsense and selfish ulterior motives. There was a simple joy in following Jesus. Her previous burdens now appeared preposterous and a waste of time. There were more important matters to attend to in Jesus' presence.

On one of their interminable walks, Matthew had shared with her one of Jesus' sermons that she loved to repeat. Her favorite line was, "Blessed are the pure of heart, for they shall see God." To be pure of heart seemed impossible. She used to think it was simply refraining from illicit affairs, but she soon began to see the little ways her love could be purer, not selfishly seeking what she wanted all the time, without thought to the others.

She thought back to Salome's proverb about having a king as a friend. She didn't care for that. While it once may have tempted her to be admired and sought by the elite of society, now she just wanted to be close to Jesus. *For me, Jesus is king enough.* He inspired her. He challenged her. He changed her. Yes, her heart was changing. It had changed already. But thanks to Salome's gentle admonition, she felt the nudge to even greater change - a way of serving and listening that sought to love more than control, to work together even if it meant giving in to her own ideas, to give without cost rather than the subtle seeking of praise and acknowledgement. *Pure of heart. That must be my way to see God.*

CHAPTER 21. YOUR LIGHT MUST SHINE

Just as the city's light upon a hill cannot be hidden, so too your light must shine in people's sight, so that seeing your good works, they may give praise to your Father in heaven.
Matthew 5:14-16

At the end of the long days, the disciples had been taking refuge in a large lodge near Cursi. Demetria's family, her baker friend, had a large farm north of the village. They were grateful to host Jesus and his disciples. After a light dinner, all were gathered outside around a large fire. She found a makeshift seat on an old upside down half damaged boat and surveyed her view to the west. Mary could easily spot Magdala thanks to the towering Mount Arbel. She sat watching a sliver of the moon and one bright accompanying star slowly duck behind the horizon as the night continued on peacefully amidst chatter and a few after dinner chores. Mary had tried to help, but Demetria's mother insisted that Mary rest.

She took in her surroundings. The farm was nestled, like Magdala, at the base of a large hill that ran into the Sea of Galilee. Close by, to the southeast she could make out flickers of light on another hill upon which sat one of the cities of the Decapolis, Hippos. She tucked her cloak around her legs, grateful for the large fire that warded off some of the cold, while still permitting a spectacular view of a star-speckled sky. She hoped the people who were camped out nearby in order to see Jesus tomorrow would be okay tonight.

The makeshift seat teetered as Jesus sat down next to her. She smiled contentedly, glad for his close company. The fire highlighted his features. His soft smile and eyes dancing with light warmed her heart.

"How is your heart tonight, Mary?"

She didn't feel she needed to answer. He knew. He gestured towards the panoramic of hills, like undulating earthy waves or upside down bowls around the sea.

"Look at those cities at the hilltops."

The hills were dotted with lights from village fires and lamps, a sign of the dwellers trying to squeeze more time out of the day, despite the night having descended.

Jesus continued, "Just as the city's light upon a hill cannot be hidden, so too your light must shine in people's sight, so that seeing your good works, they may give praise to your Father in heaven."[71]

There it was again. A Father in heaven. This idea kept warming her heart. But she was struck by his other words, "your light must shine." She was used to being seen. As Salome reminded her, she stood out for more reasons than one. She used to enjoy being admired by certain crowds, especially if she could attract them with her beauty. It gave her a thrill and a feeling of domination. But there was something different in his expression. *That they may give praise to your Father in heaven.*

She recalled the warm joy that accompanied her father's notice of the good deeds she did. His attention had been, more often than not, a result of her mischievousness. But the happiness that filled her heart to be noticed for the good deeds she had done, especially when it was her father paying attention, would send her walking on clouds the rest of the day. She thought of her labors over the last several days. It made her content, peaceful. She was tired but not weary or depleted. Her efforts had not been tainted with vain pleasure seeking. Actually, it now occurred to her, she hadn't sought anyone's eyes to admire her work. However, to imagine a Father in heaven looking with pleasure upon her, of giving glory to God, was a new experience. She looked to Jesus and, for an instant, thought she saw the look of her pleased father in his eyes.

CHAPTER 22. FROM DEMONS TO DANCING

Sing a new song to the Lord, for he has performed wonders.
The whole wide world has seen the saving power of God.
Acclaim Him, all the earth, burst into shouts of joy!
Psalm 98:1,3-4

Noise drew their attention to commotion on the other side of the circle gathered around the fire. Simon was growing more animated by the second, and all were engrossed in the story he was telling. Mary turned her attention to him. He was retelling the story of the Gerasene demoniac and the drowning of the swine. She remembered Demetria's fast and short version. She smirked at Simon's dramatics and attention-getting tactics, then checked herself for her harsh judgment. He was quite the story-teller. She secretly shook her head, remembering Salome's words that they had much in common. *Even this? Goodness,* she thought, *I never realized how very much alike we are!*

A commotion of laughter heightened her attention to the scene. It did not escape her notice that a handful of the disciples had shifted uncomfortably, watching her with side glances. John and Matthew in particular. Jesus maintained a peaceful demeanor and a jovial upward tip of a corner of his mouth. He was enjoying but not encouraging any theatrics that the animator was eager to perform.

As the story went on, her face became heated and embarrassment crept in. The laughter died down slowly as he neared the end of the story. Had Simon told the story for her benefit? Was he pointing out that she wasn't the only one who had been fiercely possessed by demons? But then, his voice sobered, and he looked right at her. He praised the man who once was a demoniac for he had become a great disciple of their Master. They didn't even know his name or where he was now, but Jesus knew his heart. The man from whom the demons had gone out had begged Jesus that he might accompany Him; but Jesus had sent him away, saying, "Return to your house and describe what great things God has done for you." So, he went away, proclaiming throughout the Decapolis what great things Jesus had done for him.[72]

Simon paused momentarily, leaving everyone wondering why he suspended his speech in midair. Mary thought it was a clever skill, but she didn't appreciate it. Finally, he looked at her and spoke.

"Great things came from one who was set free from demons. We have seen with our own eyes how the people flock to the Master. The Gentiles' hearts have been stirred. Is this not proof that one who is called out of darkness into the light is capable of great endeavors?"

Confusion replaced embarrassment. *Is he encouraging me? Affirming me?*

She felt Jesus' eyes upon her. She turned to him. Shadows danced on his face in the flickering firelight.

What is that look he is giving me? Hope? Expectation? Affirmation? Whatever it was caused a bombardment of emotions: humility, gratitude, and a semblance of courage despite being one of the few women in this band of Jesus' closest disciples. A mysterious sense of purpose washed over her. Of something more to come. Yet, she already had purpose, here, with Jesus. She was happy accompanying him, listening to him, and caring for him and all who flocked to see him. But perhaps there was something beyond this that she was meant to do?

Simon's speech came to a close. The chatter of small groups started up again and a couple of the disciples came over, pulling Jesus away from her. Simon sat down next to her, in the now empty space.

"Mary, I want to say I am sorry for our spat earlier."

"No Simon," Mary jumped in, "I owe you an apology. I was harsh and rude to you."

"You're not going to let me have the last word here either, are you?" He jested. Then he was serious. "Mary, you have been neither idle nor lazy. I see that you want, like myself, to follow the Master, to grow in knowledge and righteousness. Your passion, endurance, and devotion have not gone unnoticed. The Gentiles observe your good work and will hopefully glorify God on the day of their visitation.[73] We both have much to be humbled about, no?"

She nodded her assent and stared into the fire. A slow smile and giddiness swept over her. "Simon, did Salome give you a scolding by chance?"

He held up his hands defensively, "What? Can't a man say he is sorry without the prodding of a woman?"

She knew. Salome's wisdom and maternal ways had their effect on more than her this afternoon. Her heart warmed at the thought, but it didn't lessen her appreciation of his apology.

"Thank you, Simon."

A group of men playing assorted instruments approached the small party of disciples around the fire. The tune provoked memories of Herod's palace, washing away the pleasantness of her reconciliation with Simon. She squeezed her eyes closed, attempting to force those memories out and keep the encroaching fear that accompanied them at bay. She startled as her makeshift seat under her shifted, bobbing up and down. She opened her eyes to see Jesus once again next to her. Simon had disappeared toward the singing musicians.

"Fear not Mary," he said gently. She wondered if he had even spoken those words, or she had imagined it. His look of earlier had not vanished.

How does he do that? Look at you with hope, yet you don't feel the weight of any expectation.

"Have you heard this parable? The Kingdom of heaven is like a woman searching for a fine pearl. When she finds it, she sells everything and buys it. Mary, have you found your pearl?" She believed she understood. Her newfound faith in him as the Messiah.

"I think that I have," she whispered, hardly audible over the merry-making around the fire. She hesitated for a moment, then looked at him with boldness and certainty, "No Rabboni. I know I have."

"Then keep your eyes on the pearl. No need to fear."

The fear that had crept in vanished like smoke in a gust of wind and a new sense of strength took root. Not the boldness of her prior life that had challenged all things with defiance. It was lighter, freer, purer.

Jesus spoke. "But there is another way to understand this pearl. Are you not also the pearl that was lost and has now been found? Many who love you will rejoice that the pearl has been found."

Martha and Lazarus. Mary guessed that he was speaking of her brother and sister who had exhorted her endlessly to change her ways. She wondered what they would think of her now. *Would they even recognize me?*

Jesus turned toward the musicians who had started jumping around to their own tune. The disciples had banned together to change whatever pagan tune the original music makers were singing. They were attempting an improvised chant of a psalm[74], creating a joyful ruckus of praise and laughter.

Jesus' dancing eyes gave her a knowing invitation to rejoice. He clapped to the rhythm that had begun with uncertainty but was quickly gaining ground.

"Let us dance!" He exclaimed. He stood, leaving her almost toppling over from the bobbing of the makeshift seat. He steadied her then pulled her into motion as they laughed their way to the merrymaking. The initiative caught fire with an outburst of glee all around and they sang:

Sing a new song to the Lord, for he has performed wonders...
The whole wide world has seen the saving power of God.
Acclaim Him, all the earth, burst into shouts of joy!
Play to the Lord on the harp...acclaim the presence of the King.
Let the sea thunder, and all that it holds, the world and all who live in it...
He will judge the world with saving justice and the nations with fairness.

Mary went to bed exhausted that night, absolutely exhausted. She marveled at the new challenges she faced, so different, yet somehow internally similar. She was changing. The difference was Jesus. In his presence, one could not remain the same. His goodness, his holiness, made her want to be a better person. And not just want it. Somehow, he instigated noble desires that, if she didn't resist, flowered into beautiful acts of kindness and love.

She closed her eyes, heart full of gratitude to God. She couldn't contain the happiness that welled up from within, bringing a huge smile to her face and slipping out into an unrestrainable childlike giggle. She clapped her hand over her mouth, not wanting to wake up the other women. Echoes of the minstrels' tune and the improvised hymn to a joyful psalm brought consolation and a freedom of spirit as she settled into a comfortable position, despite the hard ground upon which all lay. Finally, she drifted off to sleep, content to rest peacefully for as long as the remaining night would permit. For she was also eager for dawn's first light. *What good things will tomorrow hold?*

CHAPTER 23. SIGNS & WONDERS

Worship the Lord your God, and his blessing will be on your food and water. I will take away sickness from among you.
Exodus 23:25

Mary awakened to the distant sound of voices almost drowning out the constant lapping of water on the nearby seashore. The hustle and bustle of feet and early morning conversations were already underway. She peeked out from under her blanket, trying to stifle the groan that gave away her tiredness and aching muscles. Dawn had already arrived. The glorious feeling of last night seemed a lifetime ago, tempting her to retreat under covers rather than face a new day. But then she recalled the large gathering that was waiting to see Jesus. She mustered up the energy to rise, performed simple morning ablutions and made her way toward the smell of freshly baked bread. Someone had been up very early. The domed oven had performed its duty and still contained a few embers, but only a handful of loaves stood in a single basket as evidence of the early morning's work. She pulled off a modest piece and ate as she went out to assess the day's situation.

Behind the lodge, a short distance away, she saw the crowds of people scattered about from the shoreline and up through the inclining hill rich with hearty grass, weeds and shrubs, although much had been trampled down with the onslaught of people. The sun was still cresting from behind the hill, leaving many in shade and chilled from the dewy night. An ensuing attraction had them all facing and migrating upward, further up the hill. Following the slow movement of the masses with her eyes, she caught sight of Jesus, sitting on the ground amidst the grassy and rock scattered terrain. He and several other disciples must have risen much earlier. The disciples were hard at work doing crowd control as small groups were permitted close proximity to Jesus. Many fell to the ground before him in a pose of supplication or were placed at his feet as they were carried and presented by others who accompanied the persons in need.

She scanned the width, length and depth of people. *Goodness, the crowd seems to have grown overnight. Where did they all come from? Did they walk through the night?* She walked through the crowds, noticing the expressions, from agony and tiredness to hope and joy. Those who had just been to Jesus were animatedly retelling their encounter with the master, feeding the hope of those awaiting their own meeting. She witnessed the lame walking, the mute speaking, and the blind able to see. Those who had no physical ailment also came away with a renewed sense of joy and peace.

She was amazed. *What would come of these miracles? This is predominantly pagan land. The Gentiles are now glorifying the God of Israel? Or at least they are believing in Jesus.*

The next two days went by like a blur. Jesus seemed to have an unending source of energy and patience for crowds that didn't dwindle, despite having seen hundreds of people already. When did he eat and sleep? He continued past her time of exhaustion when she would finally retire to sleep for a few hours. And he was already attending to requests when she arose. Her days were spent looking after the people the best she could, speaking to them and hearing the stories of where they came from, how they had heard of Jesus, and what he did for them. Most had come from the cities of the Decapolis such as Philadelphia, Raphanae, Gadara, Hippos, Dios, Pella, Gerasa, Canatha, and Damascus. She never ceased marveling at the providential ways in which they had made their way to this area, be they individuals or families with children of all ages. She was encouraged by their simple faith and hope of meeting this Jewish rabbi, despite being Gentiles from pagan traditions.

Their beliefs were not so foreign to her, having been exposed to them during her interactions in Herod's palace. The irony struck her. Having escaped the danger of it, now Jesus had, in some way, brought her into the heart of it, but with a much different interior disposition. It caused no threat to her conviction of following the one God, whom

Jesus called Father. This was something new yet familiar at the same time. It was welcome. And she hoped that these people, having met Jesus, would come to the same discovery she had.

***

Near the end of the third day of never ending crowds, Mary's patience was running thin. *Will they ever let Jesus have a break? And let me have a chance to get near him!* She had to confess that jealousy was taking hold once again. She tried to curb it, but it snaked its way into her heart. She even desired to be one among the ill, so she too could be presented at the feet of Jesus. Laughing at herself, she looked toward Jesus in the distance. Suddenly he stood and motioned some of his disciples to come.

Matthew, Simon, John and Andrew drew near. As he spoke, Matthew nodded his head vigorously, as though passionately agreeing. Simon was doing the opposite, shaking his head and flailing his arms in distress and incredulity. Andrew's hands went up as he grabbed his thick head of curls in a gesture of near panic. John remained calm. He turned and grabbed a nearby basket that had held the day's food and showed it to Jesus as the others dispersed and began ordering the people to sit on the ground in groups.

Salome approached her.

"Jesus' compassion knows no bounds. He says we are to leave tomorrow but he doesn't want to send them away hungry. I have a feeling that we are about to see another miracle, like he worked at Heptapegon, the Seven Springs, south of Capernaum a while back."

"Yes, I heard of that from Demetria. I never thought I would see such a thing."

Mary, Salome and Rachel began to work with the disciples to organize the people. As she gave orders for the people to sit, she kept her eyes on Jesus. The disciples had returned to where he had been seated. She watched John take out loaves of bread from the basket as though counting, stopping to present them to Jesus when he had seven loaves in his arms.

Is that all we have? How are we to feed these thousands of people with that?

Jesus looked heavenward in an act of praise and supplication, then bowed his head in thanksgiving as he broke the loaves into fragments and gave them to the disciples. She watched them as they began to maneuver through the crowds to hand them out. She hurried toward Jesus, looking into the basket as he held out a loaf of bread to her.

Full! The basket is now full!

She looked at him with surprise and amazement. He did not look at all surprised, only amused at her reaction.

Eyebrows lifting at her as though questioning her intent, he held up the bread for her to take. He swept his other hand toward the ocean of seated peoples.

"What are you waiting for? We have many to feed, do we not Mary?"

Taking that as her cue, she scooped up several loaves of bread and set about determined to feed these hungry people. As she passed by Matthew, she heard him excitingly count as he was handing out bread.

"We fed at least five thousand people the last time Mary! It looks like there are almost as many again!"

Five thousand indeed! She was waiting for the basket to run empty, but every time she returned there seemed to be another basket added and they remained full of loaves. Her anxiety at running out decreased every time she returned to gather more. And with each trip, her joy and incredulity increased. A song of praise surfaced and matched the joy and gratitude that was infesting the multitude. You would have thought they had given them an overabundance of wine with the ambience of festivity that accompanied the meager meal. A poor man's hunger had turned into a rich man's feast with the simple gift of bread.

***

The sun had already disappeared behind the western hills by the time they had finished, leaving the sky streaked with pink, purple and orange ribbons. It reflected on the sea, creating a majestic glow as the winds made the waters dance with a soft light. She stood for a moment taking it all in. Her stomach grumbled and yet she felt full, full to the brim with gratitude, awe, and joy. She lifted her eyes to the heavens as she had seen Jesus do and imagined a Father who provided for his children. He had done that, by Jesus' request. What could he not ask of God and attain? What could she ask of God and attain? She lifted a prayer, daring to speak from the heart as she had seen Jesus do.

Help me follow Jesus. If he is your Son, I want to help him and help others to follow him.

The beginnings of a new conversation with her God were interrupted as she heard a voice at her side. John was looking out at the skyline with her, a full basket of bread in his arms.

"'You make the dawn and the sunset shout for joy.'[75] Majestic, is it not Mary?"

"Mmm," was all she could respond. She glanced at him as he turned to face her and she could see a similar sensation in his eyes: awe, joy, gratitude, contentment and exhilaration all at the same time.

He held the basket out to her. "Here, I think you forgot to take your share."

The words of a psalm slid naturally from her tongue, "The Lord is the portion of my inheritance and my cup."[76]

"True Mary. But let us enjoy the gift that he gives us in bread to nourish and sustain our lives as we stand in awe of his signs and wonders."

Giddy with wonder, she plucked a loaf out and pulled off a morsel. "Very well. I gratefully accept!" She popped it in her mouth as she marveled at the multiplication from seven loaves to seven leftover baskets full of bread, like Jesus' goodness, overabundant.

CHAPTER 24. PETITIONS

The effective prayer of a righteous man can accomplish much.
James 5:15

Early the next morning Jesus and the disciples dismissed the crowds. Mary had mixed feelings. She was concerned for several she had met who had made the journey from far away. And yet, she was grateful that they had Jesus to themselves once again. They packed their few belongings and said goodbye to Demetria's mother with the promise of sending her love to her daughter. They were returning to the other shore. As they got into the boat, she maneuvered herself to sit near Jesus. She felt like a child with her not-so-hidden pandering for any sign of affection he might offer her. Goodness, she felt ridiculous when she recognized this, but she quickly pushed any embarrassment aside. She cared less what the others might think, especially if it won her the chance to speak to Jesus or catch anything he might say during the journey. They cast off in the direction of the district of Magadan in which lay her beloved villa.[77]

As though guessing her thoughts Jesus addressed her, "We mean to stay in your house Mary."

Joy and pride broke into a grand smile. *Finally! Finally, she could offer him the kind of hospitality she believed he deserved.*

"Thank you, Jesus! I count myself unworthy but honored among those you have chosen. You will not be disappointed. There is plenty of room for all and I will assure that we have a well-deserved rest and feast."

"I am sure that whatever you provide will be heartfelt and very welcome."

Matthew interrupted her treasured moment with Jesus with one of his common questions that seemed so out of the blue.

116

"Master, why have we been going to the Gentiles when you said you have come for the lost sheep of Israel?"

Jesus smiled, affirming Matthew for his astute question.

"I do come for the lost house of Israel if they will heed my voice. Do you remember the prophecy of Isaiah, 'I will make you a light to the nations, that my salvation may reach to the ends of the earth.'[78] This is my hope for you, to be a light for the nations, as we have done in Tyre and Sidon and in the Decapolis. And to farther reaches of the earth."

Simon elbowed Matthew to scoot himself out of the oar's range of movement so he could get the boat moving. Matthew didn't miss a word as he remained attentive to Jesus and maneuvered to a new spot.

Jesus continued, "Isaiah also prophesied, 'I have formed a people for myself that they might announce my praise. Yet you did not call upon me, O Jacob, for you grew weary of me, O Israel.'[79] You see my people? Many have grown weary. They have turned to idols. Are we not, at times, any different than the pagans whom we have just been among? They may be ignorant of our faith, but so are many of our own people. 'Those who cling to worthless idols turn away from God's love for them.'[80] They open the door to unclean spirits, not by being Gentile or Jew, but by the worthless gods they seek rather than the one God. Who then do you think will enter the kingdom of heaven? Those who have ears to hear and eyes to see and choose to use them rather than remain deaf and blind. 'Amen I say to you, many prophets and righteous people long to see what you see but did not see it, and to hear what you hear but did not hear it.'[81] Take heed then. Be that light to all nations, not hiding your light under a bushel basket."[82]

Mary's stomach had been doing somersaults as she listened to Jesus, and she didn't think it was from the waves gently rocking the boat as they made their way closer to Magdala. She knew she could be counted among those who had been deaf and blind, as one whom unclean spirits had touched because of life circumstances and her poor choices. She too could be counted among those who had turned to idols and rejected the one true God, or at least had ignored Him. And yet, she was among Jesus' closest disciples now. That must mean something. It gave her hope that the kingdom of God was not lost to her forever.

But trepidation was tying knots in her stomach with the approaching shoreline. Her previous life was about to collide with her new one. She envisioned the comforts of her home, the luxuries of her past, and the familiarity of her admirers. Then a thought seized her. *What if Gaius' friends decided to make one of their unexpected visits while Jesus was there?* A foreboding sense of darkness threatened her previous calm. She was fearful of her own reactions, despite having proven herself. Yes, proven herself. She saw it now as she looked back over the last few weeks since she had left her villa behind. She had endured the hardships, fought the doubt and frustration at not understanding all that Jesus said and did, swallowed her pride when corrected, and never shirked away from work in order to prove her worth. *To whom am I trying to prove myself? God? Jesus? The other disciples? Myself?*

As they neared the shore of Magdala, she tried to contain her mixed emotions and anxiety. Anxiety of her past and a premonition of the future? Here she was again, back in familiar ground, very likely with the same reputation or even worse off for having chased after the "rejected rabbi", as some judged him. *How will I be received or looked upon now?* Mary was suddenly disgusted with what she saw in herself. For someone who supposedly did not care what others thought, she was obviously caring now!

They beached the boat slightly north of the harbor, having decided not to dock in Magdala's port so as to avoid crowds. However, their presence had not gone unnoticed. People were already swarming to the forested terrain at the shore's edge. She caught sight of Demetria and Aharon among the growing crowd.

"Miriam! Miriam! You are still alive! Heavens! You had looked insane when I last saw you! Insane! I was frightened for you, but Tams said you went off in search of Jesus. You were with the rabbi this whole time?"

Demetria was her exuberant self. Aharon was behind her. They nodded their greetings quickly as Aharon was absorbed at the sight of

Jesus. Demetria continued her chatter, stopping suddenly mid-sentence and looking behind Mary, face aghast, mouth hanging half open.

Mary heard a voice come from behind her.

"Are you going to introduce me to your friends, Mary?"

She looked over her shoulder. His countenance belied amusement, his eyes dancing with laughter and genuine interest at the site of Aharon and Demetria.

"Rabboni, these are my very good friends..."

And before she had a chance for any formal introduction, Demetria had found her tongue and launched into another monologue, this time at Jesus' feet. She spilt out words of praise and supplication, overcome in his presence. Aharon, who was turning a dark shade of red, unsuccessfully attempted to pull her to her feet. His tall skinny frame and silent demeanor contrasted with the short plump heap of a woman whose incessant supplication revealed her heart's burden, a burden she had carried in silence for so long. Between tears, she sputtered out her desire for children, having been barren during their married years. She thought she was being punished for her previous pagan ways and begged Jesus to lift whatever curse was upon them.

Jesus stooped, took her by the hand and lifted her up, while at the same time beckoning Mary to help him. Jesus, Aharon and Mary lifted her to a standing position as Demetria wiped her tear-stained face with her head covering. She turned to Aharon, telling him to ask Jesus for the same and as they were disputing, Jesus gently turned to Mary.

"Did you know of her sorrow Mary?"

"No." Mary had never seen Demetria so discomposed. She knew they did not have any children, but she had never considered that there may be a problem, nor had she given any indication of the suffering she had been enduring for want of them.

Jesus spoke softly to Mary, "I will do whatever you ask in my name, so that the Father may be glorified in the Son."[83]

What does he mean by this? Am I to ask him for what Demetria has already requested? She didn't understand but felt prompted to act. She reached out for Demetria, touching her arm to silence her and then turned her attention back to Jesus. She spoke the words of supplication to Jesus, mustering up her faith in him, a faith that she knew had been forged in the witness of his many signs these last few days. If he wished, he could give her what she asked.

"Jesus," she spoke his name as though it held power in itself. "Demetria and Aharon would like to bear a child. I ask you to help them to receive this heritage from the Lord. Grant them offspring as a reward from him for their faithfulness to the Lord."[84]

Jesus nodded, smiling with tenderness on Aharon and Demetria.

"There is surely a future hope for you, and your hope will not be cut off."[85]

A calm descended upon Demetria's countenance and thanksgiving was uttered all around. They were suddenly interrupted by murmurings and a parting in the sea of people that had been gathering. A group of Pharisees and Sadducees made their presence known. Mary felt trouble brewing as she saw several of the same religious leaders who had been at table in Simon the Pharisee's dinner. He caught her eye, looking at her with disdain, obviously wondering at the company that Jesus was keeping. Word had already reached their ears of the signs he had worked on the shores of the Decapolis. They too demanded a sign. Mary sensed the insincerity of their request. It was a test. She waited to see what sign Jesus would work. He could prove to them his power. She looked around for John, only to find him standing right next to her.

"John, where is the bread?" She whispered insistently, hoping he would present Jesus with a loaf of bread for him to work his wonders once again. He shrugged his shoulders and showed his open and empty hands as he looked towards the other disciples. No bread among them. But Jesus did not seek out bread. He would work no signs for them. Instead, with a forced calm he spoke about judging the weather in the eve and in the morn. A plethora of emotions washed over his face: pity, ire, disgust, disappointment. Then speaking with authority, his voice carried over the rising winds.

"You know how to judge the signs of the times. An evil and unfaithful generation seeks a sign, but no sign will be given except the sign of Jonah."[86]

Mary was struck by his words, despite not understanding them. Only later, reminiscing with Salome, John and many others, would she understand the clue he had given them in this image of Jonah, three days in the belly of a whale compared to his three days in the belly of the earth before his triumphant resurrection. But at present, it remained a mystery. The tension thickened as the Pharisees and Sadducees displayed their anger and disgust. They began shooing people away as Jesus gestured to his disciples that they were moving on.

Disappointment filled her as she realized he would work no sign for them. She had hoped that he would prove to them what he could do. They walked toward her villa as Jesus broke the silent tension.

"Look out and beware of the leaven of the Pharisees and Sadducees."

Simon and the disciples murmured that they should have brought bread with them from the other side. They began blaming one another for their forgetfulness. No one had thought to bring any, and they could have shown the same miracle once again. Mary had thought the same earlier, but now it dawned on her that Jesus was not speaking of that kind of leaven. He read their thoughts and scolded them with impatience.

"You of little faith, why do you conclude among yourselves that it is because you have no bread? Do you not understand, and do you not remember the five loaves for the five thousand, and how many wicker baskets you took up? Or the seven loaves for four thousand, and how many baskets you took up? How do you not comprehend that I was not speaking to you about bread? Beware of the leaven of the Pharisees and Sadducees."[87]

Understanding dawned on the disciples' faces. Mary recalled a time when her father had taught her a similar lesson. He respected the Pharisees, his wife having grown up in this sect and he having assumed the same beliefs as though he had been a Jew all his life. But he had not been afraid to judge and question the Pharisee's demands and teachings. Her mother had cautioned him against his free thinking, warning that Mary would reap the dangers of such debate with the Pharisees. Yet here was Jesus, warning against their teachings as well.

She liked his boldness. He was not arrogant, but sincere. Simple yet with an air of authority. She experienced a newness about his teachings, and at the same time, it was familiar. In one moment, she could be overcome with excitement at the clarity she experienced, as though the truth was piercing her heart. And then, the next moment, she felt a wall go up, as if to protect herself from something. *From what?* She dared to question herself. *From disappointing Jesus? What if I am not able to live what he is asking of me?*

She thought back to her prayer for Demetria. He had trusted her to ask for a child for her friend. *Who am I to ask such a thing?* The prayer had seemed so natural as it ushered forth from her lips. But time would tell if her prayer was efficacious or not. As she walked quietly to her villa, doubts, fears, and confusion began to creep in. Noise, so much noise inside her made the past few days seem like a dream. She attempted to push away the growing fog and focus on her new task of hospitality for this strange new family she had recently inherited.

CHAPTER 25. THE TEST

For you, God, tested us;
you refined us like silver.
Psalm 66:10

The next few days went by in a blur. Mary busied herself assuring that Jesus and the disciples had everything they needed, from their lodging for sleep, to food throughout the day. She held back no coin to offer them the best and she prided herself on being able to provide for them. She had never seen Tams and Babs so happy. They seemed to lose years off of their age, displaying a new energy in service to all. Her villa brimmed with new life. Jesus taught and received the people everywhere: in the synagogues, on the nearby hill across the Via Maris, and down near the shore. The Pharisees and Sadducees kept an eye on him as well as a listening ear. But they did not intervene or obstruct the people from attending his teachings. The tension was thickening, but Jesus carried on, receiving those who wished to be healed and answering questions in his roundabout way with parables and mysterious words about how he had received everything from the Father.

When Jesus returned to the villa for the evening, she was the first to offer to wash his feet and provide him with the nourishment after a long day. She would then sit at his feet, like a child hanging onto every word.

One evening Judas brought up one of Jesus' previous teachings.

"I saw several men from Bethsaida and Capernaum today who had begun to follow you, Jesus. But then they left after your teaching in Capernaum's synagogue. Pity they aren't still with us. Our group was really growing. The sheer strength of numbers would have been enough to frighten those Pharisees and Sadducees and get them off our backs."

John looked irritatingly at Judas. "Let them leave if they cannot accept. I for one want to believe and accept this bread that you offer for eternal life Jesus."

He was referring to the challenging teaching in Capernaum. Mary had not been present, but John had recounted it to her in one of their long walks. She had been skeptical at first. It sounded mythical and superstitious, almost pagan. But she recalled the story of her people wandering through the desert for forty years and being sustained on manna that came from heaven. If God could do that, why not bread from heaven that sustained them to eternal life? Opening her heart and mind to the possibility turned her skepticism and curiosity to a sense of hope and wonder.

Judas spat back, "I didn't say I didn't believe. I just think we can be more prudent about the message we are offering and keep a few more disciples, otherwise we won't have any influence here."

Jesus remained silent, allowing the discussion to play out among the disciples.

Simon looked ready to pick a fight.'

"Are you so ashamed of the Master's teachings that you want him to keep quiet just to hold onto a few more disciples rather than speak wisdom and truth?"

He turned to Jesus, professing, "We made our choice and have professed that you are the Holy One of God, and your teachings offer truth and life."

John repeated Jesus' words from the synagogue of Capernaum which he had memorized by heart, "You are the one sent by the Father, the bread of life come down from heaven that gives life to the world."[88]

Mary was embarrassed, almost sorry for Judas, as the other disciples murmured their conviction about Jesus' previous teachings.

Jesus finally spoke, "I have known from the beginning who would believe and who would betray me. Yes, I have chosen twelve, and yet one of you is in league with the devil."[89]

Mary's stomach bottomed out. She saw a look of hatred pass through the face of Judas and just as quickly disappear. Andrew finally broke the uncomfortable silence by gently smacking Judas on the arm and suggesting that they go out and get more firewood.

***

That night, as the disciples took their leave and sprawled out around the villa for their night's rest, Mary grabbed a shawl and went out into the crisp starry night for fresh air. Jesus was sitting by an open fire pit looking solemn and pensive. She quietly drew near, longing to steal this treasured time alone with him, as it was almost impossible with the constant demands on his time and person.

She didn't have anything in particular to say but longed to sit at his side and simply be acknowledged that she was also in his presence. He turned toward her as she sat next to him, respectfully leaving him space. The glow of the fire revealed his kind acknowledging eyes, but she detected sorrow there. She questioned him back with an inquisitive frown.

"I will leave with the Twelve tomorrow, Mary."

She felt pride in the fact that he shared his plans with her.

"I will be ready to go when you say," she said with confidence, wanting to assure him that she would have everything arranged for their trip and of her eagerness for what came next.

"No, not this time. Stay here. I will return for you and then we will head towards Jerusalem for the next Passover feast."

Incredulous at his command, a protest spontaneously slipped out, "No! I will go with you tomorrow. You can't leave me behind."

"Mary, perhaps there are some preparations and things you need to put in order here first. Do not worry. I will come back for you."

Do not worry? Confusion and anger welled up inside her. *I have just offered the best hospitality I possibly could, sparing no expense, and now I am being shaken off?* She knew she was overreacting, but the hurt of not being included in the next part of his journey stung as if she had lain in a bed of nettles.

She protested. Anxiety at being left behind went unnoticed as she attempted to state her intention and decision. "Rabboni, I will go with you. I can make the journey. I am strong and won't hold you back."

Jesus was silent for a while, leaving her in suspense and somewhat ashamed at her passionate and stubborn reaction. He turned sad eyes upon her and spoke so solemnly that she felt as if his words were a sword piercing her heart, leaving her speechless.

"Mary. They don't call you the Magdalene for your grand residence here in Magdala. Your strength of character befits your name. It divulges what is both your gift and challenge. Wait here. Your time will come. But remember this. 'Whoever wishes to come after me must deny himself, take up his cross, and follow me. For whoever wishes to save his life will lose it, but whoever loses his life for my sake and that of the gospel will save it. What profit is there for one to gain the whole world and forfeit his life?'"[90]

He paused and her thoughts raced. *I have already lost a part of my life for him. I left behind my past life. What more did he want?*

He caught her attention again. "Mary, what could one give in exchange for one's life?"

She was without words, but her mind raced for understanding, for justifications and reasons for not being left behind. *What is he asking of me? I give my beautiful wardrobe, even my villa for the life he seemed to be speaking of. Why doesn't he see that?* She looked at him with pain and confusion and managed another plea.

"Rabboni, I will give you anything, everything. Just do not leave me behind."

"Mary, you may feel that I am leaving you in the desert like my Father did for our people in the time of Moses to humble and test them.[91] But it was to do them good in the end. So, I ask you, wait and pray. And do not be ashamed of me and my word. Do you believe what Isaiah said, 'They who wait for the Lord shall renew their strength'?[92] This I ask of you. Can you trust me?"

His last question seemed like a mockery. A defensive voice awoke her ire. *Have I not followed him and proven my trust? The problem is that he does not trust me!* She remembered back to his words earlier in the evening and how one was in league with the devil. *Was he referring to me? Yes, he didn't trust me. That was it. He doesn't want me with him and his group because he doesn't trust me.*

Jesus agitated the red hot coals of the dying fire while Mary's throat felt like it was being suffocated by a rising fear. *Abandoned.* Her old friends returned with a fury, unleashing terror, ire, grief, and disgust, darkening her newly bright world with shadows from the past. These were not mere emotions she could reason with. It struck the core of her identity. *Abandoned. Rejected. Unwanted. Discarded. Taken advantage of for her abundant hospitality.* The resurfacing of her old identity blinded her to the gentle, loving gaze and tone of the one she now saw as a deceiver. She interpreted his gaze as pity.

Left behind. On her own. Fear of returning to her previous life tumulted into shame and guilt and belief that he saw her for what she was. *Not worthy.* Despair crept in and then a firm decision. Her heart closed a door. She dared to return his gaze with haughtiness, her old self roaring its ugly head. She could sense it. Her heart had hardened. She covered the hurt with a resolve of vengeance she didn't know she had in her. *She didn't need him. Be gone then!* Turning her back on him, she left his presence. If she had turned around, she would have seen his heavy sigh and upward glance to the heavens as he lifted up a prayer for her to the Father, for the hurt child she was.

***

Morning came. The day of their departure was upon them. She contemplated not showing her face at all, but pride kicked in even here. She would see them off and provide all that was needed. No one would say they were left in want while they were under her reign of hospitality. The Twelve, Salome and Rachel were ready to head out. With the help of Babs, whom she had ordered to get a good supply of salted fish and fresh bread in the early morning market, she assured that they were well stocked for at least a three day's journey.

Salome and Rachel commented that they would be splitting off from the group and heading to Capernaum to visit Eva for a while, but then to Bethsaida for a rest in their home. Salome had extended an invitation to Mary to accompany them, but she remained despondently obedient to Jesus' command to remain in Magdala, thus she declined. She wondered why they were not accompanying the rest wherever they were headed. She purposely avoided eye contact with Jesus, hoping to punish him with her distant and cold attitude. Although, she wavered between the strength of her pride and the regret of her heart for one more appeal to Jesus before their departure.

John, the most attentive one of the group, after Jesus that is, noticed her mood. At times, he seemed to know her thoughts and moods better than she knew herself.

"What's ailing you, Mary? You look off."

She gave him a raised eyebrow as if to say that is not a comment you make to a woman, and it is none of your business. She covered her twinge of guilt at brushing him off with a slight smile, knowing that he meant well. But she couldn't shake the tempest still brewing inside her.

They began to head out. Some said a quick farewell. Others didn't even notice that she was staying behind, rankling her even more. Jesus was the last who crossed the threshold of her patio. He stopped, obviously waiting for her, for some sort of acknowledgement. But she remained with her arms crossed snuggly around her as if defending any chance of relenting from her present standoffishness. Her eyes darted everywhere, anywhere but Jesus' face.

She was about to turn from the group and from him when she heard his words. They were meant for her. She recognized a piece of prophecy from somewhere or other. His voice was soft, but he might as well have been shouting from the rooftop, for it penetrated through the hardness of her heart and seized her.

Losing her resolve to ignore him, she glanced over her shoulder. She saw only tenderness and love, far from the rejection she was convinced she had received the night before. He turned from her then, and she watched him disappear into the throng of the disciples as they left her property.

His words would echo in her mind and heart several days later, like a voice calling her to a new hope. But for now, they just perplexed her as she struggled to breathe. A tightening knot in her chest and the festering voices wanted to swallow her whole.

Abandoned, unworthy, no good...

In between derogatory accusations, soft and faint echoes of Jesus' voice repeated the words he had left her.

> Instead of your shame you will receive a double portion, and instead of disgrace you will rejoice in your inheritance. And so you will inherit a double portion in your land, and everlasting joy will be yours.[93]

CHAPTER 26. THE RELAPSE

Do not be misled: Bad company corrupts good character.
1 Corinthians 15:33

The weather matched her mood. Rainy, cold, and blustery. Dark clouds hung over the villa for endless days, further dampening her low spirits. The climate tormented her as much as the recurring thoughts of being rejected and abandoned. Tams and Babs' high spirits grated against her own as they incessantly recalled the previous days´ activities, Jesus' teachings and every detail of every simple encounter they'd had with him while he had lodged in the villa.

Eventually they turned somber, seeing that Mary did not match their exuberance. At first, they sought to reanimate her, confused by her forlorn state. Tams even scolded her once, but Mary lashed out in anger, feeling even guiltier than she already did for the dark mood she could not shake. Tams and Babs finally retired to their area of the property, afraid of worse verbal abuse than what they had already received. Finally, the villa returned to its silent and lonely existence.

Like an outside observer, she knew that her exaggerated passions trumped reason, but she could not stop herself from wallowing in self-pity and a general listlessness. She let the main living quarters fall into disorder. She gave into boredom, indulging herself from her well-stocked wine cellar. Due to her connections with officers of the Roman army, she had managed to acquire the newest fad in wine storage, wood barrels. Several oak barrels stored choice wines produced from pomegranate, fig, and various fruits that she had workers harvest or purchase. She boasted some of the finest quality wine in the area. It was amazing how even in her darkest moments she grasped at any straw of self-worth, even if it was pride in her wine.

Demetria stopped by a couple of times. She too was unsuccessful in pulling Mary out of her funk. The old Mary had returned, she feared. She had returned to her fits of prior days. But Mary made every effort to temper herself when Demetria showed up at her door unannounced. She managed to keep the exchange to a minimum without bordering on rude hospitality but did not encourage her to return. After several days of Jesus' absence, Mary had begun giving up hope of his return. She took to numbing the pain with an overdose of her strongest wines on a nightly basis.

One night, long after darkness had descended, a forceful knock boomed through the fog that clouded her thoughts. Whoever it was, they were persistent and were not taking the hint that she was not interested in company. A sudden hopeful thought broke through the haze.

Jesus? Had he returned?

Finally, a voice thundered through the door's barrier.

"Miriam! Open this door! I know you are in there. It's me. Please. I want to see you."

No. She knew that voice and he was definitely not Jesus. Him. He was back? She must be dreaming. Sleep it off.

The pounding continued. His voice made her teeter on the verge of stupor and consciousness of his return. She feared to say his name, and so she wavered between longing to hear his voice, to know him near, and resisting the tremendous threat that lie on the other side of that door. She held onto her desire for him, then pushed it away, unsure if she was in the midst of a good dream or a nightmare. A familiar longing swept over her, which was quickly replaced by the torment of being thrown aside like putrid fish. He had pulled her into his world. She had taken the bait. And then he had abandoned her to its follies, "kindly" sending his friends to "fill the gap" of his absence.

"Miriam. Come on. You can't hide from me! Open up. It's me!"

Pounding continued until she was certain, she was not dreaming.

Gaius. She thought the name. *There is no escaping him now. No. It couldn't be.*

A wave of mixed emotions paralyzed her. Desire, confusion, eagerness to open the door, anger. *How dare he show up after all this time, without a word or sign of promised return.* She exhaled with the hope of expelling the nightmare that was descending upon her. She should not open that door. But she felt herself giving in. Like an outside observer watching herself in slow motion, standing, staggering, step after endless step, she shuffled toward the barrier between her present and her past.

Gaius is here and Jesus is not.

At least he was something more exciting than her waiting around for...well, she didn't even know what she was waiting around for. Her eyelids sunk slowly closed and then half opened with the efforts of lifting her eyebrows. She tried to get her bearings, focusing on the door a few steps in front of her. It seemed an incredible feat and not knowing how, she found herself standing in front of the door. The knocking had turned to aggressive pounding, echoing the hammering pain in her head. She stumbled backwards, grateful that the pounding on the door disappeared as she unfastened the bolt and he barged in.

She grimaced, vanity making its way through her incoherent state of mind. She had not given her dress or state of appearance any attention for the last several days. She was half dressed in her night attire. Hair, unwashed and unkempt, spilled out over her shoulders and down her back. She huffed at the irony that dawned on her. With exception of her brief bout of insanity as she followed Jesus, she had usually been meticulous and vain about her appearance.

Her time with Jesus had certainly been a temporary lapse of judgment, she told herself. While she was with him, it had been impossible to maintain anything but basic cleanliness and simplicity in her presentation, despite her attempts for a little something more. Salome and Rachel had joked with her that she was the princess of the group. When they had returned to Magdala and Johanna visited, she had empathized with her, knowing more of her past life at court than anyone else. At present, she was far from looking like a princess.

Plumed heads and white cloaks bobbed up and down before her distorted vision. Laughter slightly sobered her as she realized that not one, but several of his compatriots began filling up the space in her living quarters. *They are drunk, perhaps more drunk than I? No, I don't think that is possible right now.* She recognized most of them, having spent time in their presence in various feasts and parties, having hosted many of them in her own place, right here, welcome or unwelcome. But it had been months since she had seen them. Now they acted as though they were the best of friends, grabbing her and twirling her around and passing her off to the next one.

She felt nauseous with all the commotion, nauseous from her excessive imbibing. It had not numbed her enough. Their greetings and remarks flew past her at an incredibly dizzying speed.

"We're back!" "It's been too long Miriam!" "Did you miss us?" "Our company is stationed in Tiberias for a couple of months." "We are destined to Jerusalem for the Passover." "Unrest." "They've called in reinforcements for the next few months." "Pontius Pilate's request." "Talk of much unrest with various factions."

"Gaius," someone shouted. The name penetrated through the overlapping voices of conversation. "We need reinforcements of wine. Where are the goods?"

Gaius. The name was spoken once again. She couldn't ignore him now. She was hoping it was just her imagination playing tricks on her. Gaius. He fell right into his old place, like a mini-god and king of the household. She felt powerless against the tide of her past life ushering itself in unimpeded. She pushed the door shut with a thud as though trying to block out what had already entered. But it was beyond her power. She hesitated, trying to make out his figure, her mind a jumble, not knowing what to feel, where to pick up the broken pieces of her heart to a past that she thought she had left behind. Now it came rushing back with a fury, inviting her right back into belonging, warmth, protection. A small voice warned her of the deception.

No, leave it in the past. He made his choice and you have made yours.

She felt helpless, uncertain except for the fact that she was woozy and unstable on her feet. She resisted making eye contact with Gaius as though it might seal her fate and affirm that this was not merely a dream. Then her eyes landed on an ominous, towering figure.

No! Vespasian. How dare he!

She sensed his wanting yet wary stare. Her supposed protector when Gaius disappeared had become her worst nightmare. Possessive. Taking liberties where he was not welcome. And he was not welcome here!

Did Gaius know? Likely not. Or maybe he didn't even care.

She had no strength to fight. Overwhelmed, she surrendered to her own incapacity. She inelegantly plopped herself onto the nearest recliner and threw an arm over her head and eyes to thwart the throbbing that invaded her entire head, depleting her energy to fight against this unwelcome invasion.

Gaius' voice disgustingly appealed to her senses.

"Miriam, Miriam. What's this I hear? It's all over the court. I leave and you replace me with that itinerant, crazy rabbi they call Jesus of Nazareth. Change your ways have you? Found your religion again? Did he guilt you into following him? Or maybe he threatened you with eternal damnation, huh?"

The men added fuel to the fire, disparaging Jesus by mocking his sayings and play-acting the miracles that had circulated far and wide. Far from reverent, their brash and insolent manners made her twinge with discomfort. She was momentarily embarrassed that they would count her as one of his followers. But that too made her cringe and was immediately followed by guilt. She did not defend him. She knew she would be ridiculed along with him if she did. *What point would it serve?*

Their raucous laughter grated on her nerves which already felt taut to the point of breaking. The other men threw out jests between compliments on Mary's beauty, despite her lack of charm at that moment. They taunted Gaius, "She caught herself a different fish Gaius, accept it!" "But where is this Jesus of Nazareth to defend her honor now?" "Maybe she learned his tricks and will work a miracle for you Gaius!" "The miracle will be if she comes to her senses and leaves that rabbi and returns to Gaius!" "No, the miracle will be if she forgives Gaius and accepts him back!" Guffawing, sniggering and howling filled the air, leaving no respite from their increasing volume.

Despite her state, she secretly hung onto the compliments like a life-line keeping her afloat amidst the chaos. Despite her closed eyes, she felt Gaius' presence. She covered her face with her hands and balled up into a fetal position on the chaise, as though this would keep her from letting reality touch her. She refused to reach out to him. But she could smell his familiar scent and felt the warmth and indentation made on the recliner as his too close body invaded her space. His near-ness brought a flood of memories and emotions. She felt lost, unable to resist returning to what had been her daily bread not so long ago. Did she want to go back to that? *Oh God!* She felt so weak, so desirous of being held again, of being treasured for her beauty and charm, of being loved.

No!

No, she had come to the conclusion that whatever they had, had not been love. She had thought it was love at the time, but his disap-pearance and lack of communication proved him to be false. None-theless, feeling adrift, she longed for security, something familiar, even if not safe.

"Miriam, look at me." His voice sounded strained, emotional, ten-der. His touch gentle as he pushed her hair back from her face and pulled her hands away from her eyes.

A vision, a lie, she thought. Gaius' face was before her, closing in. She blinked and shook her head. Then it was...*Jesus?* Refocusing again, she saw more clearly. *No, not Jesus.* It was Gaius once again. The sight of his face struck her with the full reality of his presence. He was really here, after all this time.

Don't give in!

"Stay away from me! Leave me be." She managed to sputter out, pushing him and pulling her hands from his grasp. She shook her head to try and clear it and felt a chill sweep over her. A cold wind was rushing in through the open door which she was sure she had securely slammed shut. Were more people coming to invade her home? She sat up as the revelry began to die down. A familiar voice crashed the mer-riment. It was tremulous, but demanding, nonetheless.

"Out with you all. Out, I say!"

Martha? What is she doing here?

A mixture of shame, guilt, and embarrassment overpowered her. There stood her sister, the last person she expected to see. Although Martha never gave up trying![94] Mary had constantly rejected Martha's attempts at reconciliation or refused to see her. She refused to let her in the house the one time she had shown up when Gaius was visiting years ago.

Tams and Babs were standing timidly behind Martha. She could also see Aharon and several other fishermen standing outside the door. They outnumbered the soldiers, but they didn't come forth threateningly. They stood their ground like watchmen in the night. But it was Martha who surely startled them into silence from her crazed look alone.

Gaius stood up, taking command of the situation. "It's the sister. Party's over. Get out men. We've got better places to be."

He leaned over Mary, immersing a hand in her thick mass of messy hair, pulling her head towards his as he whispered in her ear. "Send for me when the hysteric witch finally leaves. I am eager to pick up where we left off."

And with that the rowdy bunch left without incident. Mary watched her sister dismiss Aharon and his friends as Tams and Babs tried to set things right, putting some order back into the room before they quietly slipped out, leaving Martha and Mary alone. Mary's energy was quickly returning in the form of anger, channeled straight at her sister, like arrows ready to attack its prey. She didn't notice the weariness on Martha's face, nor the worry in her eyes. Mary only saw pity and judgment. And a very unfashionably dressed woman. Embarrassment at having to acknowledge her as her sister swept over her along with disgust and a tinge of jealousy. She was always the perfect one, the good one. But dressed without any pretentiousness of her station.

Just once, she wanted the upper hand with Martha. She blurted out, "I was with Jesus!"

"A lot of good it did you!" Martha fired back, then rolled her eyes at her slip of the tongue, regretting the exchange.

Fury colored everything, suddenly awakening Mary from her earlier stupor.

"Get out!" Mary screamed at Martha, moving towards her to physically remove her from her sight. "I don't need your pity or self-righteousness." She pushed her towards the door, yelling profanities and shooing her toward the entrance.

"Miriam, no. Please calm down. I want to help. Don't stay here. Those men will come back. Please, come with me. I am going this morning to Capernaum to await Jesus. Johanna is already there with Salome and Eva. She told me that you met them. You can stay with us there." Martha was desperately pleading. "I wanted to come earlier. I was staying with Demetria and Aharon and waiting for the right time to come see you. I wasn't sure you would receive me. But Babs and Tams heard the commotion and ran to tell Aharon. I couldn't leave you with them. Please, come with me. You know they will come back. Don't go back to that man. Come with us to see Jesus."

She definitely did not want to reveal to Martha that Jesus had told her to stay. Did he know that this would happen? Did he place her in this situation so she would fall into temptation? Shame overwhelmed her. But she turned it to anger and fired away blasphemies directly at Martha, unleashing a lifetime of pent-up angst. Mary appeared beside herself. She lost all control, like a crazed woman unable to possess herself. Martha feared that she would injure both of them. And she would have, had Martha not narrowly escaped. Mary hurled an amphora of wine toward her head. Martha just managed to slip out and slam the door behind her as it crashed and splintered into a hundred little pieces on the other side.

Martha was astonished. She knew that she and her sister had always butted heads even since her childhood. And a rift had been between them for several years, especially since Gaius had spun his malicious web and lured Mary into his lifestyle. She just didn't think she would see Mary this far gone. Martha had long known Jesus, hosting him in Bethany when Lazarus invited him and his disciples to dine with them. She had told him about her sister and her worries. Jesus had always assured her that she would eventually come around. Martha just needed to keep praying for her. But she wasn't one to sit back forever. She was the older sister by thirteen years and even though Mary had been raised in a very different way than herself, and became an adult during her years in Magdala, she still considered herself responsible for Mary's well-being. But now, she was at her wit's end. Mary's present state filled her with distraught. She left the villa, determined to find Jesus and demand that he do something for her right away! Enough was enough! She had already waited "patiently" for too long!

CHAPTER 27. A BLESSED FRIEND

Perfume and incense bring joy to the heart,
and the pleasantness of a friend springs from their heartfelt advice.
Proverbs 27:9

Mary's nerves were fraught. Her entire body had begun shaking. She managed to make it to her bedroom and fall into bed where she curled up into the fetal position. She desperately longed for security, a stronghold, comfort in the midst of the slow spiraling into a darkness that overwhelmed her. A pit formed in her stomach as scenes of the recent episode flashed through her mind. *It was my fault. I feel so needy.* She wanted to be wanted and was ready to throw away any semblance of a recovered reputation out the window for a brief moment of feeling herself desirable. *Am I possessed like some of the people I have seen Jesus cure?* She remembered Jesus' words about unclean spirits.

"When an unclean spirit goes out of a person it roams through arid regions searching for the rest but finds none. Then it says, 'I will return to my home from which I came.' But upon returning, it finds it empty, swept clean, and put in order. Then it goes and brings back with itself seven other spirits more evil than itself, and they move in and dwell there; and the last condition of that person is worse than the first. Thus, it will be with this evil generation.'"[95]

Fear was added to the interior storm that raged within. *Unclean. Is that what I am in Jesus' eyes?* He had told her that "blessed are the pure of heart, the kingdom of heaven is theirs." *I am so far from pure. Is the kingdom closed to me? Is that why Jesus told me to stay behind?* Shame and guilt wrenched through her soul. She felt dizzy. She was spiraling, spiraling, down, down into darkness as her body convulsed, overtaken and spent.

***

A cool wetness covered her forehead and eyes as she came to. Lifting her hand to her head she felt a damp cloth over her eyes. *Where am I?* She slid it off, wincing from the pain of light invading her room. A soft voice and gentle face came into view.

"Miriam, you're awake."

"Johanna?" She managed to squeak out through her parched throat. It felt like she had eaten sand. Her whole body ached and was completely depleted of energy as though she had swum from one shore of the Sea of Galilee to the other.

"I understand that you had a very difficult night." Johanna's eyes and smile were full of compassion and free of condemnation, which, by Mary's memory, she deserved; condemnation that is, not compassion.

"Difficult...not how I would describe the night."

She scooted into a sitting position grabbing her head with one hand and steadying herself with the other. Johanna placed one hand on her shoulder and held out a steaming and strong smelling brew of chamomile and other spices.

"Drink Miriam. This will make you feel better."

Johanna's gentleness and sympathy was Mary's undoing. She brought both hands to cover her face, doubling over as tears began to flow between sobs and gasps for air.

"Shhh." Johanna scooted closer, rubbing her back and holding her close. She allowed Mary to spill her tears, not filling the space with words, just comforting her with a rocking motion and soft shushing.

The sobbing slowly subsided, and Mary wiped her face, trying to gain composure.

"Why are you here?" Mary whispered.

Johanna managed to get Mary to sip the brew as she explained.

"I was in Capernaum. Some of us are waiting for Jesus there. We expect him back soon." Johanna tread lightly with her next words, unsure of how Mary would react. "Your sister arrived this morning, very early, and completely distraught. She told us about your, umm, trying incident last night. I came right away to see how you were faring. Tams and Babs let me in. They were quite shaken as well. They said they hadn't seen you so undone as last night. It must have been quite the trial for you Mary. I am sorry that you suffered this."

Johanna's words opened the door to something new. No anger, no frenzied desire to numb the pain. Instead, regret ushered in. She stuttered out half sentences.

"Horrible. I was horrible. Johanna. What I said. What I did. Awful. I hate myself. And Gaius. If Martha hadn't come. I don't know what would have happened. I was powerless. Gaius. How shameful! Shameful! And worse. I am a traitor. I didn't defend Jesus. They disgraced him. Mocked him. And me. I did nothing. How sinful."

Johanna was concerned by Mary's anguish, sensing that there was less sin in what happened and much more unfounded shame, despite being responsible for her present hangover.

"Shhh, Come now Miriam. Let us reason together. Remember what the Lord said through the prophet Isaiah, 'Though your sins are like scarlet, they shall be as white as snow; though they are red like crimson, they shall become like wool.'"[96]

"How? How is this possible? I left everything. Or so I thought. But Jesus knew me. I am a sinner. He left me because I cannot be like the others. I embarrass him. He is ashamed of me. He doesn't want me to be part of his followers."

Johanna peeled Mary's hands from her face as though unmasking the nonsense.

"Miriam, that is the biggest load of donkey dung, excuse my expression, that I have ever heard. Did Jesus ever accuse you or tell you he was embarrassed by you?"

Mary was taken aback by Johanna's proclamation. But it worked to reconsider her previous days of agony and she searched in her memory for something in Jesus' words or demeanor toward her that would give credence to her present conviction.

"Well, he said that one of us was in league with the devil." She searched her memory and revisited the scene again as though for the first time. "Well, he seemed to be speaking to the Twelve."

Johanna's eyebrows lifted with concern, "Well, woe to the one upon whom that truth falls. But he was not referring to you, was he?"

"No, I suppose not." She searched her memory again, then rushed on, "But he told me I had to stay here, and he refused to let me travel with him wherever they had gone."

Johanna nodded. "But did he say you were not to be his follower anymore? There is a reason for what he asks. Remember the Gerasene demoniac? He wanted to get into the boat with Jesus when he continued on, but Jesus told him to stay. And look what came of it! I have heard that the people of Hippos and so many around the Decapolis are coming to believe in Jesus as the Messiah."

Mary considered this point, rethinking her own emotional reaction. Johanna continued, "All of the women stayed behind Miriam. The rest are in Capernaum waiting for Jesus and the Twelve to return. If Jesus asked you to stay, then *Gam Zu L'Torah!* That, too, is for the good."

Mary recalled Jesus' parting words, a phrase from Isaiah that she had not taken to heart, nor considered very closely.

Instead of your shame you will receive a double portion, and instead of disgrace you will rejoice in your inheritance. And so you will inherit a double portion in your land, and everlasting joy will be yours.[97]

Did he mean these words for her people to be applied to her as well? A steady calm was taking root. But she wanted to be alone with these new thoughts. Not wanting to appear ungracious she smiled at Johanna and nodded.

"Thank you, Johanna. I am feeling much better. Please don't let me keep you."

"Very well Miriam. I do need to get back to Chuza before returning to Capernaum, but please send word to me if you need anything. And a final piece of advice to you. Fear the Lord, not with cowering and shame, but with reverence and hope. He is trustworthy. Jesus is to be trusted. As the Torah says, 'You shall fear the Lord your God; you shall serve Him and cling to Him, and you shall swear by His name.'"[98]

A growing calm was settling over Mary. She could only second Johanna's advice which resonated within her like a long overdue sense of well-being.

"Baruch Hashem," Mary spoke with reverence.

"Baruch Hashem, Blessed be God indeed."

With that, Johanna departed Mary's house, leaving her alone with herself once again.

CHAPTER 28. THE CALM AFTER THE STORM

You have also given me the shield of Your salvation,
And Your right hand upholds me;
And Your gentleness makes me great.
Psalm 18:35

Mary leaned her head against the wall, not ready to get up and face the day quite yet. Although a glimpse of pink-tinted clouds through her window hinted at a day already nearing its end.

"Baruch Hashem."

She let the expression wash over her, repeating it as she exhaled. It was like a prayer, settling her ruffled spirits and offering her new comfort. She recalled one of Matthew's many stories and lessons of which she was privy during their long walks. Jesus had taught them the Our Father and Matthew was eager to pass it on. Matthew had not hidden his enthusiasm as he helped her learn it by heart. He looked disappointed when she learned it so fast. She prided herself on having an excellent memory, something that probably got her in trouble more often than not, since she could turn on her father to remind him of the promises he had made to her if she would "do this" or "do that."

The prayer had an unforgettable beginning. "Our Father." She loved this novelty - God, our father. It made him approachable and not a far off deity to fear, despite her awareness that she often felt a certain fear and mystery when she thought of God.

"Our Father." She turned that over in her mind and began repeating it like she had done with "Baruch Hashem." The phrases of the prayer were recovered easily from her memory, coming bit by bit, each phrase acting like a balm upon her wounded heart.

"Our Father who art in heaven." She had watched Jesus pray with an upward glance, as though he was actually looking at someone in the heavens. He often spoke of "his Father," a mystery that still left her flabbergasted.

"Our Father who art in heaven, hallowed be thy name." A warmth spread over her, and she felt compelled to repeat the phrase that praised the Father, "Hallowed be thy name."

What is happening to me? She basked in the sensation of being co-cooned in the arms of a Father, her heart warmed by a tender fire within.

"Thy kingdom come." Another wave of peace invaded her, practically taking her breath away. She waited, slowly repeating that phrase again until she recalled the next line.

"Thy will be done." *Yes Father, thy will be done.* She recalled her vehement argument with Jesus when he told her to stay in Magdala and her angst at being left behind. Her face turned red hot at the revelation of her stubbornness. A psalm frequently used on her by her mother came to mind, "Blessed are all who fear the Lord, who walk in obedience to him."[99] *Obedience. Jesus is God's Son. Do I owe him obedience?* She had heard John repeat Jesus' words that he and the Father were one. Did she owe Jesus that which was to be given to the Lord God? She turned her mind's eyes to God and repeated the prayer with heartfelt conviction. "Thy will be done." "Thy will be done." "Thy will be done on earth as it is in heaven."

She never considered herself a very submissive person. Most people knew her as being far from it. But desire to be obedient to God and to Jesus was kindling a new fire inside of her. She understood that this came with consequences. She truly had to leave her old way of life. But if she had failed miserably these last few days, how could she possibly find the strength to do it now?

"Give us this day our daily bread." Bread. Jesus. The bread of life. *Give me this bread Father! I need this bread of life!* Her newfound longing for strength to obey, now coupled with an awareness of her need for Jesus. It brought a fresh wave of something new, something possessing her, but unlike her frenzied fits of the night before. It was gentle while intense. It was overwhelming while peaceful. It filled her with joy and hope, bringing her back to her encounter with Jesus on the beach, where she had experienced a new freedom. Gratitude welled up from within. Praise ushered forth as an undulating peace continued to wash over her. Then, as the intensity of consolation subsided slowly, she took up the prayer again.

"And forgive us our trespasses, as we forgive those who trespass against us." A sensation of compunction and a qualm of conscience surfaced. But it did not condemn her. Like an open door to greater freedom, she felt the impulse of firm resolution from a previous decision. She would ask Tams and Babs forgiveness. Greater pangs pricked her conscience as she thought of Martha. But there too, compunction and resolve to ask forgiveness won out over self-inflicted chastisement.

Satisfied with that petition, she moved onto the next. "Lead us not into temptation, but deliver us from evil." *Is this prayer crafted for me? I need this petition!* She felt stronger now, but she did not trust herself. It was so easy to fall back into her old ways, senselessly and without resistance. She repeated that petition over and over again, intensifying her supplication to be delivered from evil.

Another wave of peace rolled over her softly, lightly, benignly. Her fear of falling into evil was replaced with an embrace of goodness. *Where did this come from? Is this "Our Father"?* She accepted, marveling at the beginnings of a fortitude she had not experienced before. It wasn't boldness. It was a quiet buoying. That is the only way she knew how to describe it. Something held her steadfast. *Is this the hand of God upon me?* Whatever it was, she assented with gratitude and a prayer of praise, glorifying the Lord. She felt so different from just a few hours ago. She hoped that tonight would not be a repeat of the previous night. She finished the drink that Johanna had left her and settled in for a decent night's rest, allowing the prayer to lull her peacefully to sleep.

CHAPTER 29. AWAITING THE BRIDEGROOM

When I passed by you again and saw you, behold, you were at the age for love, and I spread the corner of my garment over you and covered your nakedness; I made my vow to you and entered into a covenant with you, declares the Lord God, and you became mine.
Ezekiel 16:8

The calm that had descended upon her during and after Johanna's visit remained with her. She was grateful that no more incidents took place over the next few days. Gaius and his band of followers didn't venture back to Magdala. She hoped they were busy enough in Tiberias or had made their way to Jerusalem and would leave her alone.

She finally visited Demetria and Aharon. She thanked them for their obvious intercession to Martha on her behalf and assured them that she was in a much better state than the one Aharon had seen her in recently. Even Demetria was stunned into silence upon this confession.

That being simply said, Demetria turned the conversation to Jesus. She managed to draw out of Mary stories of the days she had spent with Jesus. Retelling them helped to reinforce her conviction of the blessings she had received. And it reconfirmed what she had finally seen with Johanna. She had not been rejected by Jesus. Remaining behind had brought home the fragile state of her resolve. How much more she needed to trust in Jesus, trust his ways, despite not fully understanding why he asks what he does! Perhaps she needed to pass through the darkness and failures once again to realize how weak she was and how much she needed the Lord's help.

Doubts continued to surface every once in a while, but she strove to cast them aside, recalling moments spent with Jesus. This strengthened her resolve to be patient. She turned her days into an activity of anticipation. Tams and Babs received a profuse apology, and order was restored in the villa. A growing premonition of her life taking another turn upon Jesus' return set her in motion. She prepared for his arrival. It became a preparation of the heart, as much as being practical.

She wanted to provide for him, offering what was precious to her. A few months back, a man had been trying to convince her to sell a portion of her land for expanding his harvest north of her property. This would offer a hefty sum for their journeys. She occupied herself with a few business interactions. She refilled the ointments of her alabaster jar and a glass vial. And she made her regular stops at the harbor and Demetria's bakery. Besides that, she spent a majority of her time at home, waiting, expecting, hoping, anticipating.

As she waited, she found another occupation. She opened her chest, contemplating the white linen that she had impulsively bought in Capernaum. But then she closed it and looked around for her scarlet cloak. She must do something before she takes out that white linen. Cloak in hand she took it outdoors, determined to rid herself of anything that still bound her to Gaius. Out back was a large domed pit still left with the hot coals of a morning fire. She stirred it into flame again, adding kindling, then larger branches. Then tearing the cloak, she sent strips of the silky blood red fabric into the fire. She watched it burn until the last remnant had disappeared. She breathed easier with the hope that she could put all that behind her and prepare for Jesus' return.

Returning indoors she washed her hands and went with new resolve to the chest. Taking up the long white fabric, she envisioned a new creation. She had bought it before she met Jesus. Now everything was marked by this before and after, despite her recent relapse. Fabric and needle in hand, she sewed. The fabric would be perfect for her on her travels with Jesus. It was warm enough for the cool mornings, but light enough for the warm afternoons.

She immersed herself in the task, stopping only when Tams offered her a repast. After a simple nourishment, she took her sewing outside to enjoy the afternoon sun. Nature was in sync with her own interior world. The hills had lost their brown hue as the frequent rains alternated with sunny days allowing the dried earth to give way to greenery speckled with color. Pinkish lavender Egyptian Campion announced the persistent signs of spring. Despite the cold nights, deep red crown anemones were already in full bloom, having reached their peak when she was on the other side of the lake. And the spiny broom bushes were an explosion of yellow blossoms. Tams and Babs had been collecting them for a sweet jam. She would pack some up to take as well.

She stopped herself suddenly from her musings. Would Jesus permit her to accompany him when he returned? She very much hoped so. Doubts and fears began creeping in and she searched her memory. "I will return for you and we will head towards Jerusalem for the upcoming Passover feast." *Yes, he had said it. It is as good as a promise. I will hold him to it, just like I had done so many times with my father's promises!*

The rhythmic movements of needle in and out of the fabric eased her into further ponderings. The garment would be worthy of a bride with its simple elegance. *Marriage. The two will become one flesh.* She had a sense that marriage would not be in her future, yet she longed for that intimate union of hearts. She had fought her brother's insistence of marriage for so long and then life circumstances took her off the Jewish marriage market, not that she was sorry about that missed opportunity. She didn't understand her own self - the longing heart to love and be loved, to be fruitful and multiply, but the rejection of the traditional contract into marriage. Even from a younger age, as much as she craved the affection and attention of others, she had no inclination to enter into a marriage contract. She had surprised herself at the first thoughts of marriage with Gaius.

And Jesus? Jesus attracted her, but in a very different way than Gaius. A very different way. She had not been able to fathom it at first, the mesmerizing magnetism that Jesus held over her. The strength of it had frightened her at first. He had won her over without ever imposing himself. He never sought to appeal to her vanity by weaving a web of charm. She wanted to be in his presence as much as possible but was surprised when she realized that she lacked the need to use her typical feminine appeal on him, as she had with other men. It was indeed different. She didn't see or think of him in that way. If ever she were to understand or live the purity of heart that Jesus had preached in his sermon on the mount, it was he who would teach her. More than teach her, she simply experienced it around him.

The methodical movement of her needle, moving along the edge of the fabric, had reached its end. She picked up some colored threads, eager to give the garment a regal touch. She would add a delicate array of pomegranates and vines along the edge. Just because they lived in simple conditions didn't mean she couldn't bring along one nice piece of clothing for special occasions. As the design took shape it reminded her of a love story so popularly put to song for wedding feasts.

"How beautiful you are, my beloved. Your eyes are like doves…your lips a scarlet thread…your cheeks are halves of pomegranates…You ravish my heart, my sister, my promised bride…how fragrant your perfumes."[100] *How did the rest go?* "She is a garden enclosed, my sister, my promised bride;…your shoots form an orchard of pomegranate trees, bearing the most exquisite fruit…"[101]

She must admit, it was a bit strange that the beloved called his lover his sister and bride. But she let it pass. Despite her disappointments in love, she was a hopeless romantic and loved the poetry of the song. Her mother once heard her singing it and scolded her, embarrassed of causing scandal if overheard. But her father stepped in, giving it new meaning for her. It was a poetic allegory, he said, of God's love for his people. She had preferred the secular version, imagining herself to be the bride and a handsome and mysterious man her groom. But her father's explanation calmed her mother, and she was able to keep singing it…in the house…when guests weren't present.

Yes, the garment was definitely worthy of a bride. *Me, a bride?* To the disappointment of her brother and sister, it was something she had a notion would never be. But she would wear it nonetheless, with pleasure and delight. She would even show her sister that it was possible to maintain simple elegance that enhanced natural beauty rather than hid it under ugly frocks. Chuckling out loud, she immediately half-scolded herself and half prided herself at that determination.

CHAPTER 30. CONFESSIONS

If we confess our sins, he is faithful and just and will forgive us our sins and purify us from all unrighteousness.
1 John 1:19

More days passed and restlessness began to push away her temporary state of calm and patience. Should she go to Capernaum at least? Perhaps he was there, or she could meet up with them? She remembered Martha saying that they had anticipated his arrival there. How long would he stay? Or how long had he already been there? She half expected Martha to show up at her door again, but no. No one came. She was beginning to feel completely forgotten when the distant sound of voices and a gathering crowd increasingly drew nearer. She flew out the door, holding her breath at the hope of it finally being Jesus.

There he was. She stopped, holding back the impulsive desire to run full speed towards him. *Does he know? How will he receive me?* The thought of his incriminating look over her relapse held her in check. He was surrounded by his disciples and several women, Martha among them. But Mary's eyes were only on Jesus. He was engaged in an animated conversation with Simon, Andrew, James and John surrounding him, the rest following close behind. Jesus continued his conversation, but their eyes met. They spoke to her. She saw no condemnation, but rather, joy? And, delight? Was he delighted to see her? *Perhaps he doesn't know what happened.* She hoped that Martha had kept her mouth shut.

With tremendous restraint she closed the distance between them with a brisk walk, rather than the racing, skipping, and throwing her arms around him that she felt her heart was doing at present. Offering greetings to all, she finally embraced Jesus with a moderation she did not think was possible. He returned her hold with a secure enfolding of his arms and a gentle laugh at her exuberance. Her self-forgetfulness was suspended at the sound of her sister's gasp. *Leave it to her to scold her even in this.* She let Jesus go. He moved aside and the sisters stood face to face. But to Mary's surprise, Martha did not return a look of scolding. She appeared genuinely surprised, even joyful, disarming Mary's ready and typical defense against her sister's judgmentalness.

"Miriam." Speaking her name, Martha's expression turned quizzically tentative, as though waiting to be received.

Mary's face relaxed, her eyes softened, and her face slowly broke into a pained expression of regret.

"Martha," she quavered as tears obscured her vision. "I'm…" Her voice caught from the unexpected emotion. She felt Martha's hands on her arms, then her arms around her shoulders, a tight embrace and the drawing of Mary's head to her shoulder. Despite Mary's height above Martha, her sobbing face nestled over Martha's bosom.

"I'm sorry. I'm sorry," Mary repeated between sobs, forgetting the crowd that had partially disappeared. Finally, she raised her head, wiping her face, and saw that only the women remained. Tears still escaping, Mary let out a chuckle at her embarrassment. But her sorrow had turned to joy. She greeted Salome and Rachel, her previous travel companions. Johanna also received an exuberant embrace. Another woman stood among them whom she didn't recognize. A little woman with a big smile came forward and reached up to pull Mary's face forward, kissing her on both cheeks.

"And you are Mary of Magdala," she said as though expressing it for Mary's benefit, in case she had forgotten who she was. "I am one of Jesus' aunts, Mary of Cleophas. Or some call me Mary Jacobe since I am the mother of the other James."

Salome piped up, "The little one. Not my big James."

John was running back to the women like a delivery boy showering them with good news.

"Come, we are going to prepare a feast for Shabbat."

She saw Demetria and Aharon arriving with loaves of bread. And several others were beginning to gather, having already heard of Jesus' arrival.

Salome took her hand and placed it in Martha's. Holding them between her own hands she exclaimed, "Come Martha and Mary, let us prepare a feast to remember." Then she set off towards the house with the other women.

Mary looked down at her hand in Martha's, then glanced back up, making eye contact. Could her mere words of "sorry" and Martha's simple embrace make up for years of rift and rejection? She didn't feel that was sufficient, but a lump in her throat choked back any possibility of speaking. Martha looked uncertain too, yet hopeful. She dared to speak, "I hear that this isn't the first time you are hosting Jesus?"

Mary shook her head, no.

Martha smiled tentatively, cautiously, as though trying not to rock a precariously positioned boat. She squeezed her hand in a gesture of acceptance and spoke gently, "Then tell me, how can I help?"

Surprised, but grateful for not having to face the words that needed to be said after years of separation, Mary nodded and led the way to her villa. The disciples were already organizing their lodgings, starting a fire, and preparing the place as they had used it on their prior visit. Mary's heart rejoiced. Such a different crowd from the rowdy one that had unwelcomingly invaded her home several nights before. She welcomed them heartily and set in motion a hospitality not to be forgotten.

***

Later that evening, after having assured that everyone had their fill and had arranged sleeping quarters, Mary slipped out into the courtyard where several were chatting small groups around a cozy fire. She observed them. Having had their fill of food, they were now enjoying a fine wine she had selected as a special treat. Earlier that day, she had shown Martha barrels of her finest stock still aging and those ready to be consumed. Nathaniel, having been in the business himself, accompanied them. She realized that she spoke in great detail much more for his enjoyment than for her sister's, who knew little of the business. But she detected pride in her eyes.

Now she saw Martha and Mary Jacobe laughing in the midst of Nathaniel, Philip and Little James. It was another novelty. She rarely remembered her sister's joy and laughter. Her memories of Martha were mostly of her scolding, bossing, and constantly attending to household needs.

John pulled her out of her ruminations and motioned her over to the fireside. She had missed John. She loved his unpretentious manner. She sat down next to him, eager to tease him.

"You left me behind John. I don't think I like you anymore."

"Oh," he was taken aback as though he hadn't a clue how much it had hurt her to watch them all leave without her. "I am sorry, I thought you chose to stay back. Are you well?"

His compassion warmed her, giving her the courage to share just enough detail for him to understand that she had not lived up to the life of a disciple. John listened attentively, like the good friend he had become in the time they had spent traveling together.

"Mary, I think you are too hard on yourself. But I am certain of this: If we confess our sins, God is faithful and just and will forgive us our sins and purify us from all unrighteousness."[102]

"I feel better already for having told you John."

"Well, I am not God, but I am glad it helped."

Mary, feeling embarrassed at having exposed her failings, turned the subject to their travels. John divulged the information easily, sharing where they went, what they did, how the people had responded.

"It was probably for the best that you stayed Mary. Everyone else stayed back in Capernaum or Bethsaida as well. Just the Twelve of us went on to the region of Caesarea Philippi. And when we arrived at Paneas…" John paused, a disgusted look on his face, "well, let's just say that we went to the gates of hell."

Mary's curiosity was piqued. "What do you mean?"

Matthew, in his usual mode had stealthily drawn near to the conversation and now blurted out, "Paneas is the place of the ancient Greek god Pan, known as the god of goat herds, hunting and sexual and spiritual possession." His face turned red as he cleared his throat and stuttered, "well…I mean…uh…fertility…ummm…and battle conquests and all, but well, ummm, many think he is the only god that has ever died. Well, some believe it and some don't. There were obviously many people still worshiping him. We saw lots of altars and shrines built into the rock cliffs and caves near the natural water source for the Jordan River."

John picked up from there. "Our timing was unfortunate. Or maybe it was well planned by Jesus. I don't know." Despite the darkness of night, Mary watched John's face turn a deep shade of red.

Mary laughed and shook her head. "What are you not telling me?" She urged them to confess.

John looked around him, assuring no others were within earshot, but before he had a chance to speak, Matthew ran full steam ahead with the tale.

"They were in the height of their worship to the fertility gods that they believe return every spring from the underworld."

John tried to stop Matthew, "Spare her the details Matthew. Let's just say it is grotesque and disgusting, prostitution and other sexual immoralities are just the start of it. And for good reason it can be called the gates of hell."

"But did Jesus stop them? Did he tear down their altars?"

"No," they both said simultaneously, Matthew getting the next words in.

"Actually, Jesus simply asked us to profess who he was and our belief that he was the Messiah and the Son of Man. When Simon said that he believed he was the Son of the living God, Jesus blessed him and called him Cephas and told him that upon that rock he would build up a people he has chosen and called, and the gates of the netherworld will not prevail against it."[103]

John piped in, "I think Simon, I mean Peter now, was a little shaken."

Mary couldn't imagine Simon being rattled. He was always full of confidence and bravado. Her eyebrows lifted inquisitively.

John continued. "Jesus spoke words to Simon…Peter that were similar to the prophet Isaiah about Eliakim, the son of Hilkiah, when he prophesied that God would give him authority and place the key of the house of David upon him so what he opens none shall shut and what he shuts none shall open."[104]

Mary was confused, "What does that mean? This sounds like the rabbinic statement of passing on authority to morally bind someone." Mary didn't like the idea of having to follow some law that Simon might decide to invent with his whimsical and authoritative nature.

Matthew jumped to his defense, "Jesus said that he gives the keys of the kingdom of heaven so that whatever he binds on earth shall be bound in heaven; and whatever he loosens on earth will be loosed in heaven.[105] I think he meant that Simon, I mean Peter, is given power somehow to open or close the way to the kingdom for the Gentiles." He paused, looking perplexed and with a humph said, "Jesus has a funny way of showing his confidence in Simon though. On the way back he called him 'Satan' to his face, telling him he was an obstacle in his way for not thinking as God does, but as human's do."[106]

John now came to his defense, "Well, Simon Peter was just expressing his horror at Jesus' statement. It was hard for me to believe also." John looked concerned but didn't elaborate.

Matthew continued, "He keeps saying that he has to go to Jerusalem and suffer greatly from the elders, chief priests, and the scribes, and be killed and on the third day be raised. Peter tried to rebuke him and stop him from saying such things, but Jesus wouldn't tolerate it. He called him Satan and told us that we had to deny ourselves and take up our cross to follow him."

What was a joyful reunion suddenly took on a heavy foreboding as they stared into the fire in silence, contemplating the gravity of what was just recounted.

The profound silence was broken as Jesus and Simon Peter walked into the courtyard, looking as though they had been in a serious conversation. Mary wondered if she needed to call him Peter as John and Matthew were trying to do. Jesus placed his hand on Simon Peter's shoulder as they exchanged a few words. Then Peter nodded and left for the house. Jesus headed straight toward them.

"We should be heading to bed," John nudged Matthew who didn't budge and finally grabbed him by the arm to encourage his departure.

Jesus, offering them a night time greeting and wishing them a good sleep, sat down next to Mary.

Confess your sins. Mary heard the encouraging voice of John's earlier words echoing in her conscience. She hesitated, grateful for Jesus' presence, but nervous that he would forbid her to come along to Jerusalem with him if he knew with what ease she had fallen into temptation and how close she had come to falling completely back into her old life.

"Mary, what is troubling you?"

Mary had the intuition that he already knew but was waiting for her to confess. She glanced up at him, hesitant to meet his gaze. At once she scolded herself, not so much for having fallen, although she felt terribly contrite for that, but for having doubted his goodness.

"Fear not. Speak to me Mary," he gently invited, leaving no room for doubt that this is what she desired. As the embers of the fire glowed soft and the stars of a moonless sky shone bright, Mary poured out her confession to Jesus, feeling the weight of guilt and shame lift. A heaviness of heart dissipated like a rising fog. Peace and awe settled in. It was a full turn from how she had felt just days earlier. Now, she felt like the most beloved person on the face of the earth. She was ready to do anything for Jesus. Joy and gratitude reigned with a new hope and determination to follow Jesus, no matter that she had to "take up her cross" to do so.

Afterwards, they sat in peaceful silence, interspersed by sounds of voices as the wind snapped up tidbits of conversations from other parts of the large complex. Finally, a loud rhonchus of a snore came from the nearest group of slumbering disciples followed by a smack and guffaw as Andrew, in a not very hushed tone, whispered loudly, "Turn over James! You're waking up the whole village with your snoring!"

Jesus and Mary looked at one another, trying to suppress laughter as they began shaking with mirth. Mary finally took a deep breath and sighed contentedly.

"Rabboni." Tears of gratitude and joy blurred her vision. A lump formed in her throat. She so wanted to profess her love for him and her decision to follow him no matter what, even with this motley crew of a gang. But the words would not come.

"I know Mary. I know."

Jesus' look of gentle and unconditional love accepted the desire of her heart as he brought their time to a close.

"Time to retire. We have important days ahead of us. You especially. Tomorrow, we begin a long journey toward Jerusalem. Good night, Mary of Magdala."

CHAPTER 31. WOMEN'S INTERCESSION

Now Deborah, a prophet, the wife of Lappidoth, was leading Israel at that time.
Judges 4:4

She was leaving Magdala again and she did not know when she would be back. Jesus had returned from a solitary place of early morning prayer; they had a simple breakfast and now they were ready to head out. Mary packed a few treasures she hoped would come in handy along the way. She reached for her new tunic that she had just finished before Jesus arrived. *Is it too much to bring?* A blush of vanity overcame her. She debated leaving it behind, but her decision prevailed. Into the large satchel it went. Perhaps it could be worn for a special feast. Jesus had said they would be in Jerusalem for Passover. Perhaps she would not be back before then.

She bade goodbye to Tams and Babs who stood ready to send her off like proud grandparents. Babs held out a small money bag.

"Miriam, you were right. The far northern portion of land was worth a fortune. I found a buyer. Here is their first payment."

Mary had completely forgotten that she had entrusted this task to Babs. She looked inside. Yes, a fortune. This could surely help provide lodgings and food for the journey to Jerusalem and more.

"Thank you, Babs." She snatched out a few coins and held them out to Babs. "For you and Tams. A little something for your comfort," Mary offered as tears began welling up and threatened to spill over. *Where are these tears coming from? It's not like I won't be back and see them again.* But this felt like a different kind of parting. She really did not know when they would be back. She had spoken to Aharon and Demetria last night, eliciting their promise to check on Babs and Tams periodically, making sure they were taken care of while she was away.

Tams pushed away the offering. "No Miriam. You keep it. We have more than we need already. Be generous with Jesus or someone else you meet along the way. I know you will put it to good use." Tams did not hide her tears as she let out a little sob. She took Mary's head in both hands and kissed her cheeks, then embraced her fiercely.

Babs coughed, dissimulating his emotion over her departure. It was bitter sweet. Mary knew they had endured her ups and downs, her rebelliousness and depressions, her scandal and outrages. Perhaps it wasn't an exaggeration to say that she had put them through Sheol. And they had persevered in loving her, in silence. She surely added years to their age by taking out her fluctuating moods on them. But now they rejoiced as she resolutely followed Jesus. She tucked the money bag securely in her satchel with the thought of honoring them with her good use of the money.

They set off westbound through the Valley of the Doves, winding their way through hills and valleys, resting once for a simple lunch under the shade of a sparse tree, conveniently placed just when they most needed shelter. The days were becoming comfortably warm when the sun shone bright. Barley was already ripening, signs of an early spring. She had not thought to ask where they were headed. She was simply grateful to be a part of Jesus' followers. She thought perhaps they were traveling to Jesus' hometown in Nazareth, but soon after their respite, they turned south bound, having said farewell to Nathaniel and Philip for a temporary parting. Jesus had given them instructions and sent them off to Nazareth. The rest of the group continued the long trek, following Jesus.

By midafternoon, Mary wasn't sure if her feet could carry her much further that day. She tried to maintain the same pace as the disciples, whereas she and the other women were lagging behind. She overheard Judas.

"We should have left the women at home," he grumbled, adding to his list of complaints that day. Jesus stopped walking, not commenting on Judas' remark, but waited for the women to catch up. He led them into one of the olive orchards they had been walking beside and found a shady spot at a rock wall. He motioned to the women, "Sit down and take a rest for a while."

As everyone sat, Mary Jacobe began to pull wild strawberries and oranges out of her satchel. How her tiny frame had managed to lug the heavy load for six and a half hours of walking without complaining and without them becoming juice was a miracle in itself. She walked from person to person, offering the refreshing treats to each one as if they were guests in her own home. Salome and Mary helped her distribute the welcome and juicy treat.

They were resting in the region of Naftali, nestled between two mounts, one on which rested the town of Nazareth, and on the other side stood a very tall and distinguished mount, at which they had just reached its base. Jesus looked up the face of the large mount.

"Har Tavor. Mount Tabor. Do you know what famous battle took place at the base of this mountain?"

Matthew, eager to talk about history, barged in, "The battle of Barak versus Sisera."

Mary recalled the story, but she would have given it a different title. Having finished passing around the fruit, she sat down next to Salome and slyly whispered, "He means the victory of Deborah and Jael."

Jesus, smirking at her side comment, invited her to tell the story.

Embarrassed, she declined. But then Salome and John insisted. She mustered up courage, remembering the many times as a child she had theatrically retold the stories her father had passed onto her.

"The battle took place in the time of the judges. Israel had been oppressed for twenty years by the Canaanite king...umm...," she hesitated, having forgotten the details of the story.

Matthew, respectful of her storytelling, offered the information simply, "Jabin, King of Hazor." But then, not able to contain himself, added, "The prophet Samuel once said that the Israelites' oppression under the Canaanites was a consequence of their forgetting the Lord their God."[107]

John elbowed him, indicating that there was already a storyteller. Matthew looked apologetically to Mary.

Mary smiled at Matthew graciously, "Ah yes, thank you Matthew." She continued the story. "Sisera was King Jabin's military general, threatening to conquer Israel with his nine hundred chariots and heavily armed soldiers. But the prophetess Deborah had other plans. Under her initiative, she mediated disputes among the leaders of three tribes of Israel until she finally convinced Barak of the tribe of Naphtali to gather an army against Sisera. She told him that it was God's command that he take 10,000 men to attack the enemy starting from the high vantage point of Mount Tabor."

She looked up, imagining leading that many men up to the heights of Mount Tabor. She continued.

"Speaking in the name of God, Deborah said, 'I will lure Sisera, the commander of Jabin's army, with his chariots and his troops to the Kishon River and give him into your hands.' But Barak responded, 'If you go with me, I will go; but if you don't go with me, I won't go.'"[108]

Judas interrupted with a sarcasm, "Not too enthusiastic about his task I guess!"

Mary Jacobe jumped in as well, "I love Deborah's answer to Barak! She could tell that his courage was flailing, and he doubted that he could conquer Sisera's troops. So, she told him, 'Certainly I will go with you. But because of the course you are taking, the honor will not be yours, for the Lord will deliver Sisera into the hands of a woman!'"[109] She clapped her hands and laughed in delight as if she had just offered the punchline to a joke.

Little James chuckled at his mother's enjoyment. Judas rolled his eyes. Mary continued the story.

"Indeed, Sisera was delivered into the hands of a woman. But first the nine hundred chariots sunk into the river as if in a mud bath. The soldiers' heavy armor was no match against the rains and mud of the Kishon river. Sisera fled the battlefield and ran to the tent of Heber the Kenite, thinking he was an ally. But he found himself at the mercy of Heber´s wife, Jael. She was quite sagacious, offering him hospitality and following his orders to guard the door of the tent while he rested. But," Mary, seeing she had the rapt attention of all, paused for effect, then continued in a lower volume, building suspense, "as soon as he had fallen asleep, she drove a tent peg through his temple and into the ground."

Mary slammed one fist against her hand for effect, driving home the image, and laughing at the various reactions. Little James raised a hand to his temple with a look of pain, Thomas looked surprised then queasy, and most of the rest simply remained with open eyes of horror, despite knowing the story.

Mary continued. "When Barak came in pursuit of Sisera, Jael led him to her tent and showed him the man he was looking for. There lay Sisera with the tent peg through his temple. Dead. The words of the prophetess had come true."[110]

Peter threw the remains of his orange peels to the base of an olive tree and wiped his hands in a gesture that said he was ready to get moving. He jested as he stood, "Moral of the story: watch out for apparently kind hospitality from a woman, especially if you are on the run!"

The women rolled their eyes as the men chuckled.

"I think the moral of the story is not to be greedy," Big James chimed in. "Sisera's armies' downfall was their luxurious chariots and heavy armor. They were no match for the elements of the weather. They sank into the mud and became easy targets for the Israelites to kill."

Mary Jacobe recited scripture. "O Lord, when you went out from Seir, when you marched from the land of Edom, the earth shook, the heavens poured, the clouds poured down water."[111]

Everyone looked at her, impressed, some with their mouths agape.

"What?" Mary Jacobe exclaimed at their reaction, as though they shouldn't be surprised. "It's the song of Deborah."

Little James smiled proudly, "She loves the songs sung by Miriam, Deborah and Hannah. I've heard them so many times that I think even I could recite them by heart."

Mary Jacobe responded, "Well I just love the story. The battle was won thanks to two women. One rallied the troops and directed the general who would have preferred to flee from battle. The other made the most of the opportunity and used her feminine wiles to put an end to the beast altogether."

Little James looked aghast. "Mother, I didn't realize you had a violent side. Feminine wiles?"

She shrugged, "It was war. Perhaps I would have just tied him up and let the men deal with him. But the point is, she had courage and intelligence to cut evil off at the root of the problem."

They began to argue the moral points of the story.

Thomas interjected, "I doubt they would have won at all if they hadn't had the advance of rushing upon them from the heights of this mount."

Jesus finally broke up the conversation. "The story of these women's roles has not been forgotten by history, Mary Jacobe. And Mary, you are quite the storyteller. You all do it justice by retelling it. A bird's eye view from the top of a mountain certainly helps us gain perspective on many situations, can't it? And speaking of tops of mountains, Peter, Big James, and John, we are going up." He stood, readying to leave. "The rest of you wait here and rest for a while."

Peter began gathering his satchel, ready to go. John stood quickly. James didn't look too happy about climbing the mountain but stood and readied to leave.

Jesus let the various reactions play out, but still, he only took the three. Some had offered to join as well. James, not looking forward to the climb, was eager to give up his spot. But Jesus refused the offer of all those who insisted on taking Big James spot, telling them, "I need you here." Others stretched out and readied for an afternoon nap.

Salome fussed over her two sons, making sure they had food and water with them. She saw them off then turned and pronounced to all with great pride, "My sons went with him."

Martha, Mary Jacobe, and Mary looked at each other, suppressing giggles. They knew how proud Salome was of her sons. She wasn't one to hide her love for them. She often poured forth boasting sentiments of her beloved sons of Thunder. Mary laughed at Salome's exuberant love for them, but she also admired her. Salome had let her sons leave their whole livelihood behind to follow Jesus.

Mary made the comparison to herself. *What have I left behind to follow Jesus?* From her perspective, not much. She had gained so much more than she had left behind. She observed her travel companions whom she was still coming to know. Her sister was there among them, reunited after being estranged for so long. *Had Martha been praying for me? Had she asked Jesus to help me? Ask? No, that wasn't Martha's style. She probably commanded Jesus to do something for me.* Either way, gratitude filled her heart for being part of this strange…family? *Family?* It felt familiar, yet new. She belonged and yet was still finding her place within this group.

She looked at Martha, catching her eye. She didn't feel the same rancor towards her as before. A deep appreciation was growing for her many intercessions, as unwelcome as they had been at the time. Now she was grateful, and it was past time to tell her so. She lifted up a prayer that God would give her the right words to do so at some point during this trip to Jerusalem.

CHAPTER 32. FAITH TO MOVE MOUNTAINS

Truly I tell you, if you have faith as small as a mustard seed, you can say to this mountain, 'Move from here to there,' and it will move. Nothing will be impossible for you.
Matthew 17:20

Dusk came and night settled in. They eventually accepted that Jesus, Peter, James, and John would not be back today. Mary hoped they found decent shelter from the night's cool air. The rest of the group set up makeshift tents and were preparing their bed mats after another simple repast. A fire had been built and a lull in the conversation meant that they were slowly winding down for sleep. But Mary couldn't sleep.

Why did Jesus take only three of the disciples? What was he up to? And what are we to do in the meantime?

He had given no instructions. They were all somewhat lost without his direction. The bickering had begun as the sun was setting. They had argued about whether or not they should go to a local village. Most of the women had decided it was best to stay put, as Jesus had not indicated otherwise. Judas was eager to find better lodgings in a village. Thomas couldn't make up his mind who to side with. In the end, they all stayed. She hoped that Jesus would return early in the morning. She settled in, as best she could on the hard ground, hoping morning would come soon.

The next morning, as they prepared a hot breakfast over a fire, the group suddenly stopped their activity at the sight of an approaching crowd. A large caravan of people was invading their temporary campsite. Leading the pack was a man carrying a ten-year old boy, skinny and deathly pale. He placed the boy before the two closest apostles, Judas and Thomas.

"Please, help my son," the father pleaded. "He is suffering greatly from seizures and attacks." Many others came forward and pleaded for healing from their various ailments, others were simply curious to see if any wonders would be worked.

Judas grumbled and looked up the mount, "Oh no, they must have heard Jesus was here. He should have taken us with him. I am going to find him and get him to return." Then turning to the crowds he shouted out, "Jesus is not here, go home!"

Thomas hesitated, almost following Judas, then changed course. "Judas, let them be. Jesus told us to stay. Maybe we can help them."

Mary, feeling a mix of compassion for the gathering people and ire towards those who wanted to abandon them, reprimanded Judas, "Yes, Jesus would have us stay and help them."

Martha, Salome, and Mary Jacobe murmured their agreement as Mary approached the gathering crowd, silently nodding at Thomas to encourage him to pray for the boy. The woman followed Mary into the crowd and began speaking to each one. Matthew, Little James, and the other disciples, took their cue from the women and attended to the various pleas.

Mary approached a small group of two men and two women. The younger woman stood out for her beauty and her very Greek appearance. The three standing around her gently pushed her forward. Mary addressed her.

"Hello, my name is Mary. And who are you?"

"Bernike," she replied, her accent betraying her definite Greek heritage.

"And what do you wish from Jesus?"

Salome, Martha, and Mary Jacobe had gathered behind Mary.

Bernike looked to the man slightly behind her, gathering courage from his encouraging nod.

"I wish to bear a child. I have been barren and my husband and I have traveled in search of the Messiah."

Mary Jacobe, obviously perplexed, inquired, "But are you Jew?" Mary Jacobe looked around as though searching for others like this woman.

Mary gave her a threatening look to hush her up. But the young woman did not appear offended and explained.

"I am not. But my husband is Jewish." She reached for his arm and pulled him forward. He was a big, not so handsome man, on first glance, and appeared considerably older than the beautiful young Greek woman, which aroused suspicions in more than one of the women with Mary.

Mary Jacobe, not heeding Mary's first warning, asked the woman quietly, as though her husband could not hear her, "What are you doing here?"

The woman perceived the judgment and came to his defense. "We have travelled a long way at the bequest of his parents." She gestured to the older couple standing slightly behind them and continued. "My husband is a good man, a righteous man. He rescued me from, well, he...", her blush turned her olive-skinned cheeks a deep coral.

Mary reached out to touch the woman's arm and gave her a sympathetic smile. There was no need to explain. Mary understood. Whatever situation she had been in was painful and she admired a husband who could look beyond the judgements of others.

The man spoke up, an eagerness and gentleness in his tone. "We live in Jerusalem, but word came through my parents that the Messiah was here in the north and that he has cured many people. They urged us to come so that we could seek him out. We could not believe our ears when we heard he was spotted nearby our town! Do you think he can help us?"

Mary was moved by his faith. "We will pray for you that Jesus will heal you Bernike and bless you both with 'pribeten', fruit of the womb."

Martha grabbed Mary's arm, "Mary, should we not wait for Jesus?"

Mary hesitated for a moment, doubting her own boldness to pray for healing, but then she recalled how Jesus had encouraged her to pray for her friend Demetria in a simple faith-filled petition. He had said, "I will do whatever you ask in my name, so that the Father may be glorified in the Son." She still did not know if it had any effect, but recalling Jesus' encouragement buoyed her faith in his power. It was he who would grant their request, not her.

She grabbed Martha's hand and, with her other hand, grabbed the young woman's hand. Martha followed her lead and grabbed Salome's hand, who also grabbed Mary Jacobe's as though power in numbers would make the miracle. And Mary led them in a petition.

"Jesus, in your name we ask with hearts full of faith in your power and goodness, heal whatever ails the womb of this daughter who seeks the blessing of a child."

Salome piped in, "Yes, we ask in Jesus' name that your womb be blessed."

Mary Jacobe also spoke up, looking to the husband as she spoke, "May your wife be like a fruitful vine flourishing within your house, you sons like olive shoots sitting around your table."[112]

Mary looked to Martha to see if she wanted to add anything. Martha was staring at her, a slight smile while dumbfounded expression on her face as she squeezed Mary's hand and whispered a heart-felt, "Amen."

***

The more they attended to the people, the more the crowds increased. The disciples listened and prayed with all those who requested intercession. They were perplexed that obvious healing came to some and to others it did not, or at least not instantaneously. Mary was moved by the plight of each one. She continued praying like she had when asking Jesus for Demetria's miracle, as though Jesus was right there by her side. But she knew he was not. Her gaze frequently turned toward the inclining mount, hoping to see him, but the day continued on. No sign of Jesus, Peter, James, or John. But the people did not leave.

Hour after hour they remained, waiting for Jesus' return. Mary spent considerable time listening to various families, struck by the stories of each one, and particularly by the poverty of many. She longed to help them. Remembering the treasure she had tucked away, she went in search of her satchel. Mary could think of no better way to honor the memory of Tams and Babs' loving fidelity to her than by helping these people in need. She originally thought it would be for

Jesus' travels. *Wouldn't Jesus want me to use it for this purpose? To serve the poor?* She located her money bag and dumped several coins into her hand.

"What are you doing Mary?" Judas' presence startled her. Several coins spilled onto the ground. The sun was threatening to lower itself behind the earth's surface, making it difficult to see his face. But his agitation was audible. He hid it well most of the time, but she had begun to perceive that it was his general state.

She responded defensively but tried not to match his mood with her own reaction. "I want to offer a few families some coins. They are so poor."

"They will just come back begging for more. We need that money to get to Jerusalem."

Anger welled up inside of her, but she maintained a semblance of tact. "It won't hurt us to give a little of what we have. Besides, I brought this money from the sale of my own property."

"Well, you should have handed it over to be used for all."

Her gut tightened and her spirit riled. Suddenly they were both distracted by an increasing commotion in the crowd. All of the disciples were gathered around the father and the skinny boy, with many of the onlookers crowding around them, disputing. Mary had kept an eye on the father and boy throughout the day, her heart going out to them. She had tried to console the father as she watched the disciples, one by one, attempt to heal the boy with no success. The boy remained limp and in a dumb state. Now they were arguing about how to help him when one from the crowd cried out, pointing beyond her and up the mount, "The Master! He's come!"

Mary turned and saw him descending with Peter, John, and James. Relieved by his presence, she ran to meet him.

"Jesus, so many people have come to see you. Please help us. There is a little boy who needs you. We cannot cure him."

Before he could even answer, the father rushed in front of her and dropped to his knees before Jesus' feet, crying out, "Lord have mercy on my son. He has seizures and is suffering greatly. He often falls into the fire or into the water. I brought him to your disciples, but they could not heal him."[113]

Mary watched as Jesus silently looked out upon his apostles. He sighed and spoke with a weariness in his voice, "You unbelieving and perverse generation. How long shall I stay with you? How long shall I put up with you?" And then he spoke aloud, "Bring the boy here to me."[114]

Thomas lifted the boy from the ground. Mary interceded, motioning to Thomas to allow her to take him. Thomas transferred the boy's lightweight and fragile frame into her arms. Cradling him tenderly, she brought him to Jesus, eyes pleading to help him. Jesus laid his hand upon the boy's head and with sternness, cried out a rebuke. The boy convulsed in her arms, foaming at the mouth. She watched as the breath went out of him, and he went limp.

Suddenly the boy gasped for air. His face changed from ashen white to a healthy flushed color. He slowly opened his eyes, alight with life, blinking as if seeing for the first time. The father rejoiced and thanked the Lord as he and Mary set the boy on his feet. He looked at the crowd, bewildered. Mary was suddenly tousled by the onslaught of people crowding around her and reaching out to touch Jesus. Even those who had already been cured by the disciples pressed in on him. Peter, John, and James attempted crowd control, but Jesus allowed the people to bombard him. Mary felt a hand wrap around her arm and tug her out of the suffocating mass. Finally, she found herself on the outside, breathing freely again. John had pulled her out.

Peter, John, and James had given up their attempts to control the people's zeal and stood back, stunned at the imposing crowd. They were watching Jesus like they had seen a ghost, frightened yet in awe, restraint in their demeanor. John greeted her with a nod, holding her gaze as though wishing to share a secret. It was quickly broken as he turned back to watch the scene before him. She was in awe at the sight. As many times as she witnessed Jesus curing and driving out demons, his power never ceased to amaze her. Every time, it was as if she was seeing his power for the first time. She wasn't even sure she would call it power. It was simply presence, a presence that could make the depths of Sheol tremble, she thought to herself.

Eventually the commotion died down as the sun disappeared and the people began to leave for their villages. Mary Jacobe, ever the mother, had Little James, Jude Thaddeus, and Simon the Zealot stoking a fire and roasting some fowls that various families had brought for Jesus and the disciples. At last Jesus joined them. Mary saw his weary face and felt moved with compassion, wanting to console him, to help him rest. She brought him a choice piece of the roasted meat covered in herbs and a generous portion of bread and fresh cheese, also provided by the recent visitors. Taking it gratefully he lifted his eyes to the heavens and prayed a blessing and thanksgiving for the food.

He was beginning to dive in when Thomas and Judas, who were closest to him, insisted that Jesus tell them why they could not drive out the demons. Jesus said point blank, "Because you have so little faith." Then he directed his words for all to hear, "Truly I tell you, if you have faith as small as a mustard seed, you can say to this mountain," he pointed to Mount Tabor behind him, then gestured forward towards the hill of Nazareth, "'Move from here to there,' and it will move. Nothing will be impossible for you."[115]

How can that be? Mary marveled at such a feat of faith. Her heart ached with the desire to have the faith he spoke of. But, surely, he was simply exaggerating. *It is an analogy for the power of faith perhaps?*

He dug into his meal, as though he had simply stated how pleasant the night was, rather than scolding them for their little faith. Movement around the circle indicated that not everyone had taken his words to heart. They were distracted with the feast before them. Then Jesus set his food down. He looked serious. And he spoke.

"Listen carefully to what I am about to tell you." He paused and all movement among them ceased. A solemn silence reigned in expectation of Jesus' words.

"The Son of Man is going to be delivered into the hands of men. They will kill him, and on the third day he will be raised to life."[116]

No one dared to speak. Mary felt the weight of his words. They were shrouded in mystery. She glanced around the circle, the firelight creating dancing light and shadows on the many faces. Salome, Matthew, Peter, John, and James' looked upon Jesus with grief. Thomas, Judas, Mary Jacobe, Martha and the rest, appeared perplexed by his words. *And me?* She searched her heart and sought out Jesus' eyes at the same time. They met. A terrible ache in her heart met his sorrowful eyes. *Is he speaking of his own demise? Will he really be killed?* She knew that the Pharisees and many religious leaders disdained him, but she did not think that it would go as far as murder. Surely, he didn't mean that he would be subject to the same fate as John the Baptist. The thick silence ruined her appetite. The others finished their dinner, each in their own thoughts until Jesus spoke again.

"Mary Jacobe, perhaps you have a psalm for us to close our day." He spoke it more as a matter of fact than a request or question.

Mary Jacobe raised her eyebrows as though one dawned upon her. "Yes, one comes to mind."

A spirit of prayerfulness overtook them as she recited part of a psalm by memory.

> Surely the righteous will never be shaken; they will be remembered forever. They will have no fear of bad news; their hearts are steadfast, trusting in the Lord. Their hearts are secure; they will have no fear; in the end they will look in triumph on their foes.[117]

When Mary rose to clean up after dinner and prepare for the night's rest, she struggled against her recent agitation of spirit. She tried to return to previous feelings of awe and wonder over Jesus' healing presence. But a heaviness had descended upon them, and a foreboding of the future. She foraged in her memory for the psalm that Mary Jacobe had prayed and tried to find some consolation by repeating it to herself. She wondered if the faith that Jesus spoke of, the one that moves mountains, would be needed to face what was coming. Could faith change the fate he spoke of? Consolation did not come even as sleep finally overtook her.

CHAPTER 33. THE TREK

*Therefore, as you have received Christ Jesus the Lord, so walk in Him, having been
firmly rooted and now being built up in Him and established in your faith, just as you
were instructed, and overflowing with gratitude.*
Colossians 2:6-7

The next morning, Jesus had disappeared again, alone. He had gone
partway up the mount to pray. Mary and Martha packed their few belongings alongside one another. They prepared to continue their journey. Martha's treatment of her, so different from when she was
younger, left her dumbfounded. She was no longer the judgmental au-
thoritarian who lorded over her with vigilance. Mary felt like an equal
to her, another companion in the journey, following Jesus. This was an
unexpected novelty. *Perhaps I am not the only one who has changed*, she
thought.

Martha chatted on, revisiting moments of their childhood as if they
had never drifted apart. And so Mary hesitated in her earlier resolve to
broach the subject of their estrangement over the years. She was trying
to muster up the courage and find the right words when suddenly,
Martha interrupted her monologue of memories with an exclamation
of joy and disbelief. She began running. The other disciples also began
moving toward three figures in the distance. She recognized Philip and
Nathaniel. Between them walked a woman. She was of middle height,
thin and of a bearing that made it difficult to tell if she were young or
middle aged. Mary stayed back, observing and slowly making her way
toward the merrymaking. Back slapping and embraces accompanied
the jolly atmosphere created as they encircled the newcomers.

Martha emerged from the crowd as a way opened for the new
woman to be introduced. Mary seemed to be the only one who did not
know this new arrival. She was struck by the woman's beauty. It wasn't

an exotic beauty that made men gape or women jealous. She had a simple, modest and gentle sweetness to her as though she could do no harm to anyone. A pure innocence radiated from her eyes and yet small crow's feet around them emerged when she smiled, intimating an air of quiet wisdom. Mary was taken to her immediately.

Martha introduced her as though presenting her greatest treasure, "Miriam, this is Jesus' mother. Her name is also Miriam, or Mary! But we call her Ima, because she is also like a mother to us."

Mary Jacobe piped in, "And we are too many Mary's to keep track of!"

Ima greeted her, taking one of her hands and enfolding them in her own, "Hello Mary. Mary of Magdala. Jesus has told me much about you. I am very pleased to meet you."

"Hello," Mary suddenly felt shy before her regal dignity. But she tried out the name, "Ima."

Behind her she heard a bellowing echo of the name. Jesus was approaching with exuberant joy to greet his mother. It warmed Mary's heart to watch him take his Ima in his arms, lifting her and swinging her around as she laughed. She grasped his head in her hands and kissed both cheeks. Setting her down he almost smothered her as he wrapped his arms around her again, his whole countenance exuding joy.

"Thank you for sending Nathaniel and Philip to check on me, Son. But you will not get rid of me. I am coming with you to Jerusalem for the Passover." Mary thought she observed a twinge of concern in Mary's countenance.

"Of course, Ima. I am happy you have come and will be with us. We are all happy you have come."

Nodding heads revealed an overall assent and affirming voices sounded all around. They gathered the last of the items that they had packed and set off with their Ima in the midst of them. They crossed to the west of Mount Tabor as they made their way to Jerusalem through Samaria. Ima's presence had a calming and peaceful effect on all the disciples, as though they were on their best behavior under the watchful eyes of a mother, not from fear of punishment but to please her. Her presence, far from threatening or diverting the attention from Jesus, united them around him even more.

She felt as though the more time she spent in Ima's presence, the more she was coming to know Jesus. Many light hearted and precious moments were shared as they wrangled stories of Jesus' childhood out of her. Ima's own nostalgia would infect them, suffusing a kind of sacred listening around her story-telling. Mary also discovered an attentive heart in Ima. She had the capacity to listen as though the speaker were the only person on the face of the earth. She transmitted a genuine and sincere care of a mother, something Mary hadn't even realized she had missed.

Their trek continued as they fell into a rhythm of walking, resting, and visiting villages or stopping along the way when people congregated around Jesus. Sometimes Jesus would send a couple of disciples ahead to prepare the people. At times, they were rejected by the villagers. Other times, she wondered at their intuition. It was as if they knew Jesus was arriving. Perhaps there were prophets within the towns who knew of his coming. As they entered villages, they were greeted with either hostility or hospitality. The contrast was great, and she never knew what to expect.

Mary's walk through Samaria and then the desert matched the slow transformation of her own heart since she met Jesus. A generously rainy season had soaked the parched land, bringing life to dormant seeds. The sun and heat had given birth to soft green undulating hills, like stubble on a youth emerging into manhood. She had never felt so alive, so new. Many times during the day she would check on Jesus, expecting to see tiredness from the hot journey. Sweat had certainly drenched his tunic, front and back. But they marched on. Despite her sore muscles every morning, she loved the moment when they would set off. Jesus would turn to her, as though reading her mind. His smile belied a joy-filled acceptance of the adventures to come. He raised his eyebrows as though to say, "Ready? Are you with me?" She smiled back, hoping to convey her readiness for whatever providence would lay before them that day. Every morning, no matter how tired she was, an eager willingness was born. She was eager to attend to the first curious sojourners whom they would encounter that day.

Of one thing she was certain. Despite all the rejoicing and wonders being worked and the moments of content and delight, she perceived an increasing sadness and disturbance in Jesus' mood. He wasn't a moody person. He was always kind, despite the firmness of his statements. For example, to one he demanded they leave the dead to bury the dead if they wished to follow him. To another, one who asked to say goodbye to his family before joining them, he gave a firm warning about not looking back if he truly wished to follow. But even if some did not follow him, he never said a harsh word against them.

The number of disciples following Jesus had increased and there were now over seventy. He sent them out two by two, the women tending to remain closer to Jesus and sharing in his work wherever he went. The disciples would come back rejoicing at the miracles wrought in Jesus' name, only to be surprised at his remark, "Do not rejoice that the spirits submit to you, but rejoice that your names are written in heaven."[118]

Every day Jesus presented her with a lifetime of wonders to contemplate. And yet, a foreboding heaviness hung over her. Perhaps it was due to the fleeting glimpses of a deep sadness in Jesus' countenance. She continued to perceive it.

One day, a revelation dawned on her. She hadn't realized when or how it had happened. It came out of the blue and during the monotony of their daily walk from one village to another. She realized that her very existence was intertwined with his. Like the slow building of endurance of her body due to their simple living and long treks, her heart too had been fortified and synchronized to beat to a different rhythm. She had grown more and more attentive to Jesus' movements, moods, words, and gestures. She could not imagine a "before" without him. Or rather, she did not want to imagine an "after" without him. And that is why his words to her as they continued their trek toward Jerusalem the next day were so painful.

CHAPTER 34. THE SEPARATION

Brethren, I do not regard myself as having laid hold of it yet; but one thing I do: forgetting what lies behind and reaching forward to what lies ahead, I press on toward the goal for the prize of the upward call of God in Christ Jesus. Let us therefore, as many as are perfect, have this attitude; and if in anything you have a different attitude, God will reveal that also to you.
Philippians 3:13-15

On a day seemingly as common as others, they had been invited to feast with a group of families in a small village in the foothills north of Jerusalem. The afternoon was leisurely. Adults were gathered, lounging around Jesus as they finished their meal. The conversation took on a tone of camaraderie and trustfulness as though among old friends and family. Children of various ages were playing games nearby and running in and out of the circle of adults, older children bringing the younger ones to their parents when they were crabby or needed a firm hand. Having encountered a plethora of people, religious, simple, poor, rich, believers and unbelievers, a discussion had broken out among the disciples about the kingdom of heaven and who was the greatest. Jesus called over one of the children, a four-year old who had been more content at his mother's side than with the rambunctious group at play nearby.

"David, come," he smiled and motioned at the young one to come. Jesus tousled his abundant curls and set him on his lap. The boy leaned back, content to continue his investigation of a gadget in his hands while making Jesus his seat.

"Amen, I say to you, unless you turn and become like children, you will not enter the kingdom of heaven. Whoever humbles himself, like this child is the greatest in the kingdom of heaven. And whoever receives one child such as this in my name receives me."[119]

The father of the young one answered, "What I wouldn't give to have the cares of a child now. I am afraid for my children and what kind of country they will find when they start families of their own. The struggle for power is more evident every time I travel to Jerusalem. Tension is thick between the Pharisees and Sadducees on questions of religion, especially the debate on the resurrection of the dead. And now the Essene sect is gaining followers, dividing us further when we should be more united against Roman occupation.

Judas answered with the confidence of a commander ready to fight a battle. "Our time will come. We can't lose hope. I am certain that we are going to see a turnaround very soon."

One of the elders of the village spoke up. "We need to be free of foreign domination. If we are not careful, we will end up with something worse than the Babylonian exile. Instead of being exiled into foreign lands, a foreign way is being planted among us. Our children will face many challenges if they wish to maintain the traditions."

The mother of the four-year old interjected. "My greatest fear is that my child will not remain faithful to the covenant. The lure of the Roman's pagan mindset is very strong among the young people. They seem to choose one of two extremes. They want to raise their sword and act violently against the Romans or they let their guard down altogether and are lured into pagan ways."

Mary flushed in embarrassment, feeling uncomfortable with the direction of the conversation. They had no idea of the life she led before following Jesus. They would be scandalized. An old worry crept in. *Perhaps they will reject me? Even worse, how would it reflect on Jesus?*

John answered the mother's concern, "But we have among us one who has come to do the work of God. In him we must believe and teach our children to believe. We will tell the next generation of the praiseworthy deeds of the Lord, his power, and the wonders he has done."[120]

One of the elderly women nodded in affirmation. "Yes, we have a great responsibility to our children, to give them a future of hope and belief in the Messiah. Master, I believe you are the one we have been awaiting. If we fear anything, it should be fear of God for leading others astray in sin and unrighteousness."

Mary watched the varying reactions at the woman's profession of faith. Most granted a show of assent. A handful fixed their eyes to the ground, refusing to acknowledge the woman's statement.

Jesus spoke. "Woe to the one who causes one of these little ones who believe in me to sin, it would be better for him to have a millstone hung around his neck and to be drowned in the depths of the sea. Woe to the world because of things that cause sin! Such things must come, but woe to the one through whom they come! If your hand or foot causes you to sin, tear it out and throw it away. It is better for you to enter into life maimed or crippled than with two hands and two feet to be thrown into eternal fire. And if your eye causes you to sin, tear it out and throw it away. It is better for you to enter into life with one eye than with two eyes be thrown into fiery Gehenna."[121]

"Strong words, but true indeed," agreed the host of the party. Then he spoke harshly, spitting out repressed anger along with his words. "I pity the ones whose example leads the others astray. We have had some of our younger men leave our village in search of another way, not our own. It is better they stay away and not come to taint the little ones."

A brief silence ensued. Mary was shocked by the vehemence with which he spoke. She wondered if his own son had been among those who left the village.

Jesus continued. "If a man has a hundred sheep and one of them goes astray, will he not leave the ninety-nine in the hills and go in search of the stray? And if he finds it, amen, I say to you, he rejoices more over it than over the ninety-nine that did not stray. In just the same way, it is not the will of your heavenly Father that one of these little ones be lost."

The host spoke again. "But if that one is the poison of the ninety-nine? No, better he remains cast out, even if he was once one of our own. I wash my hands of them."

The host's wife put her hand on her husband's arm to temper his anger. She looked to Jesus, pleading in her eyes.

Jesus responded, directing his gaze to the man, "Your anger reveals your pain. There is a way to offer one you love a chance at returning. If your brother or sister sins, go and point out their fault, just between the two of you. If they listen to you, you have won them over. But if they will not listen, take one or two others along, so that every matter may be established by the testimony of two or three witnesses. If they still refuse to listen, tell it to the church[122]; and if they refuse to listen even to the church, treat them as you would a pagan or a tax collector. Truly I tell you that if two of you on earth agree about anything they ask for, it will be done for them by my Father in heaven. For where two or three gather in my name, there am I with them."[123]

Mary listened as though she were hearing the story of her own life. She looked at Martha and realized the truth. Her brother and sister had done just that with her. Well, they had left her to her own devices for a long time, but then they had tried several times to pull her out of her bad situation. They had come with the aid of friends as well. Finally, they had left her alone. But they had never stopped praying for her. Of that she was certain. And she was grateful.

Her line of thought was interrupted by Peter asking Jesus, "But Jesus, if my brother sins against me, how many times must I forgive him? Up to seven times?"

Jesus answered, "I tell you, not seven times, but seventy-seven times."[124]

Many eyebrows went up. They were incredulous.

Jesus began telling a parable, but her mind captured only the essence as her memory replayed her own rancor and unforgiveness for having felt abandoned by her siblings. And then she replayed in her mind all the times her brother and sister had tried to convince her to return to Bethany under their protective and watchful eye. Scenes of her own reactions flashed through her memory. Anger, hatred, and judgments had consumed her. She had thought that they rejected her when in fact they were loving her the best they knew how.

Mary flitted between her own memories and bits and pieces of Jesus' story, "The kingdom of heaven is like a king who wanted to settle accounts with his servants…", "settlement", "repay the debt", "Be patient with me." "The master took pity." "The servant refused to give mercy to others."

Mary thought of her own debt. How much gratitude she owed her brother and sister! The need to forgive them and to ask forgiveness dawned on her as she heard the last of Jesus' story.

"Then the master called the servant in. 'You wicked servant,' he said, 'I canceled all that debt of yours because you begged me to. Shouldn't you have had mercy on your fellow servant just as I had on you?' In anger his master handed him over to the jailers to be tortured, until he should pay back all he owed. This is how my heavenly Father will treat each of you unless you forgive your brother or sister from your heart."[125]

From the heart. Mary sensed a previously unknown wall in her heart coming into view. Like a blurred vision suddenly becoming as clear as still water. She could sense a vice-like grip around her heart that still caused subtle accusations and judgments toward Martha and Lazarus. She believed she had reconciled with Martha. But not Lazarus. She didn't know if she could face him. She closed her eyes, a torrent of unbidden and silent tears washed over her cheeks.

***

The visit had come to an end, and the disciples were taking their leave from the villagers. In their short stay, the little children had really taken to Jesus. The little ones were grabbing onto his legs, taking a ride as Jesus slowly advanced toward the village exit. Laughter and hearty goodbyes filled the air until the children were called back by their parents and all waved goodbye. They were finally off by themselves again.

Jesus walked with her and some of the other women as they spoke about the visit, laughing about the children's antics, recalling their rambunctious joy. They spoke of the different people they had met, the need for prayers for this one and that one.

Then Jesus singled her out and asked her, "Mary, what did you think about our conversation on forgiveness?"

The other women respectfully distanced themselves, giving space for a private conversation. He did this with all of the disciples throughout the trip. They were special moments that each one treasured. His attention invited vulnerability, and left her feeling known, valued, challenged and strengthened.

She hesitated. *Did he notice that I was distracted when he was telling the story of the master and servant?* "What do you mean, Rabboni?"

"Mary, we are heading to a crossroads on the way to Jerusalem, but I will go elsewhere with several of my disciples. Martha will be heading to Bethany. Ima, John, and the other women will accompany her to your family house. Would you like to go?"

Mary only heard that she was going to be separated from him again. "No," she answered quickly. "I mean, please, I will go with you wherever you go."

Jesus smiled softly, a look of concern in his eyes. "Are there not some accounts that you need to settle in Bethany?"

"Accounts?" She didn't need an answer to her question but stalled because she intuited what he was insinuating. It had already occurred to her during the conversation among the villagers. A nudging to seek reconciliation with her brother had been quietly and surely present. She couldn't ignore it, but at present, courage failed her. Her sister and her had reconciled and were on much better terms. They were almost back to their previous selves: Martha ordering her around and Mary either ignoring her or doing it her own way as she rolled her eyes. Nonetheless, Mary had surprised herself many times with her growing capacity to restrain a sassy reply and instead have a civil conversation with Martha to resolve situations. Martha was also trying to temper her older sister complex and not treat Mary like a child, but rather like the adult that she was.

Jesus had remained silent, watching and waiting for her reply. It pained her to think of being separated from him, but if Jesus had asked the question, it must be important for her to reconcile with her brother. Her mind told her it was what she should do, but her emotions cowered. She couldn't quite muster a yes, so she smiled weakly at Jesus and consented, weary of the consequences.

"Ok." She managed to say, a lump forming in her throat.

"You have a gift to offer Mary. But first be reconciled to your brother, and then come and offer your gift."[126]

A multitude of thoughts raced through her heard. *A gift? What gift have I to offer Jesus? I still have a lot of money left from the sale of the land. Does he mean that? I also have my expensive nard that I could sell in case we need more funds. But Jesus has never spoken to me about my money.* She didn't think that was what he meant, and she had no time to question him. The others had stopped at the crossroad. They were waiting for them. The time had come. Once again, she was to be separated from him. Anguish almost made her falter, but she knew she had to follow the way that he had indicated, as daunting as it seemed at present. Unfortunately, it felt like it was taking her in the opposite direction of Jesus. The consolation of his presence was already fading as she looked up the road toward her destiny.

CHAPTER 35. LOVE & UNDERSTANDING

Therefore, encourage one another and build each other up,
just as in fact you are doing.
1 Thessalonians 5:11

Eight long years. Mary had refused to return all that time. And had refused to see her brother Lazarus even when he had come to Magdala to check on her. When she stubbornly refused to open the door, he had sent messengers. His and Martha's pleas and petitions to return to their family house in Bethany had not been reciprocated.

During the trek to Bethany, the women sensed her pensive and apprehensive mood. Their presence was some consolation to her as they parted ways with Jesus and walked toward Bethany. But not enough to lift her from distraction. John also sensed a change and tried to console her with attention and humor. They knew what lay ahead for her. Mary wondered how Lazarus would receive her. Martha assured her that he would rejoice. Mary wasn't sure of her own reactions towards Lazarus, having built up a wall towards him for so long.

How might my life have been if I never left for Magdala so long ago? If I had accepted Lazarus' insistence to let him make a marriage match. The man they had proposed to her was closer to Martha's age. *Why didn't Lazarus marry Martha off? She was much older than her and still wasn't married.* So many ponderings and what-ifs.

Mary was just discovering her sister all over again. Sometimes, she recognized the Martha she knew from her childhood. Other times, it was as though they were strangers becoming friends. She thought back to several occasions since that first night Martha had stayed with her in Magdala, before they left on this journey to Jerusalem. She had observed Martha interact with others. Mary admired her spirit of service. She was a bit impulsive, perhaps like herself. But also possessed an ability to listen and respond to matters at hand with her practical mind. Mary loved to see and hear her laugh. She had delightfully observed as Nathaniel, older than some of the other disciples, made Martha laugh on several occasions. She marveled at this new Martha she had rarely seen. It seemed to take several years off of her now thirty-five years.

As they walked side by side, Martha tried to fill her in on the last eight years of Lazarus' life. Mary wondered out loud, "Martha, why did you and Lazarus never marry?"

Martha looked at her incredulously, as though Mary should know the answer. But then thought again and shrugging her shoulders began to explain.

"Mother became very ill when you were born. I was only thirteen at the time. Lazarus was fifteen. Father insisted that I care for her. We had plenty of servants that could have done this, but Father said it wasn't the same as having family at her side, especially her own daughter. It would be a great consolation to her, he had said. Mother recovered, but she was never the same. She had periods of melancholy Miriam. Such melancholy that she was not always able to cope with daily tasks. Since mother was periodically overcome with fatigue, I eventually took over the running of the household and attempted to reign you in as well. With little success there," she chuckled.

Mary had no idea. She realized now how she had drawn nearer to her father, not only because she felt a natural affection from him, but because she thought her mother preferred Martha more. Her mother had praised Martha, while she mostly received scolding and disapproval. A slightly different understanding of her family's dynamics during her childhood was emerging. Now she understood. Her mother had relied on Martha for so much.

Martha continued. "Lazarus was fifteen when you were born, but he also started being more involved in the business. When Father became ill, Lazarus pretty much took it all on. The years just passed us by, and before we knew it, both father and mother had passed away. We were left to care for you the best we could."

"I had no idea, Martha. I am sorry." Mary truly was sorry. She felt like blinders were falling off her vision of the past. How she must have made them suffer.

"Truly Martha, I am sorry for causing you so much headache. And thank you. Thank you for trying, for persisting with me. I am very glad that you never gave up. I suppose we have more in common than we realized."

Martha's horrifying look gave away her spontaneous thought. But then she tempered it and questioned, "How? What do you possibly think we have in common Miriam?"

"Our persistent and stubborn character! We don't give up very easily when it comes to getting our way, do we?" Mary nudged her with her elbow, teasing her.

Martha's guffaw brought the eyes of the other women upon them. They had gone on ahead, leaving them privacy to speak. Approval in their glances said they were relieved to hear laughter between the two of them, and not arguing. They let them be.

"Ah Martha, I love to hear you laugh. I just don't remember you laughing and enjoying life much, especially after Father died."

"No, it was all I could do to get by day by day. I threw myself into taking care of mother who seemed to disappear into herself. And once she died, well, I confess, I found ways to be even busier by taking on the task of serving the poor. I suppose it was my way of trying to save someone. I couldn't save our father or mother. I couldn't save you. But I could save some of those little ones who were starving on the street." Her countenance revealed painful memories taking the forefront of her thoughts. But then she shrugged and reciprocated the earlier elbow jabbing. With lightheartedness she teased, "Besides, you were enjoying life for the two of us!"

Mary winced. "No Martha, I think that was my way of surviving too."

They walked in silence for a while, both steeped in their own memories. It was a comfortable silence. Something had shifted between them. Yes, they had reconciled earlier, or at least they had said they were sorry. But this brought them to a new understanding. And perhaps, Mary thought, appreciation and admiration. At least for her. She looked at Martha. Her heart swelled with love and a yearning to see her happy and well cared for. Martha had been caring for others almost all her life.

"Martha!" Mary felt a bit impulsive over the thought that bubbled up, but she let it out. "What do you think of Nathaniel? He makes you laugh, doesn't he?"

"Miriam! What are you even proposing? He makes us all laugh. But yes, I must admit he knows how to aim his comments right at me to make me laugh. And I have been a willing audience. But your thinking is not correct. And please don't get any ideas or attempt any match-making for me!"

"Why not Martha? You aren't like me who refused to get married and wanted her independence. You couldn't get married. You had too many responsibilities at home."

Martha chuckled at that. "Oh Miriam, if you only knew. Now I will agree with you...how very much alike we actually are! No, no, I wouldn't even let Lazarus suggest the idea of marriage, which he tried several times. I also liked my independence. I liked being the master of my house in Bethany, which is what it became, long before father passed away."

Mary looked shocked and delighted at the same time.

"But, that is just a superficial excuse. Actually," Martha hesitated momentarily, but nodded her head as if deciding to share all.

"Miriam, I have never told this to anyone, well, except Ima. I met Jesus a long time ago. When I was little actually, but that is a story for another day. Sometimes, if he and Ima were able to come to the Passover festivities, they would stay at Lazarus' Inn and eventually they stayed with us. I don't know how your paths never crossed. I suppose because of your trips to Magdala. When father was ill, and we no longer traveled there as a family, he sent you with Tams and Babs, where he thought you would be out of trouble. And then you finally left for good."

More of her past was continuing to become clearer for Mary.

Martha continued. "I began to believe that Jesus was the Messiah long ago. Actually, Father had spoken to Lazarus and myself about Ima and Jesus, telling us that if they ever came, we were to treat them like royalty, that Jesus was very special and perhaps even the Messiah himself. I didn't believe it at first, but as he grew into adulthood, yes, I believed." Martha looked ahead, noticing where they were. "Oh, we are almost home."

They had been so engrossed in their conversation that they hadn't realized how close they were to home. Mary had almost forgotten her own jitters, but they rushed in once again as she looked upon the approaching destination.

"Miriam, what I am trying to tell you was that I decided, as I got to know Jesus, that I would never marry." Martha looked very uncomfortable, but she continued, unable to make eye contact with Mary. "I know it is rare, but it is not against our tradition. There are still some temple virgins and now the Essenes are living that way, albeit they are a little extreme for my taste. But I knew in my heart that I would serve the Lord. My husband would be my maker, so to speak." Martha's face turned scarlet red. She fumbled with her word, then rushed on, "I can't explain it. I shouldn't have told you. It is strange, I know."

Mary put a serious expression on her face and spoke firmly. "Martha! Three things. First, my name is Mary. Jesus calls me Mary, so please do the same. Miriam is my old name. Second, the scripture is not 'My husband will be my maker', but 'my maker is my husband.'[127] Remember that I have the same parents as you, and, despite you thinking that I fell away from our traditions, I have not forgotten my scripture."

"I know, I know, sorry," Martha started to interject, but Mary cut her off, holding up her hand to stay her interruption.

"Thirdly," Mary stopped walking and looked at her tenderly. "I believe I know exactly what you mean Martha."

"You do?" Martha finally lifted her eyes, making eye contact again, surprised at Mary's empathy.

"I do. I feel the same after I came to know Jesus."

"Oh."

Martha looked so vulnerable. She looked around as though getting her bearings as to where they were and suddenly perked up.

"Well, *Mary!*" She emphasized her name. "Shall I call you Mary of Magdala or Mary of Bethany then? Or perhaps you deserve the title, Mary the Magdalene! It befits you, does it not? Tall, towering, grand, in stature and character!"

Mary was amused at this teasing side of Martha that was emerging more and more. They laughed together, a silent fondness, an authentic sisterly love passing between them.

Then Martha pointed ahead. "So, *Mary Magdalene*, there is home, your other home. Are you ready?"

Mary faltered at the deed awaiting her.

Martha noticed. She slipped her hand into Mary's and led her towards the villa, closer to Lazarus, whom she had not seen for eight years.

Martha's voice penetrated Mary's growing trepidation. "And how is this for a correct scripture verse? Take strength in Isaiah." As Martha recited scripture, Mary allowed it to be balsam for her anxious spirit at the thought of the upcoming re-encounter.

"'Fear not, for I am with you; be not dismayed, for I am your God; I will strengthen you, I will help you, I will uphold you with my righteous right hand.'"[128]

CHAPTER 36. MENDING HEARTS

He heals the brokenhearted and binds up their wounds.
Psalm 147:3

They finally arrived. She stood before the grand villa, memories of her days with her father and mother rushing in, mixing emotions of joy and sorrow, fear and anger, grief and regret. The villa stood as beautiful as it was in her memory, a place where her father had spoiled her, where she had run wild and mischievous through the village, much to the dismay of her mother. It also brought memories of death, her father's and mother's death, of grief and anger, of confusion and rebellion.

Mustering up courage, she entered. A light breeze wafted familiar scents over her: the earthy spring of the open gardens through the courtyard, fresh bread from the day's baking, vinegar and lemon masking the smell of musty old rugs, and myrtle and cyclamen, evidence of a well-kept and clean house.

She closed her eyes against the overwhelming wave of nostalgia. Servants had come to greet them and were taken aback at the mirage before them. Their little Miriam was a woman now, more beautiful and elegant than her adolescent years when they last saw her. They seemed shy before her and whispered urgently to Martha. Martha's countenance turned serious. She set her hand on Mary's arm, concern and fear in her expression.

"Come Mary, Lazarus is ill."

Mary's eyes opened in alarm, her feet paralyzed in their place. John led the way as Martha and Ima ushered her forward, supporting her like pillars, one on each side. A dimly lit room greeted her as she adjusted her eyes to a corner where her brother lay. He looked so much older, still large of build, but face ashen and creased with wrinkles, hair and beard streaked with gray. He wasn't but thirty-eight years old but had the look of one who had lived a full life. Where was the energetic brother she remembered? The smell brought her back to her own father's last dying days.

No, it couldn't be!

Without hesitation, instinctually, she threw herself to her knees at his side, tears wetting his arm. She sobbed for the wasted years, wanting to take them all back.

A hand pressed down upon her head.

"Miriam?" A soft voice came from the man, hardly recognizable as her brother. She looked around. She was alone with him. Martha, John, and Ima had slipped out.

"Lazarus. I...," she choked on her own sob, trying to control the flow of emotions that beset her. "I...am...home," she managed to get out between breaths.

His raised head fell back as he closed his eyes, sighing, "Finally. Stay now."

Mary felt a tug of old anger in her at his command. She huffed through her own gasps of breath, then checked herself, tempering the old reaction that had reared its ugly head.

He spoke again, "I knew you would come back. Martha didn't think you would. But I knew someday you would finally return to us."

Mary slipped into her old role as the younger sassy sister. "Yes, well, we shall see how long I stay. But I am here for now."

A slight upward curve of Lazarus' mouth revealed amusement. Then he reached for her hand, squeezing it with all the strength he could muster up.

"Miriam, you. You will have much to do. Jesus. He's coming. Give him. Help him."

Mary felt the floodgates opening once again as she held onto him, tears pouring forth. "Forgive me Lazarus. Forgive me."

"Forgive me Miriam. Forgive me. I left you. There. In Magdala. By yourself. I couldn't care for you. I am sorry. Father. Mother. I. Just couldn't. I didn't know what to do with you."

"Hush," she tried to sooth his agitated countenance. "How about a deal? I forgive you if you forgive me?"

"Deal Miriam. Good deal." His countenance changed from agitation to peace as he gently fell into a deep slumber.

Mary stayed by his side, doing what she could, insisting that she care for him. She hardly noticed the others, with the exception of Martha, who paced ferociously and fret over Mary as much as Lazarus. There was little to be done as he had the look of one almost gone from this world. He neither opened his eyes nor spoke a word since their brief reconciliation. She soaked a cloth to cool his body, flush with fever. She sponged water onto his lips and tongue, careful not to drench and choke him as he slept. She prayed as Jesus had bid her to pray. She hoped that he would work a miracle from afar, just this one miracle. Night came and went. No sign of awakening. She continued by his side.

In the early morning, she could wait no more. After consulting Martha, Ima, and John, they decided to send for Jesus. John quickly packed a satchel and was off. No sooner had he left, when Lazarus inhaled sharp quick gasps, then slowly exhaled. And Mary knew. The end had come. His hand went cold in hers.

No, no, no. This cannot be!

Mary, inconsolable, was finally taken from the room. Ima gently convinced her to take food. She remained by her side, a silent but comforting presence. They read and sang psalms, the words washing over her.

> Lord, you have been our dwelling place throughout all generations. Before the mountains were born or you brought forth the earth and the world, from everlasting to everlasting you are God. You turn men back to dust, saying, "Return to dust, O sons of men." For a thousand years in your sight are like a day that has just gone by, or like a watch in the night. You sweep men away in the sleep of death; ...[129]

> At dawn, life blossoms and renews itself; at dusk,
> it withers and dries up. Relent, O LORD! How long
> will it be? Have compassion on your servants. Satisfy
> us in the morning with your unfailing love, that we may
> sing for joy and be glad all our days. Make us glad for
> as many days as you have afflicted us, for as many years
> as we have seen trouble. May your deeds be shown to
> your servants, your splendor to their children.[130]

The sleep of death. Make us glad? The words mocked her. At times they consoled her and other times they provoked a cry out to God. *Why?* She questioned over and over. *Why now when I have just come back to him?*

Gladness seemed distant. She knew that this was to be a time of mourning as well as praise and hope in God's power to raise up the one who died. Her father had taught them this and was a staunch believer in the resurrection of the dead. But it seemed impossible, a mere myth that was meant to buoy hope. Ima must have seen her waves of despair. She would sometimes whisper verses from Psalms as though speaking directly to her.

"Wait patiently, He hears your cry."[131]

Mary participated in the washing, embalming, and wrapping of her brother in a shroud, an honor for the women of the family. She walked in procession towards the tomb. And she listened to a new hymn she had not heard before. Or perhaps her childhood memory had blocked out from her father and mother's death. A burial and Kaddish prayer of mourning.

> May His great name be kept magnified and sanctified
> in the world that is to be created anew, where He will
> revive the dead, and raise them up to eternal life; and
> rebuild the city of Jerusalem; and establish His Temple
> in its midst; and uproot alien worship from the earth
> and restore the worship of Heaven to its place. May the
> Holy One, blessed be He, reign in His sovereignty and
> glory, during your life ring your days.[132]

She tried to muster up faith in those words. "He will revive the dead and raise them up to eternal life." She wasn't sure she had enough faith right now, but a relief of peace amidst the pain filled her with fortitude for the days of mourning that continued. She received visitors, friends and family she had not seen for years. Irritation at their presence reminded her that she was still alive and had not gone to the grave with her brother. She wondered if they were more curious to see her than to attend Lazarus' funeral.

The days of mourning went on as her response to grief wavered between a silent and uncontrollable flow of tears, a quiet resignation, and numbness. But no Jesus. He did not come. And no word from John either. She longed for him to come, not that anything could be done now. Lazarus was dead. And Jesus did not come. However, an unexpected visitor surprised her on the third day.

She had escaped the constant chatter of the continual flow of consolers who were scattered throughout the courtyard and gardens. A refuge, in a far corner of the garden behind the house allowed her a brief respite. Shrubbery behind her blocked out the view of the house. It offered a semblance of solitude at least. It overlooked the hills towards the Jordan river where she thought perhaps Jesus had gone when they last separated.

A familiar voice startled her, like claws gripping her stomach.

"Miriam," the smooth tone and accent gave him away.

"Gaius," she swallowed, turning to him and seeing Martha's fearful and steaming countenance behind him. Mary walked over to Martha, assuring her she would handle the situation and pushed her gently towards the house. Martha hesitatingly disappeared behind the shrubbery leaving them alone.

Turning back to Gaius, Mary was surprised at her own inner strength. Feeling bold, she addressed him with a relative calm and confidence, "What are you doing here Gaius?"

"So, you've come home?" His smirk, bereft of any consolation for her loss, taunted her. "I heard about your brother. Quite the sympathizer with your newfound friend, Jesus. That's one less to keep an eye on."

Fury at his disregard for her sorrow caught in her throat, ready to be spewed forth. *How I had ever thought he cared for me is beyond my understanding!*

Then suddenly she saw him for what he was. Lost. Like her. Before she had met Jesus. Lost. As promptly as the fury had been born it was extinguished and replaced with pity.

"Gaius," she said, fixing her gaze firmly but gently on him. "We are in mourning. I am mourning my brother. Please. Have you no respect at all?" She realized that he was in ordinary dress, still easily identifiable as a Roman, but not in his uniform. "I don't know what you are looking for here, but if it is me, I am not the same woman as before."

He appeared disarmed by her calm control as she spoke, breaking the arrogant facade momentarily.

"Oh no, I think my Miriam is still there before me," he challenged back.

"Don't even think for a moment that you have the right to return after disappearing without a word."

Gaius appeared confused and spat back, "I sent word. So, tell me, who left who?"

Her calm was slowly fading away at the memory of feeling abandoned. She spat back, "I received no such word from you. You are dead to me." A jolt of regret at the harshness of her own words ushered in a new effort to remain composed.

"Gaius, where is your wife?" She hoped that her clever question would serve to end the conversation.

Silence. A new expression washed over his face. Hurt. Incredulity as though she had dared to be so cruel. He spoke, a monotone matter of fact statement. "She's dead."

"Oh."

Mary had not expected that. She didn't know how to respond. For a moment, she saw her old Gaius, not the Roman officer, not the drunk carousing soldier, just Gaius.

"Miriam...I am sorry. I am sorry about your brother, your loss. But regarding your accusations, as I told you before, I sent word. Through Vespasian. It was unexpected. I had no choice but to go right away without forewarning. And then I didn't hear from you."

The old Gaius disappeared as vehemence took its place. "Vespasian told me you had moved on," he spat out the words as though he had a right to be disgusted with her. "And from what I hear, you made quite a reputation for yourself. Not missing me at all it seems. You found enough friends to fill the void."

Mary was confused by his words. *Vespasian. That brute animal.*

"What are you talking about? Vespasian told me you had taken a wife and that you had left me in his protection. I will spare you the details of how that turned out."

Mary watched hurt and confusion silence him. She did not want to open the door to further conversation on the past. Shaking off her rising irritation, she breathed deeply to calm herself, then continued, "Yes, I found a new friend."

A new strength accompanied her profession. With conviction she continued, "The Rabboni knows me for who I am. He loves me as, as." She stopped abruptly. She was about to say "as you never could" and throw it in his face but caught herself. She would not use her Rabboni's love as a weapon. She reformulated her thought. "He loves me as no one ever could. He has offered me a new life."

She paused for a moment, wondering if she dared speak further. She dared, a quiet and gentle supplication in her tone, "He could offer that to you too, Gaius."

His pompous air returned, and he snorted haughtily, shaking his head in disbelief.

"Not for me, dodi."

She was taken aback by his Hebrew use of the term of endearment.

"But I have come to warn you. Your new friends have a mark on their head from more than one group. Watch yourself. You'd be better off back in Galilee."

He took his leave, having to skirt by a fuming Martha who had remained hidden behind the tall shrubbery, on alert in case intervention was needed. Mary put up her hand to silence Martha who was obviously on the verge of unleashing a monologue of big sister advice.

Oh Jesus. Where are you? Mary cried out from the depths of her heart and returned to the multitude of visitors, a more welcome company than the solitude of her own thoughts right now.

CHAPTER 37. RESTART

I am the resurrection and the life. The one who believes in me will live, even though they die; and whoever lives by believing in me will never die.
John 11:25-26

They waited. And waited. Ima had been a consoling presence in this time. While Mary had never felt particularly close to her own mother, Ima became a new motherly presence of unconditional love. The evening of Gaius' visit, Ima approached her in a quiet and solitary corner of their gardens. Her gentle presence disarmed her. Mary felt compelled to share all that took place in her own heart during that visit with Gaius.

At first, Mary thought Ima was going to caution her against harvesting old feelings for him. But instead Ima marveled at the strength of Mary's faith and love for her son that had moved her to a genuine concern for Gaius in the midst of the varied emotions pulling her in all directions. Ima helped her see the situation anew, to believe that she was a woman of integrity and fortitude. It served to affirm her decision to love Jesus in a way, one in which she had never understood one could love another.

On the fourth day she was sitting among the multitude of visitors in one of their inner gardens, enduring their chatter once again. She marveled at how she had been experiencing moments of quiet peace and fortitude since her encounter with Gaius and conversation with Ima. But her tears still flowed freely and without warning. Suddenly a commotion turned her attention to an animated Martha rushing towards her.[133]

"The Master is here," Martha announced privately, but unsuccessfully keeping it between them. Voices silenced, heads turned. "He is asking for you," Martha accented the word "you", as though she didn't understand the mystery of that request.

Rabboni! Her heart leapt. She raced through the house as fast as her feet could carry her. Stopping at the front door she looked around wildly. She didn't see him anywhere. Martha caught up to her.

"The edge of the village," Martha motioned to her right. Mary hurried down the path, unaware that several guests had followed her at a distance. Her heart raced. She wanted to hug him, scold him for not coming sooner, ask him why her own prayers weren't able to heal her brother. She wanted to be embraced and consoled in her grief and confusion. Finally, she saw him at the village entrance coming towards her. The other disciples kept their distance, waiting behind him. Her vision of him was like a dream. Her eyes blurry from tears that burst forth like a gushing river from a broken dam. She fell at his feet, ignoring the hard clay-caked ground.

"Lord, if you had been here, my brother would not have died," she sobbed.

Mary felt his hand on her head, comforting her. She wiped her tear stained face with her sleeve, once, twice, three times, blinking in her attempt to focus through puffy, overspent eyes. Her veil had long flown away in her haste to greet him. Her disheveled hair tangled in the breeze, giving her the look of a crazed woman. She heard the crowd of mourners approaching from behind. Looking up, she saw Jesus, tears in his eyes. He sighed sorrowfully, causing a fresh start of her own tears.

"Where have you laid him?" Jesus asked.

"Come and see, Lord," several replied.

John came forward and helped Mary to her feet. His compassion was her undoing once again. They walked in procession, a familiar motion, like four days prior, toward the tomb where her brother had been laid. Mary and Martha didn't leave Jesus' side. They stopped before the stone-closed tomb. And then, Jesus wept. Silence kept vigil for a brief moment until he spoke again.

"Take away the stone," he ordered. Big James initiated a group of strong men to work at moving the stone.

Martha gasped, "But Lord, by this time there is a terrible stench. It has already been four days!"

Jesus spoke to the crowd, many of whom had heard him teaching in the Temple over the last year. "Did I not tell you that if you believe, you will see the glory of God?"

Mary wondered what he meant by this, by taking away the stone. She heard the murmuring comments through the crowd. "See how he loves him." "Couldn't he have come to heal him before he died?" "He will defile himself if he enters that grave!" "Why is he bothering with this?" "Maybe he just wants to see him one last time?"

Jesus ignored the comments. He turned his face toward the heavens and prayed quietly. John, Martha, and Mary heard his prayer.

"Father, I thank you that you have heard me. I knew that you always hear me, but I said this for the benefit of the people standing here, that they may believe that you sent me."

The stone had finally been rolled away. Then Jesus cried out, "Lazarus, come out!" Startled gasps echoed through the gathered mourners. Mary's heart beat with hope, anticipation and wonder. She mustered up faith. She wanted to believe it was possible. She focused all her attention on the entrance, willing to see her brother again. A shadow emerged in the hollow and slowly, a figure came forth from the darkness. Voices clamored their unbelief and praise. Hands raised to praise the Lord. "He truly is the Messiah." "A miracle!" "Only God can bring back from the dead!"

Jesus commanded the gapers to take off the grave clothes and let him loose. Several disciples broke free from their shock and rushed forward to unwind the bindings. Martha also rushed forward to touch and see her brother alive. Mary grabbed Jesus' arm and uttered her heartfelt thanks. Her joy was indescribable, but she felt that perhaps Jesus knew the weakness of her faith.

He smiled at her through his tear stained face.

"Mary, do you believe that I am the resurrection and the life?"

"Yes Rabboni, I believe." She gave her response without quite understanding but wanting to believe with all her heart whatever he told her.

"The one who believes in me will live, even though they die; and whoever lives by believing in me will never die."

How would they never die, she wondered. She didn't understand, but her heart was soaring at the miracle he had just performed. New tears flowed. This time, they were tears of joy. Jesus smiled and shook his head. He pulled her hand from his arm and motioned her forward. "Your brother is waiting for you Mary."

Lazarus had been unbound sufficiently to still remain modestly covered while unrestrained, setting him free to move. There was no sign of death, no sign of illness. His healthy complexion revealed a man who was fully alive. Mary rushed forward to embrace her brother anew. He welcomed her with open arms.

CHAPTER 38. THE BETTER PART

There is need of only one thing. Mary has chosen the better part and it will not be taken from her.
Luke 10:42

Mary relished the days that followed. She reacquainted herself with Lazarus and Martha, accompanied Jesus and the other disciples into Jerusalem on many occasions when he went to preach in the Temple, and looked forward to their evening meals. Jesus went between three different places each evening, attending to the crowds. He usually took his evening meal in their villa in Bethany. But sometimes he stayed in a nearby inn owned by Lazarus where several of the disciples were lodging. And on occasion he was welcomed into a public house owned by Simon the leper. It was spacious and open, useful for a larger crowd.[134]

Mary quickly became known as the woman who washed Jesus' feet. She couldn't help herself. She was moved with love watching him spend hours preaching, healing all who pleaded with faith, and attending all who sought him out. When evening came, she wished she could have him to themselves, just her and his closer disciples. But the crowds were too great. They all wanted something from him, and he never thought of his own fatigue or hunger. She took it upon herself to make sure that he received royal treatment wherever he went. She would take over the chore of washing his feet. Although, it was never a chore for her. Sometimes she was moved to tears, tears of joy at the wonders he worked, tears of sorrow over her own past, tears of gratitude for his goodness and mercy. There seemed to be no end to her copious stream of tears. She could tell that it embarrassed Martha. But Jesus quietly told Mary that tears were her gift. She was not to be ashamed.

The first night, after raising Lazarus from the dead, they had rejoiced late into the night. They retold the story of how Jesus had come to find out Lazarus had died and how he had waited two days before setting out. Martha scoffed at him, telling him that he had been testing her patience. Everyone laughed, aware that she needed the testing.

Thomas, sensitive to Martha's feelings, and not wanting her to feel that she was being laughed at, debased himself by telling about his reaction to Lazarus' death. When Jesus finally said they would go to Jerusalem the only thought that crossed his mind was, "That's the end! They are going to die like Lazarus!" So, not wanting to act like a coward, he had cried out, "Let us go up to Jerusalem to die!" An onslaught of laughter ensued at Thomas' exuberance and pride in himself for having been determined to die, knowing that he was usually so indecisive.

On the fourth night, they were still receiving visitor after visitor. They had finished their evening meal and retired to the garden. Mary, eager to not miss a word, and making the most of the crowds having dwindled as the night went on, had sat at Jesus' feet, listening attentively. Her heart was content and at peace. In the background, Mary could hear Martha bustling about, picking up dishes, straightening ornamentation, and sweeping up crumbs left by the nonstop visitors throughout the day. But Mary remained glued to her privileged spot.[135] Suddenly Martha attempted to squeeze in closer to Jesus to whisper into his ear but couldn't get any nearer with Mary sitting at his feet. Martha practically hissed through her teeth, "Lord, don't you care that my sister has left me to do the work by myself? Tell her to help me!"

Mary was concerned and embarrassed for her sister. She looked flushed and worn out.

"Martha," Jesus said with compassion.

A loud racket came from the direction of the kitchen. The sound of pottery smashing to the ground distracted Martha as she wrenched her neck around to see what had happened.

Jesus called out her name again, this time with persistence and firmness, catching her attention once again, "Martha!" Seeing that he had gained her attention, he spoke with solemn compassion. "You are worried and upset about many things, but few things are needed—or indeed only one. Mary has chosen what is better, and it will not be taken away from her."

Martha looked hurt and humbled. She retreated. Mary felt horrible for her sister, having endured the reprimand in front of others. The tables had been turned. All her life, Mary was the one being reprimanded and Martha was the perfect one, always righteous and good. But Mary couldn't gloat over it. She wouldn't trade her place at Jesus' feet, but perhaps she could help out more during the day so that the hospitality didn't rest so heavily on Martha. And perhaps she could also help Martha to relax and let the servants of the household do their work! Before going to bed, she saw Jesus and Martha speaking and prayed for her sister's peace of heart.

A couple of evenings later, after the crowd had finally gone home, Jesus stayed in the Bethany villa. Most of the disciples had gone off to the inn for the night. Lazarus, Martha, Ima, John, his brother James, Peter, and a handful of the women were peacefully enjoying the nighttime garden. Mary wanted to convince Jesus that he didn't need to go to so many places when he could stay in their villa every night. It was his home as much as theirs. Jesus surprised her with his answer.

"I know Mary. Even as a child I enjoyed your home."

She looked perplexed. "How? I never saw you here."

Ima shared. "We knew your parents since before you were born, Mary. God's providence brought us together on several occasions. When Joseph and I traveled from Nazareth to Bethlehem for the census, Joseph had found the only shelter he could under a tree near your father's inn when he and your brother happened to walk by. Your brother was just a child then, perhaps five or six. They found us there. Your father inquired kindly as to our lodgings and brought us to the inn. There wasn't room for us, but he managed to find a good pile of hay to make us a makeshift place for the night, out of the cold."

Lazarus jumped in, "And I went hunting in the kitchen for some food. Almost got my hand taken off by the cook that night!" They laughed, knowing Lazarus' resourcefulness and ability to negotiate even at a young age. He had been born with a brain for business and managed to expand the family's wealth over the years.

Martha continued the story. "I was only four at the time, but I remember Father and Mother sitting us down and sharing their excitement over their belief that Anna and Simeon's prophecy had been fulfilled.

Lazarus jumped in. "Father had guessed, correctly, that the Messiah's parents were the same couple we had helped at the inn. I remember Simeon too. Father brought him home for a meal on occasion and Simeon described you, Ima. Said that you had been lodging in Bethlehem. He passed away shortly after the news of the prophecy's fulfillment. But the news kept spreading until Herod had the children of Bethlehem massacred. Horrible day. I remember Father and Mother being so upset and worried."

Ima continued the story, "Yes, a tragic day. We escaped, while many did not." A solemn silence cast forth an invitation for a respectful remembrance. And then Ima continued, directing her words to Lazarus and Martha. "But imagine our delight to see you once again several years later."

Ima turned to Mary. "You must have been a babe then. Probably about three years old? Lazarus ran into us in the Temple area. And his generosity knew no bounds. We were searching for Jesus. He had gone missing for three days." She stressed "three days", sending a scolding look to Jesus.

Jesus laughed and winked at Mary. "I guess you could say that I too was a bit mischievous." Then turning to Lazarus, "But I had to give them a chance to meet up with Lazarus again!"

"I give thanks that we did," exclaimed Ima. "He offered us lodging every night in the Inn until we found Jesus. He even helped us search Jerusalem and the Temple area. In those three days, we forged a friendship, and we have always counted this as a second home when we passed through Jerusalem for the feast days. Of course, we missed a few years due to Joseph's health." She turned to Mary. "We just never crossed paths. While your father was ill, we stayed in the Inn, and then, once Lazarus sent you to Magdala, we began staying here when we passed through."

"I can't believe it. You were family without me even knowing it," Mary exclaimed. "Martha, you have known Jesus all these years?" Martha nodded her head with proud gratitude.

Jesus smiled mischievously. "Yes, you see, Martha had the better part for several years. It took you a while to catch up, Mary." Mary and Martha looked at each other with surprise at Jesus' joke, but fondness in their eyes. The combination of many late nights, exhaustion, and Jesus' joke broke the tension between the sisters. A contagious laughter broke out that soon turned into giggles and guffawing all around. Contentment reigned in Mary's heart as she laughed and observed Jesus' joy. But little did she know, it would not last long.

CHAPTER 39. THE RETREAT

At that time the kingdom of heaven will be like ten virgins who took their lamps and went out to meet the bridegroom.
Matthew 25:1

The ensuing days were bittersweet. Her bond with Lazarus was beyond her expectation. They felt like kindred spirits, as though they had not been apart one day of their lives. But an overarching tension tainted moments of joy. Since Jesus had risen Lazarus from the dead, they had both become the target of threats.

Lazarus downplayed it every time Mary suggested that he should retire to the villa in Magdala. No, he would say firmly, his business was here in Bethany and near Jerusalem. By business, he didn't only mean the care of his properties or negotiations. He meant the people who had begun to inquire about Jesus and come to believe that he was the Messiah. Besides, he would say, it was Jesus who received the greater threat against his life. He had been attracting much attention as he taught in the Temple or received visitors wherever he lodged. More followers, yet more danger followed him everywhere he went.

Fate seemed set in motion one fine evening. They were gathered in the garden courtyard, one of her favorite moments of the day, the treasured time after most of the visitors had finally left for home. Only his closest stayed, reminiscing of the day's events and simply enjoying Jesus' presence. A servant approached Lazarus with a message.

"It's from Nicodemus," Lazarus announced, furrowed brows revealing the seriousness of the missive.

He scanned the note as he shared pieces of it. "Some of the people who were among us these days were sympathizers with the chief priest Caiaphas and other Pharisees of the Sanhedrin. They believe that your activity is a threat to the Temple and even to the nation if the Romans intervene."

Lazarus paced back and forth. "It's true that there has already been a lot of unrest. Pilate is threatening to raise taxes so he can erect a statue to the Emperor and offer sacrifices to honor him. There is an increasingly growing group of Galileans who are revolting and perhaps planning an uprising."

Peter shared his conviction. "They mean to make a scapegoat of Jesus."

Lazarus nodded, scanning over the message again. "And they are concerned with your teachings Master. They think it borders on blasphemy." Lazarus looked up, deep lines of worry creasing his forehead. "Nicodemus thinks that they are plotting to capture and kill you."[136]

Peter stood quickly. "We need to go. Let me gather the other disciples, Jesus. Tell me where to meet you. We should go tonight."

The others were agreeing with Peter. Martha was already up, thinking of the preparations to be made for their trip. Jesus gestured for everyone to calm down.

"This should come as no surprise. But you needn't worry. My time has not yet come. I have told you many times, the Son of Man must undergo great suffering, and be rejected by the elders, chief priests, and scribes.[137] I have not hidden this from you. For this reason, I have come. The Son of Man will be betrayed into the hands of men. They will kill me, and after three days I will rise again."[138]

The air turned heavy. The weight of these words pressed upon Mary, even though she was not certain she could grasp them. Was he speaking literally or in parables again? After seeing him raise her brother from the dead, you would think she could believe anything! But should they expect Jesus to be killed and then come back from the dead?

"Nonetheless, it is wise for us to retreat from Jerusalem for a time. We will go to Ephraim at dawn," Jesus declared.

Everyone dispersed, getting ready for their departure in the early morn, just a few short hours away. Mary hung back, waiting to be alone with Jesus. But Lazarus approached him. He handed Jesus a hefty money bag.

"For Judas. More funds for your journey. There should be sufficient coins to sustain you for at least a week's journey. Do you think you will be back for Passover? Nicodemus stressed that this is very serious. The high priest himself has proclaimed that it is better for one man to die for the people than that the whole nation perish."[139]

Jesus thanked Lazarus. "Yes, we will return." He looked upward towards the heavens, closed his eyes and inhaled deeply. Opening his eyes, he sighed, looking as though he was gathering strength for a coming storm. Resoluteness washed over his countenance as he spoke again.

"I tell you, as I have told my other disciples, I have come to set the earth on fire, and how I wish it were already blazing! This will be my baptism and how great is my anguish until it is accomplished!"[140]

Mary came forward, vehemence in her heart towards the chief priest, "How could they hate you? You are only doing good for the people!"

Jesus responded, "Perhaps we have a prophet within the Sanhedrin. But I have not come to hide or to be served. I have come to serve and to be a ransom for many.[141] I will go away for a time, but I will return soon, for the Passover."

Mary interjected, "I will go with you. I will not leave you." She looked to Lazarus, hoping he would understand and not stop her.

Lazarus nodded.

"Very well Mary," Jesus assented. "But remember, if the world hates you, realize that it hated me first. If you belong to the world, the world would love its own; but because you do not belong to the world, and I have chosen you out of the world, the world hates you. If they persecute me, they will also persecute you. They will do many things to my followers on account of my name, because they do not know the one who sent me. The words written in the law must be fulfilled, 'They hated me without cause.'"[142]

Lazarus spoke up, determination and assurance in his demeanor. "They can hate us if they so desire. It will not change our loyalties to you Jesus. You are the Messiah, the holy one of God, the very Son of God who was to come into the world."[143]

Lazarus embraced Jesus as two brothers who were not sure they would see one another again. Mary slipped out to prepare herself for another journey.

***

Despite retreating to Ephraim, they remained busy. Jesus continued attracting attention everywhere he went. He preached in the synagogues, taught in open spaces, visited houses where he was welcomed, and healed the sick brought before him. Mary soaked it all in, imprinting every word and detail of his person on her heart. She observed and noticed, catching signs of tiredness or sorrow, reveling in his triumphs, content when his heart seemed at peace, agitated when she detected his growing unrest. She pondered his teachings, sometimes drawing near to ask about them or conversing with John and Matthew. Their friendship had begun in Galilee over two years ago and now she loved them like her very own brothers.

They loved to recount Jesus' teachings and deeds, pondering them together, trying to impress them more deeply in their memory so they would be able to transmit them to others. Their assistance in teaching was frequent. As Jesus personally attended to the people, they too would gather small groups or accompany individuals, speak to them and share Jesus' words and deeds. They joked that they had turned to farmers sowing the seed of Jesus' words wherever they went.

There was one conversation in particular that marked her during their long walks and talks. They had been recounting Jesus' conversation with a Pharisee in Galilee about a man divorcing his wife. It hadn't interested her at first, not having been married herself. But Jesus' final answer had struck her, resonating and tugging at her as though willing itself not to be forgotten.

"Some are incapable of marriage because they have been born so; some, because they were made so by others; some, because they have renounced marriage for the sake of the kingdom of heaven. Whoever can accept this ought to accept it."[144]

She remembered her and Martha's conversation while they were walking to Jerusalem, on her way to reunite with Lazarus. She realized that Martha had professed her decision to remain like the last one, renouncing marriage for the sake of the kingdom of heaven. *But which am I?*

She knew she was capable of marriage, but she had usually refused, or her situation hadn't lent itself to suitors with that intention. She didn't believe that she had been made incapable of marriage, however much she had been rejected by traditional society. But neither had she renounced marriage for the sake of the kingdom of heaven. She pondered what this latter one meant.

She recalled a recent encounter with a rich young man who had asked what he must do to gain eternal life. He was a law abiding and righteous young man. She had identified with him in his search to be better. She had experienced this as well, searching and longing for how to give herself more fully to Jesus but not knowing what that entailed. Jesus' response to the man had struck her.

"If you wish to be perfect, go, sell what you have and give it to the poor, and you will have treasure in heaven. Then come, follow me."[145]

She had anticipated that the rich young man would join their ranks, but instead he had walked away, a sorrowful disposition in his countenance. Then Jesus had told the disciples, "It is easier for a camel to go through the eye of a needle than for a rich man to enter the kingdom of heaven."[146]

She, Matthew, and John were recalling this encounter as they left Ephraim and headed to Jericho. They settled into a comfortable rhythm of walking, talking, sharing and pondering. They were marveling at the multitude of different people they met. Each story was so unique. Each one answered differently to Jesus' request or command. It struck her that Jesus had asked diverse things from them. To some he invited to follow. Others he told to stay behind. Still others, he asked to leave behind family or riches. And to others, he seemed to make no demand at all. They were simply to return to their homes.

Mary knew that Matthew had quite the fortune before following Jesus. She asked him how he was able to leave that all behind.

"I just had to. I knew immediately. All my riches meant nothing in the face of Jesus saying, 'Follow me.' I just knew."

John jabbed Matthew in the ribs and teased him. "Jesus might have changed his mind if he had eaten dinner at your house before he told you to follow him!"

"I beg your pardon," Matthew play acted as if insulted. "I served a fine meal!"

"Only after your mother realized the poor man's dinner you were going to serve."

"Well, I didn't have any warning that I was going to feed a garrison of disciples that day."

They laughed, content to reminisce on the past.

John recalled his own journey. "I had been following the Baptist, so I guess you could say it wasn't so hard for me. My parents are very devout and anticipated the coming of the Messiah in their lifetime. They had heard that prophecies had been fulfilled several years ago. So, since the Baptist had been preaching about his coming it wasn't too hard to convince them to let me leave home. Besides, Andrew and I had already spent some time away from home with the Baptist. And when I told them I was leaving the fishing business for good to follow Jesus, I wasn't alone. My brother came too, with the excuse that he was looking after me. But I think he was searching as well. Even as a little kid I dreamt of helping the Messiah. I hope I can pass on what Jesus has been teaching. Matthew, I saw you jotting down things that Jesus has been saying. I have been keeping my own notes and thoughts too."

Matthew nodded. "Yes, maybe there are Jews, or even Gentiles, beyond the Jordan and who aren't able to come to meet Jesus, who we could share his teachings with. I have had the opportunity to be his disciple. They haven't. But maybe there are many who would have liked to belong to the group if they had the chance. Jesus has said that even tax collectors and prostitutes will get into the kingdom of God. I am sure there are more out there like us."[147]

John grimaced, ribbed Matthew and cleared his throat awkwardly, embarrassed that Matthew had alluded to Mary's prior reputation.

"Ow! What?" Matthew protested at the assault, ignorant of the offense he committed.

Mary knew that Matthew meant no harm by his insinuation. She shook her head and rolled her eyes at John, signaling to drop it and to not worry.

Mary shared from her own heart. "I have never felt like I belonged to anything as much as I have since I met Jesus. But how do I know if I truly belong to the kingdom of heaven? If I have given enough?"

"Well, Jesus will be happy even with two pence," Matthew replied. "Remember the widow who gave a mere two pence? It was nothing, but at the same time, it was everything. It was all she had. And it was enough. Jesus was happy with her."

John added, "Mary, two pence or a thousand. I don't think it is a matter of money. Perhaps you need to listen to your heart. God is greater than our hearts and knows everything. But if our hearts do not condemn us, we can have confidence in God and receive from him whatever we ask. Perhaps that is what we give. We only give what we have received from the Lord. Anyway, that is how I feel."

They pondered in silence as they continued their downward descent toward Jericho.

After several minutes, John picked up the conversation again. "Jesus had told the rich young man to keep the commandments and then to give away all he had. He told Peter and Andrew to leave their business behind and follow. But then there was the Gerasene demoniac. He told him to stay behind and tell all that had been done for him."

John's voice became more passionate, more convicting, as though drawing from a deep reserve of something that he had been pondering for some time.

"Listen to your heart, Mary. What is Jesus asking you? It is worth giving up all the riches of the world if that is what Jesus asks. But above all, we must do what pleases him. I think his commandment to us has been that we believe in his name. He is the Christ, the Son of the living God. You have done this. You believe. He also said that we should love one another as he commanded us. Yes, above all, love one another. That is the way we know that we belong to him and to the truth that he teaches."[148]

John had gone on speaking at the ground as he walked on, like one composing an oration and practicing on whatever creepy-crawly desert insects cared to listen. He finally stopped speaking and silence ensued as thoughts continued to churn. He suddenly realized that Mary was no longer at his side. He looked up and back. Mary stood there, a few feet back, looking at him with delightful amusement and admiration at the same time.

John flustered and blushed, "What?"

"Such wisdom for one so young John." She teased him, while commending him for his profound counsel.

Matthew piped in. "Jesus didn't tell me to sell everything. But I gave him everything anyway."

Mary smiled at Matthew's simple generosity. She thought of the money she still carried with her. Should she give that up? Was that enough? What would please him?

John, seeing her reflecting, offered her one more insight. "Mary, perhaps you have already given Jesus what he asks of you. You were under the power of the evil one, he set you free, and then you followed him. You gave him your heart. You know the strength of idols and the evil spirit in the world that leads to death. Perhaps he has given you the power of discernment to know the one who is true and the one who gives life. And you, above so many others, do know Jesus. Really, I mean it. Perhaps you know him better than any of us, even though we have been with him longer. Plus, you have helped many people come to that truth. I am sure he is very pleased with that. But don't take my word for it. Ask him yourself."

Jesus had approached the group. "Engrossed in conversation as always, I see. What problems are you solving today? Have you made a new plan for our journey or convinced my Father of anything behind my back?"

They laughed with him as the other disciples joined them. They stopped to take a rest and gathered around Jesus. As they opened their satchels and passed around food to share, Jesus declared, "Let me tell you some stories, parables that you can also use to teach others."

From a corner Judas mumbled, "Stories I hope we can understand."

"Whoever has ears, let them hear,"[149] Jesus replied without turning to look at Judas.

Jesus proceeded to tell a story of a wedding feast. "The kingdom of heaven may be likened to a king who gave a wedding feast for his son. He dispatched his servants to summon the invited guests to the feast, but they refused to come."[150]

Mary listened to every word, pondering the meaning of it. Her heart had immediately desired to be invited to the wedding feast. She was appalled that some had refused to come, sad for the ones who ignored the invitation, and distraught and angered that others mistreated and killed him. When the king enacted justice she felt satisfied but then realized she was once like the guests who refused and ignored Jesus. With horror, she thought, *Am I capable of betraying him as well?*

Her mind wrapped around his last words, trying to apply it to her own situation. "Many are called, but few are chosen." *Am I called? Am I chosen? I have chosen to follow Jesus. But am I chosen by him?*

Jesus launched into another parable about three men who were given a differing number of talents. Two of them invested them wisely and gave a return to the master who rejoiced at their success. But one hoarded it in fear and had nothing to return to the master. She was horrified to hear the ending of the story. He was called a useless servant and thrown into Gehenna. Then his last statement perplexed her.

"To everyone who has, more will be given, and he will grow rich; but from the one who has not, even what he has will be taken away."[151]

This was a contrast to giving away all one's riches to enter the kingdom of heaven. *So, should I invest the money I still have left?*

He launched into a third story, again referring to the kingdom of heaven. She liked this one, being about young virgins waiting for the bridegroom. She often felt like this. She was like the virgins waiting for the bridegroom, eager to be in Jesus' presence, hanging onto every word, gesture and look. As the story went on, dividing the foolish ones who spent their oil from the wise brides who saved theirs for his final coming, she wondered which ones she was like. *Am I more like the wise or the foolish virgins?*

"Stay awake," Jesus said firmly. "You know neither the day nor the hour."[152] *Stay awake?* A desire was growing in her heart, like an invitation to receive those words and all that it implied. *Be vigilant.* It dawned on her like the wise virgins' lights brightly shining and awaiting the bridegroom.

My heart must be vigilant. Like John said, I need to listen to my heart. It was indicating when truth was speaking, when evil was threatening, when to draw near and listen to Jesus, how to love her brother and sister, how to guard herself against temptation, and how to bring others to the light and truth, to Jesus.

He had left her much to consider. And her heart was full, full to overflowing, she thought. As they readied themselves to continue their walk, she hung back, longing to have a moment of solitude to contemplate what had inspired her as she had listened to Jesus. She "retreated into herself" as they walked in silence. She was grateful for these moments when they would just breath, walk, take in the scenery, each one in their own thoughts. No one was afraid to enjoy the silence. She wanted to make the most of this time to revisit the stories. Not so much every detail of each parable, but what had stirred within her. *Is that how to hear Jesus' call? What was he asking me through these parables? What message is there in those stories for my life? What am I supposed to do to please Jesus?*

"Keep your lamp lit Mary." Jesus' voice startled her, drawing her out of her interior contemplations.

"My lamp lit," she repeated. *The virgins.* She looked at Jesus with a heart burning to show him her love. She felt like a bride already standing next to her bridegroom. But she knew he was not hers to marry. It was never that kind of relationship. They had something far more precious, mysterious, pure. It was so new to her. She felt the connection between them as something familiar and, at the same time, holy.

Her heart responded, more than audible words. *Jesus, I will give you my heart, however you ask for it.*

His tender look answered that he knew and accepted the gift. A prayer of surrender rose to her lips. It was an echo of a psalm. From it sprang acts of trust and praise for his mercies. Soon, a prayer of supplication took shape as she felt moved to pray for her people, a people she had rejected for so long, but to whom she had eventually come back. A new understanding of her place among them was dawning.

Lord, I give myself to you. My God, I trust you. Do not let me be disgraced. Do not let my enemies laugh at me. No one who trusts you will be disgraced. But those who sin without excuse will be disgraced.

Lord, teach me your ways. Show me how to live. Guide me in your truth. Teach me, my God, my Savior. I trust you all day long. Lord, remember your mercy and love. You have shown them since long ago. Do not remember the sins and wrong things I did when I was young.

The Lord is good and right. You instruct sinners to the right path. All your ways Lord are loving and true for those who follow your commandments. For the sake of your name, Lord, forgive my many sins and keep my eyes always looking to you for help. I trust you to keep me from traps of the evil one.

Turn to me and be kind to me. Protect me and save me. I trust you. Do not let me be disgraced. My hope is in you. So may goodness and honesty guard me. God, save Israel from all their troubles![153]

She offered this prayer to God as consolation enveloped her. Joy overflowed as she repeated to herself, *O Lord, keep my lamp lit.*

CHAPTER 40. DESCENT & ASCENT

You don't know what you are asking.
Can you drink the cup I am going to drink?
Matthew 20:22

They finally arrived in Jericho. Mary wondered why they were traveling there for such a brief stay. Passover was approaching and Jesus had expressed how he longed to be in Jerusalem for the great feast. *I should know better than to question the reasons why,* she thought to herself. What was unexpected for her, was obvious for Jesus. Every turn was providential. That is why she wasn't completely surprised, just humored, when, as they entered Jericho, Jesus stopped right below a sycamore-fig tree and looked up at a little man straddling precariously on a middle branch. How he managed to get up there was the real mystery. He must have asked for a boost because the lower branches were higher than his own height.

The people of Jericho had come out in full force to greet Jesus. They were crowding around him, but Jesus obviously had his heart set on meeting this one particular little person.

Matthew leaned toward Mary and whispered in her ear, "I told Jesus about him. Zacchaeus." Matthew blushed. "I met him when we were here before, but Zacchaeus wouldn't come to meet Jesus. Looks like he changed his mind." Matthew looked very pleased with himself. "He is a tax collector," he said matter of factly.

Mary understood. Matthew had been hoping that someone, like himself, would come to know and follow Jesus. She smiled, proud of Matthew and of his zeal for others.

"Zacchaeus, come down immediately." Jesus hollered up.[154]

Zacchaeus teeter-tottered on the branch, joyful surprise in his face. In his race to climb down his foot slipped. The crowd gasped in unison.

"Steady now," Jesus chuckled. "I mean to stay at your house today. If you survive the descent!"

Zacchaeus managed to slip down to the ground, fumbling with his tunic as he composed himself.

"Rabboni," he dipped his head in a sign of respect, twisting his hands nervously. "I would be honored to welcome you to my home."

Matthew approached him and slapped him on the back. Zacchaeus recognized his new friend and offered a greeting and words of gratitude for their return. Zacchaeus turned to Jesus and gestured eagerly for them to follow him to his home.

The crowd parted, allowing them passageway to follow Zacchaeus who was hurrying forward as fast as his little legs could take him. Onlookers gaped in awe, others muttering their disapproval. "He has gone to be the guest of a sinner."

Zacchaeus caught wind of their comments and stopped. He turned to Jesus, standing straight as though it would give him the advantage of greater height. Agitatedly, he searched his pockets and pulled out a rattling bag of coins.

"Look, Lord! Here and now, I give half of my possessions to the poor, and if I have cheated anybody out of anything, I will pay back four times the amount." He looked around at the crowd as though threatening to throw the money bag at them.

Jesus placed his hand on Zacchaeus' shoulder, assuring him that all was well. "Zacchaeus, today salvation has come to this house."

He looked out to the crowd and proclaimed, "This man, too, is a son of Abraham. For the Son of Man came to seek and to save the lost."

They entered Zacchaeus' house while the crowd stayed outside, eventually scattering between the various windows, hopeful to see the curious event inside. Murmurings floated around outside as the onlookers passed on the message of Jesus' proclamation and exclaimed their wonder or disdain. The approval or disapproval of the mass did not matter to the host inside. His attention was solely fixed on receiving the Lord. Since Jesus' last visit, the desire to meet him had slowly built inside Zacchaeus, turning from resistance to receptivity as he considered the stories that Matthew had shared with him. Finally, his anticipation had borne fruit in Jesus' return and he didn't dare miss this second chance.

Mary watched the camaraderie and joyful gathering. She marveled at her friends gathered around the table for this "spontaneous" meal. And she gave thanks for Jesus' disarming way of welcoming even the outcast. No one was too high or too low on the social ladder to merit the kingdom of heaven. Their difference, she reflected, was of no consequence. What mattered was their belief in Jesus. They could be literally the littlest and socially the lowest, but it didn't matter to Jesus. The kingdom of heaven was opened to all who would hear and receive him.

***

The next morning, after their brief stay in Jericho and parting with Zacchaeus, they set out to return to Jerusalem. He sent several disciples ahead of him to make preparations. Only the closer band of Twelve and a handful of women remained with Jesus. They left early as the stars were still fading into dawn's light. But they were not able to escape without notice. Slumberous dwellers crept out of their houses. As they walked, Jesus' companions grew from his small band of disciples to fifty, seventy-five, one hundred people. The noise and excitement increased as they came to the edge of the city limit.

Suddenly a man shouted out, "Lord, have pity on me, son of David!"[155]

She turned to see a blind man sitting on the side of the road, the crowd scolding and hushing him into silence. Her sense of compassion kicked in. She stepped toward him with a protective longing, wanting to defend him from the annoyed crowd. She made her way to him, then heard Jesus call out, "Come!"

She looked toward Jesus as the crowd parted, making way for the man to advance.

"Courage, stand up. He is calling you," she encouraged him.

Reaching down, she helped the blind man to his feet. His movement unleashed a stench from his filth and sweat, almost causing her to release her grip and instinctively cover her nose and mouth. She held her breath and went on, guiding the man towards Jesus.

"What is your name?" She asked as they neared Jesus.

"Bartimeus, son of Timaeus. I have been waiting for the Son of David. I know he can cure me."

They stood before Jesus.

A hush settled over the crowd as Jesus said to him, "What do you want me to do for you?"

With a conviction that didn't doubt Jesus' power he said, "Master, I want to see."

The crowd silently watched and waited. Compassion and love crossed Jesus' face as he took hold of Bartimeus' head in his hands and spread his thumbs over the man's eyes. He inclined his head toward the man speaking, "Go your way; your faith has saved you."[156]

Jesus released him. Bartimeus blinked as astonishment brought tears to his eyes and a wave of news floated through the crowd.

"He can see!" "Bartimeus can see!" "Jesus cured him!"

A procession of joy and wonder accompanied Jesus and his disciples as they continued on their path, exiting the city to shouts and songs of jubilation.

As they ascended towards Jerusalem, the crowd slowly petered out. The people of Jericho had returned to their homes, and the disciples were once again left alone with Jesus. Finally, a quiet peace reigned over them as they walked the sunbaked path.

Mary drank in the splendor of the morning, drawing strength from an inner solitude she had begun to feel during their walk through the desert. She kept her eyes fixed on Jesus. Once again, she sensed a heaviness upon his spirit.

Is he worn out from all his travel? From all the people? I certainly am. I don't know where he musters up the strength day in and day out.

He would be with the people for hours at a time, taking no food. Then he would return to the disciples and continue to teach and converse with them. She had also seen him withdraw many times from the disciples, going to a solitary place to pray. She asked him once, while she walked alone at his side, a treasured moment indeed, how he could continue and why he sometimes went off alone. To the why, he answered, "To be with my heavenly Father."[157] To the how, he responded, "My food is to do the will of the Father."[158]

As she was lost in her thoughts, contemplating what they had lived thus far, Jesus had stopped. He was beckoning the Twelve to his side. The others banded together, waiting for their meeting to finish. He did this sometimes. How she would like to know what was spoken among them in those moments. Sometimes Matthew or John would share afterwards. She watched now with curious eyes. Peter was shaking his head, upset with something Jesus had said.[159] Andrew held Peter's shoulders, calming him. They disbanded and Jesus waved to the others to follow.

Mary detected sorrow and a heaviness among the disciples now. But Salome seemed ignorant of the weighty moment. Or perhaps she had detected it correctly and was making the most of the opportunity. Whatever was the case, Salome had grabbed a hold of her sons, a hand gripped around each one's arm, and was dragging them back to Jesus. She pushed them in front of him, then suddenly knelt at his feet.

"Jesus, I want to ask a great favor of you," Salome pleaded. John and James flushed with embarrassment. They looked like they were debating whether or not to pick her up off the ground where she had prostrated herself before Jesus.

He asked, "What is it you want, Salome?"

"Jesus, please grant that these two sons of mine may sit at your right and at your left in your kingdom."

Jesus sighed, looking towards Jerusalem rather than down at Salome. "You don't know what you are asking." Turning to John and James he said, "Can you drink the cup I am going to drink?"

They nodded, eager to show their willingness. "We can," they answered.

Jesus frowned pensively and put his hands on the shoulders of John and James. "You will indeed drink from my cup, but to sit at my right or left is not for me to grant. These places belong to those for whom they have been prepared by my Father."

He stooped to encourage Salome to rise. "And you, Salome, pray for your sons and daughters that their faith may not fail."

Making sure she was on her feet once again, he turned, set his face toward Jerusalem and continued forward.

The other disciples murmured among themselves, indignant at the thought that John and James had conspired to attain privileged spots with Jesus in His kingdom. Mary was also irritated that some of the disciples were vying for positions.

Jesus turned and addressed them. "You know that the rulers of the Gentiles lord it over them, and the great ones make their authority over them felt. But it shall not be so among you. Rather, whoever wishes to be great among you shall be your servant; whoever wishes to be first among you shall be your slave. Just so, the Son of Man did not come to be served but to serve and to give his life as a ransom for many."[160]

His proclamation silenced them once again as they trudged onward and upward.

Mary peered toward Jerusalem. She couldn't see the city. They still had a long ascent ahead of them. The sun was at their back, already warming their way. All had grown silent. She followed suit, reserving her energy for the steep and long climb. She sensed she would need to conserve her strength, in more ways than one, for whatever was to come.

CHAPTER 41. ANOINTING THE KING

Rise and anoint him; this is the one.
1 Samuel 16:12

They returned, as discreetly as possible, to the villa in Bethany. Jesus sent out many of his disciples to prepare for an event tomorrow morning. Mary overheard Peter talking to Judas about several purchases, including a donkey and a colt. They were to have a procession.

If we wish to remain anonymous, this is not the way to do it, Mary thought with consternation. Speaking to the other women, they all agreed. But Ima tried to settle their worries. She spoke with great confidence that Jesus knew his hour. And if it had come, it was necessary that he reveal himself as the Messiah.

"Recall the prophecy of Zechariah and let us pray for faith and trust in the coming of salvation," she encouraged.

Mary Jacobe recited the prophecy prayerfully.

"Say to Daughter Zion, 'See, your king comes to you, gentle and riding on a donkey, and on a colt, the foal of a donkey.'"[161]

Mary added her own prayer for protection over Jesus and over them all, echoing a psalm.

"Protect us Lord from the fowler's snare. Cover us and let us take refuge under your wings. May your faithfulness be our shield and rampart. Let us not fear the terror of night, nor the arrow that flies by day, nor the pestilence that stalks in the darkness, nor the plague that destroys at midday. A thousand may fall at your side, ten thousand at your right hand, but it will not come near you. May we make our dwelling in you the Most High. Be our refuge that no harm may befall us, no disaster will come near. Command your angels to guard us all."[162]

Especially Rabboni, she added, intensely praying in the depth of her heart.

***

By late evening several women and a handful of other disciples along with the Twelve, minus Judas, had gathered together in the villa of Bethany. Judas, she assumed, was still taking care of the preparations for tomorrow. One of the upper terraces offered fresh night air and a setting for their intimate encounter. Scattered campfires dotted the hillside and valleys between Bethany and Jerusalem. Jerusalem sat like a beacon on the not so distant Mount Moriah about two miles away. Mary found it prophetic-like, a vigil for the Messiah to come.

Jesus spoke long into the night.[163] He would enter the city as a king would enter his kingdom. He spoke of how the Father had prepared him for this moment since before he was formed in his mother's womb. The womb of a virgin that bore the fruit of Isaiah's prophecy, foretold eight centuries before. Looking at Ima, he quoted it, "A virgin will conceive and give birth to a son; and they will call him Immanuel, God is with us."[164]

He spoke of the first parents' sin in the garden, of the kingdom of God encroaching upon them through a suffering to come in another garden. But death would not overcome life. Darkness would not overcome light. He spoke of a new garden of paradise to come in which sin and suffering would be no more. He spoke of himself as the one who would strike at the head of the serpent once and for all.[165] And he warned and strengthened them for what was to come.

"Truly I tell you, I have seen Satan fall like lightning from the sky.[166] But just as Eve was deceived by the serpent's cunning, be on your guard. The devil is cunning and looking to devour his prey.[167] You will suffer for believing in the one who has come so all may come to the knowledge of truth and many will be saved.[168] Stand firm in your faith[169] and do not let your minds be led astray from your sincere and pure devotion to me.[170] The Son of God has come to destroy the work of the devil.[171] He was a murderer from the beginning, not holding to the truth, for there is no truth in him. He is the father of lies[172] and comes like a thief in the night to steal and kill and destroy; I have come that they may have life, and have it to the full.[173] So remember, your struggle is not against flesh and blood, but against the rulers, against the authorities, against the powers of this dark world and against the spiritual forces of evil in the heavenly realms. Fear not. The kingdom of God is at hand.[174] But my kingdom is not of this world."[175]

She listened eagerly, trying to seal every word and expression in her heart. Everything resounded within, reminding her of remnants of her father's story-telling, various tidbits of conversations she had had with the disciples, and what she had already witnessed while accompanying Jesus. While it was familiar, it took hold of her in a new way. Hope strengthened her, hope of a victory she could not fully comprehend. Hope rose like an emotion that could not be tampered. Hope of so many others coming to know the liberation that she had received from Jesus.

It was all too much to take in. She could not contain it. Overcome by awe and mystery, overcome by the love she perceived in Jesus, she determined to fight against the evils of the world, evils she had experienced firsthand. As she listened, fear crept in like wisps of undetected smoke. Suddenly, fear of the enemy threatened to seize her. But just as quickly, faith in her Rabboni rescued her. A wave of love and reverence gushed forth like a dam bursting open. Tears flowed steadily. She reached into her satchel for the alabaster jar of aromatic spikenard that she brought with her all the way from Magdala. The conversation around her continued, but she slowly drew near to Jesus' feet, a place of privilege that she continued to claim as her own. Everyone had become accustomed to seeing her there. But this time she opened the fragrant vessel. Soothingly and generously, she poured the oil over his feet.[176] Tears mixed with oil as she bent over to kiss them. Taking a large bundle of her hair, she spread the wet mix over the length of both of his feet, drying them. A sweet, earthy, musky scent invaded the room as all went silent. The conversation had ceased.

An angry voice cut through the intimate moment. "Why was this oil not sold for three hundred days' wages and given to the poor?"

Judas had returned from his errands just in time to witness the expensive spikenard being poured out without thought of the cost. He knew of Mary's previous extravagant lifestyle and how she carried several of her costly possessions with her on the journey from Galilee to Jerusalem. More than once he had avariciously alluded to how well her items would serve them. But she hadn't handed them over. She had purposely waited for Jesus to tell her how to make use of them. But he had never asked for them. He always insisted that it was not yet needed.

"Leave her alone," Jesus firmly defended her.

Protected. Mary felt protected against Judas' harsh judgment. Her love poured out had won her the reward of security, like a shield against the enemy. Gratitude and love bore a fresh outpouring of tears.

"Let her keep this for the day of my burial. You always have the poor with you, but you do not always have me."

Grudgingly, Judas left the room.

Eventually the others dispersed as well. Mary remained, eager to speak with Jesus. Judas' words had stung. Initially she had felt defended by Jesus. Now doubts crept in. She was not doing enough. She was not giving enough. At the first chance, she addressed him.

"Rabboni, I wish to give what I have to the poor if that is what you want."

"Do not fear, Mary. I know what lies in your heart. But if you wish to offer something, I have received word that there are several prisoners in miserable conditions. They are neglected miserably. The Pharisees have driven up their debt to the point that it is impossible for their families to pay their release."

Mary nodded, speaking hastily, "I will give you the entire sum of what I have from the property I sold. And if that is not sufficient, I will sell the rest of my property."[177]

"What you have frequently offered to hand over, is more than sufficient. It is a generous gift and will bear greater fruit than you realize."

The gift was accepted. It was a hefty sum for the ransom of many. In the upcoming days Lazarus assisted in carrying out this task. As Jesus had foreseen, it bore much fruit. Several of those who were freed, along with their entire families, began to follow Jesus.

CHAPTER 42. HOSANNA IN THE HIGHEST

Rejoice greatly, Daughter Zion! Shout, Daughter Jerusalem! See, your king comes to you, righteous and victorious, lowly and riding on a donkey, on a colt, the foal of a donkey.
Zechariah 9:9

Early the next morning, Mary prepared herself. Anticipation and tiredness combined to create a nervous eagerness for the events to come. She intuited that this was a definitive moment for all of them. Jerusalem and the surroundings were already bustling with activity and people preparing for Passover. Encampments of huts and tents all around the city walls more than tripled the population. Roman soldiers were stationed at every turn. Vendors were hoping to make their fortune from the influx of pilgrims. Gates and roadways were decorated with festive garlands. The air was full of anticipation.

Mary had carefully chosen her garment this morning. It was her white linen cloak, worthy of a bride. She thought back to the prophecy Ima had recited. Jesus was to reveal himself as a king. That was how she understood the preparations. The precious and elegant cloak would be an appropriate attire to accompany a king. Her face flushed at the realization of her vanity, but she pushed it aside. She was proud of her beauty and proud that she had come to temper her past desire to flaunt it. Even Martha had praised her for the way she had embraced greater simplicity.

They walked about thirty minutes to Bethphage where they met some of the disciples. John was holding the reins of a lively little donkey colt, soothing it with whispers and gentle pattings. Its mother stood nearby, more subdued.

John pulled the small beast toward Jesus. "This one is pretty lively. It has never been ridden. I put the cloak on the mother."

Judas protested, "I wish you had let me get a horse to use. It would have made a greater impact on the people when we enter Jerusalem. I could have acquired it with a little more time."

Jesus simply stated, "Lay the cloak on the colt. He will carry me. It is as it should be."

John, perplexed, nonetheless obeyed. He removed the cloak he had draped over the donkey and placed it on the young colt. People had already started gathering at different points in the road, as the disciples had spread the news the day before. The seventy who had been gathering and ministering with Jesus, had placed themselves at different locations on the road to the city gates and up to the Temple area along the route they had planned for the entire procession.[178]

Jesus mounted the skittish colt. He looked more ridiculous than regal with his strong physique set upon the little animal. But the colt did not rebel. It calmed under his weight, allowing John to lead it forward. The rest of the Twelve went ahead, while the women followed a safe distance behind the colt.

Mary took a place at Ima's side directly behind Jesus, giving some space in case the little animal changed its mind about the burden it carried. Ima's demeanor was solemn, her eyes set contemplatively on Jesus. Her strained countenance was tempered with reverence in her eyes and gait. Mary wondered how she managed to withstand the tension that her son created with the authorities.

The procession was attracting participants. They distributed palm branches and waved them in the air as they sang psalms of praise and joy. What would have been a walk of thirty minutes became a slow snaking movement of three hours through the gathering crowds. Bethphage lay behind them as they began the descent through the Mount of Olives toward Jerusalem's city walls. They zigzagged their way through olive groves as they headed toward the Kidron Valley. The festive environment increased. Dancing and waving of branches accompanied their songs and shouts.

"Hosanna to the Son of David!"

"Blessed is he who comes in the name of the Lord!"

"Hosanna in the highest heaven!"

Men, women, young and old, approached and asked who this man was.

"Jesus, the Messiah, the one who was to come."

Others in the crowd answered, "Jesus, the prophet from Nazareth in Galilee."

A few scoffed and watched them pass by. But most ran after him, captivated by the atmosphere and the man with the bearing of a dignitary on top of a little colt. Olive trees offered their branches as homage for a king. People pulled off branches or began laying their cloaks down in front of the donkey and colt before Jesus would pass over.

The crowds thickened as they continued on their slow pace. About halfway down, the caravan stopped. She pushed her way closer, stopping alongside Jesus and the colt. To her dismay, Jesus was in tears.

No! You should be rejoicing! They are finally acknowledging that you are the Messiah, the king who was to come in the name of David!

Jesus cried out, "O Jerusalem, Jerusalem, the city that kills the prophets and stones those who are sent to it! How often would I have gathered your children together as a hen gathers her brood under her wings, and you were not willing![179] If you, even you, had only known on this day what would bring you peace—but now it is hidden from your eyes. The days will come upon you when your enemies will build an embankment against you and encircle you and hem you in on every side. They will dash you to the ground, you and the children within your walls. They will not leave one stone on another, because you did not recognize the time of God's coming to you."[180]

A surge of reverence overtook Mary at the sight of his suffering yet noble bearing. Without thinking, she untied her beautiful cloak and spread it before him, desiring to pay him the homage that was his due.

She was barely able to step back in time, avoiding harms' way. The procession continued. The colt walked on, trampling her precious cloak underfoot. She watched as it was ground into the dirt-packed road. Feet and more feet ignored the treasure she had offered.

No regret. Her favorite item was ruined. But she felt no regret. Only gratitude. She was grateful to be a part of those who came to pay tribute to him. It was a worthy homage, like a sacrifice for a king. She slipped back into line to follow the procession, noticing that Ima had waited for her. Ima looked at her with a mother's pride.

"A fine gift for a king and bridegroom Mary. A fine gift for my Son. Thank you."

Mary attempted to choke back tears. As usual, she was unsuccessful. Overwhelmed by the humility of Jesus and the grandeur of the praise he was receiving, she gave in. She did not hide their silent flow, another homage to the king, as they continued down the hill.

The path dipped into the Kidron Valley and up towards the Golden Gate that led to the Temple. As they arrived at the Temple's entrance-way, the flow of the procession halted. The sacred area had turned into a thriving marketplace. Jesus, enraged, slipped off of the colt and began overturning tables and benches. Chaos was all around. Children continued crying out, "Hosanna in the highest!" Vendors shouted at Jesus, threatening violence, agitated at having their stands destroyed. Mary sought out her other companions, afraid for herself and the women. They banded together, holding onto one another against the pressing crowds and agitated vendors. She searched the crowd for Jesus. Where had he gone? Then she spotted him. And at the same time, she observed a group of Pharisees rushing toward him. They scolded him for the commotion and ordered him to rebuke his disciples.[181]

Jesus exclaimed, "I tell you, if they keep silent, the stones will cry out!"

They rebuked him again, "Do you hear what these children are saying?"[182]

She couldn't make out his words to them. Something about children's lips and praise. She was distracted by Ima. Her face was pale as a ghost's, and she looked as though death had descended upon her. Hastily Mary caught the attention of the other women, indicating that they needed to get out of the jostling crowd and escalating tension. She caught sight of John who looked just as shocked by the frightful turn of events. He stood nearby still holding the little colt. She extracted a promise from him that he would send word to Jesus and the disciples that Ima and the women were returning to Bethany.

How quickly events had turned. From one minute to the next the tables had turned, figuratively and literally. An ominous foreboding overshadowed her previous wonder and joy as she maneuvered Ima through the onslaught of people who had quickly turned from praise to persecution.

CHAPTER 43. A TRUSTING HEART

*Trust in the Lord with all your heart and lean not on your own understanding; in all
your ways submit to him, and he will make your paths straight.*
Proverbs 3:5-6

Once home, Mary kept watch over Ima, whose countenance hadn't changed. Her eyes were closed, while her lips were silently moving. Mary had encouraged her to rest, but had the feeling that Ima was praying incessantly more than resting. Mary stayed with Ima as the other women went about the business of preparing a meal in case Jesus and the disciples returned soon. She contemplated Ima, her beautiful countenance etched in agony.

How must she be suffering, Mary thought. *Can she not do something to stop her own Son from self-destruction?* The events did not turn out at all as she had anticipated. Finally, Mary broke the silence with her pressing question.

"Ima," Mary spoke softly in case she was indeed resting. Ima stirred and opened her eyes, receptive to Mary. "Ima, how can you stand it? How can you stand that Jesus puts himself in danger? Can't you convince him to return to Galilee or at least to not draw so much attention to himself? I fear for him. How do you endure this?"

Ima sat up, reached over and squeezed her hand, holding it tenderly. Mary scolded herself internally. She should be the one consoling this mother, and yet Ima sought to console her.

"I learned long ago that Jesus has his reasons. In the moment, they are beyond my understanding. But I believe as King David prayed, 'The Lord has established His throne in the heavens, and His sovereignty rules over all.'[183] Jesus is doing what he must do. It is his Father's will. I, for my part, must trust."

Trust. Trust what? That Jesus' provocations were all part of the plan? What plan? She didn't understand why it had to be this way!

Ima brought her back to the present situation.

"Do you remember the story of Queen Esther, Mary? She had been born into a circumstance beyond her control. But the Most High prepared her to intercede for her people. She was frightened and initially resisted doing anything for them for fear of her own death. But Mordechai, her uncle, prophesied that she had come to her royal position for such a time as that.[184] Thus it is with my Son. And I believe it is the same for you and me, Mary. We cannot stop what is to be, but we intercede with supplications. We offer ourselves to be faithful to Jesus so he can carry out the plan of the Father, and we merely do our part, whatever that may be."

Ima's face was etched with sorrow. But her mouth curved into a faint smile as she recalled an earlier time in her life. "Did you know that I was a Temple virgin? My parents were God-fearing people and brought me to the Temple at an early age.[185] I was to stay there until I reached the marriageable age of fourteen. My companions would often speak of their desire to be the one chosen to bear the Messiah. There was great hope that the time was drawing near, and the promised one would be born to a Jewish bride, to one prepared as a virgin for that moment.

When I was nine or ten, a deep longing took hold of me. I often thought, 'What is the greatest gift I could give to the Lord for all the wonders he has worked for our people?' I realized that the greatest sacrifice would be to give up motherhood. I kept this inside for years until I finally shared it with one of our teachers. Ana, a prophetess. She told the high priest of my desire to remain a virgin. I just couldn't fathom myself being chosen as the mother of the expected one. But the high priest had a different opinion. He chose a spouse for me. I prayed and found peace that the God who created the heavens and the earth had a plan even in this. And a better one I could not have chosen myself. Joseph was a good and upright man. To my surprise, Joseph had felt the same way. He too desired to remain chaste. We had a holy matrimony, watching and wondering about this son, Immanuel, as the messenger of God had told me to name him. It has never been without its sufferings. But the hand of the Lord has guided us always. So, you see, Jesus was not in our particular plans."

She paused, sorrow passing over her face once again as she continued. "Being at the Temple today, watching Jesus ride in like the king of the prophecy of Zechariah, and then accosted by the Pharisees, I was reminded of another prophecy. Years ago, when Joseph and I presented Jesus in the Temple for the purification rite, we met Simeon. And I saw Ana, the prophetess, once again. Ana spoke of the babe as the redemption of Jerusalem. And I will never forget meeting Simeon. He took Jesus in his arms and praised God, proclaiming that his eyes were looking at the light for revelation to the Gentiles and the glory of the people Israel. Then he blessed us and said, 'This child is destined to cause the falling and rising of many in Israel, and to be a sign that will be spoken against, so that the thoughts of many hearts will be revealed. And a sword will pierce your own soul too.'"[186]

Ima closed her eyes again, breathing as though she were enduring the piercing of the sword right before Mary's eyes. Mary felt sick to her stomach with tension and confusion.

Ima believes what Jesus himself had foretold. Why can't I? She wanted to convince Ima that it didn't have to be like this. She didn't have to suffer. Perhaps there was another way. She opened her mouth, about to launch into her debate, but was silenced by Ima's countenance. An aura of peace and acceptance reigned, despite the deep sorrow in her eyes which Mary longed to wash away.

The shuffling of feet drew their attention to the doorway. Martha, Salome, Mary Jacobe and other women who had accompanied Jesus from Galilee entered bringing refreshments. They installed themselves in the courtyard with Ima. Their chatter chased away the silent contemplation that had preceded their noisy company.

Mary couldn't remain among them. She took to wandering aimlessly, listlessly between the courtyard and upper terrace. Dusk came and still no news. Neither Jesus, nor any of the apostles, had returned. On the eastern horizon the moon was rising, full and tinted the color of blood. A fearful apprehension threatened to choke her. She debated several times if she should return to the Temple, but she didn't want to risk missing Jesus if he decided to return by another route. Finally, she planted herself firmly on the terrace that overlooked the path to the front entrance. She would be the first to see him when he returned from Jerusalem. Like a watchman on guard, she waited and prayed for Jesus' safe return.

***

Hours later the full moon had come to its highest peak in the night sky and neither Jesus nor the Twelve had returned. Finally, a distant figure approached. A large bobbing shadow, cast by the light of the full moon accompanied whoever it was. Not Jesus. John. He came with news, sent by Jesus to let them know that he and the disciples had left the Temple and had gone to the Inn for the night. Jesus would continue teaching in the Temple tomorrow. Her heart sank. There was no stopping him. Trying to summon an ounce of peace, she mulled over her conversation with Ima. *The Father's plan. A purpose. It is as it should be.* It did not calm the nervous palpitations, but she retired to her chamber, mustering up her will to trust. She prayed for an increase of faith, to accept however the Father's plan would unfold.

CHAPTER 44. PROPHETESS

Moses replied, "Are you jealous for my sake? I wish that all the Lord's people were prophets and that the Lord would put his Spirit on them!"
Numbers 11:29

The next four days went by in a blur. Jesus and his disciples went daily to the Temple while Jesus preached. Mary went early in the day with Ima and some of the other women. They always brought food with them to assure that Jesus and the disciples ate during the day. Salome scolded her sons several times those days for not taking proper nourishment, nor stopping the constant flow of people demanding attention from Jesus, so he could also take care of himself.

Mary watched Jesus like a protective mother hen, keeping her respectful distance when he was among his listeners in the Temple. But when evening came and the disciples returned to the Inn where they were lodging, Mary accompanied them for the nighttime conversations that always took place. His closer disciples, having grown beyond the Twelve, plus the seventy whom he had sent out in his name, would converse together into the late night. Mary, eager to not miss a word, always took up her privileged spot at his feet. Martha insistently attempted to convince her to come away to their villa each night as, little by little, the crowd thinned. But Mary remained until only the Twelve, Mary, and a handful of perseverant followers remained.

Mary's emotions were like a storm tossed-sea. Like a watchdog in the Temple, she pointed out to John those she identified as deceivers in the midst of them. They antagonized Jesus, throwing out questions to trap or agitate him. Anger and a defensive instinct flared up. Ima, so often her companion these days and attuned to Mary's emotional turbulence, squeezed her hand or gently touched her arm, coaxing her to placate her rising suspicions and ire.

Since their conversation after Jesus' triumphal entrance into Jerusalem, Mary was determined to keep a watchful eye on Ima. An ever greater fondness for her was growing as she observed this humble woman draw from an abundance of inner strength. Her prior self-appointed task of caring for Rabboni's mother quickly turned to a genuine affective bond, like mother and daughter. Mary quickly realized that she was failing at the task she had pridefully resolved to undertake. *Who was caring for who?* She silently chastised herself, recognizing the natural development taking place in their relationship. Truly it was Ima who cared for Mary. And she did it through her silent, unassuming and consoling presence.

From indignation to wonderment, Mary became lost in contemplation of the men, women, and children who listened then rejected or received Jesus' teachings. Amidst the tension caused by the sharp eyed religious leaders and ominous vigilance of the Temple guards, Mary found reasons to rejoice. The Pharisees, Sadducees, and scribes skirted around the edge of the crowds, keeping a watchful eye. Mary internally celebrated when she noticed Jesus' calm composure, always answering with an authority that captivated the listeners.

The religious leaders were no match for her Rabboni. His simplicity and lack of arrogance disarmed many of the curious bystanders and they were drawn in by the combination of his noble bearing, simple authority, and gentle goodness. The contrast with his antagonists accentuated Jesus' charisma even more. Their arrogance, haughtiness, and pride left a bad taste in Mary's mouth. She wished they would disappear and leave them alone. But at least they did not obstruct anyone coming before Jesus in supplication. The sick, blind, lame, possessed, and every petition imaginable continued to draw near.

Two days before the Passover and the Feast of the Unleavened Bread,[187] as the day's light was coming to an end and the fires were lit in the Temple, John sent word to the women that they would not return to the Inn that night. Mary thought perhaps it was because of the increased speculation that the chief priests and scribes were seeking a way to arrest Jesus. It was best they didn't stay in the same place too long. The women returned to the Villa in Bethany where they were lodging every night. But as the night went on, not one disciple returned. Dusk had turned to darkness. *Had they stayed behind longer?* She thought that they were coming behind them shortly after they retreated from the Temple. *Where are they?* Anxiety rushed in like an unwelcome gecko.

She ran to her quarters and grabbed her satchel, heavy from her day's purchase. She had refilled the alabaster jar with the precious spikenard. Rushing out the door she almost crashed into John, sent as the messenger once again. She quickly extracted from him the information of Jesus' whereabouts. Simon the Leper's dwellings. He owned a large public house fit for hosting large parties there in Bethany. She knew where it was and had been there a couple of times when Jesus had used it for large gatherings. John offered to accompany her there as soon as he delivered the news to the others. Agitated at the thought of waiting a moment longer, she began to leave, shuddering at the cold. She returned to search for her cloak, then realized it was now counted as property sacrificed for Jesus. No matter, she would endure the cold.

Martha, hearing the commotion at the front door, had divinized Mary's intentions.

"Mary, wait. We will accompany you. You should not go out alone. Not now. The streets are full and there has been news of unrest with Galilean dissenters."

John stepped forward, torn between leaving with Mary and going in search of Ima. He offered once again, "I can take you. I just came to give a message to Ima. Please wait."

But Mary would have none of that. It was nearby, just a fifteen-minute walk from their own villa. She set off briskly, to the frustration of her sister. Despite the late hour, many rambled the streets. Pairs of Roman soldiers patrolled the street corners. An aura of disquiet gave rise to quicker steps. Head down to avoid being stopped, Mary steered clear of the soldiers and rowdy street mongers. She arrived at Simon's house, brightly lit, not hiding the gathering crowd. She slipped in quietly, making her way through the large public room as best she could, hoping to get a glimpse of Jesus, whose voice she already heard. Relief settled over her.

The house was packed. Familiar and unfamiliar faces were counted among the multitude, lounging wherever they could find space. Several she recognized as those who had accompanied them all the way from Galilee. They had gone out preaching and healing in Jesus' name. They nodded at her, acknowledging her presence as she slipped in further. She made her way along an outer wall toward the table where Jesus sat. She caught glimpses of him through the horde. His voice carried over the multitude, along with various voices interjecting with questions and comments.

One of the seventy was passionately stating his case to Jesus. "They are intolerable Master! We have been with you all this time. We listened to your teaching, so we are not ignorant of your message. And you sent us personally," emphasizing the last two words, "to teach and heal in your name. But these others! They speak on hearsay! How can we let these imposters do the same work when they barely know you! We even saw some of them driving out demons in your name. We need to put a stop to it before they do more harm."

A round of agreement rippled through the room.

Jesus waited for the noise to die down and spoke. "Do you remember in the times following Noah, the Most High gave the sons of Israel their inheritance. Seventy men were to go out and set up the boundaries for the people. So too are you sent. But there are boundaries which you will not reach on your own."[188]

A round of mumbling and perplexity spread over the listeners. Mary listened as she drew nearer. Jesus continued.

"And do you remember in the times of Moses how the people complained of hunger, despite having been saved from slavery. They threatened to turn back to Egypt. Moses, in desperation, cried out to the Lord to help him carry the burden of all the people that was upon him. The Lord said to Moses: 'Bring me seventy of Israel's elders who are known to you as leaders and officials among the people. Have them come to the tent of meeting that they may stand there with you. I will come down and speak with you there, and I will take some of the power of the Spirit that is on you and put it on them. They will share the burden of the people with you so that you will not have to carry it alone.'"[189]

Everyone listened attentively, some nodding and humming their assent, as though expressing their understanding of the message Jesus was communicating.

Jesus continued, "So Moses gathered the seventy elders, and the Lord came down in a cloud and spoke with him, and he took some of the power of the Spirit that was on him and put it on the seventy elders. When the Spirit rested on them, they prophesied—but did not do so again. But there were two who had not come to the tent. The Spirit of the Lord rested upon them, and *they* prophesied in the camp.[190] The Spirit gave to them what was needed to carry Moses' burden. Even now, the spirit blows where it wills,[191] preparing the way to reach all nations. Therefore, I tell you, do not stop them. For whoever is not against you is for you.[192] The harvest is plentiful, but the laborers are few, so let them labor in my name."[193]

Mary took in his words. She was not considered as part of the seventy, but she had taught in his name. She had shared Jesus' teachings with several groups of women they had met as they passed through the various villages. She had been amazed as she observed how the message went from her lips to their hearts. Their faces had transformed from skeptical curiosity to an open receptivity, and many had finally accepted the message. Their faces turned to joy and wonder as they did so. She had never experienced anything like it. Story-telling had always been a gift, but to tell the stories of Jesus' works and words had given her a new sense of purpose. She would like to count herself among the disciples, like the two extra elders in the times of Moses who had not entered the tent, but the Spirit had touched them.

She turned her attention once again to the conversation. They had picked up another thread. This time they were discussing his run in with a Sadducee earlier that day. A debate about the resurrection of the dead had arisen.

Matthew interjected, "I knew they were trying to trick you with that case…the one about the woman who married seven brothers…whose wife she would be at the resurrection. The crowd was astonished with your answer." Matthew, proud of his Master, turned sheepish as he stuttered out his question, fearful of a rebuke, "But, but...how is it possible? At the resurrection, people will neither marry nor be given in marriage?"[194]

Jesus responded, "I know this is difficult to understand now." Jesus looked around the room, smirking as he said, "An excellent wife is far more precious than jewels."[195]

Mary noticed a few of the men looking relieved, as though they had been asked to give up their wives or the possibility of one and finally realized that was not the case.

Jesus continued. "But the former way of things will pass away[196] and I will make all things new."[197]

As Jesus spoke, his gaze swept over the crowd. He caught her eyes when he came to her. He continued to speak. "In the kingdom of heaven, there will be no need for marriage, for you will be like the angels in heaven[198] who look always upon the face of the Father."[199]

His words and his look ushered in a soft ripple of joy. It was inexpressible and seized her, paralyzing her momentarily as waves and waves of the sheer love for God drove tears to her eyes. One tear, two tears, a light stream began to cascade down her cheeks as she felt compelled to honor him. Reverence and awe came over her for her Rabboni, as she so often called him. It was like nothing she had ever experienced. She reached into her satchel as she neared the place he was reclining. His gaze was still fixed upon her as onlookers watched the scene unfold, while others continued conversing, dismissing her presence. It was Mary Magdalene. She was going to take her place at his feet again, they thought.

Mary pulled the alabaster jar out, attempting to release the cork. It wouldn't budge. As if defying the devil's attempt to prevent her heartfelt adoration, she stepped behind him and smashed the flask's narrow top against the wall, releasing the balsam's power to become a gift. Mary poured her treasured perfumed oil over his head, spreading it over his hair. The fragrance wafted over the spectators. All eyes were now on the scene before them. She knelt down and took his hand in hers, palm up. She poured out more, wiping it tenderly with her hair.

She moved to his feet, expending the last drops of oil as she reverently kissed one and then the other. Tears flowed calmly. A deep joy chased away the last few days' tumultuous anxieties over his well-being. She wished she could stay there forever, like the angels who always looked upon the face of the Father. *Is this how it will be after the resurrection of the dead?*

Discordant voices grated against the peace that had consumed her spirit. As though awaking from a dream, her senses were bombarded by the stark consciousness of the mass and their indignant words flung at her from all corners of the room. The disturbance broke through the rapturous interlude like a rough grip upon her arm, tearing her from a blessed reality.

"Why this waste?", "Precious ointment", "A year's wages once again", "Three hundred days' wages at least." "Three hundred dinaris poured out!" "The woman is without sense."

She looked around bewildered, as an animal suddenly discovering itself captured in a cage.

"Why do you make trouble for the woman?"

She calmed at the sound of Jesus' voice. He came to her defense, again. Like a blanket on a cold night, protection wrapped around her.

"She has done a good thing for me."[200]

Pride swelled in her heart with gratitude, and another wave of joy and tears assaulted her.

A few among the witnesses continued to object. "It could have been sold and the money given to the poor."

Jesus responded, "The poor you always have with you; but you will not always have me. In pouring this perfumed oil upon my body, she did it to prepare for my burial."[201]

His last statement pricked her like an unexpected stab. A twinge of fear was quickly pushed aside as she rejected the thought of his burial and listened to his next words.

"Amen, I say to you, wherever this gospel is proclaimed in the whole world, what she has done will be spoken of, in memory of her."[202]

She clasped onto his words like a prophetic life line, questioning to herself how and why that would be. Mary stood, casting her glance around at the disciples gathered there. She spotted Matthew, embarrassment broke into a questioning bewilderment. Thomas sported incredulity, not certain how to judge the impressive exhibition. Big James was covering his gaping mouth with his hand. Little James shuffled his feet uncomfortably. Martha, her sister, was mouth agape, holding her breath and eyes wide with astonishment. Searching the crowd, she found John. There was John, looking at her with admiration. And Ima next to him, a warm glow on her face, approving her display of reverent adoration. All around the room she saw men and women struck dumb. And then she spotted Judas. Half lit by the torch lamp nearby, half shadowed by the darkness of the night. A cold nipped at her heart, threatening to extinguish all consolation. With a sneerful toss of his head, he slipped out the door, unnoticed by all but herself, leaving disquiet in his wake.

CHAPTER 45. PROPHECIES OF DESTRUCTION

Destroy this Temple and in three days I will raise it up.
John 2:19

Three days later (Shabbat)

Two days. Two days, she thought. She scanned her memory. The past two days merged into a blur of one long paradoxical agony. From bliss at their last supper to agony on Golgotha. Mary sat on the rooftop of Mary Mark's house, often referred to by her companions as the Cenacle, which housed an upper room. She stared into space as the Sabbath dawn emerged. The grayness of twilight had slowly disappeared. Streaks of pastels were beginning to light the sky's landscape defying the forlorn state of her spirit. Empty. Bereft of energy. Numb. Dumbstruck. Confused.

He had known.

Closing her eyes, she recollected the moment. She had anointed him that night, the night before their last supper together. *I had anointed him…for his burial.* Horror crept over her. *He told me. He said it. I anointed him for his burial.*

Guilt wrenched her stomach into knots, as though she was responsible for the absolute disaster of her Rabboni's demise.

Gone. Gone. It's over. And he knew.

"In two days' time it will be Passover, and the Son of Man will be handed over to be crucified."[203] *He had prophesied it. And it happened.*

She squeezed her eyes closed again. Intent on making sense of the nonsensical.

I should have seen it coming. I think I did see it coming.

Her mind's eye flashed back to Wednesday night. The blessed moment was now overshadowed by her remembrance of Judas. Had he gone and betrayed Jesus that night? Or was it the next night? Either way, the deed was done. And he apparently thought he could not recover from such a betrayal.

Oh Judas! Her heart cried out, anger at odds with pity over his tragic end. *Despite our clashes and the discordant encounters, I would never wish this upon you!*

He had hung himself. They had received word that he sold out Jesus for thirty silver pieces and hung himself yesterday afternoon. He must have done it about the same time that Jesus hung on the cross. Mary shivered at the contrasting images of Judas and Jesus hanging from a tree.

Mary recalled how a sudden alertness to danger had taken hold of her when she saw Judas that Wednesday night, the night she anointed Jesus. The disciples had dispersed shortly after her affectionate display of anointing and Nicodemus had arrived to speak to Jesus. Only John, Matthew, Lazarus, and herself had remained after everyone else had finally left the public house. She didn't know Nicodemus, but she had been curious about him. He had a kind face, despite being "one of them," a Pharisee. He had proven to be Jesus' friend and was respected among the disciples, despite his secretive ways of coming and going.

Usually, he simply sent messages. But that night he had arrived in person. He brought a warning of escalated danger. He feared that Jesus may be arrested. Just days earlier Nicodemus had sent a word of warning, but at that time he didn't think the Sanhedrin would dare to do anything during the Passover, especially since Jesus had become so popular among the people. Now, with the threat of the Galileans' insurrection against the Romans, the chief priests and scribes resolved to use Jesus as a scapegoat. They might try to convince Pilate that Jesus was instigating riots. They schemed to silence him and stop his growing popularity.

When she heard this, Mary didn't know if anger or fear would win the battle in her spirit. Matthew nervously wrung his hands. John, gentle John in one moment and thunder in the next, looked like he might call down the wrath of God on all of Jerusalem. Lazarus, always the practical one, suggested that they might go back to Ephraim instead of remaining for the Passover in Jerusalem.

Mary remembered Jesus' words as though hearing them for the first time. Her stomach dropped as she realized that he had offered another sign of his coming death.

"Do not be afraid of those who kill the body but cannot kill the soul. Rather, be afraid of the One who can destroy both soul and body in hell."[204]

How could I have not seen or accepted it? No, I would never have accepted it, no matter how many times Jesus warned us.

She searched her memory again, looking for more signs of Jesus' knowledge of the destruction that was closing in upon him.

Thursday.

Jesus had gone once again to the Temple in the early morning. But he had ordered Peter and John to make arrangements for that evening. They were to celebrate the feast of the Unleavened Bread and Passover.[205] They were perplexed by this order, seeing that it was a day earlier than the actual feast of Unleavened Bread, but they didn't question him, aware that he sometimes had reasons that they only understood later. And granted, some did celebrate it in their houses on that day, the day before the sacrificial slaughter of the Lambs. Providence brought them to John and Mary Mark's family house. The women gathered ingredients and went to assist in the necessary preparations.

Now she recalled Jesus' words as he commanded the disciples to secure the place. "My appointed time draws near."[206]

He must have known that he would not be alive to celebrate Passover on the actual day.[207] *How did I not register that at the time?* Her ominous premonition on Wednesday night, when she had anointed Jesus, had temporarily faded with her eagerness for the Passover celebrations. She truly had thought that Jesus was indestructible. Her mind wandered to the preparation, reliving it again.

***

Mary and the women went up to Mount Zion, a southwest section of Jerusalem. After the apostles found the man that Jesus had prophesied, it led them to a large family home. John Mark, a youthful fourteen-year-old, and his mother Mary Mark welcomed them. Their beautiful home, a tall limestone construction, sat proudly on the highest point of Jerusalem. The Passover would take place in their upper room, a large complex that would easily fit over one hundred people. The room was decorated elegantly, but without pretension. It was already furnished with tables and seats. A mosaic patterned floor and plastered walls gave it a pleasant and solemnly festive ambience. High windows let in light and air. She looked forward to the nighttime gathering. They would be all together, a family, her new family.

For once, Mary was grateful for Martha who ordered everyone about, efficiently overseeing the production down to the last detail. Mary Mark was not ruffled by the invasion into her home and let Martha rule over the domain, offering herself as one more among the women disciples wherever she could assist in the preparations. They busied themselves, moving the already existent tables to create the space for several small groups. Jesus with the Twelve at the head of the room, the women at a table all their own nearby, and three other large tables for the host's family, guests, and the poor who commonly came on this evening. Busyness increased her eager anticipation. She prepared the room. She set tablecloths and place settings, cleaned the numerous vessels that would hold the four cups of wine per person, and accommodated cushions for the various guests. She filled bowls of vinegar and salt and placed a set on each table.

Mary slipped into the kitchen, slyly avoiding any more orders from Martha that would take her away from spending time with Ima. Mary Jacobe, Salome, and Ima were hard at work on the matzo. The fiery tannur wafted out the heavenly scent of unleavened bread every time the baker slapped a flattened piece of dough onto its inside walls.

"I couldn't resist staying away from the kitchen any longer," Mary announced her presence.

"Join us, Mary!" Salome took the last of the matzos out and added them to the high stacks lined across the table.

"You've baked enough to feed all of Israel fleeing slavery from the Egyptians!"

"If they had this much bread they wouldn't have needed manna in the desert," Mary Jacobe added to the jovial jesting.

"Oh, but that would have taken away the need for God's great providence along the way to the promised land," piped in Salome.

"The Lord finds a way to provide with or without our collaboration. But I am certain he would prefer our collaboration," said Ima.

"No shortage of that here! Especially with Martha at the helm," joked Mary.

"Martha or no Martha, get over here Mary and collaborate! I have a pile of apples to prepare!" Salome ordered.

"Uff, there is no escaping the older sisters!" Mary joked.

The women laughed and continued their preparations.

As they were finally wrapping up the final tasks, they chatted more than worked. Matthew arrived unnoticed. As was his custom, he stood at the periphery, observing.

The events of Jesus' glorious entry into Jerusalem were still on the forefront of Mary's mind. "It is hard to believe that only four days ago we were in that glorious procession, proclaiming Jesus as Messiah to all of Jerusalem. It seems like a lifetime ago. How could Jesus look regal and dignified, yet ridiculous at the same time? That tiny colt must have been destined to carry him. So many paradoxes. And then the threat of violence after such a glorious entry," Mary commented.

They reminisced about Jesus' glorious entry into Jerusalem and then bombarded Ima with questions about Jesus' early years.

Mary Jacobe instigated it. "Ima, did you have any premonitions that Jesus was the Messiah, the king to come, whom we have awaited for generations?"

"What you refer to as royal dignity has always been shrouded by the threat of destruction, as early as his birth. But God has always guided us, sending us messengers to warn us or indicate our next steps. When Joseph found out I was with child, he had thought to divorce me. But in his dreams he was told to take me as his wife. Then the census forced us to go precisely where the prophecy foretold." Ima recalled the prophecy, "'And you, Bethlehem, land of Judah, are by no means least among the rulers of Judah; and from you shall come a ruler, who is to shepherd my people Israel.'"[208]

Matthew interrupted, startling the women at the sound of a man's voice in the midst of their womanly conversations. "Was Joseph in the line of David?"

Mary Jacobe jumped, knocking over a stack of bread. "Oh Matthew! You frightened me!"

Matthew moved quickly, capturing the teetering pile and setting it upright. Embarrassed from giving away his eavesdropping, he snatched a piece of the bread and turned to escape.

Ima stopped him, "Stay Matthew. You are welcome."

Matthew, appearing honored, thanked them. He piped in, "Jeremiah had prophesied about a day when the Lord would raise up for David a righteous Branch, a King who will reign wisely and do what is just and right. He spoke of Judah being saved and Israel living in safety. He would be called the Lord, Our Righteous Savior."[209]

Matthew, embarrassed again for interrupting, found a corner to lean on and continued to listen as he devoured the bread.

Salome gently ribbed Ima. "And I thought my sons were important," she laughed, making light of Matthew's statement.

Ima continued, holding back a grin at Salome's joke. "To answer your question Matthew, yes, Joseph was a descendant of David through the line of Solomon.[210] And my family also descends through the line of David.[211] But God deemed to give us another sign. Three kings came from afar to offer their homage. Soon after, we were all warned of danger. Herod heard the prophecy and saw the babe as a threat against his reign. He ordered all babes around that age murdered. The kings fled and shortly after, we also had to flee. Joseph had received another vision that we were to go to Egypt."

"The massacre," Mary Jacobe whispered. "We knew several families who lost their little ones." Then she spit out, "Herod. I call him Herod the Horrid, not Herod the Great."

A brief silent vigil ensued in remembrance of the tragedy.

Salome broke it, "Like a sacrifice made to the gods. Sounds pagan. But they were our little children, taken that one might live."

Mary was horrified, "Surely God would not do such a thing!"

Salome answered, "No, I don't believe God would do such a thing. But he certainly didn't stop it."

Mary Jacobe offered her thoughts. "The psalms say that God is not a God who delights in wickedness."[212]

Salome joined in. "Yes, and the proverbs speak of the things that God hates and are an abomination to him. Among them it mentions hands that shed innocent blood and a heart that devises wicked plans."[213]

Ima looked pained, "Innocent blood indeed."

Matthew, ignoring or unaware of the new mood, was eager to hear the continuation of the story, "You fled to Egypt then?"

"Yes." Ima turned to Mary and surprised her, revealing another past connection to her family. "Mary, the Lord provided well for us there. We received the blessed hospitality of some distant relatives of your father.[214] We were able to stay with them until the death of Herod. So, you see, the Lord's plans are even better than we could have invented."

Salome quoted a proverb, "'The mind of man plans his way, but the Lord directs his steps.'"[215]

Matthew jumped in, interrupting Mary's astonishment, "And he fulfilled another prophecy! 'Out of Egypt I called my son.'"[216] He looked proud of himself.

"Yes!" Ima laughed at Matthew's exuberance. "We did finally return but stayed clear of Jerusalem. Joseph was warned of danger in another dream, so we settled back in Nazareth." She beat Matthew to the prophecy. "And yes Matthew, it fulfills the prophecy, 'He shall be called a Nazorean.'"

Matthew nodded, quoting the prophecy of Isaiah, "A shoot will come up from the stump of Jesse; from his roots a Branch will bear fruit."[217]

The women laughed. Mary marveled at his extensive knowledge of the prophecies that enlightened her around every corner.

Right then, John Mark popped his head in. "My mom is asking if you are ready to go to the Temple?"

The stacks of bread were quickly covered to prevent unwelcome pilferers. They gathered their belongings and set off to take in the last of Jesus' teachings before the Passover meal.

***

Mary's thoughts returned to the present. It was still very early in the morning. She had gotten lost in the memory of that conversation, reliving it again. Recalling those prophecies told her mind that this was all to be, but her heart said the absolute opposite. Her emotions wafted between anger at the injustice, confusion and incredulity, then grief and sorrow at her beloved's cruel murder.

A movement down below caught her eye. It was Ima. By herself. Walking away from the house. *Where is she going at this time of the morning?* Martha and Lazarus had already warned Mary to stay put. They were concerned that the backlash against Jesus might fall upon his followers as well. They finally extracted a promise from her that she would not leave, at least for last night. And that she would wait for news of the situation before going out today. On Friday, she had desperately wanted to remain at the tomb, keeping watch like one of the Roman guards that were placed there. Anything to be close to him, at least to his body. If she couldn't accept that he was gone, at least she could hold onto his body somehow, she had thought.

Before she could even call out or follow, Ima was out of sight. *Perhaps she just needed a bit of fresh air?* Mary kept watch to make sure Ima would come back soon and safe. As she sat there, flashbacks of Thursday came once again. They had gone to the Temple after the Passover preparations. *Did I sense even then that Jesus would be arrested and killed? Had I not paid attention to the signs?* What were to be his last teachings in the Temple were particularly unsettling to some of the bystanders, in particular the scribes and Pharisees.

***

In the Temple Mary sat listening to Jesus' teachings. His words and tone reminded her of the stories of prophets of old, clamoring out warnings of destruction upon those who did not repent. More often than not, the prophets were seized, tortured and killed for their unwanted and unheeded admonitions. Over the course of the last two hours, scribes and Pharisees had begun gathering in larger numbers. She sensed a storm brewing, not in the skies but in the hearts of many.

Finally, Jesus spoke directly to them, spewing out accusations and crying out seven admonitions. "Woe to you!" "Woe to you!" With each one, a growing hostility darkened their countenances. She was frightened for Jesus and the retaliation he might be provoking. She was grateful when he finally decided he was done for the day.

They were leaving the Temple when several of his disciples stopped him. They stood on a recently constructed part of the Temple's platform, commenting and marveling at the ongoing extensions, pointing out the new buildings or old refurbished areas of Solomon's temple. It was still under construction after forty-seven years. Mary marveled at the splendor. As a little girl, when they were in Bethany, they would visit frequently, trying to guess which area would next receive its embellishments and take bets on what new addition they would find the next time they came. The disciples were doing the same, wondering what they might discover on the next Passover. But Jesus did not join in their predictions. Instead, she noticed that he was scanning the entire complex, pensively introspective.

"You see all these things, do you not?" His voice had turned solemn, and Mary detected a hint of prophetic bearing. "Amen, I say to you, there will not be left here a stone upon another stone that will not be thrown down."[218]

His prediction of the destruction of the Temple reminded her of Jesus' recent temper as he had driven out the vendors and money changers from the temple area of the Gentiles. Many scoffed at him when he told them to stop making his Father's house a marketplace. Several Pharisees had come to the entrance to see the commotion and demanded he give them a sign if he wanted them to stay out of "his

Father's house." Jesus had told them, "Destroy this Temple and in three days I will raise it up."[219]

***

Mary was brought back again to the present moment. An undulating light blue fabric on the path below caught her eye. *Ima. She has returned.* And John followed a few steps behind. Relief turned to curiosity as she noticed a light step in Mary's stride. Her veil floated in the soft breeze, making her look like an ethereal creature. Mary was about to call out to her when Ima looked up to the terrace. Her face was aglow with a mysterious peace. Mary could still see the etchings of sorrow and eyes that had endured an onslaught of tears, but it contrasted with something else, something hopeful. Ima offered a brief greeting with the nod of her head, her mouth holding back what her eyes betrayed before she quietly slipped back into the house. John followed, head down, unaware of her vigilant presence on the rooftop.

In a flash, Mary felt suddenly alert, her mind and heart racing back to the many times Jesus had warned of his death. She had dismissed it as quickly as the other disciples, not believing it was possible. But now, her thoughts sought his words after his prophecy of death.

"On the third day I will rise," he had said. In Galilee, at Mount Tabor, on their way from Jericho to Jerusalem, every time he mentioned his death, he had also said that he would rise. And again, when the scribes and Pharisees had demanded a sign, he had said, "For just as Jonah was three days and three nights in the belly of the sea monster, so will the Son of Man be three days and three nights in the heart of the earth."[220]

Was that another prophecy? Could he be alive? No, it couldn't be. The soldiers had made sure of it. His body had been completely devastated.

Grief gripped her soul once again as a flood of images of Jesus, bloody, spent, in agony, played through her memory, overwhelming her.

And like the lamb led to slaughter, he opened not his mouth.

CHAPTER 46. THE LAMB OF GOD

He was oppressed and afflicted, yet he did not open his mouth; he was led like a lamb to
the slaughter, and as a sheep before its shearers is silent, so he did not open his mouth.
Isaiah 53:7

Mary's mind flashed back once again to their last Passover preparations and to previous Passovers with her family.[221] When she had first
arrived in the upper room, the place was already spotlessly clean. Not
an ounce of leaven anywhere in the house. She had recalled the many
hours she had spent as a little girl cleaning corners. Despite the many
servants, her mother always made them participate in that aspect of
the Passover preparation. She would inspect every nook and cranny,
looking for evidence of laziness or oversight. Thankfully, that task had
been done by Mary Mark's servants.

This past Thursday, upon Martha's orders, she helped Martha rear-
range the large dining room, then snuck away to help in the kitchen.
Mary mixed nuts and bits of apple to symbolize the clay used by the
Israelites to make bricks. Then she moved onto washing and laying out
the bitter herbs of wild lettuce, horseradish tops, parsley, and mint,
symbolizing the bitterness of the suffering they endured in slavery before the Lord freed them.

Salome picked up a bundle of horseradish tops, contemplating it.
"I know we rejoice that our people were freed from slavery, but I don't
know how they managed to endure so many years of wandering in the
desert. Our walk from Jericho to Jerusalem was enough desert for me!"
She paused, then chuckled at her own thoughts, "Maybe we should eat
sand to remember the trial of our people!"

The women laughed. But Salome's comment set Mary thinking
about the fortitude needed day in and day out. She thought of the many
times her people failed to remain faithful during their trials in the desert

and the patience they must have needed amidst so much uncertainty. They didn't know where their next meal would come from or if they would even arrive to the promised land.

The bleating of a lamb interrupted her musings. John Mark tugged on the rope fixed to the neck of a little lamb, trying to coax it into a pen set right outside the kitchen door. Her heart went out to the little fellow, not John Mark, but the lamb soon to be sacrificed. She laughed at John Mark who by now was sweating from exertion and red from frustration. The little lamb had spunk, that was for sure. Mary grabbed some lettuce leaves and went to assist. Lettuce in one hand and the other hand gently rubbing down his neck, they managed to lead it into the small space. *This will be the extent of his freedom until his time comes,* Mary thought.

***

Mary's reminiscing mind returned to the present moment as a rooster crowed. The world was beginning to rouse itself. Mourning doves cooed, feet pattered, doors squeaked, and a scent of breakfast wafted on the breeze, a sign that the fires had been stoked. She remained in her contemplative seat, returning again to her memories. *That lamb. Unlike Jesus, it had no clue about its destiny,* she thought.

***

By late afternoon, the day of their Passover celebration, just before dusk, Jesus and the disciples returned to the upper room. Mary loved the Passover meal, but she was squeamish when it came time to sacrifice the lamb. She recalled a Passover with her own family. They could have brought the sacrifice to the Temple, as they lived fairly close. But her father preferred to avoid the large crowds on the day of the feast, so they celebrated it, as many families chose to do, at home.

Against her mother's warning, she had befriended the adorable creature as it awaited its fate for several days prior to its sacrifice. At sundown her father would slaughter it. Only when she was ten years old had she mustered up the courage to watch the awful event. Her father was always careful to not break any bones. Her little lamb, as she had begun calling it, was uncannily still and quiet as her father bound the feet and then did the deadly deed. She had covered her eyes, waiting for the horrid sounds of bleating and signs of its resistance. But this lamb never put up a fight. It was an odd thing. When she peeked between her fingers, her father was already draining blood into a special cup in which they would then dip Syrian marjoram and go together as a family to spread it on a door lintel, remembering the promise of God to save them from the angel of death.

When they returned to the waiting lamb, the large fire pit was already hot with red coals, ready to welcome the sacrifice. Her father skinned and opened the animal, extracting the stomach and intestines to avoid tainting the meat if they burst. Then he speared the lamb vertically, running lengthwise down the body with a pomegranate branch. Another branch was speared horizontally through the back, securing each of the front feet. She remembered the strange way the little lamb's back feet were bound together, yet the opened front feet gave the appearance of a welcome victim, as though the lamb chose to be sacrificed.

***

Like my Rabboni on the cross, she thought. Grief of the heart forced its way upward as a tearful sob escaped. She had thought it impossible to shed more tears. But the scene was etched in her mind, in her heart, reanimating all her emotions of the past into the present. She turned her mind's eye again to their Last Supper.

Jesus had surprised them that Thursday evening. He approached the little lamb, stroked its head and proclaimed, "There is no need for the lamb's sacrifice anymore."

Instead, they spent several hours with Jesus. They were intimate moments, solemn moments, surprising and reverent moments. He washed the disciples' feet,[222] and Mary, moved by his humility, followed his lead, doing the same for the women at her table. The other tables followed her lead, choosing one among them to do the same.

Jesus spoke again of the one who would betray him. Mary noticed the apostles looking at one another. Peter signaled something to John and John reclined his head near Jesus. Mary couldn't make out their exchange, but she watched Jesus dip a piece of unleavened bread into a bowl and hand it to Judas who was sitting to his left.

How odd, Mary thought. The first portion is usually offered to the one on the right, which would have been John, the youngest and therefore the one Jesus had chosen as the least among them to sit as the guest of honor. After Judas allowed Jesus to feed him that morsel, he stood and left abruptly. Initially she had thought that Judas had left to purchase something else for the feast. Now she knew otherwise. He must have gone to betray Jesus that night.

She scanned her memory of that evening, trying to recall all Jesus had said. Once again, she realized, *he knew.* She recalled some of his words, "I will be with you only a little while longer, but you are not to fear.[223] Despite the world's hatred for you, take courage.[224] I will send you an Advocate."[225]

Yes, she saw it now. *It was our last supper together. Jesus knew his end had come.* Anguish overwhelmed her again. She ached with desire to go back to that moment, to plead with him to stop the course of history, to flee Jerusalem. *Oh! If only, if only I had seen it! If only I could have stopped him! Rabboni, what have you done!?*

She searched her memory again, seeing now his concern and love for them. On the verge of his own death, he had prayed for them. She had been especially moved by his prayer. He prayed to the Father for them to be protected and for all those who would believe in him through their words. Her heart had been on fire during this prayer, desiring to make others believe in him.

But now? What is there to believe? No more teaching, no more preaching, no more healing. What was to become of their new found family? She mourned the loss not only of her Rabboni, but of this band of believers that had dispersed after Jesus' crucifixion. *Will we continue together?*

As she mourned, anger began to trump her sorrow. Anger at those who had sought to kill him, anger at those who trapped and betrayed him, anger at Jesus. *How could he let this happen?!* Time and time again she had listened and watched him confront those who antagonized him. *Maybe I should have done something to stop him. Could I have?* She recalled another moment in the Temple just days earlier.

***

Mary marveled at the people's response to Jesus' teachings. They came out in droves, more and more people gathering every day. But as the crowd increased in number, so did the tension. The chief priests, scribes, and elders broke through the mass of followers. They approached Jesus and he merely looked at them, tranquil and receptive to their advances. She wondered if they were going to throw him out of the Temple. The number of Temple guards had increased around the vicinity of Jesus' gathering crowd, drawing the attention of even more pilgrims to his area.

One of the chief priests spoke on behalf of the others. "Tell us, by what authority are you doing these things? Or who is the one who gave you this authority?"[226]

The air thickened with the possibility of conflict. The audience looked expectantly at Jesus for his response, while various children accompanying their parents continued playing, innocent and unaware.

Jesus nodded, acknowledging their question and responding calmly, "I shall ask *you* a question. Tell me, was John's baptism of heavenly or of human origin?"[227]

The crowd turned their heads to the leaders, waiting for their answer. Stunned by Jesus' comeback, the scribes and Pharisees turned to one another in consultation. The waiting escalated Mary's already taut nerves.

The chief priest turned from his consulting partners and spoke haughtily. "We do not know and could not say."

"Neither shall I tell you by what authority I do these things," Jesus countered.

She rejoiced at his triumphant victory as he responded to their provocations. The chief priest's face turned red, the others behind him muttering to each other in agitation. Mary detected danger. She wanted to rush in and scold Jesus for riling them up even more. Then Jesus spoke up again, projecting his voice out to the people who were marveling at his brush with the authorities. He began to tell a story.[228]

Mary's heart raced as she tried to concentrate, but her attention was drawn to the religious leaders. One of the scribes had left the group and headed toward a Temple guard. He was obviously irritated. Mary caught tidbits of the parable as she kept a close eye on the scribe. He was a little man, but full of rage and gall. She wondered if he was capable of inflicting harm.

"A man planted a vineyard," Jesus elaborated.

Mary wanted to warn Jesus of the little scribe and the Temple guard. She remained vigilant of the scribe as she caught pieces of the story. "...They beat the servant...", "the man sent a third who was wounded and thrown out..."

Mary watched, holding her breath. The Temple guard listened to the little man whose arms were gesturing frantically, pointing to Jesus.

Turning back to Jesus, Mary caught more of the parable. "This is the heir. Let us kill him that the inheritance will be ours. So they threw him out of the vineyard and killed him."

She turned again to the Temple guard. He was looking back and forth between the scribe and Jesus. But his feet remained planted. The rest of the crowd was enthralled, ignorant of the ensuing threat.

Then Jesus questioned the crowd, drawing her attention once again to his words. "What will the owner of the vineyard do?"

He didn't wait for an answer. Turning to the religious leaders, he spoke solemnly. "He will come and put those tenant farmers to death and turn over the vineyard to others."

Voices cried out among the crowd, "No! Let it not be so!"

Mary's heart contradicted itself. It cried out in victory as she realized that Jesus was speaking of the religious leaders and their demise. Simultaneously, she wanted to reprimand him for antagonizing the very people who could help him or seriously harm him.

Jesus turned back to the crowds and asked, "What then does this scripture passage mean: 'The stone that the builders rejected has become the cornerstone'?"

***

Her memory of that moment faded and verses of the psalm that Jesus had quoted came unwelcome to her mind. *The stone that the builders rejected has become the cornerstone. The Lord has done this, and it is marvelous in our eyes. The Lord has done it this very day; let us rejoice today and be glad.*[229]

No, she would not rejoice! Her heart felt rebellious. Suddenly her hands ached. She realized that they were clenched tight, her fingernails digging into the cuts she had attained earlier while near the cross. She thought of Jesus' words again. *The stone which the builders rejected has become the cornerstone.*

In that instant she was back on Golgotha standing with Ima, John, Mary Jacobe, and Salome. *How did they get there? How did they all end up there, watching Jesus lay upon a vertical wood beam, his arms stretched out on a horizontal beam like the lamb sacrificed for the Passover meal?* They had not had any sleep since the Last Supper with Jesus. She remembered why.

***

After supper the men went out singing. The women followed along until they headed down into the Kidron valley with plans to cross over to the Mount of Olives. Several dispersed while Jesus and the Eleven continued on to the Garden of Gethsemane. The women returned to the upper room to clean up and get some rest. Having just finished, John Mark burst into the upper room looking frantic.

"They have arrested Jesus!"

A platter crashed to the floor as Ima's face turned ashen. That was the beginning of their long night, their Passover. They followed in the footsteps of Jesus, never far away, but neither were they able to get close to him until he was carrying the heavy wood beam through the streets. Most of Thursday night Jesus was hidden from them as he was kept imprisoned in the large caverns of the high priest Caiaphas' complex. Then they saw him from afar as he was taken away.

Chains bound him at the neck, hands and feet, as though he were a dangerous criminal. He was practically dragged from Caiaphas' house to the praetorium to be presented to Pilate. Then the guards rudely pulled him to Herod's dwellings and back again to Pilate where, in the early morning, he was sentenced to scourgings and tauntings. They barely recognized Jesus as he stood before the mad crowd, a regal cape draped over his shoulders and a crown of thorns tauntingly piercing his skull. The crowd mocked him, a far off tone from the honor given only days before upon his triumphal entry into Jerusalem. Then, the verdict came. He was condemned to death. Condemned to drag his own instrument of death through the streets.

Like a lamb led to the slaughter, she thought to herself now.

And then the horrors of Golgotha. The sounds, the bang of hammer on nail, the grunts of the soldiers, and Jesus, her Rabboni, bound to that cross with steel and hatred. John held Ima. Mary Jacobe and Salome held each other, supporting one another with each blow. And then the lifting, the heaving of the wooden cross, with a live man, her Rabboni, fettered by hands and feet. The swaying of his body as it was lifted. Shouts of soldiers ordered to move this way, now that way, pull harder, heave and lift, as though they were simply constructing a house, not crucifying a man. Cussing and vulgarities filled the air as terror filled her heart. She held her breath the last seconds before the cross was erect. And then, the thud.

She groaned as she heard the thud again. Like an echo in an empty chamber, it resounded in her heart, filling it with fury and sending ripples of horror and awe that one man could endure such agony.

The thud of heavy wood and a scream of agony struck the hearts of bystanders as it slid into the rocky earth's grasp. Ima swooned. Mary's legs buckled out from under her. Silence. And then the silence was broken. Shofars from the Temple announced the slaying of the first Passover sacrifice.

In the next three hours, twenty thousand lambs would fall victim to sacrifice, yet not one was needed. *Jesus knew. He knew he would be the sacrifice.*

The next thing she remembers, there on the side of the hill, was John grabbing one of her hands. Mary found herself down on her knees, blinded by tears and gripping the loose shale rock of Golgotha in her hands. Golgotha, the place of the skull, was a small hill amidst an abandoned quarry. But the place on which Jesus was crucified, and all the way down to the area where they stood watching, was the hillside of rejected stone. It was too fragile to harvest or use for constructing. John had grabbed her hand. He pried it open to witness the shards piercing cuts into her palms, sufficient to cause a light stream of blood down their sides. She turned them, releasing the shards. Those shards were the stone that was literally rejected by the builders upon which her rock stood crucified.

***

She was jolted back to the present once again, looking at her open hands palms up. The cuts were sore and red. She welcomed the physical pain, almost a relief from her inner torment. The sun had peaked up over the horizon, toward her home in Bethany. A small portion of sun warmed her exposed face, offering heat from the contrasting cool morning air.

She heard John's footsteps behind her on the terrace.

"Mary," he said softly. "Martha sent me with orders that you eat." He handed her a plate filled with unleavened bread, olives and fresh fruit.

"I can't eat. I can't stomach anything right now."

"I understand."

They sat in companionable silence, each one carrying the burden of memories.

Mary broke the silence. "I keep seeing his body on the cross and then a lamb over the pit. And then that little lamb that Jesus told us would not be sacrificed. I can't help but think that he was the sacrifice.

John, he knew. He knew he would be arrested, tortured, killed. He tried to tell us so many times. I just couldn't believe it. I think he even knew that he would die yesterday, on the feast of Passover."

John whispered, "The Lamb of God who takes away the sins of the world."[230]

Mary looked at him quizzically.

"The Lamb of God who takes away the sins of the world," he repeated as though convincing himself that he had a clue to the puzzle. "The first time I ever saw Jesus at the Jordan, John the Baptist had cried out, pointing to him, 'Behold the Lamb of God who takes away the sins of the world.'"

Mary sat in stunned silence trying to make sense of it. John reached over to her plate on her lap. He pulled a piece of the bread off. He was about to pop it into his mouth, when he froze, contemplating the morsel. Dropping his hand, he closed his eyes. Mary looked at him, concerned.

"John?"

After a brief silence, John finally spoke. "When we were in the synagogue of Capernaum, Jesus had preached a very difficult teaching and because of that, many left. He said, 'I am the living bread that came down from heaven. Whoever eats this bread will live forever. This bread is my flesh, which I will give for the life of the world.' Many of the Jews, even those who had been following him for several weeks, some who had been followers of John the Baptist like myself, had a hard time with this saying.[231] But I will never forget how insistent he was. He said, 'Very truly I tell you, unless you eat the flesh of the Son of Man and drink his blood, you have no life in you.'"[232]

"It sounds like what he told us in our Last Supper with him. Remember? After he blessed the bread, he held one up for all of us to see and told us that it was his body, which will be given up for us. His body. What was he trying to tell us?"

"I think he was trying to tell us that his body was a sacrifice for us all. He is the Lamb of God who takes away the sins of the world. And we should remember and receive his body in the bread we bless and break."

Mary looked down at the bread on her plate, eyebrows furled with confusion. She looked back at John, whose face was also covered with incredulity, his mind racing to connect the dots and make sense of a mystery. She shook her head as though trying to clear the fog, wondering how they had gotten to that conclusion. *It's too much. Too much.*

"John, I feel horrible. One minute I feel the anguish of what happened to Jesus, but the next I am furious with him. He knew this was coming and he didn't prevent it."

"I know. I have been struggling with the same thing."

Silence overcame them again. And while they sat side by side they were in two separate worlds, each in their own thoughts, each trying to make sense of all they had lived in the last few hours, in the last few days, in the last few months with Jesus.

Mary finally spoke up. "What are we to do now? I feel like a ship adrift."

"I don't know Mary." He shook his head. Looking up to the heavens, a silent and anguished plea escaped through a sigh. Then a confession, "I cannot believe that Jesus would abandon us. And yet it feels like he has."

Mary concurred, feeling the same, yet not wanting to accept that her Rabboni would do this. Her mind was searching again for answers, trying to find a clue, something that Jesus would have said that would give direction to her unanchored spirit. Then a small spark of clarity enkindled just enough hope to make her feel she had not been cast off or forgotten.

"John, do you remember Jesus' words in our last supper with him?"

"Which ones? He spoke into the late of night."

Mary closed her eyes, picturing Jesus' face, his solemn demeanor, his loving gaze upon each of them, one by one. He had seemed so intent to communicate the depth of his heart as if speaking to each one personally. Like a sculptor who etches an image in a stone, his manner had made his words resonate and fix themselves in her memory all the more. She repeated what now came to her.

"He said, 'By this is my Father glorified, that you bear much fruit and become my disciples. As the Father loves me, so I also love you.

Remain in my love. This is my commandment: love one another as I love you.'"[233]

Mary paused, looking at John with hopeful expectation as though wanting to be affirmed that she had discovered something important. Receiving John's acknowledgement, she continued. "Then he said, 'Greater love has no one than this: to lay down one's life for one's friends.'"[234]

She felt like she was coming up for air after being submerged in water for too long. She gasped, wanting to rush forward in sharing her conclusion, but was cautious, for fear of being too bold. "He truly was the Messiah, John. He was the one our people were waiting for, right? Like a lamb led to slaughter."

Light was dawning in John's eyes as well. He spoke the prophecy of Isaiah.[235] "He was despised and rejected by men, a man of sorrows, and familiar with suffering. Like one from whom men hide their faces he was despised, and we esteemed him not."

Mary continued, "My father made us memorize this prophecy from Isaiah." She continued, "Surely, he took up our infirmities and carried our sorrows, yet we considered him stricken by God, smitten by him, and afflicted. But he was pierced for our transgressions."

Mary's voice caught as she saw him again on the cross, hands and feet pierced by nails. Head pierced by a skull cap of thorns, resembling a crown. Tears spilled forth as she continued remembering the prophecy.

"He was crushed for our iniquities; the punishment that brought us peace was upon him, and by his wounds we are healed. We all, like sheep, have gone astray, each of us has turned to his own way; and the Lord has laid on him the iniquity of us all."

John joined her as they spoke the last lines, softly, together. "He was oppressed and afflicted, yet he did not open his mouth; he was led like a lamb to the slaughter, and as a sheep before her shearers is silent, so he did not open his mouth."

They remained silent, a sense of sacred revelation overcoming them. A sliver of clarity promised a token of peace and acceptance.

And then, the spell cast over them was broken with approaching foot-steps.

CHAPTER 47. BETRAYAL & BLOOD

Forasmuch as ye know that ye were not redeemed with corruptible things, as silver and gold, from your vain conversation received by tradition from your fathers; But with the precious blood of Christ, as of a lamb without blemish and without spot.
1 Peter 1:18-19

During their conversation, the sun had fully exposed itself, practically blinding their view towards the east. But they had not budged from their spots as the revelations crept upon them like the dawn. Matthew's familiar footsteps interrupted their solemn memorial. Mary shed the cloak that Martha had kindly bundled around her during the night and turned to welcome him with a compassionate smile. Matthew dared not speak. He brought a small stool, ready to install himself among their company on the rooftop. He stopped and then decidedly sat to her left, couching her in between John and himself. He sighed but said nothing. Putting his hand to his forehead to shade the glaring sun, he scanned the horizon, like a captain adrift in the sea, looking for dry land. He sighed again.

Mary broke the silence. "Where is everyone?"

The disciples had dispersed. Many of them had run away in fright after Jesus' trial, convicting him of blasphemy and death by crucifixion. Some had put on a bold front when Jesus was arrested. They even claimed they would break into prison to set him free. Others hid in their houses or found dwelling places far away from their typical meeting rooms. Only John, and the women had returned to the house on Mount Zion after anointing Jesus' body hastily and hurrying to shelter before the three first stars announced the beginnings of the sacred Passover Sabbath. She felt as though a foundation was crumbling. She was impatient to do something about it and anxious for not knowing what.

"Peter is distraught," Matthew volunteered a semblance of an answer. "Andrew doesn't know what to do with him. We just arrived."

"Oh, I didn't see you arrive." Mary had been positioned like a sentinel on the rooftop since the night before. She would have seen all the movements between here and Golgotha in one direction and in the other she could see across part of the Kidron towards the Mount of Olives. But then again, she thought, her musings had brought her in and out of consciousness of her present surroundings. She could have easily missed them.

"We came around the back way. We were afraid to be seen coming in the front entrance in case people were on the lookout for us. Ima is with him now."

John interjected, "Ima looked strangely peaceful when I found her standing on the road this morning."

Mary recalled having noticed the same when Ima entered the house after her mysterious disappearance. Curious, she asked, "What was she doing out?"

"I don't know. She didn't say and I didn't ask. But I don't think she heard me coming until I was almost upon her. She was facing Golgotha, and I could have sworn that she was waiting for someone, but it obviously wasn't me. I thought maybe she had gone crazy and was waiting for Jesus. At that hour, I don't know who she could be expecting. She looked disappointed when she realized it was me. Then covered it up with her typical motherly greeting. I was surprised how calm she was. I don't know how she can endure this and not be completely undone."

Matthew chimed in. "Well, someone has to keep it together. Peter looks like he hasn't slept in days. Well, we all pretty much look like that."

Mary looked at Matthew and John, noticing the dark half circles beneath their eyes. Matthew's curls were matted on one side and sticking out in all directions on the other as if he had slept heavily on one side and just woken up. John had at least run his fingers through his shoulder length hair to attempt some pretense of order. She looked at

John, wondering if they should divulge to Matthew their previous conversation.

Mary wanted to see how Matthew would react and what else he understood of all the events of the last two days. He had an uncanny knack for making sense of things. "Matthew," she said. "Jesus knew."

"He knew what?" Matthew asked quizzically, then suddenly answered his own question, not pausing for them to respond. "That we would all run away?" He raised his finger, pointing over to the mount of Olives. "Yes, he must have known. When we entered the garden he said, 'This night you will have your faith in me shaken, for it is written, I will strike the shepherd, and the sheep of the flock will be dispersed.'"[236]

Matthew pondered that, his eyes fixed beyond their present vision toward the Garden of Gethsemane, despite the view being obstructed from a corner of the large mount upon which the Temple stood.

John offered an answer to Matthew's rhetorical question. "Yeah, he knew that. He also knew Peter would betray him. When we followed Jesus to Caiaphas' house, Peter stayed out in the courtyard, but I was able to slip in. It was awful. Even Annas was there, Caiaphas' father-in-law."

Matthew winced at the name of Annas. "No wonder they took Jesus to Pilate. Annas has more authority now than when he was high priest fifteen years ago! And he has been sympathizing with the Sadducees. I wonder how long they were set on arresting Jesus, especially for speaking of the resurrection of the dead."

"They arrested him for more than that," John declared. "They set up the whole thing, false witnesses, lies, accusations. They charged him with blasphemy and Jesus didn't even defend himself. Caiaphas demanded that he confess, under oath, if he was the Christ, the Son of God. Well, Jesus confirmed it, and chaos broke out."

Mary could envision the scene as though she were there. His regal bearing, neither haughty nor proud, just simple. His appearance and calm spoke the truth. She sighed, not wanting to believe that he had been the cause of his own demise.

"Of course he would confess it," she sighed.

"Well, he didn't quite confess it, but he might as well have spilt his own blood right there. He alluded to Daniel's prophecy of the Messiah's coming."

Matthew asked, "The one about the Ancient of Days on the flaming throne? And the beast that was slain and thrown in the blazing fire, but other beasts were allowed to live even though they were stripped of their authority?"

"Yes, but the other part." John indicated to Matthew to keep remembering the prophecy.

Matthew went on. "The part about one like a son of man, coming with the clouds of heaven?"

Mary cringed. She was aware of that prophecy. Her Rabboni had not permitted himself any mercy, no sign of backing down from being accused of blasphemy.

Matthew recited it. "He approached the Ancient of Days and was led into his presence. He was given authority, glory and sovereign power; all nations and peoples of every language worshiped him. His dominion is an everlasting dominion that will not pass away, and his kingdom is one that will never be destroyed."[237]

Mary wondered at the prophecy. She knew that Jesus had alluded to his power as the Messiah. *But where is his power now? Where is his dominion? His reign?* They were all flabbergasted by the contrast. He proclaimed himself a king, he foresaw his own death, he spoke with one who had authority, he healed and forgave sins, revealing the power of the Lord, and yet, gone. Gone was his presence, his power, even his many followers, dispersed. Nothing to show for the building up of the momentum that culminated in his triumphant entry into Jerusalem just one week ago. Even the one person he had chosen and given special authority to had betrayed him. Peter. He was given the power to lose and unloose, to bind and unbind, and yet he had run like a coward. Mary didn't know whether to feel pity, sorrow, or anger at Peter.

John picked up the story where he had left off earlier.

"When I was in Caiaphas' house I slipped out to look for Peter. I found him face to face with a servant of the high priest who happened to be a relative of the one whose ear Peter had cut off when Jesus was arrested. He accused him of being in the garden, but Peter denied it. And then, just as Jesus had predicted, the cock crowed. I don't think Peter even saw me. But he looked like he had just seen a ghost and he ran off. I finally found him late last night. He looked like he cried enough to fill the Sea of Galilee. I feel awful for him. I can barely see his eyes, so red and puffy."

Matthew confessed, his voice shaky with regret, "Well I wasn't much better. I ran for my life when he was arrested. I feel ashamed."

Mary tried to console him, setting her hand on his arm and squeezing. "Well, at least you are both sorry and you returned to us. I pity Judas more."

Matthew sighed heavily once again. "Maybe Ima can calm Peter down."

"Maybe," John replied. "But I am not sure even she can do that. He's high strung, devastated by his own betrayal. I went in search of him after we laid Jesus in the tomb. Found him back near Caiaphas' house weeping inconsolably. Andrew wasn't in much better shape, but at least he was able to talk. Peter wanted to go back to Gethsemane. In the end, we didn't dare. We spent the night in some caves in Hinnon Valley. I think Peter wept himself unconscious. He wouldn't budge when I tried to wake him this morning, so I left and Matthew and Andrew said they would return here as soon as possible."

Matthew, marveling at the irony of Peter's betrayal contrasted with his strength of character, thought out loud, "And he had denied that it was ever possible when Jesus had predicted it. I remember his words, because we all assured Jesus the same. 'Even if I have to die with you, I will never disown you,' he said. We all said it. We thought it was impossible to deny him."[238]

Mary thought of her own frailty not long ago. It too was a sort of betrayal; she had almost completely returned to her old life. And she might have if it weren't for Martha's zeal interceding for her. Empathy for Peter's betrayal turned to anguish for Judas' demise as she swallowed the lump in her throat that was threatening to choke her. "The blood of Jesus is on Judas' hands more than on Peter's, I fear."

Matthew, incredulously remembering the moment, spoke quietly as though not wanting to awaken spirits from the dead, "He betrayed Jesus with a kiss."

Silence hung thick upon them until Matthew broke it.

"Peter keeps repeating the prophecy of Joel, like he is trying to unlock a puzzle. 'The sun will be turned to darkness and the moon to blood before the coming of the great and dreadful day of the Lord.'"[239]

"If ever creation was going to give a sign of fulfilling that prophecy, it was yesterday," Mary said. She recalled the gradual darkness.[240] The air had been heavy with remnants of the hamsim, a sandstorm that had blown in during the night, making temperatures suddenly rise. And then another strange storm had arrived, plummeting them into frigid air. As Jesus hung on the cross, the conditions created an eerie bloody tint in the sky. The light faded and the sky darkened as her Rabboni was slipping away from them. Despite the fading light, the wetness of the blood oozing from Jesus' open wounds glistened all over his body and down the wood of the cross onto the stone platform holding him captive for all to witness.

"Yes," Mary spoke with eyes closed, contemplating the quantity of blood that had spilled from Jesus' body. "Perhaps the blood of Rabboni is on Judas' hands. Although I can't help but feel that his blood is on all our hands. I was there in the Praetorium and could do nothing."

Mary recalled how frantic she had felt. She had looked around at all the soldiers, at the religious leaders and the mass of people. Was there no one who would intercede? Scanning the crowd, her eyes had set on Gaius. He was searing her with an intense glance. He shook his head slowly. She was not sure if it was a sign of warning to do nothing or a sign of disbelief that she was still pining after Jesus. But she noticed that, unlike many soldiers around him, he was not caught up in the frenzy of mockery and jeering.

Tears began to flow once again as she recalled Jesus and Barabbas standing before the crowd, Pilate relinquishing his responsibility.

"Pilate washed his hands in front of us, claiming that he was innocent of Jesus' blood," Mary shared spitefully. "But he let it happen. We all let it happen. And all the people cried out for his death. It was like they were bloodthirsty, crying out, 'His blood is on us and on our children!'[241] Pilate was a coward. They were all cowards. But maybe we were too."

"No Mary," John defended her. "You stayed with Jesus. You did not abandon him. You, Ima, Salome, Mary Jacobe. So many women. You were all there with him."

Mary's memory flashed back to a half broken pillar upon which Jesus had been secured and mercilessly scourged. The soldiers had taken a break before releasing him from the chains that bound him. Blood pooled around his sagging lifeless body. Pilate's wife, Claudia had quickly let Ima, herself and the women into the inner area. The woman was distressed and nervous as she pressed a large linen sheet into Ima's hands.

"I am so sorry," she choked out. "I had a dream.[242] I warned my husband. I told him to have nothing to do with this. I am sorry. I couldn't stop it." She looked around, weary of being caught speaking to them and then fled. Ima, Mary and the other women barely had a chance to console Jesus before the soldiers returned and shooed them away. Despite the horrors she had witnessed, Mary was grateful that she had been there with Jesus, walking where he walked, not leaving his side.

She returned to the present.

"You also John, you were there too. You did not abandon Jesus," she tried to console John.

"No, I had my moments too. When he took us to Gethsemane, he took Peter, James, and I further in with him and told us to keep watch and pray.[243] We were all so tired. I fell asleep Mary. I saw Jesus suffering in agony to the point of sweating blood." John's voice cracked, but he went on, "and I fell asleep on him!" John relived the scene in his mind, projecting anger at himself.

"But did he tell you anything else there? Did he give you any instructions about what we were to do when he left us?" Mary hoped there was something more, some clue that would give direction to their confused state. But nothing. John shook his head, unable to speak as tears loosened from his puddled eyes.

From their privileged rooftop view they all looked out across the valley to the Mount of Olives. Part of the platform for the Temple obscured their vision of the entire mount, but she made out part of the trail that meandered into and through the groves.

"No, nothing," John finally whispered. "He just prayed. He prayed intensely. I have never seen anything like it. And he begged the Father, 'If it is Your will, take this cup away from Me; nevertheless, not My will, but Yours, be done'"[244]

Matthew questioned, "The cup?"

Mary and John looked at him, wondering what connection he was making now. Matthew continued ruminating out loud. "I thought it was very odd that we never drank the four cups of wine in our Passover meal. We didn't have the lamb or finish the cups of wine. We went out to the Mount of Olives singing hymns before the final cup. And now I remember. He had said, 'I will not drink from this fruit of the vine from now on until that day when I drink it new with you in my Father's kingdom.'"[245]

Mary was perplexed. "What did he mean?"

John began reciting the prayers over the cups of wine, trying to make sense of Jesus' action that night. "Therefore, say to the Israelites: 'I am the Lord, and I will bring you out from under the yoke of the Egyptians. I will free you from being slaves to them, and I will redeem you with an outstretched arm and with mighty acts of judgment."

John stopped abruptly, leaving one verse unspoken.[246]

Mary was struck by the prayer when she heard "outstretched arms." She contemplated Friday once again, seeing Jesus' outstretched arms and hearing him cry out "I thirst."[247] She recalled the attempts to slate his thirst along the path to Golgotha. A familiar woman, whom she realized she had met many months ago on Mount Tabor, Bernike, had approached Jesus as he carried his cross. She attempted to offer Jesus a cup of wine but to no avail. The soldiers did not permit it. But before the soldiers pushed her away, she had managed to press a cloth upon his face to give him relief from the blood trickling into his eyes.

Then as Jesus was being led to the cross she tried again. She sent a vessel full of wine and money to be given to the guards to convince them to let Jesus' thirst be relieved. But they just scoffed, took the money and the wine and distributed it among themselves. Mercy was finally offered as one soldier gave him the traditional cheap wine vinegar mixed with gall, a potion meant to offer slight numbness and relief from the tortures of the crucifixion, but Jesus had refused.

Why? She questioned. *Had he wanted to be completely conscious? Did he willingly accept the horrendous torture?* She wondered at it all incredulously, a mixture of pride and disbelief overwhelmed and confused her.

John interrupted her thoughts, looking stricken. "He did finally drink that cup of wine, but on the cross. A soldier pierced a sponge soaked in vinegar onto a hyssop branch and gave it to Jesus. He could barely move his mouth to take it in, but he took it."

"Hyssop?" Matthew asked. They all understood the connection Matthew was making. It reminded them of the story of the very first Passover. Matthew recited the first command to the Israelites that saved their people from the final plague in Egypt, a plague that killed the first born sons, but set the people free from slavery.

"Take a bunch of hyssop, dip it into the blood in the basin and put some of the blood on the top and on both sides of the doorframe. None of you shall go out of the door of your house until morning."[248]

Matthew turned to them with a pained look. "We didn't wait until morning to go out. He was the Son of God. The first born. He shed the blood of the Passover lamb that saved us from death. When Jesus went to the garden, do you think he knew he would be arrested?"

John breathed out quietly the final part of the prayer that accompanied the last cup of wine, "I will take you as my own people, and I will be your God. Then you will know that I am the Lord your God, who brought you out from under the yoke of the Egyptians."[249]

Mary's mind felt like it was flashing between various scenes: the blood draining into a cup from the Paschal lamb sacrificed before a Passover meal and his own body being drained of blood from the cross.

"A sacrifice," she whispered. "He made himself the sacrifice to set us free from slavery?"

Matthew nodded slowly, realization sinking in. "That last supper. After he said the prayer of thanksgiving and told us to drink, remember what he told us?"

Mary remembered. She had been watching Jesus carefully, his solemn way of lifting the cup. She moved to lift her own cup and knocked it over, spilling red wine onto the table setting and into her lap. She looked down now. Stains of red wine were mixed with Jesus' blood. She touched the stained fabric with reverence. The blood of the Messiah was upon her. She recalled his words. Jesus had paused briefly, catching her attention from her distraction with the spilt wine before speaking. She had been struck into stillness. Determination, tenderness, and love were poured into those words.

"This is my blood of the covenant, which is poured out for many for the forgiveness of sins."[250]

Matthew spoke the words out loud, moving within her an overwhelming emotion of awe and wonder, almost afraid to believe the truth that was dawning upon them.

John recalled the discourse in the Capernaum synagogue again. "Yes, and he also spoke of his blood as real food. In Capernaum. 'Whoever eats my flesh and drinks my blood remains in me, and I in them,'[251] he insisted."

Matthew offered another connection. "Isaiah had spoken of a new covenant the Lord would establish with us. One in which our sins would be remembered no more."[252]

"The blood of Jesus," John marveled. "It purifies us from all sin."[253]

"For the life of a creature is in the blood, and I have given it to you to make atonement for yourselves on the altar; it is the blood that makes atonement for one's life,"[254] Matthew said. "Leviticus."

Mary felt wet drops upon her hands that had tightly held onto the blood and wine stained fabric in her lap. Tears of overwhelming gratitude silenced her voice. She could hardly fathom what was being revealed as they contemplated the mystery that had ensued in less than the last two days.

Hurrying footsteps were heard on the steps up to the rooftop. Martha's voice pierced through the cloud of contemplation.

"You have to come down," she spoke forcefully, a frenzied enthusiasm in her voice. Mary wasn't sure who Martha was directing her words to, but they grated on her nerves. She just wanted to be left alone to take in all that they had spoken. No one moved. Matthew and John also seemed to be captivated, an aura of stupor reigning over them.

Martha, seeing no movement, insisted.

"There are some men here. I think you should meet them. Hear their story."

John and Matthew stood to obey. Mary didn't move until she felt John gently grabbing her by the arm, encouraging her to join them. She came back to the present moment, muscles stiff from her long vigil in the open air, a growling hollow stomach clamoring for attention. Allowing herself to shake off her state of dazed contemplation, she followed Martha, John and Matthew.

CHAPTER 48. HOURS OF AGONY

But because the Lord loved you and kept the oath which He swore to your forefathers, the Lord brought you out by a mighty hand and redeemed you from the house of slavery,
Isaiah 41:10

A tall strongly built man, reluctant and shy in demeanor, stood unshaven and unkempt. Behind him two tall lanky and awkward young men stared back at the group of men and women gathered in the hall. An air of caution hung between them. With exception of the older one's gray-streaked hair, there was an obvious resemblance between the three. Their strangely close eye sockets identified them as father and sons. She would not have recognized anyone from the crucifixion, considering she had been fully absorbed in Jesus' and her own agony, but those eyes had drawn her attention.

Her gaze fixed on the soldier, whom she now identified as a main culprit, as she drew near to Mary Jacobe. "Who are they? What is he doing here?" "He is the one who pierced Jesus' side!"

What nerve he has to come here!

He was dressed like one of them, in common attire, not in Roman garb. And yet, he had played a part in killing her Rabboni. She felt dizzy with the realization. Wrath rose within her, looking for its outlet. He must have noticed, for he cowered, holding up one hand as though to plead restraint and spoke quickly.

"He was dead. I swear he was already dead when I pierced him with the lance," defending himself from harsh accusing stares.

Mary Jacobe put a hand on Mary's arm as if to restrain her and filled her in. "He claims that his eyes were healed by the blood of Jesus."

The soldier continued to apologize profusely.

"We believe you," Martha assured him, holding tight to Mary's other arm to restrain her obvious reaction.

Ima walked forward to calm their nerves. "Come. Come and sit down and tell us everything."

Mary was bewildered. *How could Ima be so calm?* She closed her eyes and took a deep breath, following the crowd into a sitting area. She caught sight of Peter, surprisingly subdued yet cautious at the Roman soldier's presence. Perhaps Ima could work her calming effect on her also. She needed it right now, at this very moment. They sat. A lengthy and uncomfortable silence was finally broken.

"My name is Cassius Longinus,"[255] he volunteered. "I arrived in the second reinforcement. We were just changing guards when…" Cassius hesitated, then turned to Ima and said with solemn respect, "your son cried out 'Father, forgive them'. I knew then that this was not your typical criminal."

Peter cleared his throat and shifted his position as though demanding through some non-verbal communication an apology for even calling Jesus a criminal.

Cassius proved himself astute. "Sorry. Sorry. I don't mean to say he was a criminal. I had only heard of him and knew of a few of his teachings. My wife…". His countenance turned a shade of sorrow as he swallowed a lump in his throat. "She was Jewish." Cassius stopped, gaging their reactions.

That piqued Mary's interest. *A Jew married to a Roman. It happened, but was very uncommon. How did a Jewish woman come to marry a Roman soldier? Someone like myself perhaps? Being attracted to what was new and different? Falling into disgrace? Rejected by her own? An indentured servant perhaps?*

Cassius continued without explanation.

"She passed away just last year, and we never revealed to anyone that she had once practiced her traditions. But she would share with me some of her old beliefs. And I think she was still hoping for a Messiah. She kept insisting that I find out more about what Jesus was teaching. She was hopeful. In a Messiah. Well, I didn't pay it too much attention, until I was there. Yesterday." A smile broke out on Cassius' face as though he was recalling a wedding feast and not a crucifixion. Peter practically growled, bringing Cassius back to his audience.

281

"Sorry. I am so sorry!" He looked again at Ima with repentance in his eyes. She nodded, an expression of compassion and understanding encouraged him to continue his story.

"But it was extraordinary," Cassius said with greater tempered restraint. "I don't know how else to describe it. How can a man ask forgiveness for those who have treated him so cruelly? And I know Roman cruelty. This was above and beyond. Far worse than I have seen with others. I don't have...I mean, I didn't have the best eyesight, but even I could see the extent of brutality they inflicted on him. I just couldn't understand how one man could incur such wrath and hatred and then forgive his torturers."

Some of the women had been letting out small cries as he spoke. A profusion of "sorries" poured forth from Cassius once more as he sought assurance that he could continue speaking.

"Well, I began to remember some of what my wife had told me about the prophecies of the Messiah. That he would offer a new Kingdom. I never quite understood her, but I loved her and well, I tried to at least make her think I was listening," he said repentantly. "Well, I began to remember my wife's hopes when one of those thieves asked Jesus to remember him when he came into his Kingdom. And Jesus told him that today he would be with him in paradise. I just didn't understand how a man so close to his own death, and being tortured as he was, could be consoling and encouraging a thief! And then the weather, the earthquake, it was all too strange. Not normal. I said to myself right there. If there is only one God, and God has a Son, this man could just be it."

A new sensation toward this man was surfacing within Mary. Hope and wonder was fighting through the rage she had initially felt upon recognizing him.

"When I saw the other soldiers starting to break the bones of the thieves, I, well," he directed his gaze at Ima, "I just couldn't stand the thought of watching you suffer that too."

Mary had been watching Ima more than Cassius during the conversation and was in awe. Ima had a regal air about her. Her pallid face, however, gave away exhaustion. Her eyes filled with tears that flowed gently, yet she kept a tender gaze upon Cassius. A soft welcoming smile disarmed even the rigidness of Cassius' sons who seemed to relax a bit under her maternal presence.

"I am so truly sorry," sputtered Cassius. "I didn't want to let the soldiers break his bones and have you watch it. It was a sudden impulse to use my lance to show them that he was already dead. If I pierced his side and your son didn't react, then the others would be appeased with that and leave him be. But when I did. Oh! I knew. It was instantaneous. I could see perfectly. My eyesight had gotten worse very quickly over the last two years and I was afraid of being demoted or kicked out altogether. But when the blood and water poured out from your Son's side, it was as though I was cleansed. It was not just my eyes. I felt...I felt...something else. It was like I could see beyond seeing with my eyes. I knew. I just knew. He was the one my wife had spoken of, had been hoping for. He was the Messiah of whom you speak. He is the Son of God. I believe. And I have brought my sons. We want to join this, this...whatever it is. I want to help somehow."

All were stunned. Tears were streaming down Ima's face. Sorrow still etched upon it now mingled with praise to God.

John murmured, "These things happened so that the scripture would be fulfilled: 'Not one of his bones will be broken.'"[256]

Peter broke the mood with obvious irritation, grabbing the man by the arm and ushering him to the front door, his two sons following with a bewildered glance around the room.

"Look," Peter insisted as he opened the door to lead them out. "We don't have any sign up list, ok. You killed the Messiah. I don't know what comes next. But we would appreciate it if you did not let Roman officials know where we are. I don't know if they are looking for us as well. So please, go away and stay away. That is how you can help us."

He shut the door and turned to find himself face to face with John, Matthew, Andrew, Ima, Mary Magdalene and the women, all with expressions of disbelief.

"What?!" He said with raised hands defensively. "It's too dangerous to have these people coming around. I don't know how he knew we were here. Another Roman soldier, Abedanar, also found us. He came to us last night when we were hidden in the caves in the valley of Hinnom. If someone can find us so easily, we are safe nowhere and from no one."

An unexpected impatience welled up inside of Mary. Impatience over wanting to resolve their desperate situation and not knowing how. Impatience with Peter for not assuring them of the next steps they were to take. Impatience with his fear. Impatience was mixed with a sudden conviction that the visitors should not have been sent away. Something was happening that could not be stopped, should not be stopped. People were coming to believe in Jesus even though he had been crucified. But the conviction was mixed with residues of anger, and she directed it at Peter, an easy target at that moment.

"Don't you realize? These people need what the Messiah has given us. He knew he was going to be crucified. And he did this for us. He did this for them. I don't understand it either. But we can't just dismiss them when they have come asking about Jesus." Mary's ire was picking up and she unleashed it in full fury. "And by the way, where were you? We stayed with him up until his dying breath, in his three hours of agony on that cross. And where were you? You fled. You hid. You abandoned him."

Mary caught a glance at Matthew who was cowering in shame behind the women. Peter was simply speechless. Mary was breathing heavily as though on the verge of explosion. Ima stepped to her side and gently embraced her. She felt suddenly disarmed and ashamed.

Ima quietly spoke into her ear, "Have patience Mary. Each one is suffering in their own way."

Mary fled the room, ashamed to even catch the expressions in the others' faces after her outburst. She took refuge once again upon the rooftop.

Patience? She felt far from patient. She was very impatient, she realized. She felt like the Israelites wandering through the desert, freed from slavery to sin, anticipating arriving to the promised land, but uncertainty was still looming. There was no sign of a promised land. They were still adrift.

Rabboni, she groaned to herself as though uttering a prayer to him. She needed him. She needed to be with Jesus, even if it was only his body. A flashback brought her to a vivid memory of the Praetorium.[257]

Mary stood in the midst of an agitated crowd, pushing and shoving, screaming and ranting, "Crucify him! Crucify him!" Jesus stood still at the right hand of Pilate. His regal attire contrasted with the ragged attire of another man brought out of the dank prison to be presented before the crowd. Barabbas.

Ironic, Mary thought with a huff that betrayed disdain for the scene. It didn't slip her notice that Barabbas meant "son of the Father", yet the true son of the Father was Jesus. The contrast between the two could not have been greater. Proud and haughty on one side, humble and silent on the other. A man in chains, wrestling to free himself of his captors, clothed in his own filthy garments. A man in a scarlet cloak, dressed in the garment of a king with his bloody face and scourged body, and eyes that only conveyed compassion towards his own persecutors as he patiently awaited a final judgment.

Patient. Patient in suffering. How was that possible?

And then she heard Pilate cry out, words so true despite his ignorance. "Behold your King!"[258]

She longed even now to return to that moment and console Jesus in his agony. Oh, to kneel before him and anoint his feet, dark red and saturated from the stream of blood that ran down his frame. Oh, to honor the stones graced with smears that silently testified to an innocent victim. Those feet that would walk the cobblestone and rough path to Golgotha. Those feet that would be pierced. Oh, to be able to pour out precious oils and anoint him just once more! She ached with the desire to kiss him, to kiss those feet and show him the reverence that he deserved.

Her heart walked the painful path again from the Praetorium to Calvary. In her memory she felt each fall, heard each groan, longed to be that woman with the veil or the man pressed into service to carry the cross. She yearned for the honor of giving him some relief. She was afflicted once again like in that endless wait as the executioners held him in a prison cave at the side of the hill before his final execution. They forbade him the consolation of their company as he awaited the preparations upon Golgotha. She felt suspended in uncertainty and powerless, just as she had when they all longed to see him but dreaded the moment when he would be dragged from the prison only to be hung upon a cross.

She recalled how, near the cave-like prison partway up Golgotha, before his crucifixion, she saw a familiar face sitting upon a horse, watching her silently, almost cautiously. Gaius. She detected no scoffing, no arrogance. Like a silent wall, an observer, watching her more than Jesus. But her heart was elsewhere. Jesus was pulled *like a lamb led to slaughter* out of that little Golgotha prison and up the hill.

Three hours of agony awaited him. She thought they could humiliate him no more. But there upon Calvary the torture continued. Eighteen executioners for one almost completely incapacitated man. The crown of thorns, a cap of spiny branches with sharp needle-like points, was temporarily torn from his head. Clumps of bloody hair came off with it, reopening wounds that had congealed. It would be set upon him once again before raising him on high. His swollen disfigured face made him indistinguishable except for his undeniable eyes of goodness that sought to sustain them in their suffering rather than seek his own consolation from those who had not abandoned him.

The white woolen tunic that Ima had given to Jesus on the evening of the Last Supper was white no more. It had been soaked in an enormous loss of blood, now partially dried and sticking to dirt-filled wounds as a result of his falls. Without mercy, they ripped it from his body, exposing welts, lacerations, and a body completely bruised from hours of mistreatment.

Mary wrung her hands to the point of rawness, impatient to put a stop to the treachery. She began to hurl threats at the executioners. The women and John constantly tried to silence her. When the executioners went so far as to tear off his girdle, completely exposing him to public humiliation, she could take it no more. Rushing forward to shield him with her own body, she was restrained by a multitude of her companions' hands. But even this did not deter her.

Looking for some other way, she saw Gaius nearby, sitting on his horse, overseeing the entire event. She tore off her own veil, holding it out for him to see. Pulling free against restraining arms, she ran and began to climb upwards, slipping on the shale rocks beneath her feet. She fixed pleading eyes on Gaius. Something in his face changed. Compassion? Curiosity? With a swift tug at the bridle, he maneuvered the horse downhill. A moment of hope amidst desperation lit upon her countenance as he drew near.

"Gaius, please!" She half pleaded, half demanded. "If there is any mercy in your heart. I beg you, please. Show it now. Allow him to cover himself at least."

She held out her veil, shaking it for him to take. He said nothing, eyes fixed upon her tear stained face, disheveled hair flying in the wind, trembling lips. Finally, Gaius took the outstretched veil, turned and made his way back up the hill. He tossed it to a soldier with a brief order and in seconds, the soldier had undone the binding of Jesus' hands, and shoved the veil into them, ordering the executioners to let him cover himself.

Jesus wrapped himself in it, shaking as he attempted some form of modesty. Gaius had cut a piece of rope, ordering the same soldier to assist him in securing the makeshift garment. It did not go without harassment. The soldier was mocked by the executioners. Gaius let it go. The unknown soldier scowled back then ignored them. He wrapped the rope around Jesus and secured the veil as a makeshift girdle with a rough tug and knot.

The brief moment of relief and gratitude that Mary had experienced quickly faded as she watched in horror as Jesus was pushed to his knees and made to crawl upon the cross. They flipped him on his back and violently stretched his arms. Mary shuddered as one executioner knelt on his breast, while another pulled and tugged his arm into an unnatural position until they reached the premade holes in the wood. Then the sound of hammer and nail hit every nerve in her body. Cries of anguish from the women sounded out in sync with Jesus as the pain sent spasms through his entire body. The executioner simply wiped their faces of the blood spurting forth, as though it was sweat from a sporting excursion. Thirty-six strokes of hammer tortured the feet alone.

Ima's low sobs and moans of agony were a testimony to the sword piercing her own heart. At some point Mary lost the energy to sustain herself erect and fell to her knees, arms outstretched like a holocaust, an offering of her own life to God.[259] Yet she pleaded for an end to the agony as the Pharisees hovered nearby mocking them.

Her memory still held the echoes of that time, less than twenty-four hours earlier. Noises, so many noises grated upon her nerves still: Women screeching as a snake slithered out of the hole before being crushed by the cross falling into place. The thud of the heavy wood. Jesus grunting as the full weight of his body pulled upon his freshly nailed hands and feet. And then, a brief sacred silence. Only to be interrupted by the shofar announcing the Temple sacrifices. Donkeys bleating. Vendors shouting out with the hope of selling milk, profiting from curious spectators. Accusations. Curses from executioners. Instruments of torture being gathered and stored. The noise of the executioners rowdily taking their exit from the scene of their crime. Mockery from bystanders.

The woman and John had come closer up the hill when Mary had run forward. They huddled together, one supporting the other. Mary eluded the grasp of her companions again and pushed her way through the crowd and a line of distracted soldiers. She threw herself at the foot of the cross weeping. Two soldiers rushed forward. She felt the rough pressure upon her arms as she was pulled backwards. But she resisted, holding fast to the base of the cross, the top of her head just touching the tip of Jesus' feet. Mary scarcely registered a loud command and the soldiers' release on her arms.

"Leave her be. Let the mother and his friends through." Gaius had interceded for them. Mary's tears fell to the stone slab below Jesus' feet, mingling with Rabboni's own blood as she felt the presence of Ima and her friends. John half carried Ima. Mary Jacobe and Salome also approached, supporting one another. Mary shifted from her privileged spot at the feet of Jesus to make way for Ima as they knelt together.

Looking up, Mary saw no sign of life, no movement. She contemplated his feet, those feet she had so lovingly anointed. The vertical beam holding them fast was already covered with shades of bright to dark red as fresh blood oozed down the wood, dried and clotted. Ironically, it reminded her of a joyous occasion of treading barefoot in a wine press. Her own feet had been stained and sticky from red and purple grapes, sticky juice and colored pieces of skins sticking stubbornly between her toes. But there was nothing sweet and joyous about this moment. Here was Jesus, pressed like pulp, smashed like grapes to make wine.

Three hours of crushing, the longest three hours of her life. Darkness was descending as though existing candles were slowly extinguishing as Jesus' blood life was being drained. Mary felt a gathering storm within her as a strange heaviness in the weather came upon them. Then Jesus' lips began moving, praying, but his speech was indistinguishable. They began moving faster until words spilt forth for his close followers to hear. A prayer of King David[260]. Mary felt an intensity of despair and abandonment culminating in a passion ready to burst forth. And suddenly, Jesus raised his head to the heavens, heaving for air as fresh blood streamed forth from his nail piercings. He cried out, "Eli, Eli, lema sabachthani." Then his head fell forward to his chest. Silence.

Is that the end? She held her breath. The sky began to brighten as though a veil over the sun was receding. A mist played with the light, making the sun appear as a red ball of fire.[261] It appeared to beat with passion, like the devotion poured out by Ima, Mary Magdalene, John and many other women followers who remained at the cross or in groups at a distance.

At some point, Mary recalled the sound of many footsteps. Horse hooves stomped about nearby, then retreated. She dared not take her eyes off of Jesus, nor stop praying for strength. Movement all around signaled the changing of guard. Gaius watched on, uncertain of leaving, yet his troop of one hundred soldiers were ready to head out. Another troop came in their stead. Fifty soldiers commanded by Abedanar. In the commotion, the mocking began again, directed at Jesus as well as at his faithful followers. But Abedanar silenced the Pharisees and mockers.

And suddenly, Jesus heaved his body upward once again, another fresh trickle of blood oozing from his wounds. Then he sagged in exhaustion. Time taunted them, ticking slowly, marking each breath as possibly Jesus' last. One eye was completely swollen shut, yet one fixed upon his mother, then John.

A quiet voice, barely audible, "Women, behold your son." "John, behold your mother." John held Ima tighter as he nodded his tear filled assent.

In the distance, Mary could hear the Hallel Psalms being chanted in the Temple. Ima's lips moved in time to each verse. She was praying the psalms. Mary recognized some of lines. How could Ima pray such hymns of praise, of triumph and victory, when all seemed lost?

> How can I repay the Lord for all his goodness to me?
> I will lift up the cup of salvation and call on the name of the Lord.[262]
> For great is his love toward us, and the faithfulness of the Lord endures forever. Praise the Lord.[263]
> Give thanks to the Lord, for he is good; his love endures forever.[264]
> The Lord is with me; he is my helper. I will look in triumph on my enemies.[265]
> I was pushed back and about to fall, but the Lord helped me.
> The Lord is my strength and my song; he has become my salvation.
> Shouts of joy and victory resound in the tents of the righteous: "The Lord's right hand has done mighty things! The Lord's right hand is lifted high!"
> I will not die but live, and will proclaim what the Lord has done.[266]

Silence came momentarily from the Temple area and Ima raised her voice to recite what was usually spoken by the Father in the Passover.

"I will redeem you with outstretched arms and with great judgment".[267]

Her words brought fresh insult from the Pharisees who continued to watch the scene like hawks. But Abedanar silenced them once again.

Another agonizing movement from the cross, and Jesus cried out, "I thirst".

Mary looked around for something, some way to relieve his thirst. John had already sought a solution. He begged a soldier to give him water, pulling out some coins when the soldier refused. But they pushed him away. The centurion Abedanar, overhearing the exchange, ordered that they offer him vinegar at least. Another soldier stepped forward willingly to execute the command.

From the rooftop on that holy Sabbath day, Mary began to see moments of that agony anew, piecing together her newfound knowledge of Cassius, the one who lunged the spear into Jesus' side. He had stepped between the two who had refused Jesus a drink. Cassius tore the sponge out of one of the soldier's hands, squeezed out the old vinegar and soaked it in fresh wine. He made a contraption with a sprig of hyssop to help Jesus sip it more easily from the sponge and stuck it onto his lance. Holding it up, Jesus finally drank.

Then Jesus raised himself up once again and announced, "It is finished."

Heaving another breath with great effort, he lifted his head to the heavens and cried out, "Father, into your hands I commend my spirit." Then he bowed his head and gave up his spirit.[268] John and the women sank to the earth, as though offering a gesture of homage to a king, the king who had sacrificed himself for the sins of humanity. And in that moment, a droplet fell from the sky.

From the rooftop, in the present, a rain cloud played overhead with her emotions. The sun's rays warmed her face as a solitary rain cloud moved in. It prompted a flood of memories, acute details of a split second. The agony of those three hours brought fresh tears, but somehow, now, on the Sabbath, they were seen in a new light, as if time chose to linger upon that sacred moment. It sparked a brief glimmer of hope that the sacrifice offered was also received. She allowed her memory to take her back again to the foot of the cross, to that sacred space, a mere millisecond.

Silence and stillness. No more breath. Mary raised her arms to the heavens in an agonized cry for redemption from this plight of the cross. And then the heavens began to cry. Droplets fell upon her face as she turned upward in a silent plea to heaven that this entire agony be nothing but a dream, a nightmare from which she would awake. A sudden panic welled up within her. Her security, her foundation, gone. Her beloved, her life. He had given new meaning to her existence and suddenly it felt ripped away violently.

As though responding to her interior turmoil, the heavens flashed lightning and crashed thunder. The earth rumbled and the rock cracked, a fissure opening in the ground between Jesus' cross and the thief to the left who had cursed him. Abedanar jumped off his horse, knelt to the ground and beat his breast. Mary could hear him amidst a cacophony of shouts. "Truly this is the son of God," he proclaimed.

Disorder and pandemonium broke out. Horses became edgy, threatening to buck off their riders. Pharisees directed the soldiers, insisting that they break Jesus' legs to make sure he was dead. They began with the thieves, their fearful pleas and final shouts adding to the symphony of chaos. Other soldiers started dragging the women and John away from the cross. Before Mary realized what was happening, Cassius had placed himself between the soldiers and Jesus. Discussion ensued, an argument broke out, and the Pharisees intervened. Mary watched with horror, paralyzed and grasping onto Ima and John. Before they could even cry out to stop him, Cassius had thrust the lance upwards. Ima gasped, her hands flying to her own breast as though she herself had been pierced with the same lance.

Now she saw it with new eyes. It had not been a hateful attempt to provoke more agony. *It was a fulfillment?* The words of a prophecy resonated in her heart as she tried to make sense of it all.

> And I will pour out on the house of David and the inhabitants of Jerusalem a spirit of grace and pleas for mercy, so that, when they look on me, on him whom they have pierced, they shall mourn for him, as one mourns for an only child, and weep bitterly over him, as one weeps over a firstborn.[269]

From the rooftop, Mary felt agony and awe, remorse and reverence. She thought of Ima, suffering for her firstborn, her only child. She recalled her many tears, yet her deep tranquility. She recalled Jesus speaking of his Father, his Father's will, his Father in Heaven. But a gnawing question remained. *How could a Father sacrifice his only Son? Who was this God, this Father, that Jesus had spoken of so often? Who was He really? Too many questions. And no answers. Rabboni, help us!*

CHAPTER 49. THE SABBATH WAIT

But now, O Lord, You are our Father,
We are the clay, and You our potter;
And all of us are the work of Your hand.
Psalm 98:1

Signs of dusk painted the skyline, signaling an approaching end to Shabbat. The waiting felt endless. She longed to return to the tomb, anything to be near Jesus once again, even if it was just his dead body. The rooftop terrace had become her place to contemplate a myriad of memories. From there, she had seen John run after Cassius and his sons, welcoming them back to the house. Then Little James had arrived with a couple of the other disciples in search of Peter and wanting to console Ima. Ima had suggested that they at least gather the Eleven and whoever else they could find of the dispersed disciples, whoever had not fled too far away. They would reunite here in Mary Mark's house. Little James had left to see who he could gather.

The Apostles had continued arriving throughout the afternoon from wherever they had hidden. She had finally relinquished her rooftop vantage point and went below when the sun was at its peak. The atmosphere in the house was solemn and quiet. As they entered, they gravitated to Ima on the pretense of consoling her. But she was the one who consoled everyone. They whispered their greetings, as though to not awaken the dead.

Mary wondered at their suffering. Why had they fled? So many had fled. She tried not to judge. She knew her own fragility. She too had abandoned him at one point. But even if she had to relive those hours of agony, she would stay with Jesus. She would not leave him to suffer alone. As painful as it was, she felt a certain honor at having beheld

Jesus' sacrifice, at having witnessed each wound as they had washed and anointed his body.

She studied each one's face as they arrived. Expressions of guilt, fear and doubt, relief at finding solidarity and refuge among those they knew. Each one was being forged. They were being shaped by circumstances beyond their control and responding in their own way, the best they knew how.

Uncertainty loomed, but a sense of solidarity was growing. And Ima drew them together. She was like a rock, their rock, with her silent, suffering, yet maternal presence. Despite a sorrowful countenance, her inner strength and gentle peace, pacified some of the anxiety in all who approached her.

Mary Marcus continued being their hostess. At her request, Mary Magdalene helped the other women prepare a meal, expecting many hungry mouths to feed. They worked in silence, a somber mood settling around everyone. She turned at the sound of a familiar voice.

"Miriam! There you are!" Johanna entered the kitchen, John in her wake. "Dear Miriam. How are you?" Her greeting was her undoing once again. Mary rushed forward and embraced her, tears flowing from an unknown endless supply. She had always felt Johanna to be a kindred spirit and a comforting presence, almost maternal.

John waited quietly, respectfully.

"Miriam, knowing you, I am guessing you are anxious to return to the tomb, but I come with news and a warning to heed. Chuza told me that even Herod is distraught over the events and that several Pharisees have been insisting that Pilate heavily guard the tomb."

John piped in, "They are afraid we will steal the body and claim that Jesus rose from the dead. Little James has returned with the last of us. Peter is convoking us now. We are going to discuss what we should do."

"Come and join us Miriam," Johanna gently persisted.

"Yes, I will join you." She was eager to know their plans. She desperately wanted to go to the tomb, soldiers or not.

Johanna greeted the other women as they tidied up and readied the kitchen so as to join the others. She noticed Martha pull Johanna aside and heard her name spoken between them.

"Johanna, Call her Mary. She insisted on not being called Miriam. I don't want to upset her more. She's been overly distraught."

Johanna looked bewildered but agreed. Martha noticing that Mary had overheard. She cleared her throat and started shooing everyone out of the kitchen, "Come, let's join the Apostles."

They entered the upper room. Many of the same faces from just two nights previous were present, but how the mood had changed. It was still a solemn one, but the warmth of Jesus' presence lingered no more. Nerves were taut and vigilance heightened, as though all were holding their breath, awaiting an unknown fate. Groups were dispersed throughout the room, quietly discussing, while Peter, John, a few of the Eleven and the women were gathered near Ima.

She spotted Cassius and his two sons off to the side. Matthew accompanied them as if to make them feel part of this renegade group. She looked to Peter who caught her eye, a silent understanding between them. *So, he seemed to have changed his mind about Cassius.* He quickly turned his attention back to the gathered group who was starting to address him.

"I think we should return to Galilee as soon as possible," Thomas contended, a note of anxiety in his insistence. "There is less unrest there. It will be safer."

John concurred. "Jesus did say that after he had been raised up, he would go ahead of us to Galilee."

Several expressed their disbelief and mumbled disgruntledly, "After he is raised up?" "Do you really believe that after that crucifixion there was any chance of survival?" A cacophony of voices rose up. "That is what he said. We need to wait and see." "It's impossible." "He raised Lazarus from the dead. It is not impossible."

Commotion broke out among the men disputing if they should wait or not, whether or not they truly believed it was possible that he would come back from the dead.

Mary noticed Peter tense up, like an old wine skin ready to burst its fermenting contents. She felt a surge of irritation and anger at his lack of leadership turned to desperation as the noise level of the discussions climbed. She detected his attempts at self-containment and remembered how Matthew and John had shared with her that Jesus had entrusted the keys of the Kingdom to him. Anger turned to fear for them all, followed by pity and compassion, empathy at the thought of the burden he now bore.

Oh Rabboni, she silently lifted up a prayer as though Jesus were at her side, a habit that seemed to be forming over the last twenty-four hours, despite knowing that he was nowhere near. *Help us! Help Simon Peter!*

She caught Peter's glance. *Do something! Lead us! Please Peter,* her eyes pleaded. She watched him turn to the heavens and inhale, as though mustering up strength. Then he raised his voice.

"Enough! Enough! Calm down everyone! Of one thing I am certain. The less movement the better. Stay out of the streets and out of sight of the religious leaders and Romans." An embarrassed silence ensued as many shot suspicious glances towards Cassius and his sons.

"You have no need to fear us," Cassius interjected. "I can come and go carefully. I went myself to request charge of the guards at the tomb yesterday and left some others to guard it today. But this morning in the barracks, before my first visit here, I heard that Pilate was anxious and caving into the Pharisee's request for more guards to be posted at the tomb."

Mary interiorly rebelled at this news. "We must return. I will return, soldiers or not." She felt the pressure of Johanna's hand on her arm.

"It's true Mir…Mary. It is not safe. Herod also has stationed guards there. I sent one of the servants this morning to check."

"It would be best to wait at least a day or two. Perhaps with just a little more time they will lighten the guards there. I will check the situation again tonight and can let you know tomorrow how the situation stands," Cassius offered.

Mary began to protest, but Peter cut her off, looking to Ima who sat quietly. "Ima, what do you think?"

"Remember my son's words. Heed them and trust. The only thing to do now is to pray and wait."

And with those few words, she settled it. Some heads nodded. Dissenters acquiesced, bowing their heads as though accepting the order. A certain calm returned. They prepared for the Sabbath's end and prayed. Ima led the welcoming of Sabbath's end and Peter followed, leading them in various prayers. At times, he still looked on the verge of coming undone. But then she saw that he mustered up courage to lead them. It was a forced attempt, but he did it nonetheless, offering Mary some relief and making her proud of him.

Ima was the more uniting factor in this moment. It felt right that she was among them. Mary observed how often Peter looked to her for reassurance. Ima gave him discreet and maternal encouragement. They all felt buoyed up by her. Doubt plagued many. They struggled to not despair. They prayed and slowly, very slowly, a quiet hopefulness mingled with the sorrow that hung over the entire house. For her part, hope and despair, calm and restlessness took shape in her like clay that was being molded by a potter's hands. When despair and restlessness took hold, she grasped onto the memories that had once brought her hope and calm, awaiting their return.

CHAPTER 50. THE LAST ANOINTING

For when she poured this perfume on My body,
she did it to prepare Me for burial.
Matthew 26:12

Twilight had come and gone in its full splendor over Jerusalem. Now, the night lent a darkness to the senses that paralleled Mary's understanding. Stupefied, was the only way to describe it. The Sabbath had officially come to a close, but Mary's heart was far from closing the chapter of the previous days' events. Cassius and his sons had left, the disciples remained gathered in small groups, some taking turns for vigilance of the surrounding areas. The Sabbath meal had been cleared and cleaned and more bread baked for the next day. Darkness had descended, and she was restless. She wanted to prepare to go to the tomb, to anoint Jesus' body with greater thoroughness, but they had little materials left, despite the great supply Nicodemus had brought the day they left him in the tomb.

At last, she convinced Peter that they could go discreetly to the Temple area where vendors had the supplies they needed. John and John Mark were to accompany her. In the darkened night, they did not fear notice. They would blend into the crowd still present for the Passover festivities like a handful more of pilgrims not yet returning to their distant lands. She hoped the situation would be calmer in Jerusalem when they did finally leave, but for now, they could make the most of the crowd's cover.

They were just about to leave, cloaks, bags and baskets in hand when the door burst open. One of the newer disciples on guard was distraught.

"A man is here. He says he is looking for John. I think he is one of the Pharisees. He is here with a servant and a wheelbarrow of stuff."

"Nicodemus?" John rushed past the disciple, Mary following, and recognized the old man, despite his cloaked attire. He did not present himself in his traditional religious garb. Two other disciples were holding him at bay. Nicodemus waited patiently. His servant looked frightened out of his wits.

"Let him be. He is a friend. Let him pass." John escorted them into the house. Nicodemus uncovered his head. A silvery white head of hair matched his long beard. Eyes of kindness looked about, a look she had noticed the previous day when she saw him arrive with a wagon full of oils and spices.[270] She had been taken aback at the quantity and quality. She had estimated that it amounted to several months of wages and fit for the anointing of a king. Her heart had swollen with gratitude, but she had never thanked him.

Nicodemus now caught sight of Ima and approached her with tenderness, taking her hand and whispering condolences. He opened a satchel he had hidden under his cloak and pulled out a long, stained tunic. *Jesus' tunic!* The tender transfer of sacred goods between old man and mother was made. Mary rushed forward as though she were seeing her Rabboni. Ima was pressing the garment to her heart, muttering thanks as tears streamed down her face. Mary joined her side, kneeling before the precious garment, taking a piece of it in her hands and burying her face in it, kissing it as though reliving the many times she washed Jesus' feet with tears and kissed them. A touch on her shoulder caught her attention. She lifted her face and was presented with another gift. Her veil. The one she had sacrificed for Jesus' modesty. Words did not escape, but gratitude poured forth in tears.

Nicodemus addressed them. "I was able to buy the tunic from a soldier. And the veil was left in a pile when we anointed his body. It was among the things we collected and brought back home quickly upon leaving the tomb. I thought it would be appreciated in your possession. And I brought more items." He gestured to the wheelbarrow overflowing with gifts, from food to spices and more oils.

"I was able to purchase more from the Temple market, despite areas being closed. There was quite a bit of damage done from the earthquake yesterday."

Gratitude was offered by all who had gathered to witness the scene. Nicodemus was offered hospitality and installed himself in Ima's, Peter's, and John's company as several others unloaded the goods. Mary and some other women set to work preparing baskets, ready for the journey to the tomb as soon as they were able.

***

Nightfall came and attempts to rest began. Mary lay on the floor with the other woman, having made some separations for sleeping quarters in the large house. She couldn't sleep, but she dared not stir. She remained still, imagining Jesus wrapped in those linen cloths, lying alone in the tomb. She returned in memory to that tomb and its previous events.

Joseph of Arimathea, a friend perhaps of Nicodemus, paid the soldiers to assist them, and mostly to leave them alone as they prepared his body for burial. Abedanar left with the majority of his troops, leaving only Cassius and a handful of soldiers. Cassius took charge, commanding in a low, solemn, but firm voice. Slowly they lowered his body off the cross and into the arms of Ima. The image was etched in her mind. Even a few remaining soldiers took off their helmets at the sight of tender reverence with which she held her son.

John acquired a basin of water and a sponge. He dipped it into the basin and handed it to Ima. Slowly, tenderly, she wiped his blood stained head and face, kissing each piercing as it was exposed. The sponge and water quickly turned red. Mary Jacobe took charge of replenishing the basin with fresh water throughout the agonizing ordeal. Mary knelt at Jesus' feet, not bothering to wash them clean. Her tears sufficed. Her hair once again lent its service. Scraps of cloth appeared from somewhere. They continued washing Jesus' body. Mary Jacobe and Salome dabbed the body dry after the sponge cleansing, adding their own tears to the ritual.

At some point, Nicodemus arrived, his servant pushing a large cart. Jesus' body had already stiffened. When the women had done what they could, he convinced Ima to let go and let the men move his body into the tomb. He, Joseph of Arimathea, John and the servant carefully lifted the body from Ima's arms and carried him to the tomb to finish the cleansing.

The servant handed Nicodemus a large basket full of more supplies for cleansing. They emptied it all, assessed if they had what was sufficient to finish the task and to wrap the body. Mary and the women watched from outside the tomb as the men consulted and finally, John spoke with the servant. The servant ran off to fetch another clean linen. They were now making haste, for the Sabbath was approaching.

At first, Mary and the women waited. No words were spoken, only an occasional sob broke through as memories of his wounded body barraged their thoughts. But Mary could not remain idle. She grabbed the empty basket that Nicodemus had tossed aside and set out a short distance away to a wild patch of garden that was growing on the western base of Golgotha. She wanted to gather flowers.[271] It would be her contribution to the spices and other ointments that she saw in the cart brought by Nicodemus.

The blooming garden area was a stark contrast to the protruding rock surface where two of the three crosses still stood. Jesus' cross remained, standing on the highest surface. She looked up at it. The sun behind her back warned of the approaching dusk. Sabbath was creeping upon them. The holy day. And yet she did not feel bound to it. There was something holier in the sight of the cross upon which Jesus had hung. It glistened as the sun penetrated the lifting fog, giving witness to the blood spilt. *Spilt for me? Spilt for that good thief who repented?*

The weather had once again changed quickly after the earthquake. All was still, the people gone. She longed to lay down in the patch of green, decked with yellow, red and purple wildflowers and bask in the last of the day's comforting rays, forgetting the horror of the preceding hours. It was a silent garden, with exception of the executioners working to pull out the crosses, tossing them into a ravine on the back side of Golgotha where an abandoned quarry[272] received the used and bloody instruments of torture.

Basket full, she heard John call her name. At last, they could enter the tomb. Mary approached eagerly. They began the anointing. Jesus' body had the palish color of death on the few places of skin that had not been scourged, bruised or beaten. Spices and herbs were gently placed in each wound. A costly powder was sprinkled over his scourged body. The entire tomb filled with a sweet and musky scent. Mary, remembering that she still carried a small flask of anointing oil, sought it out in the hidden pocket of her dress. Unplugging the top, she emptied the contents onto his feet, washing it gently over their entirety, kissing the gaping wound several times as she did so. The men stood aside, daring not to rush the women, but evidently watching the horizon as the sun warned of the time.

At last, the wounds prepared and the body covered in a soft oily myrrh water, the servant arrived with a large cloth. It was all he could attain, he said. John said it was fine. It was the table cloth they had used for their last supper together, the one Mary remembered spreading over the long table for the Twelve, impressed with its length with no seam. It would be long enough to double under and over him. John and Nicodemus held and turned the body as the women placed half of the long linen cloth under Jesus and gently rolled him back upon it. They helped to move the arms of the stiff body in place. Joseph placed two coins on the eyes to hold them shut. Mary felt the threat of this sacred ritual coming to an end as they lengthened the other end of the linen cloth, preparing to place it over top of him.

"Wait!" She cried out with a sob, startling them all.

She grabbed her basket of flowers and began a procession-like scattering of petals from feet to head and down again, covering him in a display of color. Ima kissed his cheeks once again and pulled off a scarf she had around her neck. It was the linen cloth offered to her from Claudius Procula. She placed it over his face and stepped back, silently signaling the closing of the sacred affair. The longer linen cloth was set upon him and tucked in on all sides. More myrrh water was poured over him. Mary stayed at his feet, as a reverent and implacable adorer, until John finally lifted her arm, telling her that it was time to leave. Dusk was upon them, threatening a late return to their dwelling. Nonetheless, Mary hesitated leaving, as did the other women. To leave signified a finality they were not yet willing to accept.

The few remaining soldiers had finished discarding the crosses and were waiting for them to finish, impatiently but surprisingly respectful. John finally ushered the women out of the burial cave. Stopping opposite the tomb, they stood like sentinels, enduring the definitive moment. The soldiers maneuvered a system with a long hefty pole and ropes so as to roll the large stone into its resting place before the tomb's opening.

How would they ever be able to enter that after the Sabbath ended? Mary wondered. She had already determined to return, unwilling to leave the body unaccompanied more time than necessary. A heaving grunt and straining of the soldiers rocked the stone. It rolled and then eased into stillness, sealing with finality the truth of Jesus' death.

It hit her like a heavy blow. Sinking, drowning anguish and confusion brought her to her knees. John lifted her. Mary Jacobe took her arm. Salome clung to Ima as John led the way away from the scene of death. They began a silent procession back to Mary Marcus' house. Bethany was definitely too far to walk with the Sabbath upon them. At the edge of the garden, Mary stopped and looked back. The large tombstone was still in sight. She shook off her companions and told them to continue. She would be right behind them. Thinking she may have dropped something, they continued on with a warning to hurry.

Mary returned to the tomb. The soldiers were not in sight. But the fulcrum system had been left lying on the ground. She leaned against the large stone, head bowed against it, willing it to no longer be a barrier between her and Jesus. Approaching voices and footsteps startled her as she recognized the soldiers' movements, returning perhaps for their instruments. She turned and ran to catch up to the others.

***

The sound of snoring brought her back to the present. Quietly she stretched her muscles, stiff from the hard cold floor and the tensed stillness she had maintained as she had relived Friday's anointing. In her mind's eye, she turned her vision in the direction of that garden where Jesus was buried. Something in her heart shifted. All at once, a glimmer of hope simmered up. A restless expectation nurtured an eagerness to return. She had already determined to go back as soon as possible. Considering that sleep eluded her, she sat up quietly. No more waiting. Adjusting her vision in the dark of night, she sought the safest path out without waking the many sleepers. She tiptoed through the maze of women, a silent prayer filling her heart. *Rabboni, I am coming!*

CHAPTER 51. THE GARDEN ENCOUNTER

He will swallow up death forever.
The Sovereign Lord will wipe away the tears from all faces;
he will remove his people's disgrace from all the earth.
The Lord has spoken.
Isaiah 25:8

First Easter Sunday. Inside the empty tomb.[273]

Rabboni, where are you?!

She shivered in the chilled compartment that had once held her beloved Jesus. The cold stone underneath penetrated through her dress. Copious tears had wet her front and the linen cloth she still grasped. Her tears were subsiding, but confusion reigned. The flame in the lamp had extinguished and midnight darkness engulfed her. She pulled herself to her knees, one hand reverently holding fast to the stone ledge where they had placed Jesus just hours earlier. The other hand held fast to part of the large linen cloth.

Where is he? Did someone take him?

The darkness of the tomb was suddenly invaded by a bright blinding light. *Had the sun already risen?* She didn't think it could be so bright so early. She shielded her eyes with her hand and squinted in the direction of the source. It was coming from inside, practically in front of her, on the ledge where they had laid Jesus' body. A radiant figure appeared as a vision. Fear seized hold of her. She dropped the linen cloth, stumbled out of the inner chamber, through the first chamber and out the opening. She kept running, through the garden. She had not gone far when she saw familiar figures approaching her in the dawn's twilight. Johanna, Salome, and Mary Jacobe had arrived, carrying more baskets.

"Mary? Is that you? What happened? We awoke and you were gone! Why did you come alone this morning? You should have waited for us!"

Mary was breathing heavily, confusion and fright trumping reason. She grabbed Johanna's arms and attempted to tell them what happened, looking back with fear at the empty tomb.

"He is not there! He's gone!" She sputtered out.

They bombarded her with questions, "But how do you know? How did you move the stone? Did the guards take him?"

"An earthquake. The stone cracked in two. The guards ran away. I went in, but he is gone." She tore away from them, leaving them in a stupor, watching after her running form.

"I have to get back! I have to tell Peter and John."

She left them as she ran back to Mary Mark's house. *What would she tell them? What could they do? Maybe Cassius or Nicodemus can find out if he was taken by some of the soldiers in the night?*

Finally arriving at the house, out of breath, she burst in, startling two of the disciples who had been stationed inside the entrance. They had no time to react before she fled into the larger room where several men were still fast asleep on couches, a few were already awake, conversing in small groups. Startled by her sudden presence they all froze. She searched the crowd frantically and spotted Simon Peter and John.

Rushing forward she blurted out, tears streaming unbidden once again, "They have taken the Lord out of the tomb!"

"What!?" Peter was not sure if he should be more astonished at her words or her appearance. She looked like she had been wrestling in a garden, her hair tumultuous and without a veil, her lower garment had evidence of clingy thorns and jagged holes where the fabric had torn. Spiny branches, streaks of dirt, the wetness of dew now decorated much of her dress. And her front top side was damp, likely with her own tears, he thought.

John intervened, trying to calm her down, "Sit down Mary. Tell us. Who took him? Where did they take him?"

A chaise cleared of a now awakened disciple, and she plopped down. Her face continued searching the crowd as though looking for the culprit. Her arms raised, hands palms up in a gesture expressing uncertainty and confusion. She finally fixed her eyes on Peter, "I don't know where they put him!"[274]

Peter turned and ran out of the house without a word. John ran in his wake. Mary looked about, all eyes on her, waiting for more explanation. But she had none. She fled after Peter and John, knowing that they were racing to the tomb. She arrived on the verge of Peter entering the empty tomb. John was standing at the entrance, waiting for her. He helped her to enter before him. The morning light now lent them some vision in the obscure cave. Peter stood incredulous in the first chamber, hands running over his forehead, grasping his hair, mouth wide open as he stared at the linen cloth on the ground in the second chamber. John went in further, picking up the head cloth that sat rolled up to one side. He looked back to Mary, eyes and mouth wide open, a smile bursting forth, as though their shared expectation had borne fruit and he was on the verge of inviting her to rejoice with him. They looked to Peter who was shaking his head now, speechless. He turned heel and left the tomb, muttering. They followed him out.

"We need to regroup."

John gestured to Mary to follow Peter.

"Let's go back and tell the others," John said to Mary, as Peter had already gone ahead, obviously returning to the house.

"But where is his body?" Mary looked as though she was going to be distraught again.

"I don't know Mary. But he said he would rise on the third day. He has to be somewhere. Come, let's return to the house."

"You go. I will be right behind you. I want to get the linen cloth we wrapped him in."

John hesitated, then nodded and set off running to catch up to Peter.

She felt as if a cloud hung over her understanding. Confusion, anger, disbelief, but mostly a crazed desire to find Jesus overwhelmed her. She stooped down to look again in the cave, half expecting to see Jesus' body, as though she hadn't searched well enough the first two times. Tears clouded her vision, and her hair fell over her face, making her feel like all was a dream. She went in further to retrieve the cloth. She recalled the figure she had seen earlier and adjusted her vision. Now, in the same spot, she saw two figures, they sat on the stone couch-like ledge, one where his feet had once been, one where his head had lain.

What are they doing?! Maybe they know where Jesus has been taken? Before she could utter her plea for information they spoke.

"Woman, why are you weeping?"[275]

"They have taken my Lord, and I don't know where they have put him."

A rustle behind her startled her. She turned abruptly, almost hitting her head on the low stone separation between the two chambers. She went to the entrance of the tomb, looking about.

A gardener. Surely, he saw what happened!

Dawn's light gave the gardener an ethereal quality. She rushed toward him, intent on pleading with him to give her information. The man repeated the question of the two who were stationed in the tomb.

"Woman, why are you weeping? Who are you looking for?"

Hope momentarily tempered her exasperation over being no closer to finding him. She anticipated that help had come at last. She pleaded, "Sir, if you have carried him away, tell me where you have put him."

She suddenly became aware that he may not want to be involved in stealing away a body and added, "I will get him."

She searched the grounds with her back to the gardener, half expecting to find his body amidst the brush.

"Mary."

Her heart practically arrested when she heard the familiar voice. Like a sheep that recognizes its shepherd, she knew that voice. It registered like soft sweet honey fresh from the comb, like the sun's warm rays finally chasing away the cold dewy dawn. Her heart leapt, transporting her to the first time she heard him call her name. Back then, he was but a stranger. Yes, a Savior who was but a stranger. He would become her friend, her confidant, her Master. And now he was her beloved! And he was there, alive, right before her!

Like a fountain exploding she cried out as she rushed to throw herself at his feet and embrace him, "Rabboni!"

But he eluded her. She landed before him, unable to touch him.

"Do not cling to me," he said, half scolding, half laughing.

It hit her like a shock to the heart, yet she felt it more like an invitation than an order. She looked up at him. Now she saw him. The same loving eyes, his closed-mouthed subtle smile, almost laughing at her, delighting in her, acknowledging her love for him, as "clingy" as it was. And he loved her in return.

"I have not yet ascended to my Father and your Father, to my God and your God."

His words resonated forcefully, etching themselves in her soul.

"Go and tell my brethren I have told you these things."

In a blink, he was suddenly gone. She longed for his return. And yet she did not feel the same void. She looked around, expecting to find that he had just moved from one place to another. She peeked back into the tomb. Nothing, no mysterious figures to ask her why she was crying, no gardener, no Jesus. Just the abandoned linen cloth. She grabbed it, a reminder that she had seen the Lord and he was dead no longer. And she ran back to the house. His words resounded in her heart with every step. *My Father and your Father. My Father? I am a daughter to a Father? A Father-God.*

She remembered the day after her betrayal, when she had prayed the prayer, *Our Father,* that Jesus had taught them. But his words struck her in a new way this time, penetrating and shaping a profound sense of her identity. *A daughter to a Father-God?* What mysteries! What joy filled her heart! She could not explain the overwhelming change that seemed to pulse through her veins. And yet new tears, tears of profuse joy and gratitude fell as she held onto that linen cloth and the vivid memory of that blessed encounter in the garden.

I have seen the Lord! I have seen my Rabboni! He is alive!

CHAPTER 52. I HAVE SEEN THE LORD!

Mary Magdalene went to the disciples with the news:
"I have seen the Lord!"
And she told them that he had said these things to her.
John 20:18

"I have seen the Lord!" Mary proclaimed as she burst through the doors once again. She was exuberant. But her audience was unresponsive. Faces of shock stared back at her. But she would not be deterred. She announced again, "I have seen the Lord! He is alive! I saw him with my own eyes." She turned to Peter and John. "After you left," she said, "he was in the garden."

Some of the disciples scoffed. "Sounds like pure nonsense." She was taken aback by their reaction. She assumed they would be rejoicing as she was.

Just then Johanna, Mary Jacobe and Salome entered, returning with baskets still full of items they had intended for anointing Jesus' body.

Mary ran to them and grabbed Johanna. "I have seen the Lord! He is risen!"

Mary Jacobe looked hopeful, "You saw him? Where? We were there. We didn't see him."

"We didn't see Jesus, but we did see two men in the tomb," Johanna added.

"I am sure they were angels," insisted Salome.

Big James interrupted, "Mother, where have you been? What happened?"

"We had just entered the tomb," Mary Jacobe offered an explanation. "It was after you left Mary. We wanted to see if it was true that Jesus' body was gone. And suddenly two men in brilliant clothes appeared."

Salome piped in, "I don't think they were men. I mean, they sort of looked like men, but not like normal men."

Mary Jacobe continued. "They said to us, 'Why look among the dead for someone who is alive? He is not here; he is risen.' They told us to remember what Jesus told us when he was still in Galilee: that the Son of man was destined to be handed over into the power of sinful men and be crucified and rise again on the third day.'"[276]

"We didn't see you there," Peter commented.

Johanna intervened, "We were afraid to return and tell everyone. We," she hesitated, looking around at the incredulous stares. "We didn't think anyone would believe us. So, we went to my residence at Herod's court. I went to see what happened to the guards and if anyone had news of what had happened. Cassius and three other soldiers have been arrested for letting people steal the body of Jesus."

Mary burst forth, "No! But no one stole his body. He has risen! I've seen him!"

Peter interjected, "Let's just calm down."

Johanna tried to comfort Mary, "I don't believe anyone stole the body either, but that is the rumor going around. Many are saying that we, his disciples, have stolen the body to make it look like he survived, like he really did rise from the dead as he predicted."

"And he really did, just as he told us, don't you remember?" Mary looked around at the other disciples, frantically hoping they would believe her if she appealed to their memory. But most remained silent, expressions wary and hesitant.

Johanna continued, "Those men, the ones in the tomb, they told us that Jesus is going to Galilee and that we will see him there, just as he told us."[277]

"And," Mary added, "In the garden he told me that he is going to my Father and your Father; to my God and your God."

The groups broke out murmuring, wondering what that meant. Peter looked like he wasn't sure what to believe. John caught Mary's eyes. She felt some relief. She could tell he believed her. Good John, he had faith. He remembered Jesus' words and believed. He believed her. But it looked like many of the others did not. An argument was breaking out among the disciples as to whether or not they should go right away to Galilee.

Mary ran to Ima, kneeling before her, pleading quietly, "You believe me Ima? Do you believe that he is alive?"

Ima took her hand and nodded, "Yes, I believe you daughter." She possessed a calm joy, while Mary seemed to have left her joy behind in the tomb.

"Tell them Ima. Make them believe."

"Each one must come to believe on their own. You can't force faith."

The volume was increasing as the disciples debated their next move.

"If he said we should go, we should go right away."

Mary was heartened by the disciples' comments. It meant that some believed. But there was still much opposition.

"I want proof." "I want to see with my own eyes before we set off."

"I think it is too soon to leave for Galilee."

"We should stay put for now. There will be even more guards on watch right now."

"They are probably looking for us if they believe us to be thieves."

"No, this is the time to go. Now. There are many people returning to their homes after Passover, we can slip out unnoticed, like one more pilgrim."

Peter hushed everyone and settled the dispute. "For now, we stay. Let's be on the watch. I am going to see if I can talk to Nicodemus to get word of this rumor. And I want to go back to the tomb area."

John insisted that he go as well. But Mary Jacobe said it didn't seem safe for them to go out right now.

Little James scolded his mother, "Then why were you out there mother?!"

"Well, they aren't going to be looking for a little old woman. I can't carry Jesus' body! But they will be looking for young men, like yourselves," she pointed at John. "Be careful."

Peter settled it. "Yes, stay here John. Many of the Pharisees know you. I don't want you having a run in with them now."

And Peter departed, leaving them all to wait. A disciple securely locked the door as soon as he left.

Throughout the day people came and went, heeding, for the most part, Peter's warnings to stay close to home and be discreet if they did leave. Some went to Bethany to send word to Lazarus and to let the missing disciples, those who had fled there on Thursday night, know what was happening. Others left for more supplies. Johanna left, assuring Mary that she would return, hoping to bring Little Joanna with her, if she was able to escape her husband. He was very ill and little Joanna was consumed in his care. It reminded Mary that she was not the only one suffering right now and she lifted up a prayer for his healing and for little Joanna's fortitude in this time.

In the meantime, several guests arrived. One of which greatly surprised Mary. She had retreated to her favorite spot upon the rooftop, wrestling with impatience once again and hoping to soon hear of the direction they could take as a community. She hoped, as well, that more would believe her words. A few of the disciples looked at her like she was crazy. She felt sorry for them more than angry. She returned in memory to her encounter with Jesus in the garden. She hadn't recognized him. He was different. The same, but different. She could still hear his voice speaking her name. Like an echo that resonated in the cavern of her heart, it brought peace and joy to recall that blessed moment. In the early afternoon she was interrupted from basking in her memories.

John peeked his head up through the opening that led to the rooftop terrace. "Mary, I've got a surprise for you! A friend has come to see you!"

"Miriam of Magdala!" That voice reminded her of the Sea of Galilee.

"Aharon," she exclaimed, jumping up to greet him. "You found us!" Mary peered down the steps, expecting to see her boisterous baker friend. "Where is Demetria? Is she down below? Bring her up!"

"No Miriam, she did not travel with me this Passover. I left her with my mother. She is, shall we say...," Aharon's face turned beet red as he hesitated then finally said it, "indisposed."

Mary's jaw dropped. *Demetria...pregnant!* She had prayed for her, begged Jesus for the gift of children for them since they had been barren for many years. But it felt so long ago. She had actually given up hope that her intercession was effective. Mary threw her arms around Aharon and kissed him on the cheek to congratulate him. Aharon turned an even deeper shade of red, if that was possible, but Mary dismissed it.

"That was for Demetria, but since you didn't bring her, you will have to take my joy to her!"

"Yes, I will do that. I saw Simon, well I guess you now call him Peter. I couldn't leave without telling you the good news. I thought you might need it, seeing what happened to the Rabboni. I am truly sorry Miriam."

She realized that she was the bearer of good news as well and was bursting to share it. "Aharon, don't be sorry! You bring good news, but I have even more wonderful news for you and Demetria!"

Aharon looked almost frightened to hear her announcement. She continued.

"You were right to think that Jesus was the Messiah. And the Sanhedrin and Romans had him crucified. But I have seen him, Aharon! He told us he would be crucified and on the third day would rise. He is risen! He is the Messiah we were waiting for. The Son of the living God!"

Aharon looked confused, like he was searching in his mind for the pieces to fall into place to grasp what she had just proclaimed.

"He rose? From the dead? How?"

"Don't ask me what I don't know, Aharon. Just believe me. Trust me, please. And tell Demetria. I do not think that she will be surprised at this news. God is our Father. Jesus taught us this. And he sent his Son, the Son of man, as Jesus called himself. He was sent to liberate us, to heal the captives and he did this. He did this many times, as we have seen him heal and cast out demons. He was the lamb led to slaughter. He suffered and redeemed us from our greatest slavery, our sins. This much I know. He has done it. He made himself a victim for our salvation. And proved it by overcoming death. He is risen!"

"Where is he?" Aharon was perplexed, but somehow willing to believe.

"I don't know. I saw him near the tomb. He appeared to me then disappeared. Perhaps he will come back. We are waiting for him."

"Oh. I wish I could wait as well, but Demetria is expecting me back as soon as possible and I was leading one of the caravans from Magdala."

"You will be the first to carry this news to Magdala then Aharon."

"Yes, the first. Good news it is! Great news told by a great woman! I will tell Demetria every word you told me. Well, you are winning your title of the Magdalene for that great news!"

Aharon looked like he had been hit over the head and was still recovering, giggling from the experience rather than from pain. He grabbed her in a big hug, released her with a grin and waved goodbye.

"Consider that from Demetria. I am sure she would have wanted to do more than hug you. She would probably be dancing, despite her condition."

Mary laughed, imagining a pregnant Demetria dancing and rejoicing at the news. "Yes, I can just imagine her! Safe travels Aharon."

And with that he disappeared with John down below, leaving her alone once again, content with the knowledge of the fruitfulness in Demetria' womb and grateful to have the opportunity to share the good news and watch it being received. *Another type of birth or fruitfulness in the heart*, she thought. Hope was enkindled, nurturing her wounded and disappointed heart that still ached from the sword of unbelief. She pondered the event again. She had not expected such a negative reaction. A flame of anger began to disturb her short lived peace and joy after Aharon's visit.

Rabboni, I am sorry they did not believe!

She recalled her zealous proclamation and naive belief that her testimony would be received as enthusiastically as she had offered it. The heaviness of their unbelief felt crushing. And then Jesus' words came clearly to her mind, "All things have been committed to me by my Father. No one knows the Son except the Father, and no one knows the Father except the Son and those to whom the Son chooses to reveal him."[278]

Gratitude swelled in her heart. *He chose me. He revealed himself to me.* Her sight was a gift, as was her faith in him, a gift from the Father and from Jesus, the Son. She longed to know this Father more profoundly. Anger was replaced with sorrow over the other's disbelief. And she remembered Jesus' words that followed.

"Come to me, all you who are weary and burdened, and I will give you rest. Take my yoke upon you and learn from me, for I am gentle and humble in heart, and you will find rest for your souls. For my yoke is easy and my burden is light."[279]

Is this the yoke I am to carry Jesus?

She almost expected to hear his voice in answer to her question. She looked around hoping to see him standing behind her once again there on the rooftop. *No Jesus.* She felt foolish and disappointed. She closed her eyes and imagined him instead.

Silence was interspersed with the distant sound of conversations from the multitude of people below, doves were cooing, and a slight breeze rustled the few trees that scattered the pathway out front. Like the soft breeze, she sensed, more than remembered, Jesus' words.

"Take up your cross and follow me."

My cross? Yes, I feel their unbelief like a cross, my Jesus, my Rabboni.

Like the dawning of a new day, she knew what her yoke and cross were now and would be in the future. And she intuited that it would not be carried only by her. Others had believed. It would be a cross they would carry together, not alone. Jesus was present, somehow. These certainties came upon her like an interior prompting, like an invitation was extended and awaiting her answer.

Yes, Lord, she thought. And bowing her head, she accepted this yoke and cross as a token of her love for the Lord. In a spirit of gratitude, she would do what she could to bring others to believe. And when they would not, she would carry that burden like Jesus carried his cross for her.

CHAPTER 53. EVENING ENCOUNTERS

You, LORD, keep my lamp burning;
my God turns my darkness into light.
Psalm 18:28

They had just finished cleaning up their dinner, using the spacious upper room to feed all who were gathered and continued arriving to Mary Mark' home. They had spent the afternoon in spurts of prayer, little groups of conversations, and welcoming visitors that stopped in briefly, like Aharon. Some also came to install themselves, awaiting further news.

The women gathered in the courtyard of the house around Ima whose mostly silent countenance was like a steady beacon in their hours of uncertainty. The large outdoor area afforded breathing space, yet privacy from the prying eyes of neighbors, for which Mary was grateful, considering all the movement in and around the house. The night was chilly, but they wrapped themselves with cloaks and blankets and lit several torches. The dancing fire balls created the effects of moving shadows and light all around them. It matched her mood, she thought. It had been a strange day, full of hopes and disappointments, sorrows and joys.

That morning Martha had attempted to convince Mary to return to Bethany with her, hoping she would clean up and put on some fresh clothes. She was looking frightful. Mary refused. She would clean up the best she could while here in Mary Mark's house. She did not want to miss anything that might happen today. Martha returned before dinner with Lazarus and Maximin, one of the many disciples added to Jesus' group over the months. They were also accompanied by the last of the missing Eleven, with the exception of Thomas and Peter. Peter had still not returned, and Thomas had left to collect more supplies with John Mark. Mary was relieved that Martha had brought some fresh clothes for her. She finally cleaned herself up, grateful for her older sister's insistence. She let Martha work a miracle with her ratted knotted hair, making her presentable once again.

As Mary looked around the courtyard her gaze settled on Mary Mark, peacefully darning clothes. John Mark's clothes no doubt. He was a kind soul, but the boy was forever getting into some mess and needing the patient hand of his mother. Mary Mark was a widow, yet, like herself, she had managed the household with trusty servants and an economically sagacious talent. Her father-in-law had permitted her to maintain the house when her husband died, considering that it would be inherited by John Mark.

Mary Mark was very generous to allow them to continue lodging there. Not that she had much choice as the crowd grew ever greater. But she never complained. She graciously allowed the events to unfold around her, grateful to be a part of what she described as "the birth of something new and great." At Mary's announcement this morning, she had exuded a new excitement, far from the wrinkles of worry and sorrow that had been etched on her forehead the evening before. Mary Mark was a consolation in the midst of the heavy blow of other's unbelief and hesitancy.

With each newcomer added to the fold, Mary had been afraid it would be a strain on the woman's resources. But she took it in stride. And sure enough, every hour proved that God's providence was with them. New gifts would arrive. Some who had heard they were staying here came by to offer what they could for the cause: a sympathizer, a family whose son had been healed, Bernike, and even Simon the Cyrene.

Mary had watched as the visitors were received hour after hour. John and a few of the other apostles welcomed them in. Several disciples were hesitant to share that Jesus was risen. But they would offer them hospitality. There was always a greeting for Ima and then they would find a group to converse with. The apostles talked with them about Jesus's teachings and healings. Mary wondered why they did not just announce straight out that Jesus was risen. They were cautious, saying that some of the women believed that he had risen, but they were awaiting confirmation.

She, on the other hand, told a different story to those who would listen. Bernike had joined the women in the courtyard and Mary did not hesitate to offer the full account of the morning's adventures. She saw several skeptical disciples listening in, unhappy at her unrestrained zeal. But it was worth the judgmental glances. Bernike's sorrowful countenance was relieved. Surprise washed away her anguish over Jesus' crucifixion and joy was born. She believed. *Another for Jesus' fold,* Mary had thought. Mary rejoiced and celebrated with a big smile to Ima, who looked as though she was rooting for her to find another willing listener.

The darkness of night had descended, and people were beginning to settle in for the night. But Peter had still not returned. Everyone was of the same mind in one regard. They were to wait for him to take the lead. Andrew was pacing nervously, opening and closing the front door to check every five to ten minutes for his return.

At last Andrew shouted out to all, "I think I see him. Yes, it's Peter. He's back!"

Andrew ran into the darkness to receive him. All other activity ceased, and the little groups congregated nearer to the entrance. The anticipation heightened and finally Peter and Andrew entered, out of breath and excited. Before they could get a word out, two other disciples, Cleophas and Lucas, ran into the crowd, surprised at finding the congregated mass to meet them. Mary now realized she had not seen them all day.

They burst out at the same time, "We saw him! Jesus is alive!"

"He walked with us on the road back home to Emmaus."[280]

"But we didn't recognize him."

"He explained to us all the prophecies about himself since the time of Moses."

"We should have known it was Jesus. Our hearts were burning as he spoke, just as they did when we heard his teachings."

They rushed on, one speaking on top of the others.

"We invited him in to stay for the evening." "He opened our eyes." "We broke bread together and that was when we saw him and realized it was Jesus."

"But then he disappeared. We had to come back and tell you right away. We couldn't wait until tomorrow."

"He's risen, just as he said he would!"

Mary's heart was on fire. *He is appearing to more people! Finally, they might believe me!*

Andrew slapped them on the back as though congratulating them. "The Lord has indeed risen, and he has appeared to Simon!"[281]

Mary's jaw dropped. Simon Peter looked elated and speechless, and as though a weight had lifted. Everyone looked to him, waiting for his words.

With great conviction and solemn pronouncement, he affirmed their words.

"Yes, it is true. The Lord, who was crucified and dead, is very alive. He has risen from the dead!"

The room turned into rejoicing as though the veil of unbelief had been lifted, and they were being soaked in a downpour of joy.

The inebriation was short-lived as another figure appeared on the scene. Cassius stood before the open door looking bedraggled. John approached and brought him in, checking outside for anyone else before securely closing the door.

"Cassius, we heard that you were put in prison."

He waved it off. "A short spell, nothing to it. I told Pilate that Jesus had disappeared without explanation. Not a good idea. He had all the night guards arrested and questioned, as well as myself. But someone paid off the others to spread the rumor that his body had been stolen."

A tense silence hung thick. John broke it.

"And you Cassius? Do you believe that we stole his body?"

"No, I don't believe that. I was there. I returned at night and saw with my own eyes. It was impossible that the body was stolen. We might have fallen asleep, but the tombstone broke open with an earthquake and the tomb was empty. He would have had to pass through the rock like a ghost to get out without us seeing."

Sighs of relief swept through the crowd.

"But that doesn't mean that you are out of the clear. If people start believing and spreading news that he has come back from the dead, especially if it is a threat to Roman peace, then I think you will be in great danger. Actually, I think the threat is going to come more from the side of the Sanhedrin who insisted that Pilate crucify him. I am pretty sure that they are the ones who offered the incentive to spread the rumor. You need to keep this news to yourselves."

Mary spoke up, "Then you do believe? You believe that Jesus is risen?"

He nodded slowly as though pondering this news and realizing that indeed, he did believe. "Yes, I believe." Tears pooled in his eyes as he dropped his head. He inhaled a sob and like a dam releasing its flood-gates, surrendered. "Yes, I believe," he cried out. Hands surrounded him, patting him for his expression of faith.

Another one Lord! One more for you, Mary thought, amazed and grate-ful.

Cassius finally left late into the night. The disciples one by one found a space for camping out for the night and Peter called the Apos-tles together. Mary watched as Peter gave orders to securely lock the door after Cassius left and then they filed up the stairs towards the upper room. Ten, all but Judas and Thomas. She prayed for them. The chosen few, set apart so often by Jesus. She knew they had a difficult task ahead of them. She sensed that they would each be leaders in their own way, relying on Peter's guidance and Peter relying on them. She prayed, like Jesus had prayed that night in the upper room.

May they be one, as the Father and Son are one. May they be of one mind and heart with you Lord.

Ima and the women had been offered the few straw mats in the house. She gave hers up for her sister, since there were not enough for all of them. Mary was so exhausted she thought she could sleep through an earthquake. But the sounds of snores, creaking of the house, and the multitude of emotions that still stirred within her from the day's events left her wide awake.

A wind storm had suddenly taken them by surprise. A strong draft was whipping into their room. She snuggled more deeply under her blanket attempting once again to sleep, but to no avail. She was certain that she had lain under the covers for half the night. The windstorm had finally died down, but it was no good. She couldn't sleep. A current of cold air continued to seep through her blanket. The others must be frozen. She had one of the heavier blankets since she was the only one without a mat. She stood up, bundling the blanket tightly around her, making her way through the maze of bodies, and crept out towards the hallway.

The front door was completely opened, and cold air was streaming in. Had someone gone outside and forgotten to close it? It had been securely locked. She stepped outside to check for anyone that might simply be catching a fresh breath of air. No one. A shiver ran up her spine, not so much from the cold, but from a sense of something out of the ordinary. She pushed the heavy door closed and assured that it was tightly secured.

As she was returning to her resting place, another door creaked open from the upper room. John and Matthew were descending.

"Mary!" John descended quickly, excited to see her. "The Lord appeared to us!"

Rabboni! Mary was about to run up the stairs when Matthew added, "He already left. We heard the front door and thought it might be Thomas. Did you see him?"

Her joy for them was tempered with her own disappointment.

He came and didn't show himself to me? He didn't stay?

"Mary? Are you well?" John asked.

She shook her head, clearing the disappointment and trying to be happy for them. "Thomas? No, I haven't seen Thomas. But tell me please. What happened? What did he say? Did he stay long with you?"

"We were talking about all that had happened and discussing what we were to do about people coming to believe when suddenly Jesus just stood right there in the midst of us."[282]

"I thought we were seeing a ghost. It was Jesus, but he looked different, almost unreal," Matthew added.

"I knew it was him," John confessed. "He had once appeared to us in the same way, when he took Peter, James and I up on Mount Tabor. It was like light emanated from him."

Matthew looked at him with an odd face, "You never told me that! I want to hear that story."

"I promise I will tell you later Matthew." John turned back to her. "Anyway, he could tell we were agitated, so he greeted us with a sign of peace and then tried to prove that it was truly him, living. He showed us his hands and his feet."

"And told us to touch him and see for ourselves that he wasn't a ghost. His hands and feet still had the nail marks, but it wasn't gross. I don't know how to explain it."

"I felt the same," said John. "Just seeing him filled me with so much joy. I wanted to laugh and cry and dance all at the same time. But I was so dumbfounded, I felt paralyzed! I couldn't do anything but stare at those wounds."

Matthew and John were exuberant as they looked up towards the upper room as if they were seeing Jesus again. Then Matthew broke the silent spell.

"He asked for fish."

Mary was jolted out of the spell that the news had cast on her. "What? Fish?"

John explained. "I think Jesus must have realized we were in shock and got us moving by asking for something to eat, to show us it was really him."

"Actually," Matthew continued, "he also scolded us for being so obstinate and not believing you when you first told us he had risen from the dead. I'm sorry Mary."

Mary was greatly moved by Matthew's apology and that Jesus had in some way defended her, a reward for her attempt to witness to what she had seen.

"The Lord is gracious and merciful," was all Mary could think to say. It was just like Jesus to stun them with his miracles, teachings or demands and then bring them back to reality with something so ordinary, like asking for something to eat. She chuckled. How she loved him in his solemn splendor yet simple humanity.

They stayed for a while marveling together and then said goodnight, each going their own way to find their little parcel of space to rest amidst the multitude of growing believers spread throughout the house. Mary's heart was full, so full, and so grateful. There was still much uncertainty about what the following days would bring, but a kernel of hope was sprouting from her new life of faith in the risen Lord. She laid down to rest with her spirit full of joy, peace, and an eager anticipation of whatever was to come.

CHAPTER 54. LORD, HELP THE UNBELIEF

If you openly declare that Jesus is Lord
and believe in your heart
that God raised him from the dead,
you will be saved.
Romans 10:9

The next day, Peter recounted their experience of the previous night, how Jesus' appeared to them and what he had told them. Mary sensed a change in him. His uncertainty and fear was tempered with a newfound confidence. But it wasn't a prideful confidence that she sometimes judged as bordering on arrogance. She detected a deeper humility. He had, in reality, betrayed Jesus. She felt compassion for him and admired that he could stand before them now with bold certainty in Jesus' resurrection from the dead. I suppose seeing Jesus in the flesh can do that to you, she chuckled to herself.

The apostles and the disciples who had returned from Emmaus also shared Jesus' teachings. Just as their eyes had been opened as they listened to Jesus on the road to Emmaus, everyone who listened to their recounting of the event gained greater clarity and conviction of faith. Peter spoke of the power of Jesus' name and that repentance for the forgiveness of sins would be preached to all nations, beginning from Jerusalem.[283] Mary thought of Cassius. It was already happening! Peter told them that they were all to be witnesses to this. Her heart burnt with passion to continue giving witness of this good news. He also told them that they were to go out to the whole world and proclaim the gospel. "Whoever believes and is baptized will be saved," Jesus had told them.[284]

To the whole world! Does he mean me too? Or am I to stay in Jerusalem or return to Magdala? Should I stay with Ima?

Fear was creeping in. Now that Jesus was gone, that is, now that he was with them in a different way, she wondered what would become of her. How often would he be appearing to them? And instructing and leading them? Would she be able to go out to the whole world like the other apostles? Or would she be told to stay behind? Her heart longed to go out to the whole world, wherever that was.

Thomas had finally returned with warnings of unrest in the city. The rumors of Jesus' body being stolen had spread among many of the Jews. He listened to them recount the story of the night before but was incredulous.

The veil has not been lifted for him, she thought. She was flabbergasted by his persistent doubt, despite so many testifying to the event. They were his own friends and companions for at least three years, and he would not believe them.

They all prayed together for courage and strength, for light and wisdom. A discussion broke out regarding their plan for departure to Galilee. Salome reminded them that the angels in the tomb had said they should go to meet Jesus there. But others said it was not necessary if he was already appearing to them here in Jerusalem. Others cautioned against leaving, especially after Cassius' warning. The discussions went on throughout the day. Little groups would break out here and there in which they would reminisce, remember and piece together different parts of Jesus' teachings. Their understanding and faith were being nurtured by their memories.

***

Late in the afternoon on that second day, Mary and several of the women were resting in the courtyard when another guest arrived. Big James and John entered and made their way directly toward her, signaling for her to come. James was perturbed. John looked very concerned.

"Mary, you better come. There is someone here to see you and he won't take no for an answer," Big James told her with a scowl.

She arose and followed, curious who would ask for her directly. There, standing at the front door, two other disciples at his side like guards ready to pounce on the visitor, was Gaius. He was dressed in normal garb but looked very much like a Roman. No wonder they were concerned. Gaius had a stern look on his face. She knew that look. "No" would not be accepted. A rising fear began to take hold within.

Rabboni, help me.

The interior supplication came spontaneously. She did not want this exchange to escalate and have dangerous consequences for everyone staying here. Surprisingly, a slow soft peace settled over her. She determined to maintain a prudent vigilance but not put up a wall toward Gaius. She remembered his act of mercy upon Golgotha and the brief moment when she thought he may have let down his own wall of pride and stubbornness. They had history, a history she wanted to leave in the past, but that didn't mean she could not care for him in a new and different way now.

"Miriam," he addressed her in a low and serious tone. "We need to talk." He looked hard and steady at the four disciples standing as sentinels around her and added sternly, "Alone."

Mary nodded and assured James and John that she would be fine. They stepped outside, still under close supervision, but out of the earshot of others.

She stood tall and confident, and with a firm yet gentle voice asked, "How did you find me again Gaius? Why are you here? Do you mean to give us away?"

He smirked and raised an eyebrow. "It turns out that Cassius isn't so close-lipped as you probably thought he would be."

Mary looked alarmed, feeling betrayed by someone she had just started to believe was trustworthy.

"Don't worry. I suspected he had an interest in your group when he attempted to convince Pilate that the body of Jesus was not stolen. I told him he should keep his mouth shut if he didn't want more trouble for himself or any of your rabbi's sympathizers. But I wanted to hear the story from you. What's going on? Rumor is spreading that your people stole that crazy man's body to make it look like he rose from the dead. Even Cassius believes he came back from the dead."

He didn't give Mary a chance to interject and profess her belief.

"I don't like you mixed up in this thing, whatever it is. Pilate is weary of getting involved even more, but the Sanhedrin has been known to use their manipulative influence over him. Just look at what they did to your teacher. So far no orders have been given regarding his followers, but unless your people put a stop to this nonsense, I can't guarantee that orders won't come. Go back to Magdala Miriam. Stay out of this mess."

Mary was experiencing a gamut of emotions. Anger that he called Jesus a crazy man. Defiance against his orders. She was not his to order about. Defensiveness for "her people" as he called them. But all of that contrasted with a realization that he could have turned them in and did not. He was concerned for her. A surprising wave of tenderness came over her at the fact that he genuinely wanted to defend and protect her. Perhaps this could work in her favor, in Jesus' favor.

She sought the right words to speak, words of wisdom that might touch his heart somehow. *Is he even capable of believing what, for him, right now, was nonsense? Even many of my "own people" had not believed me. Should I even try?* She took a deep breath as though inhaling strength for whatever battle was about to ensue and turned her heart in prayerful supplication as she spoke, uncertain what arguments or words would spill forth.

"Gaius," she began softly, peacefully, feeling a new affection for him that was free of possessiveness as it used to be, and surprisingly free of fear. "Thank you for coming and for your concern for me."

She noticed his expression soften. His hard determination turned to surprise. *Disarmed,* she thought. *Perhaps there is a way to penetrate the hardness of his heart.* She continued.

"As you say, it is a rumor. We have not stolen away with his body. I myself went early yesterday morning to the tomb. I looked for him and he was not there."

"How? Did you move the tombstone yourself? Who helped you?"

She tried to calm him with a smile and shake of the head, "No Gaius. There was an earthquake as I was arriving and the stone split in two. I heard the guards run away and then I entered to see for myself. There was no time for anyone to go in and steal the body between the time the tombstone fell away from the opening and the time I entered the tomb. I tell you honestly, as I saw it, it was empty."

She could see Gaius processing this information. *Does he believe me?* She hoped, then doubted he would receive the rest of the news she wanted to share. Hesitating momentarily, she finally determined to say it. *Yes, will tell him. I will risk it.*

"Gaius, I know it will be hard for you to believe but listen to me please." She paused to perceive his reaction and openness to what she was about to tell him. He nodded his assent. *Ok,* she thought, *he isn't completely closed.*

"I was actually looking for his body, also thinking that someone had carried it away. But while I was still in the garden, outside the tomb," she paused, hoping and praying that he would receive what she was about to say, "Gaius, I saw him. Alive."

Gaius didn't respond. His brows furrowed as though concentrating on something in her eyes, trying to penetrate the truth of what she was saying, or see if she was lying to him.

"How?" He grunted out.

"How? I honestly don't know how it is possible. You saw him there on Golgotha. You had a hand in his crucifixion and death."

She was surprised to see a pained expression as though he had hurt her and was sorry.

"Yes Miriam. I was there. And I was doing my duty. Nothing more. You know what that job is. But I am sorry. I was sorry that you suffered so much."

A sudden ire escaped. "That *I* suffered? That *Jesus* suffered! He was innocent. He was the victim of ignorance, of pride, of Pilate's cowardice, of Herod's idiocy, of the Sanhedrin's power hunger and fear of losing control!"

"Hey, watch your words about Pilate if you want to keep your head!" He warned gruffly. But then he chuckled. "Well, it is good to see that the teacher hasn't changed you too much. Still the spitfire I always knew."

Feeling confident that he was more a friend than a foe at this moment, she gave him a warning, scolding look.

"You do not agree with me then that Pilate and the others killed an innocent man? Do you believe me that I saw him?"

He sighed. "I'm not paid to have an opinion about these things. I just carry out the orders I receive and give orders to make sure it is accomplished."

He paused, looking for a moment like a lost little boy, then throwing up his hands, he confessed, "I don't know what to believe anymore Miriam." He ran his hand through his thick hair with frustration. Pacing away from her, he stopped and looked up to the heavens as though the problem was his to solve. Then he returned. Facing her, he asked, "What are you and your people planning to do?"

"Plans? We have no plans. Believe me, it wasn't in my plan to meet Jesus or follow him or watch him be crucified. But here I am. I believe Gaius. I believe he is the Messiah that our people have been expecting for many generations."

"Some Messiah, getting himself killed. He didn't defend himself very well. I heard he condemned himself with his own words, calling himself the son of God. A blasphemy for your people. He should have been Roman. He might have had a better audience. One more god for us wouldn't matter much," he said scoffing.

She could see that he didn't mean any harm by his comments. Something was changing in him. The facade was breaking down revealing a vulnerable side. *Is he sincerely searching for answers? Or if not searching, at least questioning?* It was a good step. She did care for him. And determined to pray for him.

"He knew this would happen, Gaius. He isn't a Messiah in the way that many have expected. Even our own people thought he would overthrow the Roman empire. I didn't understand it at first. I still don't fully understand it. But he came to overthrow more oppressive powers. The kingdom of evil, a kingdom that we ourselves establish here." She put a finger against his heart. "We establish that kingdom with our false idols and our pride and selfishness. He set me free Gaius. I was under the oppression of much evil. Even now they call me the Magdalene from whom Jesus expelled seven demons."

Another smirk crossed his face. "I've called you worse. I knew you had the devil in you," he teased, making light of the situation. But Mary continued, not being drawn in by his old flirtatiousness.

"The point is, Gaius, that he has come to establish a kingdom that is not like the ones we have known here, not like the Roman empire. It is a kingdom that begins by believing in him as the Messiah and being baptized in living waters. Jesus has been appearing to more people than just me. Yesterday he also appeared to Peter, then in the evening to more of the apostles, the ones who were closest to Jesus and whom he has prepared to spread his message and baptize others. He is offering us a new life, Gaius. A new life in faith and peace by believing and following him."

Gaius was shaking his head now. She had lost him. Oh, how she wanted him to believe. But like Ima had said, she could not force it.

"I know it is hard to understand and hard to believe. I can only say," she held her arms out and laughed, "look at me! He changed me! For the better. He set me free of chains and darkness that I didn't even realize I had. He loved me with a pure love that I had never experienced before."

Like a door slamming, she watched his face turn from a vulnerable and searching Gaius to a hardened Roman soldier. He looked at her, a serious expression in his face, searching as if looking for some remnant of the old Miriam from Magdala whom he once knew so well.

"Yes, it is hard to believe," he said expressionlessly.

She was silent, trying to understand where he stood, hoping for some light in his eyes that indicated a little belief. But nothing. She knew, from one instant to the next, he had shut her out.

"You be careful Miriam. Don't worry, I won't give you and your people away. But you, be careful." He stood motionless for a brief moment, waiting in silence as though searching one more time for something from her. "You should get out of Jerusalem. If you do go back to Magdala, be careful. I heard what Vespasian did to you. I would have killed him myself, but he not gotten himself transferred to Galilee. And yes, I did take a wife in Rome, Miriam. When Vespasian sent me news that you had moved on." Disgust emanated from his demeanor, but she realized it wasn't aimed at her. "The cheating liar," he spat out.

"My wife," he continued, "She died in childbirth. The babe with her."

Mary wasn't sure why he was telling her this news, but she felt compassion for him and tried to show it in her gaze, careful to not give him false hopes. He searched her face as though waiting for an answer. Then, he continued speaking.

"I was going to come back to you. But yes, I see. You are...," he hesitated, searching for something from her again, then finally took a deep breath and exhaled in a spirit of resignation. "You are different."

He waited in silence again as though expecting a reaction from her. Mary was momentarily thrown off by his confession and moved by his sincerity. She nodded her head, a gesture of gratitude and confirmation that yes, indeed, she was different now. The same Mary of Magdala and yet so very different. Stronger, surer, at peace with who she had become with Jesus.

Gaius turned and walked away. She exhaled as though she had been holding her breath. She sighed with relief and marvel that perhaps she could even count on him as a friend, or at least she felt certain that he was not a threat to the growing community of believers. Gratitude and a new bud of love for Gaius, untainted and pure, turned her to prayer. *Rabboni, give him faith. Help his unbelief!*

CHAPTER 55. THE WAY IT MUST BE

For my thoughts are not your thoughts, neither are your ways my ways, declares the Lord.
As the heavens are higher than the earth, so are my ways higher than your ways and my
thoughts than your thoughts.
Isaiah 55:8-9

The next day, Martha and Lazarus returned to Bethany with several of the disciples and promised to continue the ministry that Jesus entrusted to them. Mary insisted on staying in Jerusalem, close to Ima and with the Eleven Apostles as they decided what to do next. Little did she know that a new mission was awaiting her. Several women began asking about this new way. Among them, a young girl, barely of marriageable age, disheveled and in tears, showed up at the door.

"I want to speak to Mary, Mary of Magdala," she insisted. "I heard that she is staying here."

Mary brought her in and as she gave her a meal, listened to her story. Mary's heart broke. She knew her pain. This young woman, or rather, girl, believed herself to be loved, only to be discarded and used over and over again. She convinced the disciples to let her stay for the night. But they insisted that another place be found for her tomorrow. They could not house every stray person that came knocking. They were full to the brim as it was, and feared they were outstaying Mary Mark's hospitality. But Mary Mark had no such reservations. She made room for everyone and anyone.

Nonetheless, Mary thought of the house of Bethany with its expansive land and multitude of rooms. It was a far enough distance that the girl could disappear from harm, yet close enough that Mary could check on her periodically. Surely Martha could take her in. Mary made the trip with the young girl the next day.

"Martha, I'm home!" She shouted out as she entered her childhood home.

Martha came running and embraced her wholeheartedly, not noticing Mary's companion who remained in the shadow of a corner.

"Mary, you've come home. I am so glad. Come, come. I will get you some tea and a meal. Are you hungry? How is everyone in Jerusalem? I heard that Jesus appeared to the Eleven! Oh! How I wish he would appear here!"

"Martha, Martha! Slow down. I will tell you all, but I want to introduce to you a new friend."

Mary pulled the young girl forward.

"Oh! Welcome!" Martha greeted her with warmth. "Please let me take your cloak. It is too warm these days for such a garment. Come, make yourself at home."

Martha held out her hand to take the cloak. As the young girl let it slip off, Martha let out a gasp of surprise. The woman was in need of new clothes, or better said, of more clothes.

Mary held in her laughter at Martha's expression. Martha looked at her, realizing that Mary purposely did not tell her who and what this young girl was and now she was enjoying her reaction. Martha gave Mary a look to tell her "Ok, ok, you got your revenge." Then she held herself in check, remembering that Mary was once with a similar position. She did not want to scare away this newcomer, aware that her own reactions to Mary when she was in a similar position as this young girl, had once driven a deep wedge between her and Mary.

Later, Martha scolded Mary for surprising her with such a guest but immediately laughed with her and tenderly approved of Mary's good heart and resourceful thinking. Yes, Martha would take her in. She could also use the help, and the girl was willing to help in whatever task.

This first young girl would not be the last. Word got out and thus began the first of many who came in search of refuge and healing from abuse, be it from husbands, lovers or strangers. Mary took the initiative of gathering them together, sharing with them the teachings of Jesus, and encouraging them to live and share this new found faith. And having shared the good news with them, if they truly wanted to start a new life, she delivered them into Martha's care.

As for the disciples in those first days after the resurrection, they feared repercussion from the Sanhedrin or Roman officials. But none came. Mary Mark's house became both a refuge and a central point in Jerusalem for the community. It became a place for regrouping. They entered into a rhythm of prayer, work, shared meals and discussions. In between, people continued to visit, asking if they were the followers of Jesus. Peter and the apostles were cautious, afraid some might be sent as a trap. The disciples tested the sincerity of the newcomer, then invited them to listen to Jesus' teachings. Some came because they had heard Jesus preaching in the Temple, others had been healed or witnessed his healing. Then there were those who claimed they had seen people rise from the dead the same day that Mary and the other disciples had seen Jesus.

In the evenings the Eleven would often gather, recapping their day's labors, discussing the situation of Jerusalem and how to aid those who desired to be a part of their group. On the eighth day after the resurrection, they were gathered together in the upper room, when suddenly Jesus appeared to them again.

Recounting the appearance later, Thomas, although partially ashamed of his prior doubts, boasted that he was the reason Jesus appeared to them. Oh, happy doubt! It brought them the Lord once again. But when Thomas relayed Jesus' words, it struck Mary in a new way. He had said, "You believe because you can see me. Blessed are those who have not seen and yet believe."

Every day, Mary anticipated the possibility of Jesus appearing to her again. Perhaps that was the real reason she stayed in Jerusalem. A jealous ache seized her heart when she heard that even doubting Thomas was permitted to touch Jesus. And yet, Jesus had told her not to cling to him.

Why Rabboni? Why will you not appear to me again when you appeared to the apostles twice!? An anguished desire was grasping to attain what she wanted for herself. *Surely this is a good thing, to want to see and touch Jesus once again? To anoint his feet once again?* She remembered his words, "Do not cling to me."

Then how am I to love you Rabboni?

The answer did not come, clearly, at least not immediately.

On that eighth night after the resurrection, after Jesus' appearance to the apostles the second time, they finally decided to leave for Galilee. The next day, as she prepared to go with them, Peter pulled her aside unexpectedly.

"Mary, I know you want to go with us, but the women are staying here in Jerusalem with some of the disciples. I think it would be best for you to remain. Just the Eleven of us are going north. We will wait for Jesus and his instructions there. I do not know how long it will be, as he doesn't exactly give us a timeline."

A remnant of anger surfaced. *I will not be left behind in this venture!* Mary began to argue. She wanted to be part of it just as they were. She realized that she still begrudged Peter's disbelief in her first testimony. This made her even more insistent at her decision to go with them to Galilee. "I have every right to go just as the other apostles."

Peter recognized the undercurrent between them. He did not want a confrontation. He did not engage her antagonistic spirit. This surprised her. *Yes,* she thought, *he is different. Something has changed in him.*

"I know you want to be a part of this, just as we are. And you are, Mary. You are an essential part. But we need you here. You are winning over the confidence of many women and even the men. I have asked Maximin, one of the disciples who has been with us since Galilee, to remain here and continue leading the others in our work. Would you work with him? Together? And look after Ima, although she seems to be taking care of us these days. From the looks of it, Maximin is going to need all the help he can get. People continue coming for instruction and are asking for baptism."

Mary pondered his intentions, if he was sincere or not. *Does he just want me out of his way? Would Jesus appear to those that remained in Jerusalem if the apostles left for Galilee?*

Peter could see her wavering. "Please Mary. I ask this of you. Please stay and help here. A community of Jerusalem is forming, whether we planned it or not. And those women who keep coming to look for you…they need you."

"No, they need Jesus," Mary replied.

Peter still sensed a division between them. And he knew why. "I think I also owe you an apology. The morning you came to tell us that Jesus was risen, I did not believe you, nor support you. I am sorry for that. I had to see with my own eyes. It is my downfall." His face fell as he muttered, "Along with many other things."

He was speaking of his betrayal. Compassion moved her to be the consoler, to reconcile the tension that had remained between them these last few days. They had lived in the same house amicably, but she avoided him whenever possible. Suddenly she saw clearly how her own festering anger tainted their relationship. It was a far cry from Jesus' command to love one another. Her heart had hardened toward him and feared, at times, that she had sown division with her subtle rancor. It was time to forgive, and he had opened the door to the possibility.

"I forgive you Peter."

Little did she expect the tears that would usher from his eyes. She looked around to see if anyone was watching. They had enough privacy to speak freely. She reached out, squeezing his arm as a gesture of consolation and tried to make light of the situation.

"Peter, that is my job. What are you doing shedding tears?"

He discreetly wiped them away. But a confession poured forth. "He knew I would fall asleep in Gethsemane. And he knew I would betray him, not just once but three times. I don't know what is to come, but he knows I could easily betray him again. Maybe my lack of belief was another betrayal. He sent us a message through you, and I ignored it. I am very sorry for that."

Mary was utterly and momentarily speechless. Never had she expected Peter, proud and confident Peter, to confess his faults to her. Although she supposed he had made some attempt at it when they traveled through the Decapolis and butted heads. She felt moved to confirm him in his faith.

"Peter, Jesus knew, but he also chose *you*."

"He chose Judas as well."

"Yes, but Judas did not trust his mercy and look where it led him. Yes, you betrayed him, but you stand before me now. You are here trying to follow his indications the best you can. The question is, what do you choose now?"

"Did you know that the night he prayed in the garden and was arrested, I tried to stop the soldiers with my sword?"

She had heard the story several times. They were afraid that there would be repercussions, but so far none had come.

Peter continued, "I could have killed someone. I only managed to cut off one of the guard's ears before Jesus stopped me and told me to put the sword away."

Mary chuckled lightly, teasing him, "Sounds like there's someone else who needs your apology."

Peter huffed in agreement, "You are right about that." He continued in a more serious tone. "Jesus told me many times the way things would be, but I did not listen. Or maybe I was deafened so as to not hear or remember his words. He even told me that night, after cutting off the guard's ear, 'This is the way it must be.'[285] As though my own mistakes were part of this plan of his."

Mary tried to console and encourage him. "Mistakes. If you had told me I would be here in this situation two years ago, I would have scoffed at you. Look at what Jesus has done with my mistakes. Women are coming to me who have been in very difficult situations and somehow, my own past is a way of gaining their confidence and coming to Jesus. As Isaiah said, 'For my thoughts are not your thoughts, neither are your ways my ways, declares the Lord. As the heavens are higher than the earth, so are my ways higher than your ways and my thoughts than your thoughts.'[286]"

They both stood in silence pondering this truth. *That is the way it must be,* Mary thought.

"Peter, Jesus didn't choose us because we are perfect. Maybe he chose us precisely because he knew he could lift us up, that we would stand again after betraying him. Maybe he knew we would still follow him even after many mistakes. And maybe we will keep making mistakes, and he will have to scold us and teach us how to move forward. We do the best we can. We trust him and we try to trust each other."

"Look who is the wise one now!" Peter teased her. "Well, I need to be off, but you will stay? Please?"

She assented, "Yes, I will stay."

"Thank you, Mary. Pray for us. And if Jesus appears to you again, put in a good word for me, no?"

"Of course!" She laughed and accompanied him and the apostles as they set off to Galilee.

As she closed the door, she thanked the Lord for a lesson learned. She felt heartened and strengthened by their conversation. A bridge was built between them where misunderstanding and mistrust had been festering. She had encouraged Peter. Perhaps this was also part of her mission, to be kindling for the fire to keep burning, for faith to be stronger so that those who were called to go ahead to Galilee and to the four corners of the world would not falter. She would pray for them and do what she could to nurture the new growing community here in Jerusalem, until Jesus chose to appear to her and tell her more clearly what to do next.

CHAPTER 56. THIRTY DAYS

Then Jesus came to them and said, "All authority in heaven and on earth has been given to me. Therefore go and make disciples of all nations, baptizing them in the name of the Father and of the Son and of the Holy Spirit, and teaching them to obey everything I have commanded you. And surely I am with you always, to the very end of the age."
Matthew 28: 18-20

In the end, the Apostles were gone for thirty days. During that time, the days passed by quickly, despite worrying and praying for them each day of their absence. The women began a new tradition. They walked and prayed a path through Jerusalem several times each week. The streets seemed safe now, or safer at least. Random vendors were becoming familiar faces. If they knew what the women were doing, most did not say anything, nor give them away. Only two or three sneered and spit at them when they discovered that Ima was the mother of "that crazy false Messiah."

They walked the path that Jesus tread. They prayed upon the stones where Jesus fell. It was an intimate walk, in solidarity with the women who had first followed in his footsteps. Memories brought tears, tears of sorrow for what he suffered but also tears of gratitude. Mary would often recall her own journey, thinking of each heavy and bloody step Jesus took as a continual washing away of her own sinfulness, her own persistent stubborn pride and moments of vanity that occasionally caught her by surprise. These prayerful walks were precious moments that she hated missing, but other events sometimes prevented her from joining the women.

Mary began to feel freer to come and go into the city for errands. John Mark had become her faithful companion. She let him believe that he was her guardian and protector, but she laughed at his easy distractions on the street. When a pretty young girl would pass by,

Mary spied John Mark launching nuts or dates, whatever projectile he had at hand, straight at the victim. He had a lot to learn about wooing, she laughed. Sometimes he would get so engrossed in a passing vendor cart full of curious knick-knacks that she could have left him for several minutes without him having a clue. She knew who was the guardian of who. She kept an eye out for the young mischievous, but good hearted lad. She appreciated his docility as she tried to occupy him with meaningful tasks, despite his roundabout ways of fulfilling them. She understood his restlessness. He needed a sense of purpose.

Mary also went to Bethany on occasion to visit Martha and Lazarus. There too, the community of believers was growing in number. A community regularly gathered, particularly the poor of the city. Martha was thriving in her role as mistress of the house, serving daily meals, welcoming the stranger or whomever Lazarus or Maximin would send to stay with them. Several of the disciples had taken up residence with them as they awaited the return of the Eleven and Peter's instructions. It had become a little, or better said, a large family of at least sixty people visiting on a regular basis, and not just for Martha's delicious baking, although that was surely an incentive.

Those thirty days passed by like a little cenacle in her heart. A sense of solidarity was growing among those who were eager to follow this New Way. They would break bread together. And often, Mary felt that she was that bread being broken for others. Keeping busy, helping others had become her daily bread. But Jesus had maintained his absence, and Mary felt it profoundly. Nonetheless, she was making other friends, like Maximin.

He was slowly becoming a spiritual father to her. Maximin's father and later himself, had been the steward of her family. She briefly remembered him as a young man, learning the trade from his father, when she lived in Bethany. An accident had left him blind. She had admired his resourcefulness despite his limitations and could see that her family treated him well, allowing him certain work. But she had not paid much attention to him back then. When Jesus began to visit their house at the beginning of his public ministry, Lazarus had asked Jesus to cure Maximin. He did, and Maximin took his aging father's role as steward for a little over a year, until Lazarus eventually gave him leave to follow Jesus as one of the seventy-two disciples.

Maximin was humble and wise, a leader in his gentle but decisive manners. Their difference in social status faded away. It made no difference to her anymore. She quickly began to trust him. They spoke in confidence about how they understood Jesus' teachings for their present lives. They encouraged one another, appreciating the gifts each offered when confronting their daily challenges. Maximin had a calming effect on her whenever she became restless over the fact that Jesus was not reappearing to them.

"He is still with us. Trust, daughter," he would frequently say.

She didn't understand her own heart. When she had spells of desperation for wanting to do something more for Jesus, Maximin reminded her of Jesus' words as he pointed to the women whom she had begun to help. "What you do to one of these, you do to me."

Mary would often remember her privileged place at Jesus' feet and feel a familiar wave of love come over her, like when she had poured out the anointing oil upon his feet and head. It was a brief consolation and sustained her in the hope of seeing him again. But her desire to offer Jesus this token of love could not be quenched. Maximin did not discourage her from these memories but encouraged her to look for how to pour out that anointing oil upon others. She understood he was not talking literally, but in a figure of speech.

She did not have to look far. People were coming who needed this anointing love, a healing balm. Or she would find them on the street. Her previous fascination as a child had now converted into a growing and fruitful mission. Women abandoned, made the object of a man's whims and pleasures, were scattered about on many street corners. She no longer simply took in those who came to her. Her market errands were often an excuse to win over one more. She found her way to speak to them discreetly as she pretended to be purchasing something from them. Soon they would show up at their doorstep where she continued to lodge with Mary Mark.

When more and more began seeking her out, she consulted Maximin about various situations she found women in, be it abused or depressed, or living a difficult life under what she would term an oppressive relationship. They were delicate circumstances and if she intervened, it could create backlash against their growing community. But she couldn't abandon them. He encouraged her and often accompanied her back and forth to Bethany when it was necessary to get them to safety and to check on them in intervals.

Martha and Lazarus were proud of Mary for finding ways to bring others to Jesus. The Jerusalem community quickly began to call Martha and Lazarus' place the Bethany house where the words of Isaiah were fulfilled in the name and power of Jesus. They truly proclaimed good news to the poor, bound up the brokenhearted, and proclaimed freedom for the captives.[287]

Finally, on the thirtieth day of their absence, as she was working in Mary Mark's house, the apostles finally returned. It was a joyous occasion, like welcoming back close family ties and being relieved at seeing their well-being. She caught Peter's attention, and they shared a silent exchange of gratitude when he recounted their meetings with Jesus around the Sea of Galilee. Mary detected that he was being particularly discreet or dissimulating when he spoke of one particular experience. It looked like John was expecting him to say more. No matter, she would get the rest of the story out of John later, she told herself. When she finally had a moment with John, she confirmed her intuition. Jesus had reaffirmed Peter in his chosen role as the leader among them and offered him the opportunity to confess his love and fidelity.

Mary rejoiced, but in the depth of her heart she suffered as well. *So many blessed moments they had spent with him! But why not here? Why did he not come and appear to me?* She still questioned and had to temper her anger and confusion. *Why was I not chosen to see and speak to him again?* Hearing their stories only increased her restlessness.

Mary held onto every word that the apostles repeated from what Jesus had told them in Galilee. One message in particular struck her, "I am with you to the end of times." *Could this be? Can I know of his presence? Is he with me even now?*

Sometimes the memories of her encounters with Jesus brought about a deeper certainty and consolation that he was indeed present, even now. But then fear would chase away that certainty, attacking her with doubts and accusations that she was inventing what she had experienced. Sometimes she heard echoes of accusations, "It is just your crazed womanly imagination", as many had commented when she first tried to tell them that Jesus was risen. But she fought back with determination. She clung to Jesus' promise as though it was the fulfillment of her desire to cling to his feet that day in the garden. She defended him by holding onto his words in her heart. "I am with you to the end of time." This echo nourished her faith, hope and love for Jesus.

CHAPTER 57. THE ASCENSION

You will be my witnesses, telling people about me everywhere, in Jerusalem, throughout Judea, in Samaria, and to the ends of the earth.
Acts 1:7

The next day, Mary had to go to Bethany. She would spend the night there and return the next day. Maximin and John Mark would accompany her. But before going, she had resolved to take care of some business with Peter's help. Mary Mark and she had conspired to help John Mark. They were concerned about his restless mischievousness. They approached Peter, insisting that he find some role for John Mark, a specific task that could give him a sense of purpose in the growing community.

At first Peter was dismissive. The boy was hardly a man. And yet he wasn't a child either, they argued.

"Nathaniel Bartholomew, his uncle, can keep an eye on him," Peter suggested.

Mary Mark shook her head. "Bartholomew does nothing but spoil the boy and jest with him. He needs a particular task, a mission."

Just then John Mark had come into the room, ready for the trip. Peter called him over.

"Can you write, John Mark?"

He looked perplexed at the question, "Well enough. I can speak better. I can negotiate in several languages, can't I Mary?" He looked at her expecting adulation for the several times he had assisted in negotiating with various merchants. He certainly had a way of winning people over with his quick wit and, like his mother, sagacious mind for business.

Peter replied, "That might come in handy in the future, but for now." He paused, then changed his course of thought. "I'll tell you what. Purchase what you need for documenting. I want you to record the accounts of Jesus that I share with the people. It will be important to have these records so we can send them to other communities. There are many villages where Jesus and the disciples traveled, preached and healed while he was still alive. Word has reached them of Jesus' resurrection, and some have come to believe. When we were in Galilee, we received news of various gatherings. People are coming together to share about the prophecies fulfilled and retell the stories of Jesus' teachings and healings, so this can help them. Can you write in Greek? Maybe it can serve the Hellenistic Jews of Galilee and the pagans of the Decapolis at the same time.

John Mark was excited about this new task. "Yes, I can do that!"

Mary Mark looked relieved. She immediately went to get the funds so he could purchase what was necessary as soon as possible. Mary was content for John Mark, hoping that his enthusiasm would not wane as quickly as his attention span did. For herself, she pondered the importance of having a task in the greater scheme of things. People were hungry for Jesus' message, but also eager to do something, as she had been, and for which she still felt anxious. She was impatient to do more and frustrated that she did not know what direction to take from one moment to the next. Maximin was reminding her to keep God's word in her heart. He encouraged her to let anxiety be replaced with trust.

"Remember Proverbs Mary," he often exhorted. "Trust in the Lord with all your heart and lean not on your own understanding; in all your ways submit to him, and he will make your paths straight."[288]

She didn't understand herself nor her own anxiety. She had sufficient work to do every day. God's circumstantial providence was taking care of that. And yet a restlessness as well as anxieties for the future would creep in.

"Do not worry about tomorrow, for tomorrow will worry about itself," Maximin echoed Jesus' words. "Each day has enough trouble of its own."[289]

On their journey to Bethany, she pondered those words as she watched the flock of birds overhead or saw the patches of flowers, all of whom Jesus had said his Father cares for. Little by little she noticed that her frequent supplications for trust were becoming a constant undercurrent in her heart. As she traveled with John Mark and Maximin, back and forth to Bethany, she marveled at how the Lord calls each one uniquely and yet they walk together in the same faith.

***

The next day, on her return through Bethphage, their paths separated. John Mark went in search of the materials needed for his new task. Maximin went to briefly check in with the leader of a small community that had been forming there. Mary chose to continue on. As had become habitual, a melancholic longing and vigilance for a sign of Jesus set her pace. She took her time, welcoming the quiet journey, relishing memories and anticipating possibilities. As she crested a hill that overlooked the entirety of Jerusalem, she thought she saw the apostles in the distance to the north. A familiar figure in white stood in their midst.

No! It can't be! Rabboni? She began to run in their direction, keeping her eyes fixed on him, not wanting to lose sight of him. Her legs could not take her fast enough. Still at a distance, she saw him raise his hands in a blessing. She came to a halt, a sense of something sacred happening before her. Within her. *Is he standing? Floating? Ascending before my eyes?* And in that instant, she caught his glance. It pierced her soul with an ache and unexplainable joy that brought her to her knees. She felt more alive than ever and yet undone at the same time. She reached out her arms as if to stop him, to plead with him not to leave her and yet, within, she felt him more present than ever. Then he vanished out of sight.

Her eyes fixed on the heavens, willing him to return, yet holding her hands over her breast as though she contained him within. Footsteps behind her brought her out of her trance-like state.

"Mary?" John Mark shook her. Maximin arrived out of breath behind him.

They looked up in the direction of her gaze and back at her.

"What is it, Mary? What do you see?"

"Jesus," escaped from her lips, flooding her again with the consolation of his presence as she closed her eyes, wanting to hold onto him.

John Mark cried out, "The apostles. Is that Jesus with them?"

Mary opened her eyes with the hope of seeing and speaking to him. But to her disappointment, it was not Jesus. Two men in white were conversing with the apostles. John Mark and Maximin helped Mary to her feet, and they made their way towards the apostles. By the time they arrived, the two men had disappeared.

The apostles were surprised to see Mary, Maximin and John Mark, but welcomed them with enthusiasm, their countenances exuding joy, stupor and wonder. She had witnessed it from afar, but she felt united to them in their experience and marveled at what had happened.

"Is he coming back?" She asked them all. She had not heard his words, but it looked as though they had spoken with him.

Peter answered, "Yes, we think so, but we don't know when."

Simon the Zealot answered as well, "We asked him when he would restore the kingdom to Israel, but he told us it was not ours to know the time or the day. The Father will decide that."[290]

Mary was perplexed. She had understood that he would restore the kingdom, but not in the way that many had anticipated. That the Kingdom of God was established through faith in Jesus, not by the establishment of a nation ruling over another. Had she misunderstood? She kept those thoughts to herself.

Peter continued, "Let's get home. I want to share this with everyone."

"But tell us, what happened?" Maximin asked.

"This morning, he appeared to us again in the upper room and we received instructions to stay in the city until the Father sends what he promised. He told us that he will clothe us in power from on high. And then he brought us out here, blessed us and was carried up to heaven."[291]

They were all eager to return and share this news.

"Come on, let's return home," Peter insisted again.

Home, she thought. *Where was home?* It used to be Magdala. But Jesus had turned her life upside down. Home became the place where he was. Then, home became the place where Ima and his followers were. *Home,* she thought. Home felt like it was in the depth of her soul as she experienced Jesus' eyes on her. She dared not say anything to the others. How could she explain it? She knew that she had been too far away to actually make eye contact with Jesus, and yet she had known. He had looked upon her. He had blessed her too. She pressed her hands to her heart, as though assuring that the gift would remain.

They turned towards the city, hearts full of joy and eager to tell the others.

John Mark walked next to Peter with a new enthusiasm in his step. "I can't wait to write this one down!"

Mussing up his hair, Peter encouraged him. "Yes, you do that. It will be a great way to share this good news, which we need to do more than ever now. Jesus told us that we would be his witnesses in Jerusalem, and in all Judea and Samaria, and to the ends of the earth. But first, we must wait for this promised spirit."[292]

***

For the next few days they joined together often in prayer, more frequently in the upper room and more cautiously in the Temple. They awaited the fulfillment of Jesus' promise to be clothed with the spirit. Ima was often a pillar of prayer, like a rock of fervor supplicating for all to come to believe in her Son, asking for faith, wisdom and courage for the burgeoning community of believers. They would pray daily with those who were staying in and around the city. On many days, there were over one hundred people gathered together. Mary Mark's house had turned into a main assembly of believers.

While they had chosen one man, Matthias, to replace Judas Iscariot they continued to refer to the first apostles as the Eleven. It was a sad reminder of Judas, but an important reminder of the first chosen and called to lead the others. They led the groups in the breaking of the bread, recalling Jesus' last supper and the words he had spoken. Peter often preached now, reminding them of Jesus' words and deeds and his promise of the Kingdom before they broke bread together.

Growing numbers did not change the strong sense of belonging to something new and good. Their faith in Jesus was nourished. But as the days passed, the promise seemed delayed. Mary encouraged others who began wondering if they were waiting in vain. She noticed within herself a new strength to cast aside doubts and fears, having experienced a renewed conviction from her brief encounter with the Lord upon that mount of his ascension, as she now called it. A presentiment was upon her that Jesus would return and somehow remain with them in a new and precious way.

CHAPTER 58. SACRED MEMORIES

I will remember the deeds of the Lord; yes, I will remember your miracles of long ago. I will consider all your works and meditate on all your mighty deeds.
Psalm 77:11-12

Fifty days had passed since Mary had witnessed her Rabboni taken from her by the cruel crucifixion. And almost ten days ago, he had been taken from her again, disappearing into the heavens. No one had testified to seeing him since then. No more visitations. Yet, whenever a twinge of sadness came, a living faith rushed upon her that nourished a hope of his return. Somehow, he would come back to her, she thought, even if it were only in Spirit. She did not fully comprehend the promise he had made. And she was impatient. However, there was barely a second to mourn. The days were full. She attended to the increasing number of visitors and the growing community, as well as assisted Mary Mark in managing the household that had turned into a hub of activity. She also squeezed in a few trips to Bethany, often with Maximin, to visit Lazarus and Martha and check on the situation there.

The spring days were passing by like a flash of lightning, the daylight was lengthening and the feast of weeks, Shavuot, was upon them. It was the eve of the high and holy day. They celebrated a candlelit dinner and read from the Torah. But this time, Peter added a novelty after reading the Ten Commandments. He recalled the Greatest commandment, echoing Deuteronomy and adding Jesus' teaching.

"We must love God with all our hearts, all our souls, and all our minds. And we must love our neighbors as ourselves.[293] The greatest commandment being to love."

Hearing those words again, she felt overcome with a tremendous yearning to love God above all else. But her heart ached at the thought that she did not know how to more fully express that love.

After dinner, she sought refuge once again with her friends in their privileged place upon the rooftop. The last of the day had already slipped into slumber. It was her favorite time, a few stolen minutes with John and Matthew when everyone else was settling in for the night. They would escape to the terrace and share about the day's events. They would reminisce and ponder, as they had so often done in their long walks together and in the long hours of that Holy Saturday, as she now called the endless day before Jesus' resurrection.

After the first few times that Mary, John and Matthew were making their way up to the terrace, Peter looked at them suspiciously.

"Why are you going up there every night?"

Ima broke the tension, teasing them. "They are holding a little cenacle, Peter. Let them be. They are keeping alive the memory of my Son."

Not that Mary could ever forget her Son. Jesus was the reason for her every breath, for the very existence of her life. *He IS my life*, she often thought.

From the highest vantage point of Mount Zion, they could see the activity of the Temple that would continue through the night.

"I cannot help but think back to Passover, seeing the city full of pilgrims once again," Mary reminisced.

"I don't want to go back to those days ever again," Matthew remarked impulsively.

John interjected, "As horrible as those days were Matthew, we cannot forget. Remembering is precisely what we must do. It must be our daily bread to remember and remind others of the wonders Jesus worked."

"True enough," Matthew conceded. He sighed deeply. "Fifteen hundred years."

Mary and John looked at him, wondering where his thoughts were taking him this time.

"Fifteen hundred years," Matthew said, as though they should understand exactly what he meant. "For fifteen hundred years we have been celebrating the Lord God giving us the Torah on Mount Sinai.

That is a long time to remember! I wonder if anyone will remember what happened to Jesus in fifteen hundred more years."

"We must never forget!" John spoke passionately. "To remember his name gives life. To forget is to die in our sin."[294]

"I don't just want mere memories John." Mary gave away her melancholic mood. "I wish more than anything that he would come back, walk among us. But something tells me, this will not be. But I," Mary hesitated. She didn't know if they would understand her if she shared her experience of the past few days. She decided she would try.

"I feel somehow that he is still living among us, like he is still near. Sometimes, especially after we have broken bread together, I set my eyes searching for him among the crowd as if I sensed his eyes upon me."

She closed her eyes remembering that sensation. John and Matthew's silence spoke more than words. It offered reverence in the intimacy of what she had shared.

She sighed, "But, looking around, I realize, he is not there. At least I cannot see him with my bodily eyes. At the same time, it fills me with a tremendous longing to be his witness. It is like an insistent, almost crazed desire, like when I was running back from his tomb to tell you that Jesus had risen and was alive. I just don't know how I am supposed to do that now."

"But you do know Mary. And you do it. You proclaim the Word of life," John exclaimed passionately. "That which was from the beginning, which we have heard, which we have seen with our eyes, which we have looked at and our hands have touched...".[295]

John looked down at his hands, palms open faced, as though he were stuck in contemplation. He continued in awe, "we have seen it and testify to it, and we proclaim Jesus, who is eternal life. He was with the Father yet came to purify us from all sin by his blood so we might walk in the light of truth. He has appeared to us. We proclaim, Mary, what we have seen and heard, so others may have fellowship with us, fellowship with the Father and with his Son, Jesus Christ."[296]

Mary marveled. *John's face is like an angel's*, she thought. Despite the darkness and only the firelight of a nearby torch, it was so full of light and life, exuberant joy emanating from the purity in his eyes.

"Yes John, this is my greatest privilege, to testify to all I have seen and heard. I just don't ever feel it is enough. Or that my words are sufficient to convince others."

Matthew offered his thoughts. "Jesus told us to wait until the Spirit clothes us. Maybe this will be an answer to your prayer Mary. God's Spirit is powerful. Just look at how God's spirit gave voice through the prophets and how so many prophecies have been fulfilled. They cannot all be mere coincidence. Ima told us that the Spirit helped her conceive and give birth to Jesus, and told her to call him Immanuel, which means 'God with us'.[297]

"And John, you told us that the Baptist said Jesus would baptize with the Holy Spirit and fire. That the Spirit descended upon him like a dove, then drove him into the desert to prepare for his ministry among us.[298] And he healed, rose from the dead, and drove out evil spirits all with the Spirit of God. And he sent us to do the same as we proclaimed the message that the kingdom of heaven has come near.[299]

"Like the prophecy of Isaiah says, 'God will put his Spirit upon the chosen servant.'[300] He did it with Jesus, maybe that is what he will do with us. And how can you explain that Jesus died and rose from the dead if not for the Spirit of God giving him life?"

Matthew stopped for a moment and then held up his hand, pointer finger in the air and started up again, as if another thought popped into his head.

"Oh! And he told us in Galilee that he would be with us even to the end of the ages.[301] If not by his Spirit, then how is he to be with us?" then turning to Mary he said, "And maybe it is His Spirit that will give you the right words to speak to others to convince them Mary?"

"Wow Matthew. You have been thinking a lot about this haven't you," John admired.

"Yes, much," he confirmed.

"I know he is with us, and yet, I can't help but feel," Mary winced as though she were betraying Jesus with her lack of absolute trust. But she needed to express her conflicting feelings. If not to two of her closest friends, to whom could she speak?

"I sometimes feel like an orphan. It sounds like a contradiction, but I cannot help what I feel. In one moment, I sense him near and in another I feel abandoned." Mary cringed. She didn't want to sound like she had no faith in Jesus and his promise, but those brief moments of doubt sometimes came over her.

"Yes, I think I know what you mean Mary," John consoled her. "But remember his teaching? He told us that there would come a time when we would no longer see him, but that he would not leave us orphans. He promised to send the advocate, the Spirit of truth. Perhaps when that time comes we will see more clearly the way forward. Actually, I thought it strange that Jesus said we already know him, for he lives within us, but will be in us. Like it already has happened and yet is still to come."

John paused at that contradiction, shaking his head. "Anyway, I am eager for that day. He told us that on that day we would realize that he is in his Father, that we are in him, and he is in us. And that he would reveal himself to those who love him."[302]

Matthew patted Mary's arm in an attempt to console her. "That is it then. You will see him again, Mary. Because I don't know anyone who loves him more than you. Except Ima, of course."

"Speaking of Ima," John added, "I know exactly what she would tell you right now."

"Patience Mary," the three of them said at the same time.

They chuckled. The voice of Ima speaking that phrase had become a constant echo in her heart.

John continued, "And remember. Jesus said that when the Advocate comes, whom he will send to us from the Father—the Spirit of truth who goes out from the Father—he will testify about Jesus." John set his hand on her other arm, shaking her lightly as though to assure she was listening. "And you also must testify, for you have been with him almost from the beginning. You are one of his closest disciples, his Magdalene."[303]

Mary offered a nod of gratitude to both, unable to speak from the threat of tears on the verge of being unleashed. She was so grateful, she thought. So grateful for her brothers in the Lord. How she loved them. She was touched by their attempts to console her in a moment when she didn't even realize how much she needed it. It came unexpectedly, like the Lord's great day of consolation that was upon them.

CHAPTER 59. PENTECOST

And afterward, I will pour out my Spirit on all people.
And everyone who calls on the name of the Lord will be saved;
for on Mount Zion and in Jerusalem there will be deliverance, as the Lord has said,
even among the survivors whom the Lord calls.
Joel 2: 28-32

The great day came, like a storm set upon them without warning. The day of Pentecost. It was morning. They decided to forego the visit to the Temple that day. Too many people were in search of them. Pilgrims had come from far and wide for the festivities, but many also went in search of the so-called New Way that had been forming. They were curious and eager to reunite with someone who reminded them of the Messianic rabbi, the one who had cured them, whom they had heard preach, or they simply had heard of through other believers.

Fifty days had passed since Passover. The Eleven, many women disciples, and various families of the other disciples had gathered in the upper room. The grain had ripened, and the first fruits were ready to be offered. A basket full of grain and bread, freshly baked with the first of the harvest was laid in the midst of them. Mary's presentiment had begun the night before, with a heightened anticipation. She could feel it in the air. The others perceived it too. This was to be a Pentecost like they had celebrated with their forefathers, and yet there was a newness to it, something different. The breaking of the bread, their anticipation, the excitement of coming together, united as a community, united around Ima as a reminder of how the Spirit had ushered in the Messiah whom she had carried within her very womb, the Messiah in whom they believed, their new and growing congregation...it all reminded her of the scripture Peter was reading to them that morning.

God's command to obey and offer the first fruits was ripe with the fulfillment of a promise. The Lord would "open the heavens, the storehouse of his bounty, to send rain" upon them and bless all the work of their hands.[304] Peter was a great orator, bringing the story alive before them. Making them feel as if they were present on that tremendous day fifteen hundred years ago, the great coming of the Lord upon Mount Sinai when he spoke the law into their hearts.

Peter recalled the ancient Pentecost. "The people had 'stood at the foot of the mountain while it blazed with fire to the very heavens, with black clouds and deep darkness.'[305] In the days of old, 'the Lord spoke to the people face to face out of the fire on the mountain,'[306] but 'what mortal has ever heard the voice of the living God speaking out of fire, as we have, and survived?'"[307]

Peter then cried out, "My dear brothers and sisters in the Lord, they could not see! But we have seen!"

Suddenly, the doors flew open, the window shutters flapped like the wings of a rooster trying to take flight. A violent wind rushed in all directions, swirling their clothes and hair, knocking over anything that wasn't firmly fixed to its spot. She knew not from where it came, nor where it was going. It came from outside and from within, from the rooftop and through the very floor, in through the doors and out through the windows and back again. A sound came from the heavens and filled the entire house. An overpowering presence spilled into exuberant joy that set hearts on fire to praise the Lord.

Am I dreaming?

Tongues of fire appeared over the heads of many as they stood in praise, wonder and adoration.[308] One danced for joy, others spoke in foreign tongues, yet Mary understood every word. The Spirit of God! His promised has been fulfilled. She felt Jesus at her side, in the very core of her being. His Spirit within! The Holy Spirit they had been promised!

Slowly the wind died down, yet the joy did not subside. Couples embraced, Peter appeared impassioned with fever, John laughed like a child, Matthew was stunned into stupor. And all continued to praise the Lord. She marveled. People from various lands declared the wonders of God in their own tongue and yet, they knew with clarity the same message, the prophecies fulfilled, salvation was in the name of Jesus, the Lord of heaven and earth.

Another sound caught her attention. It came from outside. Her ears did not deceive her. A large crowd was accumulating outside the house. People moved about the house, in and out, wondering at and sharing the good news of the Spirit's coming. Like wildfire catching, the Spirit continued to set fire to more hearts as one after the other received the news and more joined the ranks of rejoicing.

However, not all were set ablaze. Taunting and disbelief loomed like a cacophony of dissonance, attempting to extinguish the ardor of praise.

"They have drunk too much wine!" "They are just trying to get attention!"

Rebuttals exclaimed the truth of the matter. "They all speak their language and yet we understand what they say. They are Parthians, Medes and Elamites; residents of Mesopotamia, Judea and Cappadocia, Pontus and Asia, Phrygia and Pamphylia, Egypt and the parts of Libya near Cyrene; visitors from Rome, both Jews and converts to Judaism; Cretans and Arabs. How is that possible if they are drunk?!"[309]

The apostles spread themselves out into the crowd, zealous to defend the Lord. Peter climbed to the terrace rooftop. He bellowed out, addressing the crowd, believers and nonbelievers alike.

"Fellow Jews and all of you who live in Jerusalem, let me explain this to you; listen carefully to what I say. These people are not drunk, as you suppose. It's only nine in the morning! No, this is what was spoken by the prophet Joel: 'In the last days, God says, I will pour out my Spirit on all people...Your sons and daughters will prophesy...Even on my servants, both men and women, I will pour out my Spirit in those days, and they will prophesy. And everyone who calls on the name of the Lord will be saved.'"[310]

Mary did not know from where they came, but the streets were filling to their maximum capacity. They invaded the house and filled the garden courtyard. *It is impossible to receive more people*, she thought. Mary looked for Ima among the crowd and maneuvered her way to her side. Her face was radiant. Their attention turned again to Peter. Peter's voice could be heard from the rooftop into the street, through the house and into the garden courtyard. Despite the number of people continuing to stream into the vicinity, they listened with eagerness or curiosity. His voice resonated with a power of its own.

"Fellow Israelites, listen to this: Jesus of Nazareth was a man accredited by God to you by miracles, wonders and signs, which God did among you through him, as you yourselves know. This man was handed over to you by God's deliberate plan and foreknowledge; and you, with the help of wicked men, put him to death by nailing him to the cross."[311]

A murmuring rippled through the crowd "We had nothing to do with his crucifixion."

Mary grabbed Ima's hand. An unspoken understanding between them set them praying that all who were present would receive Peter's words and come to believe in Jesus. The murmuring died out quickly as others hushed the grumblers and Peter went on.

"But God raised him from the dead, freeing him from the agony of death, because it was impossible for death to keep its hold on him."[312]

As Peter recited a psalm of David,[313] heads nodded and even children recited the words with him. Joy spread like a contagion. And Peter went on, as passionately as ever.

"Fellow Israelites, I can tell you confidently that the patriarch David died and was buried, and his tomb is here to this day."[314]

More heads nodded, for the tradition held that David's tomb was buried very nearby. Pilgrims often wandered over to Mount Zion while they were in Jerusalem for the festivals. They paid homage to the anointed king and prophet David. While Mary Mark's house was not on the main street of that typical traffic, it was nonetheless in a privileged spot for that very reason.

Peter continued, "But he was a prophet and knew that God had promised him on oath that he would place one of his descendants on his throne. Seeing what was to come, he spoke of the resurrection of the Messiah, that he was not abandoned to the realm of the dead, nor did his body see decay. God has raised this Jesus to life, and we are all witnesses of it. Exalted to the right hand of God, he has received from the Father the promised Holy Spirit and has poured out what you now see and hear."[315]

Recitations of another of David's prophecies undulated like waves over the people. Like a choir of angels, Mary thought, a beautiful harmony sprung forth. It further enkindled their hearts with the fire of the Spirit, setting aflame once again a chorus of praise. No one was alone. The multitude was simmering with the same fire of faith.

Peter shouted out again as the choir quieted to a symphonic hum.

"Therefore, let all Israel be assured of this: God has made this Jesus, whom you crucified, both Lord and Messiah."[316]

A new hum rose among them, setting something in motion. A singular question surfaced. They addressed the apostles, "Brothers, what shall we do?"[317]

Peter replied, "Repent and be baptized, every one of you, in the name of Jesus Christ for the forgiveness of your sins. And you will receive the gift of the Holy Spirit. The promise is for you and your children and for all who are far off—for all whom the Lord our God will call."[318]

There were still unbelievers among them. As if written on their faces, Mary saw belief and unbelief. Peter cried out a final warning, pleading with them to save themselves from corruption. In that moment, Mary perceived with clarity whose hearts were hardened and whose were opened. She saw those who came forward to be baptized out of fear or sheer curiosity, those who came out of insistence or encouragement of a spouse or parent, and those who eagerly desired to enter into the fold of believers. Their joy was the greatest. Mary, Ima, and the other women disciples spent the next several hours ministering to the crowds, praying in gratitude for those who came forward to be baptized, praying for those requesting healing or further faith, speaking words of wisdom and encouragement to those on the brink of choosing.

Mary had never been a mother, but in that moment, she knew the joys and pains of giving birth to a living being. Her labor pains, while not physical in nature, were sufferings that she bore when people walked away, unbelieving. However, her joy was a hundredfold upon receiving a new brother or sister in the faith. New life was everywhere, and she welcomed each one with the kiss of peace.

***

Exhaustion accompanied exhilaration as the last of the newly baptized finally left, late into the night. Ima gathered them together. She was the first to serve a nighttime meal, replenishing their hungry bellies which had gone without all day. And she was the first to draw out of each one their stories. Fatigue would not snuff out the fire of zeal. They shared their experiences of that day.

"Three thousand people Ima!" Matthew exclaimed. Mary didn't know how he even had time to count or keep track of how many people they had baptized.

"I can't believe it," Thomas exclaimed, "And from the four corners of the world!"

"Jesus had told us to go to the four corners of the world. I didn't know he was going to bring the ends of the earth to us!" Nathaniel marveled.

Contentment flowed into a prayer of gratitude as they finished their meal. Peter already gave hints of what he foresaw in the upcoming days.

"We have much work to do, many to teach in this new way, many we must strengthen in their faith. This house is not large enough to contain us anymore."

"We must go into the Temple courts," Matthew offered. "There we could easily preach to thousands a day. We could separate them by groups, or you could speak again like you spoke from the rooftop Peter."

Where once Peter might have cowered, he now spoke with bold certainty. "Yes, we must preach the word of God. We risk the wrath of the Sanhedrin, but the greater tragedy would be losing the opportunity to bring the inheritance of the kingdom to all, the inheritance prepared by God and received by faith in the Son of God. The Spirit is raising up living stones[319] and building us into a spiritual house. If the Spirit has strengthened us, we too must strengthen others in the faith."

All agreed. After discussing practical aspects of this new initiative, Peter divided the tasks among them. They would begin tomorrow with a sense of urgency, fortitude and courage uniting them in the Lord.

CHAPTER 60. FRUITS & FOREWARNINGS

By this everyone will know that you are my disciples, if you love one another.
John 13:35

Every day, the apostles went out to the Temple. Peter had assigned them various positions in and around the gates. Newly baptized, as well as the newly curious, came to listen to their teachings. Signs and wonders were worked. And the number of followers increased daily. Several of the original seventy were commissioned by Peter to form communities and strengthen the faith in their own hometowns and surrounding villages, be they in Jerusalem, the surrounding area or in Galilee. The conviction of faith was strong.

During these days, Mary was reunited once again with her old friend, Little Joanna. Her husband, considerably older than Joanna, had passed away on the great day of Pentecost. Joanna had been barren and despite being young and eligible for marriage once again, she convinced her aunt and uncle, Johanna and Chuza, to allow her to join Mary and the faith community in Jerusalem. Like many new believers, she sold what had remained of her belongings from marriage and put it at the service of those in need. Since then, little Joanna had taken up her old post as Mary Magdalene's companion. This time in a much different venture. Her aunt Johanna was pleased with this new arrangement, grateful that little Joanna had a place in the community and a model and friend in Mary Magdalene.

The very first day of the apostles' Temple preaching, Mary wished to be sent as well. Not willing to be left behind, she convinced Peter that she would be the perfect disciple to be sent into the women's court. Little Joanna eventually joined the ranks. Almost daily, the Apostles frequented the Temple. Mary and Joanna accompanied Peter,

John, Maximin and John Mark, Peter's very faithful scribe, to the Beautiful gate. Then they parted ways. Mary quickly gained a reputation among the women. It was a time to pray, be prayed over, and to listen to the stories of Jesus that she shared to any who would lend an ear. Many women joined their ranks. Despite their husbands' warnings against associating with her, the women's court became a type of refuge for many who came to believe.

One evening, gathered together in Mary Mark's house, they were sharing the fruits of their endeavors. But John, Matthew and John Mark were missing. Matthew and John Mark slipped in halfway through the shared meal. *Where was John?* Mary was concerned. He and Peter had already been called in for questioning by the Sanhedrin and accused of spreading lies and superstitions, especially because of the growing belief that even Peter's shadow could heal the sick.[320] They were ordered to stop preaching the name of Jesus. But Peter and John had refused. Nonetheless, they had been let go and continued to boldly teach, preach and heal in the Temple area. John Mark had estimated that at least five thousand believers could now be counted in and around Jerusalem.[321]

She caught Matthew and John Mark stealing glances at her, as though they had an unpleasant secret they were unwilling to tell but belonged to her to know. They remained quiet, not interrupting the dinner conversation. Thirty minutes passed and still they offered no clue as to their strange demeanor. Peter wrapped up the evening meal with his final counsel and distribution of the next day's tasks, who would go where and how to follow up with the various requests that had arisen. Yet still, she would catch Matthew and John Mark glancing at her, then at the door and back again, as though awaiting some threat, toward her, to enter through the doorway.

The disciples broke up. The cleaning of supper began. And John finally entered. He approached her.

"Mary," he said discreetly. "There is someone here to see you. Please come with me quietly. I don't want to attract the attention of the others."

"Who is it?"

John, not wanting to say aloud for others to hear, gently took her arm and escorted her to the front door. Before opening, he looked back to see that they were alone. Only John Mark and Matthew had noticed their escape. They stood stiffly, watching Mary.

Before opening the door John addressed her solemnly, "It is Gaius. Please, I ask you to hear him out."

"Were you with him this whole time during dinner John?"

"Yes. We had a long conversation. I didn't trust him at first, but I think he means well. I think he wants to help us. Well, not so much us, but you. He came to see you. I just wasn't certain that we should let him."

"I can take care of myself John."

"I know you can. I was just afraid he might..." John stopped abruptly. "Well, never mind. He is out there now, waiting to talk to you. I didn't want Martha getting upset if she heard about him coming around."

It rankled her that John might not trust her own conviction at the sight of Gaius. But she tried to temper it with the thought that he meant well. She brushed him aside to open the door.

John quickly offered, "Do you want me to stay with you while you talk to him?"

"No," she said determinedly as she opened the door.

Gaius stood tall like a sentinel at the corner of the house, away from the torch that lit the front entrance. He waited in expectation, vigilant of his surroundings. He was dressed in ordinary garb that made him blend into the darkness of the moonless night.

John came part way outside with her. "Keep the door open, so we can hear if you need anything."

"Fine."

John did not move. Mary pushed him into the house. "Go have dinner John. I will take care of this."

She left the door open but walked out to meet Gaius. His half shadowed face revealed weariness and concern.

"Gaius. How can I help you?" She maintained calm, remembering their last conversation. He had been such a mix of the old vulnerable

Gaius and the hardened Gaius. He had confessed the death of his wife and babe and, in her shock, she had not even offered a word of consolation.

"Miriam. I wanted to see that you were alright." He hesitated, then went on, a surprising humility in his demeanor, or at least a lack of arrogance. "I know this is not my right, but I am worried for you. There is word going around of, of your, well, what shall we call it?" His note of concern turned to humor. "Your new occupation? Provocations? Scope of influence?"

She didn't know if he was insulting her, belittling her, or teasing her.

"You mean my teaching and work with the women in the Temple?"

"Yes, that. It isn't enough that those friends of yours are drawing the attention of the Sanhedrin by their preaching and healing? You have to do the same? You know that the Sanhedrin have the right ear of Pilate. They practically own half of him with their offering of the Temple treasury to construct an aqueduct to Solomon's pools.[322] But then, you probably know this, considering their influence over Pilate to have your teacher killed."

"I know Gaius. Peter and John have already been warned. But there is no stopping them. And there is no stopping me as well. We must speak about what we have seen. It is a matter of life and death. Eternal life and death Gaius. I wish you could understand this."

Gaius' face flashed frustration, then a calmer resolve. He shook his head. "You have always been strong headed Miriam. But granted, I can see in that friend of yours, John, your same conviction. All I ask is you be careful. I am warning you. The Temple captain is on high alert and even requested for a reserve of Roman soldiers to stand guard in case it is needed."

"Thank you, Gaius. I will keep this in mind and let the others know. I just don't think it will change our course of action."

"I can't protect you Miriam," he said with a hint of sorrow and frustration.

"And I am not asking for your protection." A sense of gratitude and tenderness overcame her. "But I do thank you Gaius. And I am sorry. Sorry for all that has happened between us. And I, I am sorry for your loss." She hesitated, wanting to do more for him. "I pray for you," she said quietly, hoping he would at least accept these words.

She was surprised that he didn't throw it back in her face. He looked pensive. "Well, I won't refuse it. If your God exists, if your teacher is really the Son of God as you people claim, your prayers can't hurt."

A spark of hope was ignited. "You...You believe?"

"Believe? No Miriam. I wouldn't call it belief. But I have seen your friends praying over people. There is something different about it. Different than the Jews. Different than our rituals to our Roman gods."

"Because Jesus is with us. His Spirit is with us. His Father provides us with all good things."

"Good things?" He humphed. "Crucifixion and the threat of being arrested are the good things your God gives you?"

She didn't have time for any rebuttal. He continued with conviction in his voice, neither angry nor ridiculing. She detected sincerity.

"I am not so sure about your God. But," he hesitated, looking up to the heavens as though searching for the right words or the strength to continue. Then, he looked at her intensely. "I believe in you Miriam. Or I believe in the person you have become. This, this Mary Magdalene. That is what I hear everyone calling you. I see you, my Miriam, but I also see something else. Something unshakeable. Not just stubborn independence. I see courage. A calm courage. I always loved your impetuosity and astuteness. Now I see...I'm not sure what to call it, but it is unwavering. If only my soldiers had half of your determination!"

Mary was overcome with his profession. It partly frightened her, to be the object of his belief. But at least he acknowledged her decision. He accepted that she believed. It was not what she hoped for or had been praying for, his faith in her God, but his words touched her. She was left speechless.

He continued. "Miriam, when I accused you of infidelity, you said you were faithful to me. Well, I can see you are still faithful."

Mary started to protest, but he stopped her.

"Wait. I see your fidelity. And I know it is not for me. I accept that. I respect that."

He hesitated, then continued, "I even think you still love me." He waited for her reaction, but she said nothing. She was silently lifting up a prayer for him.

"But that too is not as before. Something different. I don't understand. But that too, I will try to respect."

His face changed to a quiet agony as he grabbed her arms as if in a desperate plea.

"Oh Miriam. Your heart is too good. Please listen to me. I know you are courageous, but please, don't be foolish. Vespasian is returning to head up this group of soldiers. I don't think he will be as kind as me. He is not interested in protecting you, as you well know. He has a taste for vengeance and is not afraid to spill blood. Perhaps his hatred is more for me since I returned from Rome, and for having some influence in his demotion once he went north. But I am certain he will take it out on you, or on your friends. And I am being sent back to Rome. I cannot protect you or warn you. Maybe you could go back to Magdala. At least for a while. Until the situation calms down here."

"Mary?" John was using his thundering voice to interrupt Gaius' passionate plea.

Gaius released her from his grip.

Mary pacified John. "I'm fine John. I am coming." Turning to Gaius, she now sought his eyes in the dancing light of the nearby torch-fire.

"Be not afraid for me Gaius. My Lord is with me. He is my shield and protector. I do not fear persecution. I do hope you will understand someday. Go in peace."

She turned, a prayer still in her heart begging God to give him faith, as she entered the house.

John did not enter the house with her. Not right away. She went up to the rooftop, her emotions too awake to cooperate with sleep. From the obscurity of her perch, she could see John and Gaius in conversation. She was tempted to return. She wanted to know what they were speaking about for so long. But she determined to stay and pray.

Lord pour out your Spirit upon them both. Give John the right words to speak.

Perhaps John's words would bear fruit in Gaius more than hers did. Finally, she watched them shake hands. John turned toward her and searched above for signs of her presence on the rooftop. Gaius, not aware of her silent and prayerful observation, turned and walked into the darkness of the night.

She heard John's footsteps coming up to the terrace.

"Mary?" He whispered, "Ah, I knew it. I thought I would find you here."

Mary wiped away tears that she only now realized had slowly accumulated. It didn't escape John's notice, despite the night's shadows.

"What's wrong? Did he hurt you?"

"No, not at all," she defended him. "No, I doubt he would ever hurt me. Well, not anymore. I am just so grateful." She didn't know how to explain her sentiments. "But tell me. What kept you so long? I was praying for you to have the right words to speak to him. Maybe someday he will also believe."

"Hmm, maybe someday Mary. Keep praying. At times, when we were talking, I thought he might just believe, and then he would say something that made me realize he was far from it. But he is brave to risk coming here and warning us. He even gave me a way to contact him in Rome, if there was ever anything he could do for us. Well, really, for you. Although I am not sure there is much he can do if Pilate decides to side with the Sanhedrin to stop us."

"Uff, Pilate! I have to confess that I would love to go to Rome myself and give Caesar a piece of my mind about him! Having an innocent man crucified!"

John remained silent.

"Well, wouldn't you John? Maybe Gaius could do something about that?"

John remained in silence, making her curious where his thoughts were wandering.

"John?"

"Do you still love Gaius, Mary?"

"Were you listening to our conversation John?" She asked, wondering where this question was coming from.

He didn't answer, just waited for her answer.

"I think I do still love him. At first it frightened me. But I realized, it is not like before. It is very different. I feel a new love for him. And I love Jesus. With all my heart, I love Jesus. But for Gaius, it is like a deeper and more genuine care for him. I desperately hope he will someday believe what we believe."

"I don't think you need to fear that kind of love. I have been thinking a lot about this lately. I have come to understand that God is love. And perfect love drives out fear. If we live in him and he in us, then we live in love. And we can love because he first loved us."[323]

Both remained silent, lost in their own thoughts, a peaceful stillness between them.

Then John asked, "Does that make sense Mary?"

She nodded contemplatively, "Yes, I think so."

John sighed. "Well, we have another big day tomorrow. More surprises, I am sure. So, I'm going to rest. Good night, Mary."

"Good night, John. Rest well."

John's footsteps faded away, leaving her in solitude. In that pregnant silence her heart longed to sit at the feet of her Master and ponder the wonders of the last few days, weeks, months, years. She thought back to her first encounter with Gaius after his return from Rome, after she had already met Jesus. Her two worlds had collided and clashed. A violent tug of war had taken place within her soul. She compared that experience with her recent meeting, perhaps her final one with Gaius. Her heart ached for him with a new desire, a desire for his eternal salvation, for his faith in the living God, in her Rabboni.

Her two worlds, past and present, had collided once again. But somehow, she felt them reconciling. She could see purpose and the Lord's providence. For the first time, she realized, she could look upon her past and not want to change anything. Her failings, her sins, even her lack of faith had all been overcome in the Lord. It had been a long journey, a transforming journey. And she was certain it was not the end. Not yet.

A fire burned in her heart for the Lord, a fire she hoped and prayed would set more hearts ablaze for her Rabboni. She lifted up a final prayer to the heavens and at the same time, felt that she was turning to her Rabboni who dwelt intimately in the center of her being.

Thank you Rabboni. I love you with all my heart, all my soul, and all my strength. I surrender to you. I entrust to you all those under my care and ask you to watch over and guide them. Send me your Spirit and let me always be your faithful disciple.

EPILOGUE. THE CONSUMMATION

Look, I am coming soon!
My reward is with me...
I am the Alpha and the Omega,
the First and the Last,
the Beginning and the End. [...]
The Spirit and the bride say, 'Come!'
Rev 22:12-13

A letter to the Apostle John from Little Joanna

Anno Domini 77, Sainte LeBaume, Gaul

My dear brother John in the Lord,

Greetings from the land of Gaul. I sit in the humble abode of father Maximin, Mary's faithful friend and spiritual father during all these long years in which we have been separated. He has graciously insisted on surrendering these dwellings to Mary and myself. All is peaceful here on the edge of a mystical-like forest, at the foot of the holy mountain, Sainte LeBaume, as some have begun to call it. A small lamp is lit, enough to continue my writing without awakening Mary. As you relayed, thanks to Maximin's missive several months ago, Mary is quite ill. It is a miracle that I arrived when I did. The Lord has given us a chance to reunite while she still breathes, but now, I fear her time is near.

She is lucid. She has not forgotten her little Joanna, as she still calls me. I am grateful that you insisted on me making this journey. It has been too long. It is hard to believe that almost forty years have passed since Mary and I parted ways in Rome. We are older and hopefully wiser for all we have endured. You once said that there were not enough books to contain all that Jesus did and said. I almost feel the same about our beloved Magdalene. Maximin, bishop and friend to both the rich and poor in Aix and the surrounding areas, has used his influence to gather papyrus, ink and pen so I may attempt to memorialize the confessions I have been privy to these last four weeks. I have much to tell you!

Listening to her now, I realized that I never truly understood her so many years ago. As you know, Mary and I were reunited during those two years after Pentecost. But we parted ways at the end of our adventure to Rome. I was always grateful for her letters during those ten years of faithful labor with you and the other disciples upon her return from Rome. Would you believe that, even now, she prays for our enemies, especially that beast Vespasian. I struggle to imitate her in this. His constant threat seems many lifetimes ago, yet I still think of him with disdain. But Mary reminds me that God's providence worked even through that.

"Remember little Joanna, how the Lord prompted us to leave Jerusalem and return to Magdala?" she scolded.

I do not know how she sees God's loving hand in all things. Vespasian's threats, especially upon her, were worrisome. And as Gaius predicted, she had no protection against him. She finally agreed to leave Jerusalem only due to Aharon's petition with the growing number of people requesting baptism and to know the Lord in and near Magdala.

She even sees Tams and Babs' illness as working in our favor. As I sit beside her, watching her life fade away, I hope I can care for her with the same tenderness she showed Tams and Babs in their final days. Those were difficult days indeed. While she felt the futility of her prayers that could not cure them, a new peace came over her upon their final rest. She confessed to me, with a mix of humor and seriousness, that after their death she was jealous of Tams and Babs. They were now with her Rabboni, and she was once again left behind in this land of exile. I do not mean to say that she was depressed. Her joy and zeal for living gave little hint of the interior pain she endured. It was like a sword that pierced her heart, as we used to say of Ima. Why must great love be united to suffering? Please write for me an answer to that!

Well John, she cared not for her villa the same way after that. She was grateful, and she still loved it in a way, but she saw it all in a new light. She sold much of her land which funded our eventual trip to Rome and aided the new community in Jerusalem. And the villa was left to Aharon who had taken leadership of the growing community of the New Way in that area. I do wonder what has become of them all, there in Magdala, after suffering another Roman invasion due to the rebellion.

Oh John, too many memories! I must send this letter as soon as possible. And after putting all of my notes in order, countless pages will follow. Or perhaps they are better kept safe here, with Maximin? So many stories of her past, of before and after she met Jesus! You can guess how difficult it was to obtain this from her. I pleaded, I pried, and I even attempted underhanded questions. She saw through my ruse. She would not speak of herself. She wanted only to speak of the love of God. She reminds me of you! Finally, after several unsuccessful attempts, I gave up. Then one day, I was lamenting, interminably lamenting, over my own faults and how little I had done for the Lord, how weak and sinful I felt. From her humble bed, if you can even call the simple straw mat a bed, she grabbed my arm.

"My little Joanna!" She scolded me in her loving and maternal way. "Can you not see what the Lord sees? Yes, dear one, confess your sins. And believe that he looks upon you in mercy. But do not stop there. He sees so much more than your past. Do you not feel his gaze resting upon you? He delights in you. He recreates in you!"

Now don't think that I didn't catch the double meaning of that last expression! You and Mary are very clever with words, but I have also learned over these last several years. I believe she was speaking of what she herself has experienced in the Lord. He takes his recreation, so to speak, his rest, by inviting us into intimate friendship. He creates his garden of Eden within us. I know that Mary has been a privileged one to know the Lord's eyes upon her, delighting in her, as though walking hand in hand in the garden of paradise. And in that walk, he rejoices in carrying out his re-creation! You see John. I have grown up. I have attained some wisdom since I joined the ranks of Jesus' followers.

Well, would you believe that, after this, the floodgates suddenly opened! Time and solitude have nurtured her sacred memories, for what she spoke could have come from the lips of angels. I saw her life from a new perspective.

It was a confession of sorts, of both her failings and triumphs. But above all she recounted the wonders the Lord has worked within her. Truly, it is a tribute to his fidelity. And this is what she made me promise, that if I speak to anyone of these things that she shared, it must turn their hearts to Jesus. Therefore, I fear I will not do it justice. Perhaps Father Maximin will review the stories I have documented. He knows her better than anyone, not just the history of her travels, but the transforming and very interior journey of her soul. He has been privy to the more personal and intimate aspects of her history, how she matured because she knew herself loved unconditionally by her God in the midst of the messiness of her life.

***

Oh, dear John! I had to pause while Mary stirred. She takes no food anymore, surviving on the Eucharist that Maximin brings her daily. Yet even with the little energy she still possesses, she thinks of the well-being of others. She asked me what I was writing. I cannot tell her that I have taken detailed notes on all that she shared. So, I told her I was writing you a very long letter. She wishes to do the same but has not the strength to even sit up. The best she has to offer is her pain and the hope that you continue persevering in the love of the Lord. She is still the apostle to the apostles, always praying for those who shepherd our people. She confessed that she was delighted by that endearment that Ima used for her before the two of you parted for Ephesus!

As I pen these words, I fear that she is quickly fading away. But this does not deter her. She prays for more to enter the fold. I sense that, for her, death is a mere passageway to her beloved. I confess John, I was a bit irked when I arrived, and after my long travels her first reaction upon seeing me was disappointment! But she masked it well, and I knew for whom she held vigil. Her heart is enkindled with hope like a torchlight in the night. She is a faithful virgin who has kept her lamp lit. She awaits the beloved bridegroom. How pleased he will be to find her ready and eager for his eternal embrace.

One thing is certain. She will be reunited with her beloved Martha and Lazarus once again. You would be proud of the work they started in the name of the Lord here in Gaul. They are to be admired. I have seen for myself and Maximin told me of the fruits of their labors since they arrived on these shores. Alas, it is for another letter, and we are short on time and writing supplies. Maximin and I are both in need of a scribe here, a faithful John Mark, to take note of the wonders taking place.

I don't know if you will still be in Ephesus, but I hope that this letter will find you, eventually. The Lord's providence seems to find a way to make this great big world very small by sending messages between the new and growing communities. Our little churches spring up in unexpected places, don't they? This land of Gaul is one such example. Who would have foreseen that the emperor Caligula's persecutions would send Mary, Martha, Lazarus, Maximin and several others into the sea to drown, only to land upon pagan lands ripe for the Good News. I wish my own eyes could have seen it those thirty years ago: Mary Magdalene preaching about our Lord and Savior to the pagans, even with the threat of the local ruler's wrath.

The people say that she worked a miracle for his wife, first interceding for the fruitfulness of her barren womb, and then saving the babe in childbirth. She did the same for Demetria, remember? You witnessed her prayer for Demetria's barren womb on the shores of Magdala, but I witnessed the birth myself. I had lost all hope that the babe would survive, but Mary's supplications to her Rabboni brought breath once again to that tiny creature. It is no wonder that women still look to her for her prayers in times of barrenness or perilous labor.

***

I had to stop again. Maximin checked in on us and began reminiscing. Mary insists that I share with you the good work that her brother and sister did in this land. I confess, I have found such a strange mix of people here. When I arrived in the port of Massilia,[324] it reminded me of Jerusalem, with Roman soldiers visible as a sign of their conquest and a warning against any threat of rebellion. But the fruits of Lazarus' efforts are also present, even if he is not upon this earth anymore. The small but firm foundation of believers in Massilia welcomed me and even escorted me through the hills and forests to this treasured spot with Mary. Maximin tells me that Martha also worked tirelessly near the Roman colony of Arles, called Tarascon.

The mix of Roman, Greek and Gallic tribes lends itself to pagan influence even amidst the modest beginnings of the New Way. Perhaps this taints the tales they have woven about our dear Martha. They say she saved men, women and children from a terrible dragon that lurked about the River Rhone. I do believe that it was one of those exotic Roman imports, those wretched creatures, half reptile and half fish. It likely escaped from the colosseum in Arles, and Martha, ever the problem-solver, stunned it with the mere sight of the holy cross and bound it with her own girdle. I laugh at the thought John! It has all the qualities of our Martha whom they say was also a great preacher.[325]

They tell stories of our beloved Magdalene as well. Fact and myth merge together. But I see my Magdalene in them. And oh John, I had heard rumors, but it was shocking to see the truth for myself. Her cave dwelling is a sight to see. She has been almost thirty years serving the Lord in this land, but in such a different way than before. Maximin says she spent most of those years in that cave, accessible with only the greatest of efforts up the steep and rocky incline. I was fortunate to be in good health to climb it myself but needed the help of two good and strong brothers in the Lord to bring her down the cliff-like mountain into the sheltered forest. Here, in Maximin's little dwelling, I can better tend to her.

Why would she hide herself away like that, I asked. She sought solitude, she said. However, her desire was not altogether granted by the

Lord. Visitors sought her out, from princes to paupers, men and women, young and old. They sought her counsel and prayers, her intercession for healing and her company. You were right. She cannot stay hidden. She gains a reputation wherever she goes.

As with any good story, legend has filled in the gray areas around the truth. They think she comes from a lineage of kings. Albeit, she still maintains a noble bearing despite her luxurious raven black hair now turned to a silvery white, and her once youthful face has graceful wrinkles of wisdom, which she so deserves to flaunt, in my opinion. Of course, she would not. Any traces of vanity have disappeared from the Miriam I once knew. However, many still claim that she remained impetuous. Thinking back to the early years of our labors after Pentecost, I suppose one would assume she was so. But I would disagree. She had a quick intuition coupled with determination to act on her convictions. Like the time she decided to travel to Rome and give Caesar a piece of her mind about Pilate.

In memory, Mary and I revisited our adventure, laughing and praising God for his providence on our way to Rome to see Caesar. Truly we were not in our right minds to even venture such a task! Nicodemus almost forbade us, but there was no stopping Mary. I will spare you all the details. She likely shared much of our months' long journey with you already.[326]

But these memories brought Gaius to the forefront of our conversation. She remains ever grateful and in awe of your prayerful intercession for him and his practical intercession for us. When we thought all was lost and we would be detained in a Roman prison, he not only attained our release, but also an audience with the emperor's right hand man.

Even at the miraculous transformation of the egg from white to red, I still don't think either of them believed that Jesus rose from the dead, not at that point. But at least the emperor finally did something about Pilate. Many say that Pilate was recalled to Rome due to the slaughtering of the Samaritans on Mount Gerizim. Perhaps that was the final straw. But I like to think that her persuasive words of his unjust treatment of Jesus had some influence.

Of course, I gave her the bittersweet news John. And you were right. It was well that I did. I told her all.

"Your prayers have finally been answered Mary! Gaius came to believe that Jesus is the Messiah! I am sure John's letters helped to tip the scales in favor of conversion."

Yes John, I told her how you continued to encourage and write to him, as well as pray for him. Then I told her how his conversion came about.

"Another Mary was his undoing this time! His daughter Mary. I do wonder if he named her after you. Either way, your name's sake is just as determined and bullheaded as you. Courageous too! When she was only twenty-two, she convinced her Father to intervene for the Apostle Paul and get his sentence reduced. Thank God Gaius did! He managed to attain a lesser punishment, house arrest. His two years in Rome, even under those circumstances, were a blessing. He taught us much, and Gaius' daughter was the first to care for his needs and share his teachings. Paul had a special fondness for her, and she became quite the leader among the Roman community.[327]

But John, I couldn't hide the uglier truth from her. She insisted I tell her all.

"The persecution increased. Nero was ruthless. And in his third year of reigning[328] a great fire broke out in Rome. Nero blamed the Christians. Gaius´ daughter and many others escaped, but Nero´s fury knew no bounds. He went on a rampage. First Peter, then Paul and finally anyone among his cabinet who professed themselves Christians was tortured and killed. Gaius was offered no mercy. But he was brave, Mary. He never denied his faith. And while he lived, he did what he could for the Christians who remained in Rome under the threat of death. I, myself, am a beneficiary of his courageous protection. My own husband, my second one that is, escaped Nero's wrath thanks to Gaius. I count Gaius among the blood that was shed so others might live."

This is what I told her. And John, I thought for certain I would have to bring her a large amphora for her tears. But surprisingly, they were few. I almost did not recognize our Mary Magdalene. She simply closed her eyes and lifted up a prayer to the Lord. I would even dare to say that a contentment washed over her countenance. And then, oh John, the joy on her face was angelic as she began to thank and praise the Lord effusively. How can she react with such faith? Her way of seeing all things anew is beyond my understanding.

***

As if to move fate along, I was interrupted by the visit of a humble woodworker. He says that Mary's prayers saved his wife and baby. He left a tribute to her, and it comes not a moment too soon as every breath is agony and may be her last. It is a modest but polished piece of wood, fashioned from a tree in this mystical-like forest that nestles under her cave dwellings. He has burnt the words, "Here lies the body of the Blessed Mary Magdalene." It is sealed in wax to be preserved for perpetuity, as I hope her story will be as well. Personally, I would have added much more that these simple word, but I could not diminish his pride in the gift he offered.

***

Oh John! It is finished. My own tears now stain this paper as I am confounded with a bittersweet sorrow and joy. As though the Lord Himself in all his splendor came to take her into his abode, her countenance was glorious as she took her last breath.

"I have seen the Lord," she cried out.

And then expired. I have no more words. She now truly sees the Lord, her Rabboni, her light and her life.

FINAL NOTES

History versus Imagination

Surely the reader would like to know what is true and what is imagination? I couldn't tell you. It has all, certainly, made its way through my imagination, but gathered together from elements of history and tradition. Mary's walk through Magdala is inspired by the actual archaeology of the first century town uncovered in 2009. I have walked to Tiberias, the same path I had her take in her visit to Herod's palace. Her dream in the cemetery is inspired by the actual tombstones that are carved into large boulders, still visible today, a short distance from Magdala.

Mary's background is based on various traditions and theories, as well as the visions of Anne Catherine Emmerich. Since a hagiographical study that influenced the liturgical reform in the 1960's, there has been a gradual disassociation of Mary Magdalene, Mary of Bethany, and the "sinful woman" who anointed Jesus' feet. I do not see them as incompatible traditions, as is evidenced in the story.

As much as possible, I attempted to follow the gospel of Matthew's timeline. But Gaius, Little Joanna, and Vespasian are pure fabrications of my imagination to facilitate the story's plot line. The other biblical characters I used are imaginatively fabricated around their traditions or based on their actual words and actions within scripture. Mary's various acts of anointing Jesus and elements of the passion are imaginative creations inspired by the gospels and the visions of Anne Catherine Emmerich.

If you have ever been to the Holy Land, you will have recognized sights, smells, sounds, and even the touch of such things as the shale rock of Calvary, the undulating hills of Galilee, the spattered colors of wildflowers, the flocks of migrant birds, the sudden rain storms that disturb the Sea of Galilee, and much more. The topography, geography and the use of nature of first century Galilee and Jerusalem are all indicative of reality. The anointing of Jesus' body is based on aspects of the Shroud of Turin. Even the directions, movements, times and types of the sun, moon, sunrises and sunsets are researched to create as accurate a vision as possible with the current scientific knowledge we have of these elements of nature.

The Last Supper, Jewish customs, the food and lamb, the setup of the dining area are all based on research of the Pasch. And any other reference to events within salvation history have been researched and scriptural passages integrated into conversations in order to offer a deeper understanding of these salvific events.

A Personal Note: Dreams Fulfilled

Have you ever looked back on your life and realized that God had fulfilled one of your childhood dreams in a surprising way? From the age of twelve I aspired to write a book. It took more than thirty years to fulfill that dream, over which time I didn't take that aspiration seriously…until one day.

The inspiration for my first book came to me as a surprise. I was sitting in the newly opened holy site, Ancient Magdala, sipping coffee with our media coordinator in November of 2017. We were swapping stories of strange things we had heard people say about Mary Magdalene, from tour guides, to visitors, to the media. As the coordinator of tours and hospitality, I noticed that visitors were requesting books on both the site of Ancient Magdala and about Mary Magdalene. We lamented over the fact that we didn't have any good books in our gift store on either of those topics. Israeli customs and a tight budget made it difficult to ship books from the United States to our modest gift store; and published information on Magdala's archaeological discoveries was primarily limited to academic journals and detailed reports, not so friendly to the lay reader.

Spontaneously and with bold certainty I declared, "I'm going to write my own book on Mary Magdalene." Prophetic words? Holy Spirit or not, the deed was done less than a year later. On July 22, 2018, Mary Magdalene's liturgical feast day, my first book was released and available for purchase in Magdala's gift store. I departed from Ancient Magdala three days later, the end of four years of service in a place that left an indelible mark upon me. But that was not to be the end of reflection on my friend, Mary Magdalene, nor my connection to her ancient hometown.

My first book *Mary Magdalene: Insights from Ancient Magdala,* offered insights gained from over three years of study, prayer, and discovery of this fascinating saint while I lived and served in Ancient Magdala. In it I captured big and little discoveries that I had stumbled across as I explored archaeological treasures, studied first-century Jewish culture, and learned of ancient texts and historical traditions related to both the town and her person. All of these things gave me a new and deeper insight about this woman. Eventually I also wrote a reflection novena, *Nine Days with Mary Magdalene,* painting with large brush strokes her transforming journey. That became a springboard for this present work, *Becoming Magdalene.*

My hope is that *Becoming Magdalene* has provided insight into your own walk with the Lord, for Mary Magdalene's story is a paradigm for every Christian's spiritual journey. I leave you with this final prayer that I crafted in Ancient Magdala, desiring to express what I believe would come from the heart of this great saint.

Lord Jesus, transform my heart with your personal and unconditional love. Heal my brokenness, restore my dignity, and cast out all that prevents a deeper relationship with you. Through the gift of Redemption, may I experience authentic freedom. Grant me fortitude so that I may faithfully follow you, even in the shadow of the Cross. Pour out your Spirit upon me that I may passionately witness to the good news of your victory over sin and death. And at the end of this earthly pilgrimage, may I be with you forever in your Kingdom. Amen.

Saint Mary Magdalene, pray for us.

[1] 1 Kings 19:12.

[2] The gospel accounts of Mary Magdalene and the women discovering the empty tomb vary slightly in their details. They may be found in Mt 28:1-10; Mk 16:1-11 (verses 9-11 are considered a later addition to Mark); Lk 24:1-11; Jn 20:1-18). This prologue uses creative license to piece various elements of the gospels together in a plausible sequence.

[3] With exception of the location of her villa, the story's scenes of walks through Magdala follow the town's layout according to the archaeological discoveries. A preliminary archeological report was published by the Israeli Antiquities Authorities of Israel in 2018, authored by Marcela Zapata-Meza, Andrea Garza Diaz Barriga and Rosaura Sanz-Rincón.

https://www.academia.edu/37686689/The_Magdala_archaeological_ProjecT_2010_2012_a_PreliMinary_rePorT_of_The_excavaTions_aT_Migdal. The description of the town, used throughout the book, is based on archaeological findings, while the specific villa of Mary Magdalene is fictitious. However, the Franciscan owned site, to the south of property owned by the Legionaries of Christ, claims to have found remains of a Byzantine church that venerated the spot of Mary Magdalene's house. For a summarized description of the historical and archaeological context, see Part I of Mary Magdalene: Insights from Ancient Magdala by Jennifer Ristine.

[4] Tiberias was built around the year 18 or 19 AD.

[5] This description of her parents has some similarities to the visions of Anne Catherine Emmerich. Although I have used creative license to develop some details of her parents' life and temperament along different lines. *Mary Magdalene in the visions of Anne Catherine* Emmerich. (Illinois: Tan Books & Publishers, Inc., 2005), 1-6.

[6] Vinalia Urbana (April 23) is a wine festival shared by Venus and Jupiter, king of the gods. Participants asked for Venus' intercession with Jupiter, who was thought to be susceptible to her charms through the effects of her wine. Venus was the patron of ordinary wine for daily consumption. Jupiter was patron of the stronger and purer wine. It was believed that he also had power over the weather, influencing the autumn grape-harvest. At the festival, people honored Venus by drinking the new ordinary vintage that was pressed in the previous year's festivities. Upper-class women gathered at Venus's Capitoline temple and poured last year's more sacred vintage into a nearby ditch, dedicating it to Jupiter. Common girls and prostitutes gathered at Venus' temple. They offered her gifts of myrtle, mint, and flowers and requested beauty, charm, wit and popularity.

[7] Around 103 BC.

[8] Jesus' home-base in the region around the Sea was Capernaum, about a two hour walk from Magdala, or quicker by boat. This is the setting for much of Jesus' public ministry around the lake. After John the Baptist was arrested, Jesus "settled in Capernaum beside the lake" (Mt 4:13). "From then onward, Jesus began his proclamation with the message, 'Repent, for the kingdom of Heaven is close at hand'" (Mt 4:17).

[9] A large living complex in Ancient Magdala boasts of the remains of several rooms and a central courtyard. It held evidence of fishing equipment and a room with six bread ovens, as well as hints of Roman occupation. It leaves the imagination open to ponder the possible inhabitants. A fisherman's family perhaps? A modest sized bakery as a family business? In this book, it becomes the setting for Aharon and Demetria's living area and bakery.

[10] Ps 104:1-3, NABRE.

[11] Is 43:1.

[12] Ps 104:5-9.

[13] Ps 104:24-25.

[14] Ps 104:27-32, NIV.

[15] Ps 104:35.

[16] Ps 37:4-5.

[17] McNamer, Elizabeth. *The Case for Bethsaida after Twenty Years of Digging: Understanding the Historical Jesus.* Cambridge Scholars Publishing (2016). p. 69, 93.

[18] Magdala, Migdal in Hebrew, meant "tower," perhaps named after that towering Mount Arbel under which the town is nestled.

[19] The Israeli Antiquity Authorities has a scanned letter from November 24, 1934 reporting the discovery of several sarcophagi uncovered from flooding in the Tiberias region on the west side of the Tiberias-Safed road. As of my time in Magdala (2018), one of those sarcophagi could be seen as you drove along the newer paved road that hugs the side of Mount Arbel, between Tiberias and Magdala. There were also rock hewn coffins carved into large rocks that sat in the ground. They are accessible even today by simply walking into the field. http://www.iaa-archives.org.il/zoom/zoom.aspx?folder_id=13176&type_id= &id=79061 (Accessed May 10, 2020).

[20] Literary creativity is exercised here. The actual site of John the Baptist's beheading is believed to be Machaerus, a desert fortress east of the Dead Sea in current day Jordan. Both the Jewish historical, Flavius Josephus (first century) and the Christian historian Eusebius of Caesarea (fourth century) wrote of John the Baptist's beheading in Machaerus. For more information see, https://www.vaticannews.va/en/world/news/2022-02/uncovering-the-site-of-john-the-baptist-s-martyrdom.html.

[21] Daniel 12:2.

[22] Isaiah 26:19.

[23] Isaiah 9:1-2.

[24] Isaiah 53:4.

[25] Leviticus 16.

[26] Ezekiel 18:4.

[27] Exodus 34:6-7.

[28] Hosea 6:6.

[29] 1 Samuel 15:22-23.

[30] Mt 13.

[31] Lk 11:19-21.

[32] Lk 11:24-26.

[33] Lk 11:43.

[34] Mt 23:23.

[35] Ps 139:2.

[36] Lk 13:12.

[37] Ps 72:18.

[38] Lk 13:16.

[39] Lk 13:10-17.

[40] Ps 51:11, 12, 16, 14.

[41] Ezekiel 36:25-27.

[42] Julian Norwich: "When God sees sin He sees pain in us."

[43] Shabbat is the Hebrew pronunciation for the Sabbath which begins on Friday eve.

[44] Mt 15:2.

[45] Mt 15:7-9.

[46] Variation of Mt 15:19-20.

[47] The following scene references Luke 7:36-50, the passage of the "sinful woman" who anoints Jesus' feet. A few things to consider about this association: 1) Who is this woman? While she has long been associated with Mary Magdalene, it is unclear if this is her or not. In the subsequent passage, Luke 8:1-3, we see Luke's first mention of Mary Magdalene, along with Johanna, the wife of Chuza, and other women who accompany the Twelve and provide for them out of their resources. One theory is that, if the sinful woman is Mary of Magdala, she is not named as such because it was her previous life. She is however named in the very next passage as the first in the list of women who were healed. 2) Where did it take place? This is also unclear from the passage itself, but Luke's placement suggests that it takes place amidst Jesus' travels in Galilee. Prior to this passage, Luke tells the story of a centurion's slave being healed in Capernaum and the raising of the widow's son in Nain (chapter 7). The passages in chapter 8 are traditionally associated with a geographical location between Magdala and Capernaum, with exception of the Gerasene demoniac's cure on the opposite side of the Sea of Galilee. This nestles the passage of the anointing in between events that took place in the Galilee area. For my story, I place it in Magdala, in the house of Simon the Pharisee. 3) Finally, while this passage may or may not be Mary Magdalene, I make use of Luke's passage here to illustrate the overflowing gratitude of heart that we can attribute to Mary Magdalene and any benefactor of Jesus' unfathomable mercy. I also integrate Jesus' conversation with the Pharisee's into the dinner conversation (Mt 15:1-19), as it fits the schematic movement I am following in Matthew's gospel to illustrate Mary's journey.

[48] Lk 7:44-46.

[49] Lk 7:47-50.

[50] Mt 19:29.

[51] Mt 15:20-28.

[52] Mt 6:26.

[53] Mt 6:27.

[54] The Hebrew name of the flowers are in parenthesis. They bloom as early as January in some regions of Galilee: Anemone (Kalanit), Cyclamen (Rakefet), Dog Chamomile (Kahvan).

[55] Mt 6:25-34.

[56] Mt 8:19-20.

[57] Mt 8:21-22.

58 Mt 10:9-10.

59 Mt 10:22-23.

60 Daniel 7:9.

61 Daniel 7:13-14.

62 Mt 6:26; 7:11.

63 Jn 3:34-35.

64 Jn 10:22-30.

65 Jn 10:24.

66 Jn 10:30.

67 Jn 5:21.

68 Jn 5:27.

69 Proverbs 11:2.

70 Proverbs 22:11.

71 Mt 5:14-16.

72 Lk 8:38-39.

73 Adaptations of 2 Peter 1:5-8 & 1 Peter 2:12.

74 Psalm 98.

75 Psalm 65:8.

76 Psalm 16:5.

77 "Magadan" or "Dalmanutha" is believed to have been located south of the plains of Gennesaret along the western hills. This places it in the vicinity of Magdala or another name for Magdala itself. https://bibleatlas.org/magadan.htm (accessed August 23, 2022).

78 Isaiah 49:6.

79 Isaiah 43:21-22.

80 Jonah 2:8.

81 Mt 13:17.

82 Mt 5:15 variation.

83 Jn 14:13.

84 Echoes of Psalm 127:3-5.

85 Proverbs 23:18.

86 Mt 16:4.

87 Mt 16:8-11.

88 echoes of Jn 6:33, 58.

89 echoes of Jn 6:69-70.

90 Mt 16:24-26.

91 Deuteronomy 8:16.

92 Isaiah 40:31.

93 Isaiah 61:7.

94 According to a vision of Anne Catherine Emmerich, Martha, Mary Magdalene's older sister by seven years, had spoken to Jesus with great concern for Mary's situation. Jesus encouraged Martha to not stop praying for her and exhorting her to change her life (Vol. I, p 401, 404).

95 Mt 12:43-45.

96 Isaiah 1:18.

97 Isaiah 61:7.

98 Deuteronomy 10:20.

99 Psalm 128:1.

100 Song of Songs 4:1,3,7,9,10.

101 Song of Songs 4:12-13.

102 1 John 1:19.

103 Mt 16:16-18.

104 Isaiah 22:20-22.

105 Mt 16:19.

106 Mt 16:23.

107 1 Samuel 12:9.

108 Judges 4:6-8.

109 Judges 4:9.

110 Judges 4:14-22.

111 Judges 5:4.

112 Psalm 128:3-4.

113 Mt 17:15-16.

114 Mt 17:17.

115 Mt 17:20.

116 Lk 9: 44-45, Mt 17:22-23.

117 Psalm 112:6-8.

118 Lk 10:20.

119 Mt 18: 1-4.

120Echoes of John 6:29 & Psalm 78:4.

121 Mt 18: 6-9.

122 *Ekklesia* is the Greek word that is used for church, meaning an assembly or congregation that has the authority for discipline.

123 Mt 18: 15-17, 19-20.

124 Mt 18:22.

125 Mt 18:23-35.

126 Echoes of Mt 5:24.

127 Isaiah 54:5.

128 Isaiah 41:10.

129 Psalm 90: 1-6.

130Psalm 90 variation, https://www.sinaichapel.org/tools-resources/traditional-readings-prayers.aspx.

131 Psalm 40:1.

132 Diamant, Anita. "Development and History of Kaddish", in *My Jewish Learning*, https://www.myjewishlearning.com/article/development-and-history-of-kaddish/, https://prayerist.com/prayer/thedeadhebrew, (accessed September 10, 2022).

133 The following scene reflects John 11:17-46.

134 Anne Catherine Emmerich, in her visions (Volume Four), mentions these three places of rest and preaching in the evenings while he was visiting Jerusalem.

135 The following scene reflects Luke 10:39-42, although this passage is often speculated to be a different Mary than Mary Magdalene.

136 Echoes of Jn 11: 46-48.

137 Lk 9: 22-27.

138 Mk 9: 30-32.

139 Jn 11:50.

140 Echoes of Lk 13:49-50.

141 Echoes of Mt 20:28.

142 Parts of Jn 16: 18-25.

143 Echoes of Jn 11: 27.

144 Mt 19:12.

145 Mt 19:21.

146 Mt 19:24.

147 Echoes of Mt 21:31.

148 Echoes of 1 Jn 19-24.

149 Mt 11:15.

150 Mt 22:1-3. The story continues to verse 14.

151 Mt 25:14-30.

152 Mt 25 1-13.

153 Psalm 25 adapted from the International Children's Bible. https://bible.com/ bible/1359/PSA.25.1-22.ICB, (accessed September 11, 2022).

154 The following story reflects Lk 19:1-10.

155 The following scene reflects Mk 10:46-52.

156 Mk 11: 46-52.

157 Mt 5:48.

158 Jn 4:34.

159 Mt 20: 17-19.

160 Mt 20:25-28.

161 Zechariah 9:9.

162 Echoes of Psalm 91.

163 Very loosely based on visions of Anne Catherine Emmerich (Volume 4) and Jesus' teachings before his passion.

164 Isaiah 7:14.

165 Echoes of Genesis 3:15.

166 Lk 10:18.

167 Echoes of 1 Peter 5:8-9.

168 Echoes of 1 Timothy 2:4.

169 Echoes of 1 Peter 5:8-9.

170 Echoes of 2 Corinthians 11:3.

171 1 Jn 3:8.

172 Jn 8:44.

173 Echoes of Jn 10:10.

174 Mt 4:17.

175 Ephesians 6:12.

176 This scene echoes John's account of the anointing at Bethany in the house of Lazarus and Martha, six days before the Passover before the entry into Jerusalem (Jn 12:1-11).

177 Loosely based on Anne Catherine Emmerich's visions.

178 Elements of this scene echo the visions of Anne Catherine Emmerich.

179 Mt 23:37-39.

180 Lk 19:42-44.

[181] Lk 19:39-40.

[182] Mt 21:16.

[183] Psalm 103:19.

[184] Echoes of Esther 4:14.

[185] Based on a tradition of the early Church written in the apocryphal *Protoevangelium of James*, 7, https://www.newadvent.org/fathers/0847.htm, (accessed April 17, 2025).

[186] Luke 2:29-35.

[187] Mark 14:1.

[188] Echoes of Deuteronomy 32:8.

[189] Numbers 11:16-17.

[190] Numbers 11:25.

[191] Echoes of Jn 3:8.

[192] Lk 9:50.

[193] Echoes of Lk 10:2.

[194] Reference to Mt 22 23-33.

[195] Proverbs 31:10.

[196] Echoes of Revelations 21:14.

[197] Revelations 21:5.

[198] Mt 22:30.

[199] Echoes of Mt 18:10.

[200] Mt 26:10; Mk 14:6-7.

[201] Mt 26:12.

[202] Mt 26:13; Mk 14:9.

[203] Mt 26:2.

[204] Mt 10:28.

[205] Lk 22:7-8.

[206] Mt 26:18.

[207] Scholars continue to posit theories about the dating of the Last Supper and whether or not it was the traditional Seder meal with the sacrifice of the Lamb or not. After much research I base this story on the theory presented by John P. Meier and summarized by Pope Benedict XVI in *Jesus of Nazareth – Holy Week: From the Entrance into Jerusalem to the Resurrection.* A summary is provided in the following article. "Pope Benedict XVI: The Last Supper", In *The Catholic Herald,* March 2, 2011, https://catholicherald.co.uk/pope-benedict%E2%80%88xvi-the-last%E2%80%80%88supper/). (accessed July 2021).

[208] Mt 2:6; Micah 5:2.

[209] Jeremiah 23:5-6.

[210] See Mt 1.

[211] Tradition as early as Tertullian (*De carne Christi* 21, https://www.newadvent.org/ fathers/0315.htm).

[212] Psalm 5:4.

[213] Echoes of Proverbs 6:16-19.

[214] Invented. Although according to Anne Catherine Emmerich's visions, Mary Magdalene's father was of Egyptian descent. And he did have some early encounters with the Holy Family giving a connection with their family years before Jesus and Mary Magdalene had met.

215 Proverbs 16:9.

216 Mt 2:15; Hosea 11:1.

217 Isaiah 11:1.

218 Matthew 24:2.

219 Jn 2:19.

220 Mt 12:40.

221 Exodus 12 & 13 describe the First Passover requirements.

222 Jn 13:1-20.

223 Jn 13:33; 14:1.

224 Echoes of Jn 15:18.

225 Jn 14:16.

226 Lk 20:1-2.

227 Lk 20:3-4.

228 Lk 20:9-17.

229 Psalm 118:22-24.

230 Jn 1:29.

231 Jn 6:51.

232 Jn 6:53.

233 Jn 15:8-9, 12.

234 Jn 15:13.

235 Isaiah 53:3-7.

236 Mt 26:31-33.

237 Daniel 7:13-14.

238 Mt 26:35.

239 Joel 2:31.

240 Lk 23:4.

241 Mt 27:25.

242 Mt 27:19.

243 Mt 26:41.

244 Lk 22:42.

245 Mt 26:29.

246 Exodus 6:6-7.

247 Jn 19:28.

248 Exodus 12:22.

249 Exodus 6:7.

250 Mt 26:27-28.

251 Jn 6:55-56.

252 Isaiah 31:30-34.

253 1 Jn 1:7.

254 Leviticus 17:11.

255 Anne Catherine Emmerich identifies the man who pierced Jesus' side as Cassius and attributes a miracle of perfect sight to the moment the blood and water poured out onto his face. (pp. 109-11; Vol 4, pp. 312-315).

256 Jn 19:31–36.

257 Various descriptions of the passion of Jesus will echo scriptural texts as well as visions of Anne Catherine Emmerich.

258 Jn 19:14.

[259] This scene was inspired by the mosaic on the Franciscan side of the Calvary chapel in the Holy Sepulchre in Jerusalem.

[260] Psalm 22.

[261] See Volume 4, Anne Catherine Emmerich.

[262] Ps 116:12-13.

[263] Ps 117:2.

[264] Ps 118:1.

[265] Ps 118:13.

[266] Ps 118:13-17.

[267] Exodus 6:6.

[268] Jn 19:30.

[269] Zechariah 12:10.

[270] Jn 19:39.

[271] The Shroud of Turin, a linen with a miraculously imprinted image of a crucified man, had signs of flowers around the head of the body. Professor Avinoam Danin, a leading Israeli botanist, identified several species of flowers, due to pollen residues. Approximately 300 flowers, with stems removed, were placed around and on the head. Four of the identified flower types bloomed within a 6-12-mile radius around Jerusalem and Hebron in March and April, the time of Jesus' crucifixion.

[272] Remnants of the quarry can be seen in the Holy Sepulcher, down several flights of stairs in Saint Helena's chapel. Tradition holds that Saint Helena, upon her son Constantine's conquest of Jerusalem, commissioned the search for the holy cross amidst several remnants of crucifixes in that quarry.

[273] The following chapter weaves together an account by making use of the four gospels, which seem to tell the story from various perspectives and moments. It also integrates some ideas from the visions of Anne Catherine Emmerich. See the *Companion* for a chart comparing the four gospel accounts of the scene at the tomb.

[274] Jn 20:2.

[275] Jn 20:11-13.

[276] Lk 24:5-7.

[277] Mk 16:6-7.

[278] Mt 11:27.

[279] Mt 11:28-30.

[280] The following scene reflects Lk 24:13-35.

[281] Lk 24:34.

[282] Lk 24:36-43; Jn 20:19-21; Mk 16:14-18.

[283] Lk 24:47.

[284] Mt 16:16.

[285] Mt 26:54.

[286] Isaiah 55:8-9.

[287] Isaiah 61:1.

[288] Proverbs 3:5-6.

[289] Mt 6:34.

[290] Acts 1:6-7.

[291] Lk 24:29.

[292] Acts 1:8.

[293] Deuteronomy 6:5; Mt 22:37-39.

[294] Echo of Jn 8:24.

[295] 1 Jn 1:1.

[296] Variations of 1 Jn 1-7.

[297] Mt 1:23.

[298] Mt 3:11, 16; 4:1.

[299] Mt 10:7.

[300] Mt 12:18; Isaiah 42:1-4.

[301] Mt 28:20.

[302] Jn 14:16-21.

[303] Jn 15:26-27.

[304] Deuteronomy 28:12.

[305] Deut. 4:11.

[306] Deut 5:4.

[307] Deut 5:27.

[308] Acts 2:1-4.

[309] Acts 2:11-12.

[310] Acts 2:17-21.

[311] Acts 2:22-23.

[312] Acts 2:24.

[313] Psalm 16.

[314] Acts 2:29.

[315] Acts 2:30-33.

[316] Acts 2:36.

[317] Acts 2:37.

[318] Acts 2:38-39.

[319] 1 Peter 2:4-5.

[320] Acts 5:15.

[321] Acts 4:4.

[322] The reasons for Pilate's removal from office have been debated among historians due to discrepancies in various texts or traditions between the Roman historian Josephus, the Christian historian Eusebius, traditions that have surfaced as legends, or various apocryphal texts that offer seven different accounts of Pilate's death, one of which is called the Gospel of Nicodemus or the Acts of Pilate.

[323] Echoes of 1 Jn 4:13-19.

[324] Massilia is Marseille, France. The French Tradition holds that Mary, Martha, and Lazarus, Maximin (one of the seventy disciples and Mary Magdalene's spiritual father) as well as various others, were set adrift in the Mediterranean Sea due to Christian persecution. They miraculously landed in Gaul, present day Saintes Marie-Mar in Provence (southeastern France). They eventually separated. Martha headed to Tarascon and Lazarus to Marseilles where he became bishop. (Archbishop of Genoa Jacobus de Voragine (1275), *The Golden Legend* or *Lives of the Saints*, First English Edition by William Caxton, 1483, Vol. IV, (accessed July - December 2023).

[325] Ibid., https://sourcebooks.fordham.edu/basis/goldenlegend/goldenlegend-volume4.asp#Martha, (accessed July - December 2023).

[326] Many Eastern Orthodox icons of Mary Magdalene reveal her holding a red egg in one hand. Their tradition holds that approximately two years after the crucifixion, Mary traveled to Rome to speak the truth about Pilate´s unjust punishment

of Jesus. When she spoke of the resurrected Christ, he claimed that a man being raised from the dead was as likely as the white egg on the table turning red. Mary picked up the egg and it did indeed turn red. This story illustrates her presence at Jesus´ crucifixion and her passionate testimony of the Risen Lord. However, if there is truth to this story, the Emperor Tiberius had already withdrawn to the isle of Capri before this date. Caligula, his nephew and future emperor from ca. 37-41 would have received her. The character of Gaius, the Roman official throughout the story, is fictitious. The apocryphal gospel of Nicodemus relates a conversation in which she is determined to travel to Rome and gain an interview with the emperor in order to seek justice.

[327] Romans 16:6. Paul mentions a Mary who treated him well and labored much among the Christian community. We do not know who this Mary is. For this story, she is the twenty-two-year-old daughter of Gaius.

[328] 64 AD.

9798888704226